THE FALCON
TATTOO

ALSO BY BILL ROGERS

BILL ROGERS
THE FALCON TATTOO

f THOMAS & MERCER

Text copyright © 2016 Bill Rogers

Published by Thomas & Mercer, Seattle

www.apub.com

Amazon, the Amazon logo, and Thomas & Mercer are trademarks of Amazon.com, Inc., or its affiliates.

ISBN-13: 9781503941151
ISBN-10: 1503941159

Cover design by Stuart Bache

Printed in the United States of America

I had a dove, and the sweet dove died
And I have thought it died of grieving:
O, what could it grieve for? its feet were tied
With a single thread of my own hand's weaving;
Sweet little red feet, why should you die
Why should you leave me, sweet bird, why?

John Keats "Song. I had a Dove."

Chapter 1

Her heart was pounding, the sound of each breath magnified by the respirator. She repeated the mantra they had been taught:

Fast is slow, slow is fast. Move slow, think fast, focus.

She could feel the first beads of sweat forming where the visor met her hairline. A voice erupted in her earpiece.

'Stand by!'

Another adrenaline spike. Nerves at screaming point, she breathed in again, slow and deep, breathed out, relaxed her grip a fraction on the polymer handle of the Glock. Victor appeared at her side, the menacing black bulk of the Enforcer raised to smash their way in.

'*GO! GO! GO!*'

The door flew open. She was first through, Romeo close behind. A passageway, a door to the right, two doors to the left.

'Hall clear!' she said. Keeping low, she moved into the room on the right. A table. Two seated. One standing behind. *Gun? No gun? Gun!*

She squeezed the trigger once, controlled the recoil, squeezed again. A fluid movement. Double tap.

'GR One. One Tango down, two Charlies present.'

Back across the hall, she scanned to check that it was still clear. The barrel of Romeo's MP5 brushed her hip.

She scanned the second room. Three chairs, a coffee table, a television set, a bookcase. Another doorway. She was about to declare the room clear.

A figure stepped out from behind the bookcase.

Fast is slow, slow is fast . . . Gun? No gun?

Gun!

She fired two shots. The body fell back.

Count the shots. Six remaining.

'GR Two. One Tango down,' she said, heading towards the second doorway. As she drew closer, there was the sound of automatic gunfire from within the room.

Romeo touched her on the shoulder.

'Flash-bang,' he said.

She leaned back against the doorjamb and closed her eyes as Romeo lobbed the stun grenade into the room. The bright white magnesium flash left a ghostlike impression behind the tinted eyepiece as she moved through the doorway.

Two hooded figures were standing in the left-hand corner, another in the right-hand corner. Both were armed.

She fired one headshot at each of the figures to the left. There was an instantaneous burst of automatic fire from Romeo on her right. She fired a second shot into each of her two targets, and they fell.

Count the shots. Two remaining.

'GR Three. Three Tango down. Room clear!' she said.

Back through room two, and into the passageway. Still clear. One doorway on the left. Romeo was still behind her. She moved to the door, and kicked it open. It was an empty toilet.

'GR Four clear!' she said.

The hostages? Where the hell were the hostages?

The passageway led into a small hall. There were stairs. The stairs were empty. She began to move up them, hugging the wall. The landing was clear. There were four doors, and a ladder to the roof. Two of the doors were open. She checked the first on the right. A bathroom.

'U One clear!' she said.

Romeo had entered the second of the rooms. She moved into position behind him.

'U Two clear!' he said.

She stepped back out on to the landing. A figure holding an AK47 appeared at the far end. She fired two shots. He fell backwards. *Count the shots. None left!*

'One Tango down,' she said, ejecting the magazine and tearing the spare from its clip. Another figure appeared at the end of the landing. She had to turn the spare so that it presented correctly.

'*Shit!*'

As she fumbled with the magazine, there was a burst of fire. The figure fell back. She rammed the magazine home. Her hands were shaking.

'One Tango down!' said Romeo.

He was already moving to the next doorway. Jo followed him. He stood to the right of the door, waiting for her to enter the room first. Her face was bathed in sweat. Condensation was forming inside her visor. She moved into the room.

A hooded figure stood in the middle of the room. His left arm was around the neck of a young woman. Her head lay pinned across his left shoulder. He had a gun inclined across her face.

Jo fired two shots into his head.

'Tango down,' she said. 'One Charlie present.'

Count the shots.

She was breathing heavily as she exited on to the landing. One by one, she entered the remaining two rooms. They were both clear.

Angling the Glock upwards with her right hand, she began to climb the ladder to the roof above, followed by her colleague. Three rungs from the top she stopped, and raised her left hand to shoulder height, palm upwards, fingers pointing to the rear. Romeo slapped a cylindrical grenade like a relay baton on to her palm. Her fingers curled around it. He began to count.

'One, two, three . . .'

She hurled the grenade through the hatch. The sound of the explosion echoed around the barrelled roof above them. She launched herself through the aperture and turned through 360 degrees, sweeping the roof space with her pistol.

'Clear! Clear! Clear!' she shouted.

'Romeo, Juliet, stand down!' said the voice in her ears. 'Stand down.'

Senior Investigator Joanne Stuart holstered her Glock, and removed her balaclava, visor, ear protectors and respirator. Her hair was wringing wet, her face and chest bathed in sweat. She wiped her face on the back of her sleeve, took a deep breath and began to cough.

'There's bugger all fresh air in here,' said Romeo.

Jo looked up at the hangar-like ceiling above them. They were still underground, safe from prying eyes and passing satellites. It had been easy in the heat of the moment to forget that the SAS Killing House was concealed in a bunker.

They retraced their steps. There was a hum from extractor fans dispersing the smoke from the stun grenades. The building was suddenly a hive of activity as staff made their way in and busied themselves removing bullets from the rubber walls, checking and fixing targets, setting the furniture ready for the next exercise. The scene reminded Jo of the firearms skills house at the GMP Clayton Brook Complex in Manchester, modelled on this facility, where she had gained her first such experience. But this had felt entirely different.

Romeo and his colleagues had been battle-tested around the world, and were in a constant state of readiness. But then, she reflected, these days who isn't? That was why the National Crime Agency had sent her here.

Chapter 2

'So, how do you think you did?'

'I don't know,' Jo replied.

'Right answer,' said the instructor. 'Let's find out, shall we?'

They were seated in front of a row of screens. A technician was operating the video. The picture was paused on the exterior view of the Killing House. One click, and the playback started.

'Initial entry good,' said the instructor. 'Let's have a look at ground floor one.'

Jo was fascinated by how slowly she seemed to be moving on the screen. Everything had felt so fast in real time. She was secretly impressed by how cool she appeared as she took out the first of the targets. The instructor agreed.

'Good reaction times,' he said. 'Classic double tap. Both shots on target. However . . .' The pause was ominous. He asked the technician to go back, and then freeze the action at the moment Jo began firing. 'What do you notice about your position?'

Jo stared at the screen. She thought she had a strong stance: left foot slightly forward, weight balanced on the sole of each foot, arms locked into the firing position, yet loose.

'I'm not sure?' she said.

'What about Romeo's position?'

She was barely a yard inside the room. Romeo was trapped between her and the doorway.

'I should have wheeled left, or gone much further into the room,' she said. 'I'm sorry.'

'We don't apologise here,' said the instructor. 'We learn. Run it on, Mike.'

Her performance in the corridor and the second room was declared fit for purpose. Next came the room in which she had faced three hostiles.

'Three things you got right here,' said the instructor. 'First, there's the decision to take the two targets on the left and leave the other one to your buddy. Then there's the decision to give each of them one headshot first, and then a second, rather than two double taps. If you'd gone for a controlled pair with the first Tango, the other one would have had time to take you out, and possibly Romeo too. Finally, there's your accuracy, but we'll come to that later.'

He turned to the SAS trooper who had partnered her as Romeo in the exercise.

'Did you notice anything untoward, Ginger?'

Ginger nodded. 'When Mike plays it back, Jo,' he said, 'watch what you did with your Glock after you finished firing, and as you turned to exit the room.'

This time, Jo spotted it straight away.

'I swept the muzzle over your head, and then your legs as I turned to leave the room,' she said. 'If there'd been an involuntary trigger squeeze, I could have shot you.'

'Exactly,' said the instructor. 'Imagine if there had been four of you in that room? It's all about muzzle discipline and control. You can forget all that hype about safety triggers – in the heat of the moment, anything can happen.'

He tapped the technician on the shoulder.

'Next.'

The remainder of the ground floor and her passage up the stairs passed without comment, but Jo knew what was coming. The instructor allowed the playback to continue until the second Tango had been hit, and then turned to Jo.

'I don't need to tell you, but I will. At least you knew you were due a reload, but it took you far too long. What's more, you remained in clear sight while doing so. If this had been a live Op, you'd be dead.'

'I know,' she said. 'I'd placed my spare mag the wrong way round in the clip. I fumbled, trying to turn it one-handed.'

'Well, don't do it again,' said the instructor. 'This is why we practise over and over again.'

Her performance on the ladder and accessing the roof received grudging approval. Next, the instructor tapped the keyboard in front of him.

'Now let's see how accurate you were.'

A screen was filled with the head and shoulders of the first of the targets at which Jo had fired. Numerals in red identified the placement and sequence of the shots.

The instructor used the digital mouse to move through each of her targets in turn. Jo realised with mounting relief, and just a hint of pride, that not one of her shots had missed its target, and they had all been lethal headshots. The instructor smiled for the first time.

'Bloody impressive,' he said. 'Although after your performance on the ranges yesterday, I suppose we should have expected this.' His smile faded. 'Mind you, if you'd been one of my guys, you'd have failed today's little exercise on that reloading debacle alone, and had to repeat it.'

He eased his chair back, and swivelled to face her.

'We repeat these exercises until it becomes second nature. Question is, now the Home Secretary is talking about plain-clothed officers walking the streets wearing concealed sidearms, will they get the same level of training? I doubt it.'

'I don't expect I'll be authorised to carry a weapon unless we're engaged in a counterterrorism operation, or there's a specific known threat,' Jo said. 'But in any case, they'll insist on regular refresher courses.'

'I hope they do,' the instructor replied. 'For your sake, the public's, and ours.'

Fed, showered and changed into civilian clothes, Jo was on the train back to Manchester. After two action-packed days with the SAS Regiment in Sterling Lines, she was glad not to be driving.

She checked her BlackBerry. No new texts. No missed calls. A succession of emails, all of which could wait until she was back at base. Nothing from Abbie. It had been over a week since Abbie had left. Since then they had only communicated by text. Jo's phone calls had gone unanswered, her voice messages lost in the ether. Abbie's texts had been formal and abrupt. She was staying with Sally, the sister of her friend James from uni, who was the intended sperm donor for her baby. Abbie would call at the apartment for some of her things when Jo was at work. She would continue, for the time being, to pay her share of the mortgage through direct debit.

For the time being. What the hell did that mean? For a month? Two months? Until Jo came to her senses? Jo didn't even know how she felt about the situation. Okay, she was angry that Abbie had presented her with an ultimatum. Abbie was going to have a baby, and she was going to have it her way. And there would be more babies, at least another two. Abbie wanted them to become a proper family. If Jo wanted to be part of that, fine. If not, they were finished. That wasn't fair. Jo had never said that she didn't want it, only that she could not yet see how they could make it work.

Jo knew that she was being dishonest. Deep down, she was still worried about the world she lived in and the work she did. About not being there when Abbie needed her to be. About the prospect of any children they decided to raise losing one of their parents. Losing her. And there was James bloody Warburton. How did Abbie expect her to feel? Selecting as the father this former friend from her time at uni. What role was he going to have in their growing family? What role might he expect to have? Despite all that, Jo really missed her. She missed her touch, her feel, her smell, the sound of her voice. The comfortable silences they shared. Her absence was a physical ache in the pit of her stomach. Jo sighed and reached for her book.

The matronly woman sitting across from Jo nudged her partner, and nodded in Jo's direction. The movement, slight though it was, had not escaped Jo's attention. The two had taken in her black hair with its annoying tendency to curl, intelligent dark brown eyes, attractive face and tall athletic build. But their attention now focused on the cover of the book. They looked surprised and uneasy. It was, after all, a catchy title: *The Evil That Men Do! FBI Profiler Roy Hazelwood's Journey into the Mind of Sexual Predators.*

Jo lowered the book and smiled serenely.

'It's my homework,' she said.

The woman prodded her partner.

'I need to go to the loo,' she whispered.

He shuffled along his seat, and stood in the aisle to let her out. Then he followed on behind.

Ten minutes later, neither of them had returned. Jo wondered how they would have felt if they'd seen her a few hours ago in full combat gear, reeling off the rounds. She smiled and turned the page – *Chapter 4: The Dead Speak.*

Chapter 3

Early next morning, Jo's team, the Behavioural Sciences Unit, gathered in the meeting room around the smaller of two oval tables. Harry Stone, Deputy Director of Specialist Services, their boss, was seated opposite his team, a pile of folders in front of him.

'A series of rapes,' he said. 'Five to be precise. In every case, the perpetrator was believed to be a single unidentified subject. All of them were stranger rapes. All of the victims were students. There are sufficient markers to suggest that they may be part of, or develop into, serial offences. Hence they fall within our remit.'

'Which markers in particular?' asked Andy Swift, the team's behavioural psychologist. In his cargo pants, trainers and favourite *LIFE BEHIND BARS* T-shirt, he could not have made more of a contrast with the Boss's dark grey suit, white shirt, and brick-red tie. Mad scientist versus Corporation man.

'We'll get to that,' said Stone.

He opened one of the folders, and handed each of them a set of papers stapled in one corner. 'This is the case file detailing the first of these offences. It's typical of the others, which are believed to have been committed by the same unsub. As you can see, it's from Lancaster PPU.'

'PPU, not the CID?' said Max Nailor, Jo's fellow senior investigator.

'That's right. They made the decision to put another thirty CID detectives on to pursuing paedophile investigations, and let the Public Protection Units handle all the other sexual offences, including rape.'

'That would make sense,' said Jo. 'It would make for more consistency and focus in both cases.'

'But do the PPUs have enough experience?' wondered Ram Shah, their slim, youthful unit intelligence analyst.

'Not when it comes to a case like this one,' Stone replied.

The name of the investigation was printed in bold on the first page: *Operation Juniper.*

'Random computer generation,' Ram surmised.

Stone carried on talking while the team read the files for themselves. 'Sareen Lomax. Eighteen years old. Freshers' Week pub crawl in the city centre, with a bunch of girls she's only just met. You know the scenario. Chance to let your hair down, start to socialise, maybe score if you're that way inclined.'

'Sharks circling,' muttered Max, struggling to get comfortable in the mean-spirited chair. At six foot three and close to fourteen and a half stone, Jo could see Max on the rugby field.

She nodded. It was a good metaphor. These students were a shoal of innocent seal pups playing in the surf, blissfully unaware that a great white shark was preparing to take one of them out.

'She gets carried away,' Stone continued, 'as they do, and gets left behind when the others move on to another pub. They don't notice she's missing till it's time to get the coach back. She turns up the following morning six and a half miles away in the middle of a bridge, in a place called Samlesbury Bottoms. And you can spare us the comments, thank you, Ram.'

'Wasn't going to, Boss,' said Ram, holding up his hands in mock surrender.

'Good. Passing motorist, a farmer's wife, almost knocks her down on the bridge when she lurches in front of her Land Rover. She's incoherent, sweating and shaking. Motorist takes her to A&E. They call the police. When they ask her about her movements the previous evening, she has no memory of any of it other than starting out with the other girls. When they carry out the medical examination and she finally realises that she's been raped, she's panic-stricken.'

Max flipped to the forensic report.

'No evidence of excessive force,' he observed. 'No internal or external bruising. No evidence of restraint or defensive wounds.'

'She was drugged,' noted Jo. 'Gamma hydroxybutyrate showed up in the urine. There's a new test for GHB that has trebled the number of positive results. Another few hours, however, and they still might have missed it.'

'He used a condom. Absence of perpetrator body hairs suggests he shaved them all off,' said Andy. 'There's also a chance he either wore a hairnet, or is bald.'

'No sweat traces either,' said Ram. 'Forensics reckon he must have bathed or showered her afterwards, then dressed her, and dumped her close to where she was found.'

'She could easily have stumbled into the river,' Jo pointed out.

'No trophies taken from her person,' said Stone. 'But he did leave a calling card.'

'The tattoo,' said Max, holding up one of the photographs. 'What kind of bird is that?'

'A falcon,' Stone told him. 'A raptor in the species *Falco*. Specifically, a peregrine falcon.'

'What do we know about peregrines?' asked Andy.

'You'll find a note on the back of the photo,' Stone replied. 'In essence, it's the most common of all falcons, found almost everywhere from the Poles to the Tropics. It lives off small to medium-sized birds. The female is larger than the male, and at two hundred miles an hour the peregrine is the fastest animal on Earth.'

'That's two reasons for him to be angry,' said Ram, grinning. 'Envy and premature ejaculation.'

'Ram!' said Stone.

'Sorry, Boss. Just trying to lighten it a bit.'

'I doubt that's how either the victim or her parents would see it.'

'He thinks of himself as a hunter,' said Jo. 'A natural predator. Instead of taking a trophy, he leaves a signature in the form of a tattoo, and as a symbol of his control over his victim. I hope for her sake it isn't permanent?'

'That would have taken too long. You'll find that in the notes too. They believe he used a stencil and an inkpad. Then he used hairspray to fix it. Her own hairspray, would you believe? It washed off, but it took some scrubbing.'

'I suspect that he *did* take a trophy,' said Andy. 'In the form of a photo or a video.'

'Like the guy in the States who had a place full of photos? The one who appeared on *The Dating Game* after he'd already killed two women?' said Max.

'Rodney Alcala,' said Andy. 'Except that they were never able to prove that any of the women in the photos were his victims.'

'Maybe not, but some of them were of girls, women and even boys who'd gone missing. And he did admit to a further thirty murders.'

'Let's stick to the facts of this case,' said Stone. 'Few witnesses came forward. Most of the men caught on camera in the pubs and clubs she and her friends visited together that night were subsequently identified, and they've all been eliminated from the investigation. There were some who it was impossible to identify. Dark lighting, backs to the camera. She hadn't made any male friends in the short time she'd been in the city. There were no boyfriends that might have followed her from Bristol where she lives with her parents and a younger sister. Fairly extensive analysis of traffic cameras and CCTV at and near the club has produced no leads whatsoever. There was no evidence on her laptop or in her emails that she was being stalked, groomed or harassed in any way. Seven months on and they've made no progress whatsoever.'

'They do have some trace evidence though,' Max pointed out. 'The foreign fibres and a single strand of hair found on her skirt.'

Stone nodded. 'The fibres are from upholstery that was supplied to Adam Opel AG and Vauxhall Motors, both subsidiaries of General Motors. There's a list of relevant models and years at the back. They're all saloons or estates registered between 1996 and 2013. A total of eight hundred and sixteen thousand cars, according to the manufacturers. Just under half that if you exclude foreign registrations.'

'Four hundred thousand registrations to check,' said Max. 'The senior investigating officer might have got approval for that if it was a murder investigation, but not for a single rape.'

'You're right, they didn't. As for the hair, it was identified as belonging to a female Caucasian, who drank alcohol on a regular basis and was an occasional user of cocaine.'

'Could it have belonged to one of her friends?' asked Jo.

'No. They were all eliminated, but she could have picked it up in any of the places they'd been that night.'

'Or it could have come from the same upholstery in the same vehicle as the fibres?'

'Exactly. But without that vehicle, they'll never know. So, Jo, tell me – why do you think they want our help, and what do you think they expect us to do?'

The others all stopped reading, and stared at her. 'Like you said, Boss,' Jo said, 'this case has multiple markers that suggest that the perpetrator, if he's not already one, is likely to develop into a serial offender.'

'The markers being?'

'The perpetrator is not known to the victim. The attack was premeditated. He's organised and methodical, in that he came equipped with GHB to render his victim unconscious and powerless; he was able to remove her from the scene undetected; he took precautions against leaving trace evidence; and he had a stencil and ink pad ready to leave his signature in the form of the tattoo. That signature alone, like that of a graffiti artist, would indicate that he's confident, proud of his handiwork, craves attention, and intends to strike again.'

'He didn't though,' Stone said. 'Not for over six months. That's a long time between attacks for a serial perpetrator.'

'Not if it was his first,' Jo pointed out. 'His apprenticeship as it were. He would have been waiting to see if he'd really got away with it, and how the police responded. Following everything that was written about the investigation in the media and on social media, and learning from it.'

'I agree,' said Andy. 'How long was there between the second and third victims?'

Stone opened the second of the files and distributed sheets with photos, descriptions, names, dates and locations of the five offences.

'Victim two's last known sighting was in Preston, twenty miles away from the first abduction. She's American: Wallis Grainger, age nineteen, five feet tall, blonde, blue eyes. Different university. On a Freshers' night out, just like the first victim. Only she staggered outside saying she felt a bit sick and needed a wee. She was seen going round the back of the club.'

'And she didn't come back?' said Ram.

'She came round in the grounds of a former psychiatric hospital near Goosnargh, five miles away,' said Stone. 'Following the attack, she packed up and went back to the States. Six weeks after she was assaulted, he struck again nineteen miles down the motorway in Bolton. Hayley Royton, victim three, was left on the moors near Darwen. Four weeks later, he abducted another girl in Salford. She turned up in Worsley Woods. And the latest victim was plucked off the street in Bradford last week, and left unconscious in a wooded copse in a farmer's field near Denholme.'

'A classic escalation pattern,' said Andy.

'The gap between numbers two and three fits exactly with the university summer holidays,' said Jo. 'All of the attacks occurred in term time.'

'Maybe it's a member of staff,' said Ram.

Stone looked sceptical. 'At five different universities?'

'They're all within a radius of forty miles or so,' Ram said. 'That's less than the Yorkshire Ripper covered. And they're all connected by motorways.'

Jo was staring at the colour photographs and the sketchy details beside each of the victim's names.

'There's another thing that connects the victims,' she said. 'Besides their being students. They're all blonde and short. The tallest is five foot three, the shortest four foot nine.'

'I noticed that,' said Andy. 'In my view, we're looking at a collector. One with a very specific set of criteria. Somewhere in his past there'll be a trigger that explains why he selects these girls in particular.'

'A fact, Andy, that I'm sure will figure in your behavioural profile for Operation Juniper,' said Stone. 'But we're getting ahead of ourselves. First I need to tell you where we're going with this.'

He flipped open another of the files and handed them each a sheet of A4. 'We're not going to repeat the mistakes that were made in the Ripper case. Forces failing to share information with each other, data collection and analysis all over the place, interview and search procedures poorly conducted.'

He shook his head and raised his eyebrows in disbelief.

'Sutcliffe was interviewed ten times before he was finally arrested, and even then it was by accident. That's not going to happen this time.'

He held up the sheet of A4. 'The Operation Talon team has set up a Major Incident Room here in Manchester, specifically for Operation Juniper. They'll collect and collate all evidence as it comes in, and feed it directly to a satellite MIR here in the Behavioural Science Unit. Jo will be the NCA senior investigator with free rein to carry out victim and prime suspect interviews, request analysis and operational resources. Where Talon cannot supply the resources, the NCA will.'

'Talon,' said Ram. 'Is that to do with him using a falcon tattoo?'

'No,' Jo told him. 'It's the name of the Greater Manchester Police team tackling sexual crime across the region. There are nine hundred specially trained officers and staff.'

'That's what I call a resource,' said Ram.

Stone turned to the psychologist.

'Andy, as usual, will work on a behavioural profile for these assaults, and at the same time postulate what the behaviours of the perpetrator and other features tell us about the unsub and his likely future offending behaviour, and advise Jo accordingly. And you, Ram, will interrogate our unique national database of unknown motive sexual attacks by strangers, and identify any matching patterns of behaviour or other aspects relating to this case. You will also carry out other analyses requested by Jo, including geolocation analyses.'

Max raised a hand. 'What about me, Boss?'

'I know you're tied up helping to review the sequence of unexplained male drownings in north-west waterways,' said Stone. 'But I want Jo to know that she can call on you whenever she needs to. And if she does, you're to give this your immediate attention. Is that clear?'

'Yes, Boss.'

Her fellow investigator had said it without rancour, and had even managed a smile in Jo's direction. *Things are looking up with Max*, she thought. *Maybe he does have a cheerful side after all.*

Chapter 4

Sareen Lomax was fragile. It was not the pale face, the paper-thin hands, or the fact that her camouflage jeans and matching hoodie hung limp on a fleshless frame. It was her eyes. They were cold and blank, even as she smiled and shook Jo's hand.

'I'd like to help,' Sareen said. 'But I'm not sure that I can. I told the police what little I remembered at the time.' She hesitated. 'And that was over a year ago.'

She seemed surprised that it had been that long. Jo realised that there was plenty going on behind those eyes after all, but it was happening in another place, a long way away. *That's it*, she thought, *a place of safety. Out of range.*

They sat down in two comfortable chairs in an office the college counsellor had vacated for their meeting.

'I understand, Sareen,' said Jo. 'And there's really no pressure for you to try to remember something new, far from it. It's just that I'm now in charge of this investigation and it would really help if I could hear your story for myself.'

The student nodded. Her short hair, newly dyed chestnut brown, limp and badly conditioned, barely moved. Jo wondered if she'd been told that she'd been chosen for her looks. That her abuser had a penchant for blondes.

'But if you'd rather not, Sareen,' she said, 'I'll understand completely.'

'No, it's okay,' Sareen replied. 'Sometimes it can help to talk about it. That's what I've been told.' She didn't sound convinced.

'It can,' said Jo, 'and more often than not it does.'

Something flickered in the student's eyes as she picked up the hint of personal experience in the detective's voice.

'So,' Jo continued, 'take your time. Starting with how that evening began.'

'It was the end of Freshers' Week. There were two mixed pub crawls organised. One was around the campus bars, the other was around the town.'

Her voice, low and faltering at first, became stronger and more assured as the story unfolded. 'The group of girls that I was with from our college, well, my hall of residence mainly, decided to go into town. There were coaches arranged.'

She looked up to check that Jo was following her.

'You were all girls? No male students?' Jo asked.

'There were plenty of boys. I mean, it's a mixed hall, it's just that it was early days, and we'd sort of bonded, the six of us.'

Jo nodded. It had been the same when she'd started at Manchester Uni. You found your feet in a group of like-minded girls, and then people gradually began to go their own way. But some of those earliest liaisons were the ones that endured. It was how she and Abbie had met.

'Besides,' Sareen continued, 'only one of the girls wanted to go round the campus bars.' She paused, and Jo guessed that she was probably reflecting on how different things would have been if she had gone with her instead.

'There were three coaches. Ours dropped us outside The Bobbin on Cable Street. We had one drink in there, but it was heaving. And with it being a real ale pub the lads were all ordering pints, so we decided to leave first and get to the next one ahead of them. We had a map.'

Jo held up the copy of the map from the case file that she had brought with her. She held it up so that Sareen would know that she was following the route they took.

'What were you drinking, Sareen?' she asked.

'Vodka fruit drinks mainly. In a bottle, obviously. Because it's easier to put your hand over the top? Stop someone dropping something in it?'

She frowned. In the end it hadn't made a damn bit of difference.

'I should have asked before,' said Jo. 'Had you preloaded before you set out?'

Sareen shook her head. 'No. We would normally have done. Saves you a fortune, but with us having only just got together and it being a last-minute decision, it wasn't something we'd had time to arrange.'

'So you left The Bobbin ahead of the guys?'

'That's right. Then we headed up the hill. We had one drink in each of the next six.' She counted them off on her fingers. 'The Three Mariners, The Pub, The Robert Gillow, Merchants 1688, Ye Olde John O'Gaunt, The Penny Bank. After that I couldn't say if we had more than one in each of the other pubs.'

Jo had printed off a satellite map of the city centre from Google Earth, and traced the route they had taken from the map in the file. All of the pubs had been in the centre of the city, on or close to a main road. Several had been in side streets or ancient lanes, but never far from cameras or prying eyes at that time on a Friday evening.

'Then someone, I think it was Penny, suggested we finish off at The White Cross. It was on the route, and close to where the coach was supposed to be picking us up.'

'Do you remember leaving the last of the pubs?'

Sareen shook her head.

'Vaguely. It's all a blur. I'm not even sure how much of what I've told you is what the others said we did, rather than what I really remember.'

'But you never actually arrived at The White Cross?'

'Not according to the others.'

Jo looked at the satellite map. It was a direct route, down George Street, across the junction, down Quarry Street and over the broad bridge by the canal. Just over two hundred yards. So near and yet so far.

'Did you buy your own drinks, Sareen?' she asked.

The student looked puzzled for a moment.

'Yeah,' she said. 'That's what we agreed.'

'Sorry, I meant did you have your bottles handed to you by one of the bar staff?'

Sareen's expression alone would have sufficed as the answer. She was already beating herself up for her stupidity.

'We had a kitty,' she said. 'In any case, there was never enough room at the bar. One of us bought the drinks and then handed them down the line to the rest of us.'

'Through the crowd?'

She nodded miserably.

'He must have been there watching us. Waiting his moment.'

Then how come he wasn't picked up by any of the CCTV cameras? Jo wondered. Or had he already scouted the different pubs and worked out how to avoid being filmed? Or maybe they'd got it wrong. Perhaps there were two of them. One, a woman who did the legwork and slipped the drugs in the drinks, the other a man who carried out the abduction and the rape. It seemed inconceivable that a woman would stoop to that. She knew better. Fred and Rose West, and Hindley and Brady proved that when it came to human behaviour, nothing could be ruled out.

Jo suddenly realised that Sareen was waiting for a response.

'That is one possibility,' she said. 'But you mustn't blame yourself. There is no way you could have known. And even if you had, there is only one guilty party here, and that's him.'

'But if I hadn't drunk so much . . .' Sareen began.

Jo cut her off.

'Stop that!' she said. 'Don't ever fall for the excuses men try to make. It's never about what you drink or how much, about what you wear or how you behave. In the end it comes down to one word. *No!*'

'But I never got the chance to say it.'

It came out as a whisper. It was as though she had shrunk into herself.

Jo shook her head.

'You were never given the opportunity to say yes. It comes to the same thing.' She softened her tone. 'Come on, Sareen, you must have been told this a hundred times.'

The student smiled weakly.

'Being told is one thing,' she said, her tone sad and regretful. 'Believing it is something else entirely.'

Jo looked at the notes on her tablet.

'You told the police you had no memory of having been abducted. No sense of someone holding you up perhaps, or helping you into a car. Is that still the case?'

'I spent the first two months trying to remember,' Sareen said. 'So hard that it hurt. Since then I've been doing my best to forget all of it . . . until today.' She looked around the room distractedly, as though wondering what she was doing there.

Jo realised that it was not only pointless to ask if Sareen remembered anything about the assault itself, or how she came to be beside that bridge in Samlesbury Bottoms, but also cruel.

'Thank you, Sareen,' she said. 'I'm really sorry to put you through this again.'

'It's alright,' she replied. For the first time since Jo had entered the room, Sareen's smile had a trace of warmth to it. 'This wasn't as hard as I'd expected.'

'How are things at the moment, Sareen?' Jo asked. 'How are your studies going?'

The question appeared to take her by surprise. She had to think about it.

'I'm alright, I think. I can't remember when I was last hysterical. I don't cry any more. I haven't had a panic attack this month.' She looked up. 'The last time I had a nightmare was during the summer holidays.'

Jo was concerned that this came across as so matter of fact and devoid of any emotion.

'And your studies?'

'My grades are okay. I'm on top of it, I think.'

Jo stood up and held out her hand.

'Good,' she said. 'I'm glad you're getting there, Sareen. It takes a long time, but I promise you can put all this behind you.'

The young woman's hand was like a feather. Jo was afraid that even a gentle squeeze might shatter the bones. She held it lightly and waited until she had eye contact.

'We *will* get him,' she said.

Sareen's pupils dilated.

'He's done it again, hasn't he? That's why you came?'

There was no point in lying. It would shortly be all over the media.

'Yes, Sareen, we believe he has. Several times. But not here. Elsewhere in the region. And, although it may sound strange, the fact that he may have committed more offences is the reason that I know we're going to get him. And soon.'

Jo felt Sareen's hand shake as it was withdrawn, and saw in her eyes not fear but fathomless sorrow.

———

'She's a long way from resolution, whatever that may mean.'

Helen Merry, the student counsellor, stared out of the window and across fields to the heather-covered hills rising beyond the motorway. There were premature strands of grey in her shoulder-length hair that hinted at disappointment. Jo wondered how any-one could bear to listen to an endless litany of unhappiness. Helen turned and smiled wanly.

'Compared with where she was immediately following the attack, Sareen has come a long way. Once the initial trauma passed, she was in a state of permanent numbness. We were really worried about her. We thought she might self-harm, or worse.'

'What about her parents, her family?' asked Jo. At least she had had Abbie after her own abduction.

Helen Merry shook her head.

'I tried to persuade her to go home, take some time out, but she wouldn't. It's not unusual, I'm afraid. They came up here as soon as they heard, but her mother was in almost as bad a state as her daughter, and Sareen couldn't bear to look her father in the face. She felt that she'd let them down, and of course they were beating themselves up that they hadn't been there to protect her.'

Jo nodded. She had known families to be torn apart by the aftershock of serious sexual assaults.

'You've noticed how thin she is?' said Helen Merry. 'Well that's my current concern. She's not anorexic, not yet, but she will be unless she starts to eat at regular intervals, preferably in the lounge or the residence dining room with other students. I've got some of her housemates onside, so hopefully it's only a matter of time.'

'She mentioned that she'd managed to carry on with her studies?' said Jo. 'Her grades are good apparently?'

'In a way that's symptomatic of her problem. She's thrown herself into studying to the exclusion of all else. She fought the nightmares and insomnia by studying into the night until she dropped off at her desk. Now it's become a habit. She has no downtime, no leisure pursuits, she doesn't go out with any of the other students. Basically, she's become distrustful of the friends she'd begun to make, and hyper-wary of making any new ones, especially with male students. She's in a prison of her own making.'

Helen saw the expression of disapproval on Jo's face.

'By which I meant,' she said, 'that she now has choices about how to move forward from this. That's my job, to try and help her break out of her cocoon.'

The counsellor reached across to her out tray and selected a slim document. She held it aloft like a barrister before the jury.

'Did you know,' she said with barely controlled anger, 'that one in three female students in the UK report having been sexually assaulted or abused. Forty-three per cent of students said they did not report it. And one per cent of students of both genders have been subjected to rape. That's twenty-four thousand rapes! The vast majority are what the media likes to term date rapes, where alcohol, drugs and unwarranted coercion are involved, only five per cent involve violent stranger rapes such as the one that Sareen endured. But, believe me, the effect is just as damaging.'

Jo knew the statistics. She had worked closely with Manchester's Sexual Assault Referral Centre, but it wouldn't help to tell Helen Merry that.

'It's an epidemic, and it isn't getting any better,' the counsellor continued. 'We have to eliminate the laddish culture in our universities, support women and girls to better protect themselves and – most important of all – educate boys from an early age about respect and consensual sex. And do you know what? It isn't even a compulsory part of the school curriculum!'

'Have you had any more incidents like Sareen's in the past twelve months?' Jo asked.

'Stranger rape? No.'

Helen Merry threw the document down on the desk.

'There have been other sexual assaults, and complaints of sexual harassment. We take a zero tolerance approach to them all. The victims are encouraged to report all allegations to the police. They investigate, and at the same time refer victims for specialist crisis counselling. We provide ongoing counselling here, for as long as it takes. Our record is better than most. We came fourth in the Safest University rankings in 2013.' Helen Merry sighed. 'But, of course, one case is one too many.'

'Thank you for persuading Sareen to meet with me,' Jo said. She stood up. 'And for the use of your room. I just hope that I haven't set her back by coming here.'

'It may have done,' Helen Merry replied. 'But it's never a straight road to recovery. More like a rollercoaster. I can tell you one thing that will help her,' she said. 'Finding the bastard who did this.'

Chapter 5

Jo parked on the Booths' supermarket car park just as the heavens opened. Her regulation windcheater was in the trunk and so she decided to make a dash for it.

Inside she bought a couple of bottles of wine, a ready-to-cook fisherman's pie for dinner, and a chicken sandwich for lunch. It was only when she came to put them in the trunk that she realised that she had picked up a meal for two. It was going to be a difficult habit to break.

In her heart of hearts, she still believed that Abbie would be back. She shrugged on her windcheater, pulled the hood up over hair that was already drenched, set the alarm on the Audi, and walked down Cable Street until she reached The Bobbin, and the start of Sareen's fateful pub crawl.

Fifteen minutes later, Jo stared east down Quarry Road towards the bridge over the canal, rain dripping from the peak of her hood on to her shoes. She was none the wiser. One of the bottles from which Sareen had drunk could have been spiked in any one of the pubs.

Jo tried to put herself in the mind of the perpetrator. He could have chosen to wait in any of the dark, narrow lanes and back passages along the way, following the group of young women at a discreet distance. Perhaps he had seen the pub crawl event advertised on the university website, and brought along a copy of the route identical to the one that she now held in her hand? If so, it would have made sense to wait here, towards the end of the route, where his already heavily intoxicated target would be at her most vulnerable.

She began to walk towards the canal. On the opposite side of the road loomed the severe, almost windowless, side elevation of the city police station. At the junction with tree-lined Thurnham Street she crossed over and stood on the corner by the car park for the Magistrates Court. She tried to imagine this spot in the early hours of the morning. It would have been easy to lead a girl as slight as Sareen, confused and unsteady, up the blue cobbled banking, between the bushes and into the concealed car park.

Another hundred paces brought her to the canal bridge. The towpaths on either side were ideal locations for an opportunist rapist. But the unsub was not an opportunist. She was certain of that now. He was arrogant, confident and resourceful. He had to be, to take a young woman off the street within yards of her friends, by a busy pub, along a street close to the central police station. It beggared belief. But then, she reflected as she folded her map, serial sexual offenders always do.

Jo drove back to Manchester, bypassing Preston, from where the second victim had fled back to her family in New York State. Then it was Bolton, where there had been a string of alleged student rapes over the past three months, only one of which was clearly connected to Operation Juniper. This was another victim she would not be interviewing. The divisional senior investigating officer had told her that the twenty-year-old was off sick, so traumatised that her family and GP had requested that she not be subjected to any more questioning in the foreseeable future. Her account, already recorded in the files, was more or less identical to that of Sareen.

Half an hour later, Jo was back in the BSU offices. One of the meeting rooms had been transformed into a satellite Major Incident Room, complete with display boards and an interactive SMART Board. A PowerPoint projector had been installed on the ceiling. Dorsey Zephaniah, the unit administrator, Dizzy to her friends, was bursting to show her round.

'Two dedicated telephones, two additional PCs with Internet and intranet access, a dedicated fax machine and printer, and a Home Office Large Major Enquiry System version two terminal – HOLMES2.' She pointed to the far wall. 'Those are three secure lockable storage and filing cabinets to ensure the integrity of all first-hand material generated by this team.'

'This is amazing,' said Jo. 'How on earth did you manage to get it set up so fast?'

Dizzy grinned. 'I'd love to take the credit, but it was part of the standard set-up.'

'What's the TV screen for?' Jo asked.

'Video-conferencing with the Major Incident Room, and whoever else you please. And another thing, you have a dedicated email account for Operation Juniper.'

The door opened, and Ram entered.

'Not bad, is it?' he said. 'Not that we aren't worth it. Dizzy's worked another miracle.'

'Get away with you!' she said, punching him playfully on the shoulder as she passed him on her way out.

Ram pulled out a chair and sat down.

'I think you'll be pleased to learn,' he said, 'that while you've been busy at the sharp end, we've made some progress, Andy and I. Shall I ask him to join us in here?'

Jo began to shrug off her jacket. 'That would be good,' she said.

Ram returned, carrying two mugs of coffee. Andy accompanied him. They made an unlikely pair. The psychologist wore his usual beige cargo pants, brown hoody and Jungle Book plimsolls, contrasting with Ram in his leather jacket, ubiquitous cashmere scarf, and black skinny chinos tucked into lace-up Jacob boots. The English eccentric and the Asian urban fashionista.

Ram handed a mug to Jo.

'Thought you might need this,' he said. 'I'll be using the SMART Board, so I suggest you sit there.'

'Thanks,' she said, and sat down next to Andy at the small table while Ram set up his presentation. The coffee reminded Jo that she was ravenous. She took the chicken sandwich from her bag and got stuck in.

'I've been working on that behavioural profile,' Andy told her. 'I'll be interested to see how it chimes with what you discovered this morning.'

'I'm not sure that I learned anything at all,' she said. 'Aside from the fact that he's clever, highly organised, arrogant, is not averse to high-risk scenarios, and he gets kicks from wrecking young women's lives.'

'That just about covers it,' he said. 'You don't need me at all.'

'Come on, Andy,' she said. 'We knew all those things about him before I went up to Lancaster.'

'No, we didn't. We surmised. That's not the same thing at all. Everything we do here needs to be tested in the field, and either confirmed or refuted. Your interview confirmed it.'

Andy poured water from a small flask into a beaker, took a sip and observed her closely. 'That's not all you got out of that visit, is it, Jo?'

She stared at him.

'I don't know what you mean?'

'When you set off, you had a mystery to solve. A riddle to unravel. But now you're on a mission.'

'Is it that obvious?'

'Oh yes,' he told her. 'Whenever we pick up a cold case, or are called into an investigation part way through, it feels as though we've been presented with a puzzle. In your former role with GMP, you were there from day one. Seeing the murder victim, attending the post-mortem. It's only when you're confronted with the human misery these people cause that it becomes personal. And when it does, it's reflected in your eyes, your manner, your impatience.'

'Is that a bad thing?'

'That depends.'

'On what?'

'On whether it sharpens your senses and intensifies your motivation, or clouds your judgement.'

'Is that a warning?' she asked.

He shook his head. 'No. Just an observation. It's the same for all of us.'

Jo hoped to read the truth in Andy's eyes, but his head was already bowed as he leafed through the papers he had brought with him. She would not have been surprised if he had meant it as a warning. After all, in the first case they had worked on together, she had thrown caution to the wind, rushing off alone to rescue the victim before backup had been organised. Hardly surprising, given that she was still haunted by the conviction that complacency had led to her own abduction.

'I'm ready,' said Ram, sitting down beside her, and placing his laptop in front of him. 'I assume you've had experience of geographical profiling before, Boss?'

'Substantial experience,' she said.

'Good. That saves me having to explain it. So, let's see what it tells us in relation to our unsub.'

He tapped his keyboard, and a map of the North West of England appeared on the SMART Board. He tapped it again and five red circles appeared.

'Each of these circles marks the last known sighting of one of the unsub's known victims,' he said. 'As you can see, they're quite widely dispersed. However, they tend to follow an arc starting in Lancaster in the north, and running south through Preston and Bolton, ending up with two victims within five miles of each other, in Salford and Manchester, and then up again to Bradford.'

'Following almost exactly the M6, M61 and the A6,' Jo observed.

'Correct,' said Ram. 'Many analysts believe that the proximity of the victim's place of residence to the unsub's home is the most critical factor.' He grimaced. 'Unfortunately, motorways tend to complicate these analyses. They make it too easy for a perpetrator to travel quickly and easily between their base and those they prey on.' He pointed to the board. 'Based solely on the first four attacks, and applying the geographer's principle of *nearness* and the psychologist's principle of *least effort*, where would these suggest our unsub is most likely to live or have a base?'

'Chorley,' said Jo, not least because the crime scene from her last case was still fresh in her mind. 'It's almost exactly equidistant between the locations of the first and the fourth attacks.'

'What if I add the locations where the unsub left his victims after he had abducted, raped and tattooed them?'

Ram pressed the return key. Four green dots appeared in a tighter cluster to the west of Preston, in an arrowhead from the Trough of Bowland in the north, to Darwen in the south, and Burnley in the west. Ram pointed to each in turn: 'Samlesbury Bottoms, Cow Ark, Pickup Bank, Love Clough. Sick sense of humour or what?'

He stepped back from the board and turned to face them.

'For the sake of consistency, I'm calling these the dumpsites. Some analysts believe that over time the dumpsites will move ever closer towards the perpetrator's home base, and therefore this is the best indicator of where the unsub might reside. Either way, the perpetrator is likely to live within a one-mile radius, angle or sector of a circle from the centre of the cluster of dumpsites or the victim's homes.'

'Blackburn,' said Andy. 'That becomes his new epicentre.'

Ram nodded. 'Tap the Return key for me, Jo,' he said.

Another red circle appeared, this time on the outskirts of Leeds. He joined up the red dots with one finger, to create a continuous curve equal to a quarter of a circle.

'Now he's spread his wings and followed the M62 into Yorkshire,' said Ram, 'how does that change the mix?'

'It could be somewhere around Burnley,' said Jo. 'If he didn't use the motorway. My money is on him living somewhere in that tighter circle around the dumpsites. After he's abducted them, he clearly takes them somewhere he considers safe to assault and tattoo them. And, given that he has to release them in the early hours before anyone's reported them missing, that only gives him a limited distance that he can travel.'

'If you're right, that would give us approximately seventy thousand males between the ages of seventeen and forty as potential suspects.' Ram looked at Andy. 'Assuming that's an appropriate age range to use?'

'Close enough,' said Andy.

'However, if you're wrong,' Ram continued, 'then we're talking about an overall population closer to four million, and approximately seven hundred and seventeen thousand potential suspects.'

'The whole point of a geographical profile is that it adds another lens for us to look at suspects through when they actually come to our attention,' said Jo. 'So the closer any suspects live to these loci, the closer we'll look at them. That's what they failed to do in the Ripper case. Every time Sutcliffe appeared on their radar, they accepted what he told them without checking it out properly. Armed with an analysis like this, and a behavioural crime profile as well, they'd have caught him three years earlier, and saved at least five lives and possibly as many as twenty.'

Andy sat up straight and stretched his arms.

'That sounds like my cue,' he said.

Chapter 6

Jo opened Andy's report. *Operation Juniper: Unsub Crime Behaviour Profile, Version 1.* The psychologist was now perched on the edge of the table nearest to the SMART Board. His flask and beaker were on the table beside him.

Andy reminded Jo of a university professor. Bespectacled, intense, radiating an air of exceptional learning. Whenever he found himself reflecting on his findings, he would remove his glasses and suck one of the temple tips, before putting them back on again.

'I know that you're both bursting to flip to the end and read the summary profile,' he began. 'But context is everything, as is engagement. So, I'd like to begin by inviting questions.'

'How old do you think he is?' asked Ram.

Andy raised his eyebrows.

'How do you know our unsub is a man?'

'I don't follow?' said Ram.

Andy looked at Jo.

'Jo?'

'If it is a man,' she said, 'we know he must be using a condom because we don't have any semen or seminal fluids. And, because he bathes or showers his victims, we don't have any DNA either. So, theoretically, it could be a woman. Or a man and a woman.'

'Very good,' said Andy. 'And since all of the victims are intoxicated, drugged and petite, it would not require a great deal of strength to subdue them.'

Ram was not convinced.

'A woman. How likely is that though?'

'Highly unlikely,' the psychologist replied. 'For lots of reasons. Which is why we will continue to refer to the unsub as *him*. But we mustn't discount the possibility that we're looking for a woman.'

'What age might they be?' asked Jo.

'The average age of a convicted rapist is thirty-one,' Andy replied. 'The majority fall within a window that stretches from seventeen to the late forties. Repeat rapists tend to be younger than average. However, the most successful serial rapists – committing assaults over many years during which they are undetected, are generally older, often in their mid- to late forties before being arrested.'

'Was Sareen Lomax's abduction and rape his first offence?' asked Ram.

Andy removed his glasses, and sucked at the arm before replacing them.

'My hunch is that he has raped before,' he said. 'Almost certainly during his adolescence. Having got away with it, as many young and silent rapists do, he has developed his methodology over the years until he has felt confident enough to draw attention to his crimes, and arrogant enough to believe that he will continue to get away with them.'

'So, do you think this has been a linear progression?' Jo wondered. 'Or might he have been active and undiscovered for a number of years, or stopped, and then been triggered by some event or other into starting again?'

Andy nodded. 'Either is possible. The abduction and rape of Sareen Lomax was too meticulous in the planning and execution to have been our unsub's first. Nor do I think that the gap between that attack and the next one was accidental. It was a classic cooling-off period, during which he waited to see how the police proceeded, and to give him time to fine-tune his plans.'

He removed his glasses again, took a blue microfibre cloth from his pocket, and proceeded to clean them as he talked.

'Since then his attacks have escalated. Again, this is typical. It can be explained in several ways: he's experiencing diminishing returns of satisfaction from his attacks, and becoming increasingly desperate to recapture the excitement and release that his first crimes gave him. On the contrary, the thrill that he experiences is driving him on in the way that a drug might. Or it may be that this is becoming as much an emotional and intellectual exercise, as a physical one. This is a game of risk that he's playing with the authorities, with us. The more frequent the attacks, the greater the risk, the grander the achievement, and the more superior he proves himself to be.'

He put the cloth back in his pocket, and replaced his glasses.

'There are two aspects of his modus operandi that lead to me to veer towards the latter explanation. Firstly, the fact that he tattoos his victim is symbolic. A reminder of his control over, and possession of, his victims. Secondly, that he has been choosing locations to release his victims that have names full of irony, given the ghastly nature of his assaults on these young women. Taken together, these behaviours represent a metaphorical two-fingered salute in our direction.'

'What type of rapist is he?' asked Ram.

'He's almost certainly a silent rapist. As far as we can tell, he does not use the con approach of those who pose as police officers, authority figures or taxi drivers, for example, nor does he seem to use the blitz approach of the violent predator involving knives, gas, stun gun devices or other forms of physical threat.'

'Why does he abduct his victims overnight and then release them?' asked Jo. 'Don't most rapists who abduct their victims end up by killing and disposing of them?'

Andy smiled at her.

'It is true that almost all victims of rape held for more than an hour or so are murdered. This unsub has a need for intimacy with his victim, albeit that she's drugged. He fools himself into thinking that she's a willing partner. The tattoo he applies is a symbol of possession, a stamp of identity and a challenge to the police, and in his mind it also implies a degree of intimacy. But that does not imply empathy on the part of the unsub.'

'Why does he release them?' Jo asked. 'Surely that would make it more likely that he'll be caught?'

'Not necessarily. Murder deposition sites are much more likely to provide useful trace evidence.'

That was often true in Jo's experience, but not universally so. She hoped that they didn't have to wait for a murder before they caught this animal.

'Do you think he might progress to murder?' she asked.

Andy's expression was not what she had been hoping for. 'If there's a risk of his being identified by a victim,' he said. 'If he's cornered in some way. If the victim fights back. Then I think he might well kill – and if he does, that'll make him angry and confused, and his future behaviours unpredictable.'

He took the silence with which that was greeted as a sign that they had run out of questions.

'You may now turn to the summary,' he said. 'As you can see, I've divided this into two sections. The first summarises what I regard as his typology as a rapist based solely on his behaviours to date. The second is intended to act as an aide-memoire when considering potential suspects.'

He stepped to one side, and brought up on the SMART Board a copy of the first of the two sections.

'This is a typology of rapists,' he began. 'One that is commonly accepted in academic literature, based on extensive research into sexual assault. I'd categorise our unsub as a Power-Assertive, Exploitative, Selfish Perpetrator. I base that on the following behavioural markers.'

He touched an icon on the side of the SMART Board. A copy of the first of the two summary lists appeared. He reached into the pocket of his hoody, and pulled out a red pencil-like stick. On one end was a white-gloved hand, index finger extended.

'My daughter bought me this,' he said. 'They use them in school apparently. So much more appealing than a cursor or a laser pointer.'

He used it to focus their attention on each bullet point in turn, sometimes adding a brief comment like a codicil.

He has an overwhelming desire to dominate an impersonal sexual partner.

'Impersonal, because she's both a stranger to him, and unconscious at the time of the assault, which links with the next one.'

He prefers his victims to be passive.

'Then we have . . .'

His behaviour is aggressive, but not lethal.

'Not lethal yet. We have to hope that it stays that way, or that we catch him before it changes.'

We believe that he selects victims younger than himself.

'This is not typical of the standard typology, which makes it a unique, and therefore extremely important, feature.'

We know nothing about the nature of his sexual behaviour other than it involves non-consensual penetration.

He transports his victims to a different location, where he carries out the assault.

He is mobile within a specific geographical region.

He leaves his traumatised victims beside a road where they will eventually be found, but heedless of their continued vulnerability.

'And finally . . .'

The cycle, or pattern, of his attacks is shortening.

'Which in the case of our unsub is of real concern.'

He touched another icon and another list appeared.

'Now,' he said. 'The final summary, or aide-memoire.'

He paused to make sure that he had eye contact.

'Jo,' he said, 'you'll need to stress to anyone using this that it should not under any circumstances be used to eliminate suspects. Only to ring alarm bells in their heads when a potential suspect – including witnesses – appears to meet a number, not *all* but a *number*, of these criteria.'

Jo nodded. In her experience, most officers still regarded such profiles with a high degree of scepticism, and rightly so.

Andy removed his glasses and placed them on the table in front of him. He rubbed his eyes and then pinched the bridge of his nose. His eyes remained closed as he spoke in a deep, measured voice.

'Our unsub is likely to be male, over twenty-five but under forty. White Caucasian, solely on the basis that he is more likely to blend in. Above average in height, between five foot seven and six feet tall. He will be of muscular or athletic build, and weigh between one hundred and fifty and two hundred pounds. He will come from what are now termed the *technical*, or *established* middle classes. His IQ is in the higher range. He will score on the Wechsler Adult Intelligence Full Scale between one hundred and ten and one hundred and twenty-nine, thus falling within the "bright normal" and the "very high" range. He has been educated at least to a level of further education, and quite possibly to graduate degree standard.

He may be married, divorced or in a partnership with a woman, but could just as easily be single. He will be employed or self-employed, and his work or leisure pursuits will take him into universities or their environs. He's comfortable working among women, and when he does so, he will be popular.'

Andy refilled the beaker and replaced the lid on the flask. When he began to speak again, his eyes were open and his voice had returned to normal.

'There is a misconception that all sexual predators have indulged in precursor activities that will have brought them to the attention of the police. Either because they have been abused themselves, or committed petty but escalating crimes such as shoplifting, petty theft, indecent exposure, arson, assault. Statistics tell us that this is most likely the case for first-time opportunist rapists who are almost always arrested before they become repeat offenders. The true serial rapist is successful because he is, more often than not, unknown to the police. I believe that is the case with our unsub.'

Andy lifted the beaker, and took a sip.

'We know very little about the workings of a serial rapist's mind. Those who are in captivity tend to be too arrogant and disdainful to allow us to study them. What I can say without fear of contradiction is that he has an antisocial personality disorder. He is narcissistic and deeply misogynist. He may have a history of aggressive behaviour, but it is just as likely that he has managed to find ways of relieving his aggression in non-public settings that haven't brought him to the notice of the authorities. He sees himself as completely normal. One caveat, he will be aware that his sexual behaviour is atypical, but will have rationalised this in ways that overcome his own internal and external inhibitions, such as public morality, parental attitudes and religious beliefs. As an undetected serial perpetrator, he's likely to appear normal. Just another man in the street. He may appear friendly, charming even. A ready smile, a reassuring hand on your arm.'

Andy took another sip.

'Which brings us finally to the vehicle he uses to transport his victims to the place where he assaults them, and then to the place where he releases them. The favoured vehicle would be a small to medium-sized delivery van, preferably with a sliding door, and without rear or side windows, or markings of any kind.'

Andy put his spectacles back on, picked up his flask and beaker, and came to sit beside them. Jo thought he looked exhausted, as though emotionally drained.

Ram turned to Jo. 'Now that you've seen both of our reports, what do you want us to do next?' he asked.

'I have a meeting scheduled in an hour in the Major Incident Room,' she said, 'to share your reports with the team from Operation Talon, and to agree next actions. Ram is already using HOLMES2 to filter the data they sent over of all known sexual offenders held in the Police National Computer using our unsub's specific behavioural markers. Since the first attack on Sareen Lomax, officers have already carried out over three hundred interviews across Lancashire, Greater Manchester, and parts of Cheshire and Merseyside. The geographical analysis and your behavioural crime profiles will help them to review some of those interviews, and target future ones.'

She turned to Andy.

'Do you think it would make sense for you to take a look at the list Ram comes up with, and see if it's possible to identify those that most closely match your profiles?'

'It would make perfect sense,' he said. 'And I'll see if I can fine-tune those profiles while I'm about it.'

'Thanks,' she said. 'As for me, based on what you've just shared with us, I'm going to ask for a list to be drawn up of any males known to travel regularly between the universities that have been targeted so far. I assume that will include academic staff, suppliers of equipment, books and services, including things like materials, chemicals, security systems and software. And I assume there'll be some students too, such as Student Union officials?'

Ram looked sceptical. 'That could take forever,' he said, 'and involve a hell of a lot of people.'

'Jo's right,' said Andy. 'You have to start somewhere, and it'll focus people's minds, both in the universities and in the team itself.'

Jo pushed her chair back.

'I'll have to go and prepare,' she said. 'I've arranged to interview victim number four in Salford this evening.'

She stood and picked up the two reports.

'Thanks for all your hard work. I have a feeling that it could make all the difference. Not straight away perhaps, but soon.'

'I hope so,' said Andy. 'I sense that time is not on our side.'

Chapter 7

Jo and DI Sarsfield left the Major Incident Room in Central Park, and made their way to the CCTV- and video-viewing room.

'Congratulations on your promotion, Gerry,' said Jo. 'I heard you made Inspector within a year of joining the Serious Sexual Offences Unit.'

He grinned.

'You've done alright for yourself, Jo. You don't mind if I call you that?'

She smiled back.

'Not at all.'

He laughed, and brushed a hand through his curly black hair.

'I bet you were hoping you'd be working with DCI Caton?' he said.

'Not at all.'

The truth was that she would give anything to have the support right now of her former boss. And not just professionally.

'Good,' he said. 'Because I get the feeling I'm going to enjoy working with you.'

Jo frowned.

'I'm impressed with the team you've put together,' she said, 'and how hard they're working, but it's not as though we've made much progress, is it?'

Sarsfield shrugged. 'It's early days, but I know what you mean. All those interviews with so-called witnesses? None of them seem to have witnessed anything worth pursuing.'

'I'm not surprised. Unless they happen to be looking to pull, young people out on the town only have eyes and ears for their friends, and their focus is on consuming as much alcohol as possible in the shortest period of time. Our unsub was never going to draw attention to himself. He'll have been "Mr Normal" right there in plain sight, head bowed, avoiding eye contact, or lurking in the shadows.'

'Funny you should say that,' he said. 'Because that's why I brought you in here.'

He put his hand on the shoulder of a middle-aged man in shirt-sleeves sitting in front of the nearest of the monitors.

'This is DC Jack Withers. Jack has been going over the only useful footage we managed to garner from over a hundred hours of CCTV retrieved from the pubs and clubs the victims were known to have visited.'

Withers shrugged.

'I wouldn't get your hopes up, Ma'am,' he said. 'It's the usual story. There were too many pubs whose CCTV was down at the time, and those that weren't had most of their cameras aimed at the top of people's heads rather than their faces. Surprise, surprise, the best coverage was of the tills and the stock.' He shook his head. 'Profits first, customer safety second.'

He pulled out a chair for Jo and the two of them sat down in front of the bank of screens.

'Just show SI Stuart what you do have, Jack,' said Sarsfield.

The man pressed play, and the first of the sequences appeared on the monitor screen.

'This is from the fifth of the pubs visited by the first victim,' he said.

Jo leaned closer. The images were in black and white, and nowhere near as sharp as she had hoped. There was no sound. She guessed that the camera was sited above the door, and trained in such a way as to capture those customers at the bar. The pub was packed solid, with people four and five deep vying with each other to be served. It looked like a scene from a Tube train at rush hour, only worse.

'This is her,' said Withers, touching the screen with a tablet stylus.

Sareen Lomax was only just in view. She was standing towards the back of the crowd with four other young women, none of whom seemed particularly steady on their feet. They swayed in unison as they were jostled from every direction. Two of them had open bottles in their hands. Because she was so small, the camera frequently lost sight of her as the bodies surged and shifted.

'Here we go.' Withers touched the screen with his stylus.

A tall girl at the bar, hair down to her shoulders, half-turned with a bottle held high in her left hand. She appeared to be shouting something to the girls behind her.

'Can you tell what's she saying?' asked Jo.

Withers paused the footage.

'It was difficult to tell because she's almost in profile, but our speech analyst reckoned she was saying something like "*Sreens*".'

Jo nodded.

'Sareen's.'

'Makes sense,' said Withers, 'given she's had a few. It also fits with what happens next.'

He pressed play.

The bottle was passed from hand to hand over the top of the heads of the crowd, until it reached one of the girls beside Sareen Lomax, who then handed it to her.

'This is the one we're interested in,' said Gerry Sarsfield.

He had paused the footage again, and was pointing to a figure with his back to the camera, standing halfway between the counter and Sareen Lomax. Jo leaned even closer. There was very little to see. Just the hair on top of a head, and an impression of size and build that could only be gauged by the amount of space he appeared to be taking up. Even that was difficult, given the tightly packed crowd.

Withers ran the footage back a few frames, and pressed play again. At the point at which the bottle reached the figure he had highlighted, he paused the action.

'He's wearing leather gloves,' said Jo. 'If it is our unsub, he doesn't want us managing to get a close-up of his hands.'

'He's not wearing a watch either,' said Sarsfield. 'But there's something else, even more interesting.'

'He's holding the bottle with both hands,' said Jo. 'He's the only one so far who has. He's trying to make it look as though he's steadying it, but I'm prepared to bet he's actually spiking her drink.' She was trying hard not to show her excitement. 'Can you get a close-up of that left hand?'

'We've tried over and over again,' the detective constable told her. 'But there's nothing conclusive.'

He found the relevant frames anyway, and zoomed in and out several times. Jo could see what he meant.

'Does he appear in the other clips too?' she asked.

'See what you think,' said Withers.

He played the remaining clips of footage, one relating to victim three, and the other to victim four. The positions of the cameras varied only slightly, and the pubs were as crowded and chaotic as the first had been. The scenarios that played out on the screen were more or less identical, with one exception. Jo sat back down in her chair, her excitement waning.

'None of them have the same man's hairstyle, height or build,' she said. 'Even their gloves aren't the same.'

'But they're all wearing gloves,' Sarsfield pointed out. 'And all those other things can be changed. Okay, his build seems to go up, but that's easy to fake with fat suits and shoulder pads, though it never reaches the point where he's so large he stands out. As for the hair, all that would take is a change of parting, a bit of styling gel, a blow-dry.'

'I see that,' said Jo. 'And there was a piece on one of the break-fast TV programmes about the use of cork and jelly shoe inserts that can boost your height by up to two and a bit inches. Celebrities use them a lot apparently.'

She pointed to the picture frozen on the screen.

'Can you print a still of that, Jack? I'm just about to interview the victim. I'd like to show it to her. See if it might jog her memory.'

'Despite interviewing the victim's friends, and all of the witnesses that have come forward, we haven't been able to identify any of these three men so far,' Sarsfield told her. 'But then we haven't identified fifty per cent of the males in each of those frames.'

Withers handed her the printout.

'Thanks, Jack,' she said.

Jo followed Sarsfield out into the corridor. They walked towards the lifts.

'It must be him, modifying his appearance each time,' Jo said. 'It's too much of a coincidence that all three of those men are wearing gloves. And nobody is that careful to avoid appearing on CCTV. He'd probably checked those pubs out in advance.'

'He'd be stupid not to,' Sarsfield agreed. 'And whatever else our man is, he's not that.'

Jo stopped short of the lift doors.

'I've just realised,' she said, 'that the one thing that seemed to be constant about him was the size and shape of his head. Is it worth someone having a look at that? Then we'd have something to go on, regardless of the hairstyle he chooses?'

'Good idea,' he said, as he pressed the call button.

The doors opened and Jo entered the lift.

'I'll see you later at the press conference,' she said. 'My Boss is coming.'

'Mine too,' he said. 'It should be interesting.'

Chapter 8

Hope Bellman was twenty years of age, five feet two inches tall, with ash-blonde hair, and grey eyes set in an oval face. Had she been smiling, she would have been exceptionally attractive.

She was not smiling. Her face was devoid of make-up, and the studio bed along one wall remained unmade. Her lips were pursed into a thin slash. She was sitting on a sofa wearing a pink onesie buttoned to her neck. When she inclined her head to look up at Jo, a tattoo in the shape of a feather was visible beneath her right ear.

The young woman who had introduced herself as Veronique Akubilo at the door to the student flat pulled a chair out from under a desk.

'I'm sorry, but this is all we have.'

'This will do fine,' said Jo. 'Thank you,'

When the young woman sat down next to Hope, the contrast between the two of them could hardly have been greater. Veronique stood head and shoulders above Jo, and sitting down she towered above her friend. Where Hope's skin was waxy pale, hers was the colour of burnt umber. Her lips and nose were full, while thin arching eyebrows set off oval eyes with dark-chocolate centres. Her hair was an unruly halo of wiry black curls. When Veronique spoke, Jo's attention was irresistibly drawn to two rows of perfect white teeth.

'Well. Have you caught him yet?' she demanded.

Jo already knew from the case notes that Veronique had accompanied Hope on the ill-fated night out. She guessed that her anger was guilt displacement. Jo had encountered it many times before from friends and relatives who believed that they had let their loved ones down – that there were things they could and should have done. Invariably, they were wrong.

'Not yet,' Jo replied. 'That's why I'm here – to see if there's anything else you or Hope may have remembered.'

She looked at Hope, inviting her to reply. Veronique raised her eyebrows. Her response was scornful.

'Remember?'

She placed a long graceful arm around her friend's shoulders, and pulled her close.

'Hope is trying to forget. Every time a police officer turns up asking if she's remembered anything yet, it sets her back. Can't you understand that?'

'Of course I can,' said Jo. 'And as I explained when I rang you, Hope, I'll do everything I can to minimise any upset that my questions may cause. But we have to catch this man. Not only because of what he did to you and to other students, but also on behalf of all those young women he's going to abduct and assault if we don't stop him.'

Veronique was about to respond again, but Hope pushed her delicate arms up through those that enveloped her and prised them apart. Her friend stared at her with surprise as she edged away, took a cushion from behind her back, and placed it on the sofa in between them. The message was clear.

'That's why I agreed to see you, officer,' she said. 'But I don't see how it's going to help, because I don't remember anything I haven't already told your colleagues.'

'Of course you can't remember anything,' muttered Veronique, folding her arms. 'You were drunk, and drugged.'

'Veronique,' said Jo, 'I appreciate that you're here to support Hope. And I'm sure that you're a tremendous source of comfort and reassurance, but this isn't going to work if you keep answering for her. Either I'm going to have to ask you to go into another room while I speak with Hope, or you're going to have to promise not to interrupt.'

Hope placed a hand on her friend's knee.

'She's right, Veronique,' she said, 'and I'd prefer it if you stayed.'

Veronique placed a hand over Hope's.

'I'm sorry,' she said. 'I can't help myself. You know that. Of course I'll stay. And I promise to shut up.'

'I'm not asking you to do that,' said Jo. 'If you could just confine your comments to when I ask you a direct question?'

'Okay.'

'Good. And it's Jo, by the way. "Officer" makes it sound like I'm in the army.'

That managed to drag a smile from both of them.

'So,' she continued, 'Hope, can you start by telling me what you were wearing when you embarked on the pub crawl?'

She saw the expression of surprise on Veronique's face, and hastily added, 'The only reason I'm asking is that this may help us to jog the memory of some of the people who were in the pubs or the vicinity at the same time as you. At the moment, it isn't clear from the notes I have, and the CCTV images are indistinct and in black and white.'

'I deliberately dressed sensibly,' Hope replied. 'I had on a pair of jeans.' She looked down at her legs and frowned. 'Not these – the police kept the ones I was wearing. I had a plain white blouse tucked into them, and a black cagoule over the top. The advice from the Student Union was to wear sensible shoes, so I wore a pair of trainers. White, with green frogs on.'

'When did you decide to go on the pub crawl?' said Jo.

'It was a last-minute thing. Veronique knocked on my door just before lunchtime. She said that she and a couple of other people we'd got to know in this block were going, and did I want to come along?'

Jo nodded. It reinforced her deductions about the reason why Veronique felt so responsible for Hope, and it also suggested that the unsub had singled Hope out on the night, rather than stalking her in advance. It supported Andy's view that he was a collector. She looked down at the notes on her tablet.

'You had quite an early start?' she said. 'Why was that?'

'Because there were fourteen different pubs in all. The idea was to take our time, and have something to eat while we were going round. That way we wouldn't feel that we had to drink fast, and end up drunk halfway round.'

A hot pink blush brought her cheeks to life. She bowed her head and stared at the floor. Veronique squeezed her hand. When she looked up again, there was a hint of shame in her eyes.

'You did nothing wrong,' said Jo. 'Nothing that hundreds of thousands of students haven't done before you. And in any case, as Veronique pointed out, he managed to spike one of your drinks.'

Hope's eyes widened.

'I know, but how? We were so careful. We followed all the advice we were given at the start. We only drank out of bottles and we never let anyone else buy us a drink.'

'I think we may know the answer to that,' Jo told her. 'But I'm hoping that your story of that night will confirm it for us.'

Hope looked up at her friend.

'Could you get me some water, Roni?'

Veronique stood up. 'Would you like a drink of some kind, Jo?' she asked. 'I should have asked when I let you in.'

'Water would be great.'

Veronique went into the kitchenette and returned with three half-pint beer glasses. Jo smiled. She'd been a student herself, and had a pretty good idea where those had come from. When they had all taken a sip, Hope began.

'We arrived at Atmosphere, that's the bar at the Students' Union, at two in the afternoon. We had our first drink in there while we waited for everyone who'd booked on the tour to turn up. It was about three o'clock when we set off.'

It took Hope five minutes to recount their tour through some of the best pubs Salford and Manchester had to offer. That was half as many minutes as it had taken them in hours. She only stopped to have a drink of water when her mouth dried up. Her voice remained clear, and confident.

She'd started off with good intentions, planning to have a bottle of water or a Red Bull in every third venue. However, it seemed that she'd lost count halfway round, and settled for whatever bottle was passed to her. She'd eaten a Greek veggie burger in the Knott Bar at around 5pm, and shared a plate of saag aloo with Veronique in The Garratt on Princess Street at around 8.30pm.

'We only had three more pubs to go to the end of the official tour,' Hope said. 'I was feeling proud of myself for having stayed the pace.' Here, she smiled grimly. 'After all, it's not as though I'm going to have the same alcohol tolerance as someone the size of Veronique?'

Her friend feigned hurt, but both she and Jo knew that Hope was right. She may have been carried along on a tide of peer pressure, but her peers should have known better than to expect this slightly built young woman to keep pace with them.

'By the time we reached Sinclair's Oyster Bar on Cathedral Approach, I knew I'd had more than enough. I remember being unsteady on my feet, and having to sit down at one of the outside tables. I sat there for quite a while. I don't think I had a drink?'

'You didn't,' Veronique confirmed.

'Someone suggested we finish off at The Crescent, because it was on the way home?'

'It was Keira's idea,' Veronique reminded her. 'We did go into The Crescent, but they refused to serve us because they said we'd already had far too much.'

Good for them, thought Jo. What a pity that hadn't happened a lot earlier. Not that you could blame the bar staff. It must have been impossible to decide who was with whom.

'I think you'd better take it from here, Roni,' said Hope. It was the first time that her voice had faltered.

'Carla invited a few of us back to her place in the Student Village, on the other side of the Irwell,' said Veronique, 'to sober up with a pizza and a box set of the first season of *Girls*. I said I'd better stay with Hope, but she said no, she'd be alright, and I should go. Carla ordered a taxi to pick us up in the bus lay-by. We walked with Hope towards the Towers while we were waiting for it to arrive.'

She looked down at her friend. Hope, head bowed, clasped the glass of water tight with frail hands as though her life depended on it. A look of pity flitted across Veronique's face. When she turned back to face Jo it had been replaced by a different one. *Regret*, Jo thought, *or guilt?*

'The bloody taxi came too soon,' Veronique said. 'Carla and the others ran back to the taxi. Hope was holding on to the railings by the park. The others had the door of the taxi open. "Come on, Roni!" shouted Carla. "She'll be alright."' She shook her head as though reliving the moment. 'I didn't know what to do. Then Hope said, "You go, Roni. I'll be alright, I promise."'

She turned her head, and stared out of the window.

'Only she wasn't, was she?'

Jo stood up and walked over to the window. Even this late on a slate-grey winter's afternoon, the view was impressive. From up here, Salford merged seamlessly with Manchester, her bigger brother. The glass and steel monoliths that had come to define the twin cities were set into stark relief by a pale sun breaking through the leaden sky over Kinder Scout, twenty miles away in the Pennine Hills.

'Show me,' she said, 'where she was when you last saw her.'

'You can't quite see it from here,' said Veronique. 'It's just beyond that corner where the road curves around the trees.'

'In each of the pubs that you visited,' Jo said, 'was it always you that ordered the drinks for your friends, Veronique?'

The young woman looked surprised by the sudden change in direction.

'Yes,' she said. 'They asked me to hold on to the kitty and get the drinks in. I do most weekends, because I don't drink that much. You see, it's nearly always packed at the bar then. When there's an organised pub crawl, even more so.' She grinned self-consciously. 'You may not have noticed, but I have the advantage of being tall. I can pass the drinks back to them over people's heads. It's the only way to do it. Besides, if the bar staff reckon one of your party's had too much to drink, they can refuse to serve all of you.'

'How often does that happen?'

She shrugged.

'Sixty per cent of the time.'

Jo was pleased that the drive to make bars act more responsibly seemed to be working, but it didn't help if the punters kept finding ways around it.

'And more and more of the pubs,' Veronique continued, 'have bouncers on the door to weed out people who look like they might cause trouble, and turn away anyone who's had too much to drink.'

Jo returned to her seat and retrieved the still photo of the video footage from her bag. She handed it to Veronique.

'Yeah,' she said immediately, stabbing the picture with a long red-varnished fingernail. 'That's Kelly and that's me. And look, that's you, Hope, just in view.'

Hope stared at it briefly, and then turned away.

'And this man?' said Jo. 'The one wearing gloves. Do you remember seeing him?'

Veronique stared at it, nudged her friend, passed her the photo, and pointed to the man in question.

Hope looked at it and shook her head. Then she looked at Jo. Her hand trembled as she passed it back.

'Is it him?' she asked.

Jo had no idea which reply she had been hoping for.

'We don't know,' she said. She placed the photo back in her bag. 'In the week before the night in question, Hope, did you ever get the sense that there was someone watching you?'

'Someone?'

'A man?'

'Of course there were men watching her,' Veronique retorted. It could easily have sounded belligerent, but she didn't mean it to be. She was simply pointing out the obvious.

'Have you seen her? She's beautiful! Do you know how many students there are at this university? Over twenty thousand. Half of those are male. Then there are all the lecturers, and technicians and builders. Everywhere we go there are men leching.'

Over the years, Jo had been made well aware of how attractive to men she was. Nowhere more so than within the force itself, including men who were well aware of her sexual orientation. Those with the biggest egos had regarded her as a challenge. Until she'd put them straight.

'I appreciate that,' she said. 'Even in a crowded room, we women tend to know when someone is paying us close attention. You get this sense that someone is watching you. You look up, and there he is, staring straight at you? That must have happened to you, too?'

Both girls nodded.

'So, Hope, did you get any such feeling in the week or so before that night? That someone was watching you or following you?'

'I'm sorry. No.'

Jo could tell that Hope was tiring, physically and emotionally.

'One last thing,' she said. 'Could you just close your eyes, rest your head back, and try to relax.' She waited until Hope had done that, and her breathing had become shallow. 'Now, Hope,' she said. 'Take yourself back to the moment that Roni and Carla got in that taxi, and you were standing there on your own. Is there anything at all that you remember?'

There was a distant hum of rush-hour traffic on the A6, and the low, steady, heartbeat thump of a subwoofer in the flat above. After an age, Hope opened her eyes. 'I'm sorry,' she said, 'I still can't remember a thing.'

She looked disconsolate.

'Don't worry,' Jo told her. 'I'm sure you've already been told that it's completely normal not to remember anything after a trauma such as you have suffered. Your brain is protecting itself, that's all. You've been really helpful. Both of you.'

If only that were true, she told herself as she headed for the lifts.

Chapter 9

Jo decided to retrace the steps that Hope Bellman would have taken to reach the entrance to the flats. Presumably she had been taken somewhere along that route. She had covered thirty-five yards when something made her stop, turn around, and look up at the tower block.

Two faces stared fleetingly down at her from a tenth-floor window. One deathly white, ghostlike, the other a black shadow barely discernible in the dark interior of the room.

Jo turned, and carried on counting. She had reached one hundred and fifty-six by the time she arrived at the spot that Veronique Akubilo had described. For all but the last forty yards, Hope Bellman would have been visible not only from her own tower block, but the one set back a little beside it, and five more blocks that lined the south side of the street.

Jo stood by the railings beneath the line of trees where Akubilo had left her friend. It wouldn't have helped to tell her, but it had been a bloody selfish thing to do. Besides, Akubilo already knew that. It explained why she was sleeping on that fold-up camp bed in Hope's lounge.

Jo stood with her back to the railings, and began to scan the area with the eyes of a predator. Twenty-five yards in front of her in a gap between the trees, across a road, a verge, a broad pavement, another verge and a set of iron railings, cars sped past on the A6 dual carriageway. She tried to envisage it at night. Eyes fixed on the road ahead, the headlights of their vehicle barely spilling beyond the railings: it would have taken less than half a second for a driver to pass by. The likelihood of anyone, even if endowed with the best peripheral night vision in the world, noticing Hope Bellman being bundled into a vehicle was less than the odds of winning the EuroMillions lottery.

Jo looked to her left. The bend, and overhanging trees which must have been in leaf at the time, would have obscured the vision of everyone unless they were rounding the corner at the precise moment that Hope was abducted. Behind her, across a wide area of grass, was a low building that she knew to be a Sure Start Children's Centre.

She turned to her right. The trees ran out in less than fifty yards, as did the far verge and the railings. She could see the bus stop and the lay-by where the taxi had pulled in. Two hundred yards further down the road stood several more high-rise blocks of flats, and the slip road from the dual carriageway. From this direction, the predator would have been far more exposed. And yet, what lighting there was had been trained on the A6 rather than this stretch of road, as was the only camera that she could see, high up on a stanchion.

There was no way that the unsub could have followed the girls on foot, waited until Hope was alone, and then gone back for his car in order to abduct her. Perhaps he had an accomplice who followed in a vehicle at a distance, and who was called up when the opportunity arose? If not, he must have parked his vehicle close to the end of the pub crawl, or his intended victim's rooms. But that would entail him knowing where she lived. That would also have required a back-up plan if Hope had been accompanied to her flat? Or a willingness to abort his mission. *How many times does he have to gamble and fail,* she wondered, *before he makes a successful abduction?*

Jo shook her head. There were too many ifs and buts. If nothing else, she now knew for certain that the unsub was a high-risk predator. A gambler who planned meticulously in order to reduce the odds, and had the ability to think on his feet when things did not go exactly to plan. That sounded like every serial killer she had studied, and several she had experienced first-hand. Not that this suspect had killed anyone. Not yet. She walked back to her car, and drove the six miles that her satnav said it would take to reach the spot in Worsley Woods where Hope Bellman had been found.

It was raining. A miserable drizzle rather than the torrential downpours of the past few days. A blue-and-white streamer fluttered from the branch of a tree, the only clue that this had been a crime scene. It had been raining on the morning that a dog walker had discovered Hope lying curled up on a bed of leaf mould beneath these trees, beside the broad metalled path of the Route 55 National Cycle Path.

Hope had been barely conscious. Dressed in the clothes that she had worn the night before, she was freezing cold, wet and shivering. According to the paramedics, in less than an hour she would have succumbed to hypothermia.

Dense woodland bordered the cycle path, which stretched ahead in a straight line for two hundred and fifty yards, before curving away to pass beneath the M60 motorway a similar distance away. It was close to sunset, and the light all but gone. It must have been this gloomy the morning that Hope was left here.

Jo found herself shivering, less from the chill wind and rain than from this unwelcome reminder of another wood and a different time, and how close she had come to a worse fate than that of the student. As she shook her head to chase the memory away, droplets of water sprayed from the peak of her NCS cagoule.

A warning shout made her turn. A man and a woman, sporting helmets and capes, powered towards her on their mountain bikes. Jo stepped aside as they passed, the spray from their wheels soaking her boots and the bottom of her trousers.

She squelched her way back to the bottom of the wooden steps that led up to Greenleach Lane, where she had to wait for a middle-aged woman, already halfway down, accompanied by a Westie and a Labradoodle. As soon as the Labradoodle's feet had reached terra firma, it proceeded to shake its woolly coat, soaking Jo's trousers to her knees.

'Molly!' said the owner, with an apologetic smile, before striding off with her dogs, waving a black-handled pooper scooper and a bulging plastic bag.

Jo climbed to the top of the steps and stood by the wooden fence on the bridge at the corner of Roe Green Junction. This had to be where the unsub had entered the woods. From the map on the board, Jo surmised that no vehicle larger than a bicycle could have entered the woods, and come within half a mile of the spot where Hope was left. Too far and too risky for him to have carried her. Theoretically, he could have parked on the hard shoulder of the M60, carried the student down the maintenance steps and then a further five hundred yards, before placing her on the grass beside the path. But the cameras that had been installed for the 'smart' motorway improvements would surely have been too great a deterrent. In fact, she was fairly sure that the hard shoulder was now coned off at that point – something she would check on the way back.

Instead, Jo's instinct told her that this was definitely the place that he had chosen. Beside a bend in the road, shaded by overhanging trees, with woods on either side, and a hundred yards across the village green to the nearest large suburban house hidden behind a row of beeches, it gave quick and partly concealed access to the woods. He would have been unlucky to encounter a walker or cyclist that early in the morning, and yet he must have known that within an hour or so, one or the other would find her.

Presumably that had been his plan. Each of his victims had been left where someone would come across them before too long. And yet every one of them had been vulnerable in one way or another. Sareen Lomax might easily have stumbled into the path of a speeding car – in the same way that Hayley Royton could have fallen on to the rocks at Pickup Bank, or Hope Bellman might have crawled deeper into the woods and perished of hypothermia.

Whoever this unsub was, his behaviours were contradictory. He planned meticulously, yet left crucial elements to chance. An opportunist rapist seized his moment. This perpetrator had an overall design, a strategy, and an array of tactics that he employed according to changing circumstances. Andy was right. This was an elaborate game. A game of chess, she decided, in which the victims were his pawns, and the police his opponent.

Jo returned to the car, removed her boots and placed her sodden socks inside them. She dried her frozen feet with the micro towel in her sports bag, slipped on a pair of her training socks, put on her shoes, closed the trunk, and set off for GMP Headquarters in Central Park, deep in thought.

Chapter 10

If the number of people packed into the media suite was anything to go by, Operation Juniper had gone viral. Jo had read that Manchester was the second largest media centre, including digital and creative industries, outside of London. She counted three national TV crews, another three representing local stations, and a host of radio reporters. The national broadsheet and tabloid newspapers were all here, as were the locals.

'If any more turn up, we'll have to go outside to the car park to accommodate them all,' whispered Gerry Sarsfield.

'What was that?' demanded Helen Gates, the newly promoted Assistant Chief Constable, who was sitting to his left.

'I was just saying to SI Stuart that we seem to have attracted quite a crowd, Ma'am,' Sarsfield replied.

'Mixed blessing,' Gates said, pursing her lips, and scanning the crowd for a friendly face or two. 'It means we should be able to get our appeals out to a wide audience, but on the other hand they tend to start trying to outdo each other with snide comments and unbridled criticism when the big guns are here. Then there's a danger that the sniping is what gets into print, on to screen and out on the airwaves, and our message gets lost.'

Harry Stone slipped into the seat beside Jo. He looked harassed. There were dark shadows beneath his eyes.

'Sorry I'm late,' he said. 'The traffic was appalling, and the taxi driver wasn't much better. Doesn't know the city and couldn't work his satnav.'

'It's good to see you, Boss,' she said. 'How are you?'

'I'm fine.' He grinned ruefully. 'My hair got soaked running between the taxi and reception. I had to dry it under one of the hand dryers in the men's toilets. That's the other reason I'm late.'

Stone looked around the crowded room. 'Are you ready for this?'

Jo pointed to the cards in front of her. 'As I'll ever be.'

'Good,' he said. 'Because it looks like they've sent the A team. I suspect that you're going to have to field some bloody difficult questions.' He smiled weakly. 'But you can always deflect the impossible ones.'

'Deflect to whom?' she said.

He leaned forward, and looked past her down the row of officers and media advisers.

'Who's that, next but one, the attractive Assistant Chief Commissioner?' he whispered.

'Helen Gates. She took over from Martin Hadfield when he retired last month, Boss. I thought you were in the observation room with her when I interviewed the Operation Hound suspects?'

'I must be losing it,' he said. 'I knew I'd seen her somewhere before. I'm surprised I didn't recognise her straight away. Anyway, to answer your original question, that's who to deflect them to, ACC Gates.'

Jo was about to reply, but Helen Gates tapped her water glass several times with her biro. Gradually the hubbub in the room subsided. Lights appeared on video cameras. The hush was charged with expectancy. The senior press officer began by thanking everyone for coming at this time in the evening, introduced the panel and explained the procedure.

'This investigation is being coordinated and led by the National Crime Agency, in conjunction with the Greater Manchester, Lancashire, and West Yorkshire Police Forces. Greater Manchester Police have provided a Major Incident Room in the North Manchester Divisional Headquarters next door. Assistant Chief Constable Helen Gates will take all questions regarding policing logistics. Deputy Director Harry Stone will respond to those relating to the role of the National Crime Agency. All questions regarding the current progress of the investigation should be addressed to Senior Investigator Joanne Stuart.'

She paused and looked around the room at the seasoned hacks, and the keen young bloods straining forward like greyhounds in the traps.

'You have all been given a briefing sheet and a prepared statement. We will now take questions. This will be followed by an appeal to members of the public with which we need your assistance. Now, who would like to go first?'

A sea of hands appeared. The press officer pointed to one at the front.

'Dave Grice, BBC North West,' the reporter announced. 'SI Stuart, can you confirm the number of young women who have been abducted and raped by this man?'

Jo leaned into the microphone.

'We have reason to suspect that five young women have been victims of the same perpetrator.'

'Over what period of time?'

'Fifteen months.'

'So you're investigating a serial rapist?'

'We believe so, yes.'

'What makes you think it's the same man?' asked a woman from one of the broadsheets.

'The modus operandi.'

'Which is what exactly?'

Helen Gates signalled to Jo with her hand, and simultaneously leaned forward.

'We will only answer that in general terms,' she said.

'What, where and how would be a start,' one of the journalists muttered.

It was greeted with murmurs of agreement from his colleagues.

The Assistant Chief Constable looked sideways at Jo. Her expression warned her to be careful.

'Go for it, Jo,' Harry Stone whispered.

Jo took a deep breath.

'To date,' she said, 'the crimes we're investigating have all been committed in university towns and cities in the North West of England, on Friday and Saturday nights between midnight and two o' clock in the morning. The victims have either been in a party, or with one or two friends from whom they have become separated. All of the victims have had a significant amount to drink prior to their disappearance, but we believe that their drinks are likely to have been spiked.'

'Significant amount?' said one of the TV reporters. 'Are you implying that the victims were culpable in some way?'

'Absolutely not!' Jo replied firmly. 'To quote the Operation Talon website, "Drinking Is Not A Crime – Rape Is!"'

'But you don't deny that drink was a contributory factor?'

'Yes, I do deny that. What a woman drinks or wears has no bearing on the act of rape. Neither is it an invitation to be victimised.' She held up a hand to forestall a response. 'I agree that anything that is likely to make a woman or a man more vulnerable to sexual assault should be avoided. For example, accepting lifts from strangers, including taxis that haven't been booked by telephone; walking home alone in the dark; becoming intoxicated with alcohol or drugs such that your senses are seriously impaired. But none of these things can be used to attribute any responsibility to a victim of the abhorrent crime of rape. To do so would be to become an apologist for rape.'

'Well done,' whispered Stone.

An ITV reporter was selected.

'ACC Gates, if these crimes began fifteen months ago,' he asked. 'Why have you waited until now to call in the National Crime Agency?'

'Firstly, because there were twelve months between the first and second abductions. Secondly, it was only within the past month that these were designated as serial offences. Thirdly, because both Lancashire Police and my own force have dedicated teams for serious sexual offences. And finally, because it is only in the past week that the perpetrator has been active outside of this region.'

'And what exactly is a National Crime Agency takeover going to add to the investigation?'

Everybody stared at Harry Stone. He leaned into the mike.

'I'd like to stress from the outset that this is not a takeover. This is a joint operation coordinated by the National Crime Agency. You have already heard about the existing expertise of the dedicated sexual offences units in this region. They will continue to work on this investigation. However, between them they currently have ongoing investigations into over two thousand alleged sex offences against children, and a thousand allegations of rape.'

There were gasps around the room as reporters checked with each other that they had heard correctly. Stone hurried on.

'Clearly, under these circumstances any additional resources would be advantageous. The National Crime Agency has already committed additional staff in the Major Incident Room, and the expertise of our Behavioural Science Unit staffed with intelligence analysts together with senior investigators, including SI Stuart.'

'Are we talking profilers?' someone shouted from the back of the room.

'Forensic behavioural psychologists,' he replied.

'So have you got a profile yet?' someone else shouted against a general clamour for the details. Jo had seen this kind of reaction before, whenever mention was made of a profiler. It almost always derailed a press conference, something she had been dreading.

The press officer stood up.

'Unless we're able to continue in an orderly manner, with questions directed through me to members of this panel, then I'm afraid we will be unable to take any more questions.'

A hand shot up. It was a reporter from one of the tabloids.

'Larry Hymer, Manchester Evening News. I have a question for Mr Stone.'

'Go ahead.'

'Do you have a profile yet?'

There was a chorus of approval from his colleagues.

Poker-faced, Harry Stone leaned forward.

'No comment.'

Another hand went up.

'Is it true he tattoos his victims?'

'No comment.'

'Only we've heard he tattoos them with the image of a bird of prey. Is that true?'

'No comment.'

Jo tried to see who had asked the question. She'd always known that it was a matter of time before that detail was leaked to the press. The problem was that this was going to boost the unsub's vanity and feed his craving. Not only that, but it could lead to copycat offences that would only serve to cloud the investigation.

'Maybe he keeps birds of prey,' joked someone. This led to a flurry of asides.

'Maybe he's a birdwatcher?'

Several of the reporter's colleagues laughed nervously. The majority of them looked uncomfortable. A woman turned towards him and shouted 'Shame!'

Before Jo had time to think, she found herself responding.

'If anyone here,' she said, 'believes that this is a subject for humour, then I invite them to come with me to meet some of the victims, and to hear first-hand the life-changing impact of these horrific crimes.'

Helen Gates whispered to the press officer, who leapt to her feet.

'I will now call on Senior Investigator Stuart to make a direct appeal to the public.'

Jo took a deep breath and picked up the card on which the appeal was written, more for reassurance than anything else; she had already committed it to memory.

'We are asking any young woman who has been approached by a stranger in any of the North West and West Yorkshire university towns, perhaps offering to give you a lift home or to a hospital or to walk you home, especially if they have attempted to force you into a vehicle, to ring the following dedicated numbers where your call will be taken in strictest confidence by one of our specialist officers. Those numbers are as follows.'

She read them out slowly, while at the same time they appeared on the screen behind the panel.

'Alternatively, you can ring CrimeStoppers on 0800 555 111. The information that you provide will be sent anonymously to our Major Incident Room. You can also provide the information anonymously using the online form on the CrimeStoppers online website at www.crimestoppers-uk.org.'

More hands shot up. The press officer stood up.

'Thank you for coming,' she said. 'And thank you for your cooperation in ensuring that this appeal reaches the widest possible audience. You will all be kept informed of future developments as they arise. In the meantime, please direct all related enquiries through the press office. Good afternoon and thank you again.'

The panel stood as one and began to file out before any of the reporters could accost them. Stone whispered in Jo's ear, 'You're a natural.'

'Thanks, Boss,' she said. 'Thank God it's over.'

She heard him sigh.

'If only,' he said.

Chapter 11

The debriefing took ten minutes. Jo brought Harry Stone up to date, and then joined Gerry Sarsfield and the Incident Room Manager.

'There is one action I'd like to propose,' she said, 'but it's going to require the cooperation of all three Forces.'

'Go on,' Sarsfield sounded apprehensive.

'Automatic number plate recognition. I'd like ANPR cars patrolling areas around universities during the window in which we believe that he operates. Midnight till three am, Fridays to Sundays.'

The DI frowned. He led them over to the board on which a large map of the region had been attached.

'Red pins denote the previous known sighting of each victim,' the Incident Room Manager explained. 'Blue pins mark the location at which each victim was discovered, green pins the victim's universities, brown pins all of the remaining universities.'

'There are twelve universities in the North West,' said Sarsfield. 'Five in West Yorkshire. Most of these have multiple campuses. That's a minimum of seventeen cars. And what if he decides to spread his wings?'

'The universities tend to be close to each other,' Jo pointed out, 'and we're only talking five cities and two rural communities. What if we concentrated on those universities in the region where he has not yet struck – that would narrow it down to just eleven?'

'*Just* eleven?'

'One in Cumbria, three in West Yorkshire, five in Merseyside, and two in Greater Manchester. But since neither Cumbria nor Greater Merseyside are involved as yet, that would leave only five.'

Sarsfield pursed his lips, as though he'd bitten on a lemon.

'I can try, but you know what they're going to say?'

Jo nodded. 'Scarce resources, needle in a haystack, come back when you've got a better idea of what you're looking for.'

'There you go then.'

'I see one problem,' she admitted. 'We don't know what to tell them. Normally we'd be talking about a van, a covered pickup or an estate car with tinted windows. All of his victims have been small enough to hide in the trunk of a Nissan Micra. The only forensics we have relate to GM Vauxhall and Opel models, but they may not even be from the suspect vehicle.'

'Sounds like you're talking yourself out of it?'

Jo allowed herself time to think. Even if they turned her down, at least her proposal would be logged. If the worst came to the worst and he struck again before they caught him, they couldn't say she hadn't tried.

'No,' she said. 'Go ahead and ask. And tell them we're working flat out to try and identify suspect vehicles. And remind them that if nothing else, a marked car cruising around should work as a deterrent and reassure the public.'

It took another half an hour for her to log the reports of her interview with Hope Bellman and Veronique Akubilo, and her visit to Worsley Woods. It was ten past ten in the evening when she finished. She had been on the go for fifteen hours, and suddenly realised that the only food that she'd had was that sandwich ten hours before.

'I'm off home,' she told the Incident Room Manager.

'I don't blame you, Ma'am,' he said. 'You look . . .' he pulled himself up short, '. . . exhausted.'

She smiled wearily.

'Shit is the word I think you're looking for,' she said. 'It's also how I feel. Tell DI Sarsfield I'll be at the Quays first thing in the morning.'

Five girls abducted and raped already, she reminded herself as the lift descended. He was not going to stop. At times like this, she'd work around the clock seven days a week if she could. There was no such thing as too early or too late, only too exhausted to continue. It was something that Abbie had never been able to understand. Something that had begun as a mild irritant, and developed into a festering sore.

Caton had drummed into her the importance of sleep during a major investigation. It gave your body a chance to rest, and your unconscious mind the opportunity to process everything. That was when moments of clarity occurred. When critical insights surfaced. When the blindingly obvious slapped you in the face.

The lift doors opened. A member of the Reception desk staff looked up and waved Jo over.

'That bloke's been waiting for you for over an hour.'

A man in a black leather jacket was seated on a couch, his back towards her. He was looking at something in his lap.

'He's one of those reporters who were at the press conference. Insisted on waiting. If you want to slip out while he's not looking, Ma'am, I can give it five minutes and then tell him he's missed you?'

'Thanks,' she said, 'but I'll see him on his way.'

He saw her reflection in the plate-glass window as she walked towards him, stood up, and turned to face her. The man was in his late thirties she guessed, tall with an athletic build, mid-blond hair cut in the angular fringe popular with professional footballers, blue eyes, designer stubble and an overconfident smile. He wore a blue sweatshirt under the jacket and skinny jeans. A black-and-silver scarf trailed across the back of the couch. He held an iPad in his left hand.

'SI Stuart,' he said, 'I accept.'

She took a step back.

'I beg your pardon?'

His smile broadened.

'I accept your invitation to meet one of the victims. I think it could help with your appeal.'

Had she not been so tired, she might have told him to bugger off there and then.

'Who are you?' she said instead.

'Sorry. Rude of me.' He fished in his inside jacket pocket, produced a laminated photo ID card, and handed it to her.

Anthony Ginley. The photograph had been taken seven years ago. The same face, less the smile, the same designer stubble. According to the accreditation he was with *Independent Press Consultants, UK Ltd.*

'Never heard of them,' she said, 'or you.'

He smiled serenely.

'No reason you should have. We're all freelance investigative journalists. IPC UK handles our accounts. We sell our services and stories to the big boys for big bucks.'

'Good for you,' she said. 'Now if you don't mind, it's been a long day.'

She turned to go.

'What about it then?' he said. 'Your invitation?'

'It was rhetorical. I'd have expected an investigative journalist to get that.'

'Make a great story,' he called after her. 'It would harness public sympathy and help your appeal no end.' His tone hardened.

'I assumed you'd prefer to be there, but I can always talk to the victims without you.'

She turned to face him so that he could see the anger in her eyes.

'You do anything that hinders this investigation, or causes any of those victims further distress, and I'll make it my job to ensure that you regret it.'

His smile never wavered.

'Is that a threat, SI Stuart?'

'No, Mr Ginley,' she said, 'it's a promise.'

The door to their Northern Quarter apartment block closed silently behind her. The residents' management committee had been busy. The fifteen-foot ornamental tree that always dominated the central foyer had been adorned with twinkling white lights and topped with a star. Jo suddenly realised that she had forgotten that the season of peace, goodwill and ringing tills had arrived.

Under normal circumstances, she and Abbie would already have spent an evening exploring the Christmas Markets, strolling from stall to stall between Albert Square and The Shambles, drinking mulled wine, listening to the brass bands and carol-singers from the Royal Northern College of Music, and buying a new decoration for their own Christmas tree.

She walked wearily across to the floating stairway. The sound of her footsteps on the wooden treads bounced off the brick walls and steel columns, a hollow reproach that followed her to their apartment on the top floor. As she put her key in the lock, someone opened a door on the floor below. The muted strains of Wizzard's 'I Wish It Could Be Christmas Everyday' floated briefly around the mezzanine, ceasing abruptly as the door slammed shut.

Jo entered the apartment, cancelled the alarm, closed the door and stood for a moment with her back against it. A week ago, she had stood just like this as she plucked up the courage to face Abbie. Now it was with the dread of entering the empty apartment. She took a deep breath, picked up her work bag and the Booths bag-for-life, walked into the lounge and switched on the lights.

It was just as she had left it. She placed her bags on the kitchen table, removed the two bottles of wine and placed them in the rack. She turned the fisherman's pie over and read the instructions. Forty-five to fifty minutes in an oven. She wasn't sure she could stay awake that long.

She popped the meal in the oven, and then checked the phone for voice messages: there were none. She went into the bedroom, threw her jacket on the bed, stripped, and left her clothes in a heap on the floor.

The shower's nebulizing mist spray drenched her body, along with wave after wave of foaming shower gel flushing away the accumulated sweat and grime of the past sixteen hours, and the stress that came with it. Jo wrapped a towel around her head, shrugged on her bathrobe and stepped back into the bedroom.

An uneasy feeling came over her. She sat on the bed and looked around. She had no idea what it was that was so disturbing. The bed was made, the room neat and tidy, but for the pile of her discarded clothing. The dressing table was just as she had left it. She stood up and opened the fitted wardrobes one by one. Nothing had been disturbed. The two rails where Abbie hung her winter clothes, and all of her drawers, had been emptied six days ago while Jo was at work. The remaining rail still held her summer dresses, skirts and trousers. She closed the door and looked around the room again. Something prompted her to go back into the wet room.

Jo's eyes were drawn to the tiled shelf above the twin sinks. The year they had moved in together for the first time, they had bought a pair of matching mugs each with a red heart beneath their name. She was certain that Abbie's mug had been there this morning. Now it was gone. Jo felt dizzy and clutched the doorjamb for support. The absence of that tiny object threatened to engulf her with an overwhelming sense of loss, of grief, that Abbie's physical presence had not. She took a moment to compose herself, switched off the light and lay down on the bed. She closed her eyes and invited sleep to rescue her.

An insistent beeping told Jo that the pie was ready. With a sigh, she rolled over, swung her feet off the bed, and went through to the kitchen. She removed the pie from the oven, spooned half of it on to a plate, took it through to the lounge and switched on the television.

She caught the depressing tail end of the *Ten O'Clock News*, and was about to channel-hop when the presenter segued to Regional updates. The Operation Juniper press conference was the final North West item.

Jo hated watching herself at the best of times, but decided to stick it out if only to see how her appeal had been received. Judicious editing had cut out most of the Q&A session, with the exception of her angry response to the TV reporter. She winced as the camera zoomed in on her face, and then cut away to catch Helen Gates's expression. But at least the appeal was shown in its entirety.

The weather forecast followed the news. There was no good news for those in Cumbria, struggling to recover from the devastating floods following Storm Desmond. Another would be hitting the UK mainland within the next few days. Jo switched off and returned to her meal. After a few mouthfuls she realised that her appetite had disappeared.

Jo took her plate into the kitchen, scraped the remains into the food caddy, and then did the same with the remaining half. Delicious as it was, she could not face reheating it in the microwave like some sad and lonely spinster. She set the alarm, went into the bedroom, switched off the light, and crawled beneath the duvet.

She lay in the dark, lost in their king-size bed, listening in vain for the soothing sound of Abbie's breaths beside her. The silence was implacable, a brooding force that weighed down on her, and brought tears to her eyes. An eerie creaking sound startled her. Jo sat up, and reached for the light switch, before realising that it was only the hot-water pipes contracting in the walls as the temperature dropped.

She lay down again, rolled on to her side, closed her eyes, and prayed for a deep and dreamless sleep. But the dreams came thick and fast. None of them memorable. With one exception.

She was walking in a wood on a path of pine needles, springy beneath her feet, each step wafting scent into the air. Birds were singing, and shafts of sunlight filtered through the trees. Then the path began to narrow, and the trees crowded in on either side. The wood became a dark and impenetrable forest. She turned and began to run back the way she had come, tripping over a root and sprawling on her hands and knees. When she got to her feet, her shoes were missing. Now every step was agony, the naked soles of her feet pricked and probed by the bed of needles. A wall of branches blocked her path. Someone screamed.

Jo woke bathed in sweat, knowing that it was she that had screamed. When she checked the time, she realised that she had either slept through the alarm or had failed to switch it on, so that she was an hour later than she had intended. Worse still, she felt physically, emotionally, and mentally drained.

Chapter 12

'Did you sleep okay?'

Ram sounded genuinely concerned. Jo smiled. 'Yes, thanks.'

'You need to go back home and sleep some more,' Dorsey Zephaniah called over from beside the fax machine. 'You look . . .'

'Terrible, I know,' said Jo. 'But I'm fine, honestly.'

'Well, I'm fixing you a big mug of coffee,' Dizzy said. 'Did you have breakfast?'

Jo's face was a giveaway.

'I thought not,' said Dizzy. 'I'll fix you toast when I've done the coffee.'

Jo was too tired to argue. She put her jacket over the back of her chair and her bag on the desk, sat down, and stared at her ghostlike reflection on the monitor screen.

'Here you go, dear.'

Jo looked up and saw Dizzy standing there, a coffee in one hand and a plate of buttered toast in the other.

'Zeph, you're an angel sent from God,' she said.

Dizzy beamed one of her gleaming smiles.

'I know it. Where do you want this, Ma'am? On your desk or in the rest area?'

Jo moved her bag to make space.

'Here's fine. I need to get started before people start wondering where I am.'

The administrator raised her eyebrows.

'Too late for that,' she said. 'Check your emails.'

By the time the computer booted up, and she had logged in, Jo had demolished both slices of toast. *At least*, she thought, *my appetite has returned.*

There were fifty-three emails. It took her two minutes to delete the dozen or so that the spam filter had failed to block and mark as read another dozen that looked like NCA administrative circulars. The remainder, from Gerry Sarsfield, Harry Stone, and the SIOs from Lancashire and West Yorkshire, she quickly prioritised.

Gerry had sent her seven, each of them expressing growing frustration at her failure to respond. She decided to ring him rather than reply to his emails.

'Thank God, I was beginning to think something had happened to you,' he said.

'I'm sorry, Gerry,' she replied. 'It's a long story. I've only just got into the office. The appeal certainly seems to have had an impact?'

'You could say that,' he said. 'But how exactly remains to be seen.'

He didn't sound as upbeat as she had expected.

'Seventy phone calls, and two allegations of rape,' she pointed out. 'That sounds like a result to me.'

'Mmm. Depends where they take us. They've all been collated, and I've got a pair of specialist detectives from the Operation Talon syndicate following up the most promising. But I wouldn't get your hopes up.'

'Why, Gerry? What are you saying?'

'Half of them are historical. Go back anything up to twenty years ago. If your lot are right, our unsub would have been at primary school.'

'And the other half?'

'Five have all the hallmarks of time-wasters and, before you jump down my throat, yes, we are going to talk to them.'

'I never doubted that, Gerry.'

'Fair enough,' Sarsfield said. 'I'm sorry, Jo, it's just that I've got accustomed to having to defend every action we take just because of the way allegations of rape and sexual assault were treated in the past. It's not easy being a man.'

'It's not just male officers who face this kind of thing. How would you like to be accused of betraying the sisterhood?'

'That's never going to happen, is it?'

She sensed him smiling.

'Anyway,' he continued. 'Seven of them are the wrong age, inasmuch as they don't fit his current pattern. In their thirties and upwards. One of them's sixty-three.'

'It doesn't mean . . .'

'I know. We're doing a second-level triage on all of those, and a further seventeen that fall outside the pattern. We will follow every one of them up within the next forty-eight hours.'

'And the remaining six?'

'You've been counting. I'm impressed. Those six are the ones that are being interviewed today. Not that any of them set our pulses racing.'

'When you say outside the pattern, what markers are you using?'

'Students, attending a university or college in the North West or West Yorkshire, late teens to mid-twenties, petite, blonde, been out drinking, and approached in the way you described in the appeal. We've broadened it to include any responses from Cheshire and Derbyshire.'

She couldn't fault his logic.

'What about the two allegations of rape?'

'Those are being processed in line with our standard procedure. I have to say from the outset that neither of them appear to be connected to our man.'

'Because?'

'Because one of them has the hallmarks of a date rape. We have a name and location for the alleged offender. We expect to have him in custody within the next hour or so. The other one looks like an opportunist attack, in an alley near to a host of student lets. We're pretty sure this is the same person who made an unsuccessful attempt last weekend. We have a good description. He's a teenager, South East Asian, thin, five feet three or four, and he was brandishing a knife.'

Jo felt suddenly deflated. He must have sensed it from her silence.

'Jo,' he said, quietly, 'last year, in the first three months of the university year, we investigated thirty student rapes across Greater Manchester. Sadly, these two are nothing out of the ordinary.'

'I know,' she said, 'but those committed by our unsub are. Do you know what my colleague Ram found when I asked him to research rape abductions?'

'No. Surprise me.'

'That it proved impossible to come up with a reliable figure. Child abductions are classified separately in the UK, but those involving adults are hidden within "violence against the person". Even so, with the exception of abduction for sex slavery, which includes rape, and kidnapping for forced marriage, genuine abduction for the purpose of rape is as rare as hens' teeth.'

'I read in the Manchester Evening News that a geneticist at Manchester University has discovered hens with teeth,' he told her. 'It's a mutation, apparently.'

Jo was too tired to hide her exasperation. 'This is rape we're talking about.'

'Sorry,' he said, sounding genuinely chastened. 'Inappropriate.'

'Accepted,' she replied. She gathered her thoughts. 'Furthermore, Ram found that cases involving kidnapping for rape in which the victim was later released were the rarest of all.'

'Much more likely to be murdered and the body hidden.'

'Exactly.'

'Like the Moors Murderers and the Ripper.'

'There is one exception,' she told him. 'It's a current unsolved investigation. The Batman rapist.'

'He started back in the 1990s,' Sarsfield said.

Jo imagined him nodding as he searched his memory bank.

'Almost exclusively in Bath,' he continued, 'carjacking lone women. He made them drive him to a different area where he assaulted them, and then made them drive him back to the area where he'd abducted them. Also referred to by the press as The Riddler, on account of the baseball cap with a question mark on that he deliberately left at one of his crime scenes.'

'Either you've an excellent memory, or you've just been going through the case.'

'Neither. The Head of Operation Talon told me about it when I joined the team. They've always had an interest in it, not least because the Somerset and Avon operational name for the Batman case is Operation Eagle.'

'I'm surprised you didn't mention him before?'

'I would have, except that if he's still alive, he'll be somewhere between fifty-five and seventy-five years of age. Plus, all of his offences were committed in the same area, he's a tights fetishist, and he appears to have been inactive for over a decade.'

'Even so,' she said, 'there may be a connection. Operation Eagle, Operation Talon, and our unsub leaving a falcon tattoo on his victims? Is he making a point?'

'If he is, he's taking the piss.'

'Let's hope that's his undoing.'

In the silence that followed, the two of them reflected on the fact that it had not been the undoing of the Riddler rapist.

'Aren't you seeing victim number five today?' he asked.

Jo looked at her watch.

'Five minutes ago.' She logged off, scooted her chair back from the desk and grabbed her bag. 'I have to go, Gerry. I'll ring you as soon as I've finished.'

Chapter 13

Jo had hoped to remain inconspicuous, but the Chancellor's Building lecture theatre was packed, and she had to stand at the back with a handful of other latecomers. *At least they haven't started yet,* she thought, as she scanned the room.

The room was elegant and circular, with high walls and a domed roof. The walls were clad with geometric-patterned acoustic tiles, and the floor was carpeted. The audience were sitting on concentric rows of chairs facing a table directly opposite Jo at which were seated two young women and a slightly older man. She estimated that between two and three hundred people were present, the vast majority female, and almost exclusively of student age and appearance. The woman at the centre of the table stood up. As if by magic, the buzz of conversation ceased.

'My name is Miriam Hood,' she said. 'On behalf of the National Union of Students, I'd like to welcome you to this *Say No And Stay Safe* seminar. Before we begin, I'd like to thank the University of Manchester for offering this venue without charge, and the Salford and Manchester Metropolitan Universities for also helping to sponsor the event.' She now adopted a serious expression and tone. 'It is an indictment of the society in which we live that we have to resort to a series of seminars such as this.'

There were murmurs of agreement.

'An indictment of parenting, of the education system, of policing, and of the criminal justice system.'

The murmurs grew louder. The speaker paused, and looked slowly from left to right around the room.

'It is gratifying,' she said, 'to see so many of you here today, and to know that you will spread the word among your own institutions. But I can't help feeling, and I say this while acknowledging the handful of courageous men in this audience, that I'm addressing the wrong people. Specifically, the wrong gender!'

The room erupted with cheers and applause. Jo wondered if there wasn't a danger that this was going to turn into an evangelical meeting. Not that there was anything wrong with that per se, only that in her experience, when emotion drowned out reason, some of the most important lessons were lost. The speaker waited patiently for the noise to subside, and then nodded in empathy with her audience.

'As things stand, these seminars have little option but to focus on what we can do to protect ourselves. And yes, I'm addressing the men in this audience too. As you'll discover shortly, male rape is also on the increase. What the rest of society – parents, schools, the medical profession, politicians, the media, the criminal justice system – have to do is get their act together in addressing the issue of prevention. Put simply, we need to change the mindset, the culture and the behaviour of men!'

This time Miriam Hood cut the applause short by raising a hand.

'If there is anyone here who doubts this, consider the following data from just two of the scores of studies in recent years into societal attitudes towards rape in the Western world.'

She picked up a sheet of paper and read from it, ignoring as she did so the growing chorus of angry comments elicited by the evidence.

'In one study, over thirty per cent of male students said that they would force a woman to have sexual intercourse if they could get away with it. When asked the same question but using the term rape, the percentage fell to under fourteen per cent.'

She looked up. 'See how men delude themselves when it comes to sex?'

She returned to her text.

'Another large survey found that forty per cent of female undergraduates regarded rape as an exercise of male power over women.'

Miriam Hood looked at her audience.

'A figure that I personally find worryingly low, but what percentage of male students do you think agreed with them?'

The replies predictably ranged from less than thirty per cent down to the '*Zero*' a student standing next to Jo shouted out.

The speaker shook her head.

'Eighteen per cent,' she said. 'And do you know what the male undergraduates were more concerned with? I'll tell you. With protecting their fellow male students from false allegations of rape!'

Now there were cries of '*Shame! Shame! Shame!*' Miriam Hood waited for them to subside. When she began to speak again, she was calm, measured and empathetic. Jo could see her having a stellar career in politics a few years down the line.

'I could go on,' she said. 'But I doubt that any of the research findings would come as a surprise, living as we all do with these attitudes day to day. However, what none of the statistics absolve us from is our responsibility to listen to, support and learn from those who have suffered directly from rape or serious sexual assault. And so,' she paused, smiling at the young woman seated to her right, and then turned back to the audience. 'I can't say, under the circumstances, that it gives me great pleasure to introduce our first speaker, but having spent just a few minutes with her, I can confidently say that I'm full of admiration and respect for her courage, resilience and determination. Please welcome Orla Leanne Lonergan.'

She remained on her feet, leading the clapping as the young woman beside her stood up. Finally, Miriam Hood sat down and an expectant silence filled the room.

Chapter 14

Jo found it impossible to reconcile the photo attached to the crime report for victim number five with the woman who stood before her. The girl in the photograph had long blonde hair, no make-up, a pallid complexion, and sad eyes the colour of cobalt; her height was given as five feet three. This woman seemed taller. She had short flame-red hair, subtle make-up and a lightly tanned complexion. When the light caught her eyes, Jo could have sworn that they were green. Either this was a different person, or she had reinvented herself.

Orla Lonergan placed her fingertips on the table, and stood tall. There was something magnetic about her composure, and the way in which she radiated confidence as she surveyed the audience. When she began to speak, her voice was electrifying.

'My name is Orla. Orla Leanne Lonergan. I'm twenty-one years old, from Derry in Northern Ireland, and I'm currently a third-year student at Bradford University where I'm studying Geography and Environmental Management. Ten days ago I was raped.'

It took a millisecond or so for what she had said to register, and for a communal gasp to ripple across the audience. She waited for them to settle.

Orla's accent struck Jo as well-matched to the pace and style of her narrative. Despite the subject matter, it had the feel of a gentle tale told by an open hearth in an Irish country pub. The student walked behind the other two speakers and came to stand between them in front of the table. She was wearing a cobalt blue, ruched, twist-front jersey dress that sat on the knee. It had elbow-length sleeves. On her feet was a pair of pointed silver glitter shoes, with a two-inch heel that explained her extra height.

'It was a friend's twenty-first birthday celebration.' She paused. 'I wore this.'

There were muted gasps as the implication hit home.

'Not this dress, obviously,' she said. 'The police have the one I wore that night. Well, the forensic science service to be precise. But it is identical. I sent for it the day before yesterday. I thought it important that you should see it, so that you can judge for yourselves.'

She held her arms out to the side, and turned slowly through 360 degrees.

'What do you think?' she asked. 'Is this provocative?'

There were indignant shouts from the audience that echoed what Jo was thinking.

'*No!*'

'*No way!*'

'*It's demure!*'

She raised her eyebrows.

'Not an invitation then?'

'*No!*'

'*Never!*'

'*No!*'

'*No way!*'

Orla waited for the noise to subside.

'Thank you,' she said, her voice so soft and low that Jo almost missed it. 'I just needed to know for sure.'

She turned and walked slowly back to her place, and stood in front of her chair. *This is one of those occasions,* thought Jo, *where the phrase 'you can hear a pin drop' rings true.* Orla's fingertips found the table again. It seemed as though she was drawing strength from the ground beneath her.

'We started the evening off in my room at seven fifteen pm, with a bottle of champagne and some nachos. There were only six of us, so just one glass each. Then we had two Jägerbombs apiece.' She smiled. 'I want you to keep count, because it's important. Then we hit the city. Our friend whose birthday it was had booked a table in our favourite Indian restaurant. I ate the poppadum and chutneys, mixed starters, and a Karahi Palak Paneer. To drink, I had one bottle of Tiger beer. We left there at around ten fifteen. We visited two pubs, and two wine bars. In each of the pubs I had a bottle of Lime-a-Rita. In the wine bars, a white wine spritzer.'

Jo found the level of detail remarkable. Orla needed them to know exactly what had happened.

'Around two am,' Orla continued. 'Two of the girls decided they'd go on to a club with a couple of guys who'd been chatting them up. The rest of us decided to call it a night.'

She reached for the glass in front of her, and realised that it was empty. Miriam Hood hastily unscrewed the top from a bottle of water, and filled the glass. Orla nodded her thanks, picked up the glass and took a sip. She placed the glass back on the table, and addressed her audience.

'If you've been keeping count then you'll know that I'd consumed at the most eleven units of alcohol. Given the passage of time, I'd have had around five units still in my system. Enough to be over the drink-drive limit, but far from senseless.'

Given the student's size, Jo was certain that she had overestimated the speed at which her body would have processed all that alcohol. Even so, she would still have had her wits about her.

'Certainly,' Orla continued, 'capable of giving, or refusing, consent to . . .' here she paused, and looked up at the circular oculus in the centre of the dome, staring down on them like the all-seeing eye, '. . . sexual intimacy.'

She took a deep breath, raised the glass to her lips, sipped, and then placed it with exaggerated care on the table.

'I made two mistakes that night. Neither of which I intend to agonise over. If I could go back, of course I wouldn't repeat them. But I can't.'

She paused, not for effect, Jo realised, but to draw on her courage.

'All night I had drunk from bottles. Sat there with my hand around the neck, my thumb over the top. Of all of us, I think I was the most cautious. Hypervigilant, I suppose.' She shook her head acknowledging the irony. 'When I changed to white wine spritzers in the two wine bars, they both arrived in a glass.' For the first time there was a hint of sadness. 'I never gave it a second thought.'

She nodded her head as though having an internal dialogue, smiled thinly and continued.

'The second mistake I made was to walk back on my own. Not all of the way, just the last quarter of a mile. You see, I share a house in the city with five others, two of them were the girls who went on to the club with the guys they met. The other two girls live in the same hall in the Student Village. I'm not sure what I'd have done differently. Joined the queue for taxis, and waited half an hour in the cold? Gone on to that club, played gooseberry, and hoped the other two didn't cop off?'

She shook her head.

'The thing is, I didn't know that the drug he'd managed to slip into my drink had begun to affect my ability to make any decision at all. I guess I was just unlucky, that he'd chosen me.'

What would the unsub have done if she had made either of those decisions, Jo wondered, or if she had gone back to the Village with the other students? In a way, Orla was right. He had been playing a game of chance with her, and she had lost.

Orla's tone changed. She spoke without emotion, at a pace that seemed as though she wanted to get it over with as quickly and as clinically as possible.

'The last thing that I remember about that night was feeling sick, dizzy and drowsy, all at the same time, and thinking that there must have been something wrong with the curry. I leaned against a parked car, and I remember sliding forwards, and downwards. Five hours later I woke up cold, wet and shivering on the edge of a copse in a farmer's field in Denholme, just fifty yards from the road. I sensed immediately that I had been raped. There was no pain, nothing physical anyway, and my clothing was intact. I just knew.'

There was another pause, and that little shake of the head.

'The police told me that the tests indicated I was a victim of DFSA, which is short for drug-facilitated sexual assault. Someone had used GHB, a form of ketamine, to render me unconscious. Apparently it's also known as liquid ecstasy.'

Orla grimaced.

'*Liquid ecstasy?* Only a man would call it that. You see, there was no intercourse, no intimacy, no bonding. Because these all require more than one person. And there was only one person there. One person and one animal. *I* was incapable of giving consent. *He* did not need it. He simply took what he could, because he could.'

Another pause.

'I told myself that I was lucky. I was not conscious when he assaulted me. He used a condom. Not, I suspect, out of any consideration for me, but so that he could avoid detection. He left no physical scars. I was already sexually active so I do not have to cope with him having stolen my innocence. And I'm still alive.'

She paused and looked down at her hands, before raising her head and continuing, 'I went through that checklist in my head to see if it would help. If it would lessen my anger. It did not. Violation is still violation, however carefully it comes wrapped. Then I imagined his defence lawyer presenting that same list as grounds for leniency, and some hoary old judge nodding away in acknowledgement. My anger leached away, and was replaced by something else. A sense of purpose. A determination to make something good, something positive, come of out what I went through.' Her voice faltered. 'What I'm going through.'

Orla breathed in, pressed her hands firmly on the table. She drew her shoulders back. When she spoke, her strength and confidence had returned.

'I read a book this summer that I found inspirational. A biography by someone who's used a far worse experience than mine to galvanise the world. Her name is Malala Yousafzai. The title of her book is *I am Malala*.'

She waited for the buzz of conversation and the nods of recognition to recede.

'I'm not comparing myself with Malala,' she said. 'Simply acknowledging the role her example has played in my decision. I'm resolved to campaign to change the way in which men view non-consensual sex, and the way in which society colludes with the status quo. I'm determined that our voices are heard. Today I'm launching a social media campaign initially, with a dedicated Facebook page, a Twitter account and a YouTube video. If you want to join me, you know how to find me.'

Her gaze slowly swept the room, taking in each row in turn. She was challenging her audience to harness the emotion she had stirred in each of them. To come together in a public roar of indignation, for justice and for change. Jo felt herself sucked into the vortex of passion that seemed to spiral upwards as the silence built to a crescendo. The young woman pushed herself back from the table, took a final deep breath and declared:

'I am Orla.'

Chapter 15

As Orla sat down, the room erupted. Some were cheering, others crying, everyone applauding. Jo was close to tears. She found her view of the speakers hidden by the head and shoulders of two women standing on the back row. A man behind her was pressing into her back as he craned forward to see. A jab with her elbow persuaded him to back off. It was a long time before the noise subsided, people settled down, and Jo was able to see again.

Miriam Hood was on her feet, waiting for the few remaining people still standing to sit down.

'Any comment from me would be superfluous,' she said. 'I think your reaction has said it all. Orla will now take a few questions, through me, please, and I have to stress that she will only respond to questions relating to her campaign.'

A sea of hands went up. Predictably, people wanted to know how they could help, where they could get more information, details of her social media sites. Several wondered if she would be prepared to speak at their university or college. They were dealt with quickly, then Miriam Hood looked directly towards Jo.

'Yes?' she said. 'You have a question for Orla?'

A male voice erupted in Jo's ear.

'I do,' he said, 'although you need to know that I'm here in my capacity as a reporter.'

Jo turned, and stared into the face of Anthony Ginley.

'You,' she hissed.

He squeezed past Jo into the space in front of her, more concerned with responding to the cries of indignation around the hall than to her. He had to shout to be heard above the uproar.

'I promise,' he said, 'that I will report this conference as positively as I can, in order to support Orla's campaign. I'm on your side.'

Orla Lonergan tugged Miriam Hood's arm and whispered in her ear. Hood straightened up, and held out both hands to quell the angry tumult.

'Miss Lonergan is prepared to take you at your word,' she said. 'But if you let her down in what you write, you will have to answer to all of us.'

This produced a cheer, during which Orla Lonergan stood up.

'I will answer one question,' she said, 'and only one. So please choose carefully.'

Ginley nodded his understanding.

'My question,' he said, 'is, if you had the opportunity to address the man who attacked you—'

'*Raped* me,' she said.

He inclined his head.

'Raped you. What would you say to him?'

The atmosphere changed in the room, as the audience waited to hear how she would answer. She took her time.

'When I see him,' she said at last, 'and I *will* see him, because he *will* be caught, I will tell him that whatever it was that he set out to do that night, he failed. Did he think that he was exercising power over me? How? By waiting until my ability to resist had been weakened by alcohol? By sneaking drugs into my drink? Did he really believe that was a demonstration of power, of dominance, of control? I will tell him that if he thinks that has left me crippled emotionally or psychologically, and that he has destroyed the rest of my life, then he's very much mistaken. I will tell him that I refuse to be his victim. Far from it. He has made me determined to expose people like him. Men whose only way to feel alive is to come like a thief in the night, drug their victims, take them and toss them aside. Men who are cowardly, spineless, unable to attract, to love, to empathise with other human beings. Because that is what he is, and how I will always remember him. With contempt and with pity.'

This time, the applause was louder than ever. Ginley turned to face Jo. His smile was self-congratulatory.

'I told you it would help,' he said. 'But I'd rather work with you. What do you say?'

'Go to hell,' she said.

He shrugged. 'Have it your own way.'

He squeezed past her, and headed towards the exit.

As she waited for the audience to settle, Jo reflected on what Ginley had said. Would Orla's campaign really help, and if so how? She was in favour of anything that would make people sit up and listen. It might just move the debate on to educating men. Not that that was going to impact on serial perpetrators like their unsub, or the man who had abducted her two years ago. But then ninety per cent of rapes were by men known to the victim, and they were every bit as devastating. As for Orla, despite having been deeply affected by her words and her manner, Jo was still not sure to what extent her apparent strength masked a dangerous fragility. A brittleness that might shatter at any moment. She wondered if she was ready for the storm of vitriol her campaign would unleash from mindless trolls. As brave as Orla's performance had been, Jo couldn't help feeling that it was too soon after the event. She remembered the force psychotherapist warning her that she should not confuse putting on a brave front with being strong. That acknowledging and dealing with your feelings required a different kind of strength. One that in the end was more likely to bring a resolution with which she could live.

Miriam Hood was on her feet.

'I'd now like to introduce our second speaker,' she said. 'I have no doubt that some of you will have been wondering why we have a man on the platform. Well, there are quite a few reasons. Firstly, men are also victims of rape and, as I mentioned earlier, male rape is on the increase. Secondly, since the perpetrators are exclusively male, it might help us to hear from a male perspective how better to protect ourselves.'

She acknowledged the murmurs of dissent, but did not respond to them.

'Thirdly, if Orla's campaign, which we have already pledged to join, is targeting men, then it will surely help to have men on board. Above all, we have invited this speaker because of what he brings to the table professionally, and as a person.'

She picked up a sheet of paper, and referred to it as she continued to speak.

'Sam Malacott left university with a degree in Psychology and Business Studies, and a burning desire to make a positive contribution in the world. Over the past sixteen years, he has worked with and for eight different charities. He's the owner and managing director of SM Charity Management Ltd, a human resources consultancy dedicated to supporting voluntary organisations. This work currently includes the specialist training of call centre staff for a range of women's charities. Five years ago, Sam completed a part-time MA entitled "The impact of sexual victimisation on society and on the individual".

'Since then, in his spare time and at his own cost, he has been a regular *Say No And Stay Safe* speaker and trainer.'

She put down the briefing sheet and placed her hands together in readiness to lead the applause.

'It gives me great pleasure to introduce Sam Malacott.'

Malacott reached behind Miriam Hood, placed a hand on Orla Lonergan's arm and said something that made her smile and nod. Then he withdrew his hand and stood up.

He was tall, with an oval face, pale blue eyes and a slightly cleft chin. His light brown, medium buzz-cut hair was spiked with gel. Designer stubble suited him. He looked elegantly casual in a silver-flecked, grey woollen jacket, and blue-striped open-necked shirt. He looked strong and athletic. *I bet he keeps himself fit*, Jo thought. When he spoke, his voice was cultured and engaging. There was a slight trace of an accent. *Cheshire perhaps?*

'Thank you, Miriam,' he said, smiling down at her, 'for raising expectations way beyond my ability to meet them.'

Cue polite laughter.

'As if having to follow Orla wasn't hard enough.'

More laughter, warmer this time. *It's not a competition, you prat*, thought Jo unkindly.

'Seriously though,' he said, 'as I sat listening to Orla, I thought how privileged I was to be here, to see and hear you speak, and to witness such a passionate, moving and seminal performance. My only regret was that it wasn't being streamed live to every smart-phone, tablet and television set in the world.'

Someone began to clap, and then everyone else joined in. Including Jo, who was beginning to wonder if she had rushed to judgement. He held his hands up and waited.

'Then I remembered that courtesy of that camera,' he pointed to a woman standing off to the right with a video camera trained on the speaker, 'and your social media campaign – tomorrow it will be out there, and the revolution will begin. That, Orla, is why I feel doubly privileged to be invited to follow you today.'

Hmm, thought Jo, *nothing to do with the fact that she's filming you as well?* When the audience had calmed down, he began in earnest.

'I'd like to start with a quick overview of my presentation. I will remind you of some of the cold, hard statistics that prove that we're dealing with an epidemic of sexual assault that has far-reaching implications for individuals and for society as a whole. Then I will share with you a range of tips and measures drawn from research, police advice and common sense, which will help to reduce your risk of becoming a victim of sexual harassment and sexual violence. After lunch, I will facilitate a World Cafe event in which you will have an opportunity to share your experiences, your concerns, and your ideas about how to stay safe, and how to engage with Orla's campaign. And finally, there will be a practical session on self-defence.' He paused, smiled, made sure he had their attention and added, 'So don't eat too much at lunch.'

It was a weak joke, but this audience was now ripe for anything. Jo decided not to stay to hear the rest of it. She already knew the depressing statistics. Half a million adult rapes every year in England and Wales alone, only twelve per cent of them on men. Half a million sexual assaults. Twenty per cent of females aged between sixteen and sixty having experienced some form of sexual violence. And eighty-five per cent of such crimes never reported to the police. And that wasn't counting the abuse of children under sixteen. She wove a path through the crush, and out into the peace and quiet of the corridor.

Chapter 16

Jo found a quiet corner of Chancellor's lounge bar, and used the time to catch up with DI Sarsfield on her BlackBerry.

'I'm sorry to disappoint you,' he said, 'but the three potential victims we've been able to interview so far are non-starters.'

'And the other three?'

'One of them, the detective constable who was going to interview her, his pool car broke down outside Oldham, and he's still waiting for a replacement. Another one insists on having a mate present before she's willing to talk. The mate's gone AWOL. They're trying to track her down as we speak.'

'And?'

She heard him puff his cheeks, and blow out slowly.

'The one we thought was date rape? She took an overdose last night, not long after she contacted CrimeStoppers.'

'So why did she contact them?'

'Who knows? But it turns out it wasn't the first time she'd been raped. Poor kid.'

'How is she?'

'Alive, more by luck than judgement. One of her mates needed to borrow a book for some work she was behind with. She went to this girl's room and found her fully dressed on the bed, with an empty bottle of wine on the floor and an equally empty bottle of paracetamol on the bedside locker. Another couple of hours and they wouldn't have been able to save her.'

It was a scenario with which both of them were all too familiar, but they gave it the moment's silence it deserved.

'So, how did you get on, Jo?' Sarsfield asked.

'I'm not sure, to be honest. The victim, Orla Lonergan, didn't tell me when she agreed to meet that she'd be tied up all morning speaking at a conference.'

'Bloody hell,' he said. 'She must have some balls.'

'You may want to rephrase that, Gerry.'

'You know what I mean. How long is it since she was abducted?'

'Ten days.'

'What was she speaking about?'

'Her rape.'

'Bloody, bloody hell!' he said.

'If you think that's impressive, I hate to imagine what you'd have said if you'd been here.'

'What did she say?'

Jo gave him the potted version.

'Sounds like you don't need to interview her,' he said. 'Between the case notes and her account, it doesn't sound like there's a lot more she can tell you.'

'That's what I thought. But I may as well hang on just in case. They'll be breaking for lunch shortly.'

'Do yourself a favour,' he said. 'Grab a bite to eat yourself, it sounds like you need it.'

Jo's next call was to Ram. She brought him up to date, and then told him there was something she wanted him to do.

'Sounds intriguing,' he said.

'What makes you say that? I haven't told you what it is yet.'

He laughed.

'I can tell from your voice. I bet you weren't even aware that you'd lowered your tone, as though afraid of being overheard.'

He was right, she realised. Not that it had been a conscious decision.

'You're very perceptive,' she told him. 'I want you to run a background check on Anthony Ginley.'

'That investigative reporter who waited for you after the press conference?'

'He turned up here today. Asked victim number five what she would say to the rapist if she got the chance, and then tried it on with me again.'

'Cheeky bugger.'

'Exactly.'

She could almost hear his brain working overtime.

'You don't think he might be our unsub?' he said.

'I have no idea, Ram. But it wouldn't be the first time that a serial rapist hung around one of his victims. Demonstrating his omnipotence. Getting a secondary thrill from seeing her continued suffering.'

'From what you've told me he'll have been disappointed with the way that Orla Lonergan's come out fighting.'

'I'm not so sure,' she said. 'You take my point though: there are precedents?'

'Sure. Like murderers turning up at their victims' funerals. Or dogging the police investigation. There are plenty of examples of those.'

'So you'll do it?'

'Of course I will. You're the boss.'

'Don't forget to tell the loggist.'

'Would I?'

She smiled as she remembered Detective Inspector Gordon Holmes' favourite response to that – '*Don't call me Wood Eye,*' from his repertoire of classic jokes. What would she give to have Tom Caton's team around her right now?

'Thanks, Ram,' she said. 'Got to go. I think they've stopped for lunch.'

Some of the delegates were coming into the lounge for a pre-lunch drink. Others were making their way outside on to the decked area for a smoke. Jo put her phone and her tablet in her bag, and went back towards the conference hall.

The speakers were still at their table, surrounded by a clutch of delegates desperate to speak with them. Orla Lonergan was the centre of attraction. Jo decided to take a seat, and wait until she was free. After a couple of minutes, Sam Malacott leaned over to say something to Miriam Hood and then stood up. He picked up his satchel and walked towards Jo.

He was loose-limbed, and his gait exuded the same confidence as had his opening remarks. The closer he came, the more attractive she realised him to be. He had the sort of penetrating gaze that ought to have made her feel uncomfortable, but did not. When he stopped in front of her and smiled, his face lit up.

'You're Senior Investigator Joanne Stuart,' he said.

She felt a jolt of alarm. How the hell did he know that? Her face betrayed her. He immediately looked embarrassed.

'I'm sorry,' he said, 'that was rude of me. Only I saw you on television. That appeal you made?' He smiled again, more tentatively this time. 'You were bloody good, by the way.'

She stood up so that he was not towering over her.

'Thanks,' she said, 'you were pretty impressive yourself. What I saw of it.'

He pretended to look hurt.

'I know. I saw you leave.'

Now it was her turn to feel awkward. 'I'm sorry,' she said.

'Don't be daft,' he replied. 'You must have heard it all before. You'd have probably done a better job than I did with all the experience you must have had.'

Jo decided it was time to put an end to this mutual admiration. 'Orla Lonergan was really impressive,' she said.

Malacott looked back towards the table. Orla Lonergan and Miriam Hood had extricated themselves, and were walking towards them.

'Yes, she was, wasn't she? Magnificent.' He shook his head. 'God knows where she found the strength to do that.' He lowered his voice. 'To be honest, I'm a bit worried about her.'

Jo thought she knew what he meant, but there wasn't time for him to elaborate. The other two were almost upon them. She stepped to one side, and held out her hand.

'Miss Lonergan, I'm Senior Investigator Joanne Stuart.'

Jo detected a flicker of anxiety in those bright green eyes. *I was right,* she thought, *the bravado is a mask concealing the depth of her suffering, as are the contact lenses, and the dramatic change to her hair.* Jo wondered if someone had let slip that the unsub had been deliberately targeting blondes. Orla's hand was cool, and her grip less firm than Jo had expected.

'I'm sorry you had to wait so long,' she said. 'I should have warned you.'

'Not at all,' Jo replied. 'I'm glad I heard you speak. I thought you were inspirational, Miss Lonergan.'

'Call me Orla, please.'

The student disengaged her hand, and turned to the others.

'Can you save me a place? I'll join you as soon as we've finished.'

'You're welcome to join us for lunch, Miss Stuart,' said Miriam Hood. 'You could have your meeting afterwards. There'll be plenty of time.'

'That's very kind of you,' said Jo. 'I'd love to.'

Only when the first course arrived did Jo realise just how hungry she was. She had to make a supreme effort not to show herself up by shovelling the food down at a rate of knots. The four of them had a table to themselves, and the conversation was deliberately polite, none of them wishing to pre-empt the discussion that she and Orla would be having. At the end of the meal, while the coffee was being served and Orla and Miriam were busy discussing the plans for the campaign, Sam Malacott turned to Jo.

'If you ever think I could be of some assistance,' he said quietly, 'don't hesitate to give me a bell.'

She tried hard to hide her surprise.

'I'm not sure I follow?'

'With the investigation.'

'Oh.'

'Only I've had a lot of experience talking with victims, and even with some perpetrators when I was conducting my research for the MA. You'd be surprised what I've learned.'

'I see.' She hoped she sounded non-committal.

'For example,' he said, warming to his subject, 'have you considered concentrating your search on men who regularly travel between different universities?'

'Like you?'

It had just slipped out. To her surprise, he didn't take the slightest offence.

'Exactly!' he said.

'As a matter of fact, we have,' she told him, 'but I'm afraid that I can't discuss any details of the investigation with you. And I do already have a team of extremely experienced officers. But thanks anyway.'

'I understand completely,' he said. 'But the offer's there, just in case.'

Chapter 17

She looked very different up close. It wasn't just the heavy-handed make-up – exaggerated eyebrows, blotchy artificial tan, excessive lipstick, and coloured contact lenses – it was as though a mask had slipped, revealing someone lost between her real self and the alter ego she was trying so hard to project.

'I'm sorry,' said Orla. 'I don't remember anything else. Nothing at all.'

They had been talking for over ten minutes. Gone was the confident and commanding voice that had so transfixed her audience. Now the adrenaline that powered her performance had leached away, she looked exhausted. Jo's heart went out to her.

'Don't worry,' she said, 'it's almost always the case with GHB. Four out of every five women we interview have no memory of what happened, and those who do have such a confused recollection that it's impossible for us to act on it.'

Jo realised that it was going nowhere. As with the other victims, the perpetrator must have used a massive dose of the drug on her, not only to ensure that she was submissive, but also so that she would remember nothing. Jo was aware that there was a fine line between sedation and overdose. Mixed with alcohol, it had led to numerous cases of coma, and several resulting in death.

'Not even a smell that was out of place?' said Jo.

Orla frowned.

'Sorry, no.'

Jo decided to wind the interview down.

'How have your parents taken it?' she asked.

'I haven't told them yet.'

Orla read the look on Jo's face.

'I know,' she said. 'They're bound to find out when my campaign begins.'

'That's tomorrow,' Jo gently reminded her.

She nodded.

'Tomorrow.'

Orla sighed and looked down at her hands. The blue varnish, to match her dress, was already chipped where she had chewed her nails.

'I'll ring them tonight.'

'Were you hoping to protect them from this?'

'Not them,' she replied, 'me. I've been trying to protect myself.'

'From what?'

For the first time, Jo saw the pain in her eyes.

'Mum will scream and rage, and then cry and cry until she's exhausted. Then she'll want to treat me like an invalid, suffocating me with love and care and protection. And my dad . . .'

She faltered. Jo could see the tears welling up, and the student battling to keep them at bay. Orla swallowed, took a breath, and continued.

'My dad will be calm, sympathetic and understanding. He'll hug me and tell me not to worry. That it's not my fault. That I'll be alright. But his eyes will tell another story. I'll catch a glimpse of them when he thinks I'm not looking, and they'll be full of hurt and disappointment. Like the time he found out I was pregnant by the boyfriend I'd just dumped.'

'You have a child?'

A teardrop swelled, teetered on the edge of her eyelid and then tipped over.

'No,' she said. 'I miscarried.'

Orla reached for her handbag, and searched in vain for a handkerchief. Jo took a small pack of tissues from her bag and handed them to her. Orla took one and dabbed her eyes. Jo waited until she had regained her composure.

'I gather you turned down the offer of victim support and you've refused to see a counsellor?'

The student stuffed the crumpled tissue into her bag while continuing to clutch the rest of the pack. Her knuckles were white with tension.

'You heard my presentation,' she said. 'I refuse to be a victim.'

'So you should, but that shouldn't prevent you from coming to terms with what happened.'

'It's *how* I've come to terms with what happened.'

Jo considered her bloodshot eyes, the pale streaks where her tears had caused her tan to run, and the desperate charade of her new incarnation. It was a dangerous kind of denial. One to which Jo had almost succumbed herself.

'*I* thought it was that easy,' she said, 'but it wasn't.'

Orla seemed not to have heard, her mind somewhere else as she stared at the pattern on the carpet. Jo waited. When the student looked up, she seemed confused.

'What did you say?'

'I said that I also thought it was easy to refuse to accept that I'd been a victim. To simply carry on as though nothing had happened. To put a brave face on it. But I discovered that it wasn't.'

The confusion was replaced by surprise, and something else. A hint of relief?

'You've been raped too?'

Jo shook her head.

'Not raped. Abducted, tied up, sexually assaulted. Told that I was going to be raped, and that when he'd finished he would kill me.'

Orla's hands went to her face, and a little gasp escaped her lips.

'How did you get away?'

'My colleagues arrived just in time. I'd been working undercover. Only he was smarter than we were.'

'You're alright now though?'

It was said with a hint of certainty, and of hope.

'Most of the time,' Jo told her, 'but only because my boss insisted that I go for counselling.'

She saw Orla beginning to retreat back into her protective shell.

'I wouldn't dream of trying to tell you how to deal with this,' Jo said. 'But please believe me, you need to give yourself permission to grieve for the child you lost, and the way in which the rapist has changed how you look at life and at yourself.'

She retrieved her bag and stood up.

'Thank you for agreeing to talk to me, Orla,' she said. 'And you're right – we *will* get him.'

She held out her hand. The student stood up and grasped it. This time her grip was firmer.

'Thank you,' she said. 'I know it's not what you came here for, but you have helped.'

Jo smiled.

'I'm glad. And I hope you take the help that's being offered to you. To do so is not a sign of weakness, Orla, it's a sign of strength.'

Chapter 18

Jo returned to the Quays, to find the rest of the BSU team assembled in the meeting room. Harry Stone had spent the morning in Warrington at the NCA Regional headquarters, and then hotfooted it over to Salford. She was glad to see him. She would need his influence to stand any chance of obtaining more resources to ramp up the investigation.

'Jo,' he said, as she entered the room. 'Good timing. Come and sit here.'

He relinquished his place and took an empty seat beside Andy.

'You don't have to move for me, Boss,' she said, flustered at being the last to arrive.

'I know,' Harry replied, 'but this is your investigation. It's only right that you should chair the meeting.'

Jo placed her tablet on the table, then lined up a biro with the top of the pad of tear sheets in front of her. The top sheet was blank. Jo hoped that it meant they had only just started.

'I've asked Dorsey to sit in on the meeting and record the main action points,' said Stone. 'It'll make it easier for the rest of us to think. Especially you, Jo. It's a bugger trying to chair and contribute both at the same time.'

Jo felt herself visibly relaxing.

'Can you please read out the agenda we've just agreed, Dorsey?' Stone said. 'Then Jo can decide if there's anything she wants to add.'

Dorsey Zephaniah slipped on a pair of tortoiseshell-rimmed glasses. Jo had never seen them before, but they gave the administrator an air of gravitas that completely transformed her.

'Item one,' she read, 'behavioural profile issues, Mr Swift. Item two, analyses of potential suspects, Mr Shah. Item three, responses to press appeal and issues arising from latest victim interviews, Senior Investigator Stuart. Item four, availability of Senior Investigator Nailor. And finally, agree next actions.' She removed her glasses with a flourish.

'Thank you,' said Stone. 'Obviously you can change that order as you see fit, Jo. Over to you.'

'It looks fine to me as it stands. Except I'd like to leave my feedback to the end if that's alright.'

This was greeted with nods around the table except for Max, who simply shrugged.

'So,' she said, 'Andy, would you like to kick off?'

'Unfortunately there's not a lot to add at this stage,' said the psychologist. 'We have no information from any of his victims about his physical characteristics, his speech or his behaviour. I take it that's still the case after your interview with victim number five, Jo?'

'I'm afraid so.'

'In which case, I'll just be reiterating what we already know. So I'll keep it short. Profile number one still stands. Our unsub is likely to be Caucasian or mixed race, well built, average to above average in height, above average intelligence. He's comfortable in the company of women. He may, or may not, be single.'

He looked around the table. 'That's the part that I'm least comfortable with. There are examples of serial killers and rapists managing to juggle a stable relationship with planning and carrying out their attacks without their partner having a clue, but they're the exception rather than the rule. On the other hand, he may not be working alone, in which case his partner may also be his partner in crime.'

He looked down at his notes to see where he was up to.

'Employed or self-employed, although I'm tending towards the latter, narcissistic, misogynist, charming, and to all appearances completely normal, whatever that is.'

He tossed his notes down as though disgusted with the lack of progress he had made.

'Of the four main categories of rapist – eighty-seven per cent commit date rape, thirteen per cent are stranger rapists, ten per cent are local opportunity rapists, and three per cent are hunter-predators – the unsub is a perfect example of the latter. The hunt is an essential and increasingly important aspect of the experience, and therefore of his modus operandi, as is the tattoo. But we'd already established that.'

He opened and closed his hands. A habit that Jo had come to recognise as an expression of his frustration.

'In the absence of anything concrete from his victims and crime scenes, Jo, the best I can do is take a close look at any potential suspects, providing you come up with some.'

Jo thought he was being a little hard on himself, given that the triage team was already using his initial profile, sketchy as it was, to prioritise that list of suspects.

'Thanks, Andy,' she said. 'That brings us neatly to Ram.'

The intelligence officer sipped some water from his plastic beaker, then cleared his throat. 'There are two different sets of potential suspects,' he said. 'Those that were thrown up by the public appeal that Jo made, and those that I've been compiling based on the criteria she gave me.'

'Those criteria,' said Stone, 'remind me.'

'Males known to travel regularly between different North West Universities.'

'Known by whom?'

'By the universities themselves.'

'That can't have been easy to establish?'

'It wasn't,' Ram agreed, 'or should I say it isn't, because it's really slow-going. So far I've barely scratched the surface. Having said which, I've identified the following forty-seven names.'

He pressed the space bar on his laptop and turned to face the far end of the table, where the overhead projector had displayed a list of names on a white screen suspended from the ceiling. There were eight names on each page, with three columns stating the age, occupation and ethnicity according to the 16+1 self-defined codes used by the police.

Ram gave them time to read each page before moving on to the next one. When all eight pages had been displayed, there was a final summary sheet.

'As you can see,' he said, 'of the forty-seven, twenty-eight are white, and nine are of mixed ethnic background. Those are the ones at which I'm going to take a closer look.'

'How are you going to do that?' asked Jo.

'By running background checks and cross-referencing the information against Andy's behavioural profile. Cross-referencing their visits to individual institutions with the location of the crime scenes we know about. Mapping their home addresses on the geo-location map I drew up.'

'It sounds like you're going to have your work cut out,' said Stone.

'I'm hoping the rest of you are going to help out,' said Ram. 'Dizzy has collated a set of the names for each of you.'

He nodded to Dizzy, who passed the sets around the table one at a time.

'I'd like you to take a look at these,' said Ram, 'and see if anything jumps out at you. Obviously I'm not expecting miracles, but we all know that five minds are better than one.'

'I've had a thought,' said Jo. 'Why don't we ask all of them to volunteer a sample of their DNA?'

Max raised his eyebrows. 'We've nothing to compare them with,' he pointed out.

'But they don't know that,' she said. 'If any of them refuse, then Ram can put them under a microscope.'

This would have significant cost implications. They all looked at Stone.

'I'll think about it,' he said. 'It'll take some explaining, especially if you're thinking of doing the same with names thrown up by the appeal.'

'I'm not,' said Jo. 'I had a quick word with Inspector Sarsfield on my way here. The number of responses to the appeal has risen to seventy-five. Three of them involve recent historical allegations of rape. Only forty-two of them included a name. At first glance, none of them appear to have any connection with our unsub. They're all being followed up, but I won't propose DNA tests without a clear link to this investigation.'

Jo checked the agenda.

'That covers items three and four, which brings us to your current status and availability, Max.'

Max had been lounging in his seat, his long legs stretched out under the table. He eased himself into a sitting position.

'That won't take long,' he said. 'The Manchester Force has become increasingly defensive about the number of males found drowned in the local canals and waterways over the past six years. It hasn't helped that parallels have been drawn with the Iowa Smiley Face Murders theory. Apparently the fact that the National Crime Agency has been helping them to review some of the cases is felt to be stoking the claims that there's a serial murderer at large. So I've been politely told to get lost.'

'The official version,' said Stone, 'is that with the exception of a few cases where the coroner recorded an open verdict, none of the others have been identified as suspicious. Consequently, the much appreciated services of Mr Nailor are no longer required.'

'I think I prefer Max's version,' quipped Ram.

'So do I,' said Stone, 'but don't quote me.'

Ram grinned. 'Smiley Face Murders?' he said. 'Sounds intriguing.'

'Forty-five young males of college age,' said Andy. 'Whose bodies were found in a variety of stretches of water across the Midwest back in the 1990s, after they'd been drinking in bars or at parties. All of them had drowned. A couple of former New York policemen came up with this serial killer theory based on smiley faces having been discovered in the general vicinity of some of the drownings.'

'General vicinity?' said Ram.

'In some cases, over a mile away from where the body was found,' said Max. 'And they had no idea where most of the bodies had entered the water.'

'Neither the police nor the FBI give any credence to the theory,' said Andy. 'As far as they're concerned, it has been statistically proven that alcohol and water don't mix.'

'Can we get back to Operation Juniper?' said Jo, who had never understood why it was that male colleagues felt it okay to go off at whatever tangents occurred to them. 'As far as this investigation is concerned, there's no doubt whatsoever that we're dealing with a serial rapist.'

'Sorry,' said Ram. 'My bad.'

'So, Max,' Jo continued, 'does this mean that you'll be able to concentrate on Juniper?'

Her fellow investigator looked at Stone, who nodded.

'Looks like it,' Max confirmed.

'That's great,' said Jo, while secretly wondering how it was going to work, given that he was far more experienced than she. 'So,' she continued, 'that just leaves me.'

She gave them a concise account of the conference session, and her subsequent interview with Orla Lonergan.

'Just like all the others then,' observed Max when she had finished. 'Saw nothing, heard nothing, felt nothing, at least not until it was all over.'

'That's about the size of it,' she agreed. 'And the unsub was just as careful to cover his tracks with her as he was with all the others. In her case, not only had she been showered or bathed, but because she'd been lying in the rain, what little if any DNA there might have been was washed away.'

'It's pretty remarkable,' said Max, 'that there's not been any trace evidence so far. Presumably he must have shaved himself, worn a condom, had a shower, worn barrier clothing after the event. Even then, there's always something left behind.'

'There was,' said Ram. 'It's called a tattoo.'

Max glared at him. 'You know what I meant. For example, how come they didn't recover any footprints from the Bradford and Salford deposition sites?'

'The farmer's field was so wet that all they had was a series of ill-defined footprints full of muddy water and cow shit,' Jo told him. 'And whatever footprints he may have left on the metalled cycle path in Worsley Woods had been ridden over, trampled on, and washed away by the rain long before the crime scene investigators got there.'

There was moment of silence as they pondered the lack of evidence.

'What I haven't told you,' said Jo, keen to move on, 'is that I've asked Ram to run a background check on the reporter Anthony Ginley.'

'On what grounds?' asked Stone.

'She doesn't need grounds,' said Ram, 'he's a reporter.'

That drew a smile from everyone except for Stone.

'Because he's made it his business to try to get close to the victims,' said Jo. 'Because he made it clear he'd like to get close to the investigation under the pretext of being helpful. Because as a self-employed freelance investigative reporter, he almost certainly knows his way around the university campuses. And finally, because there was something about his manner that I found disturbing.'

Max leaned forward. 'Ram has got a point,' he said. 'It seems to me that you could say all of those things about most reporters.'

'What was it about his manner?' asked Andy.

Jo didn't need to think about it.

'He has a veneer of charm, but he made it clear that he's prepared to fight dirty if he doesn't get what he wants. He pretends to be concerned about the victims when in reality all he's interested in is a good story. He's supremely confident, and I hate the way in which he keeps turning up out of the blue. I don't think that it was coincidence that he ended up standing right behind me at the conference. And finally, call it a woman's intuition if you like, but I get the impression that at best he's a chauvinist.'

'Believing women to be inferior isn't the same as hating them,' said Stone.

'True,' Andy acknowledged. 'But Jo did say "at best". If he's the unsub, he's hardly going to let people see that he's a misogynist.'

He removed his glasses, and sucked one of the tips. They waited for him to continue.

'Then there was the question he asked the victim,' he said. 'That was really interesting. Not the obvious one you'd expect of a reporter. But it's exactly the sort of question a serial killer might ask.'

'Not the answer he'd be hoping to get though,' said Ram.

Jo shook her head.

'I'm not sure about that. What Orla Lonergan said, and how she looked close up, weren't the same at all.'

'I can understand the unsub turning up at the meeting, and hiding in the crowd,' said her fellow investigator, 'but why take the risk of deliberately standing out like that?'

'Because,' said Andy, 'as Jo has already pointed out, he's supremely confident. We know that's a characteristic common among serial perpetrators.'

He unscrewed the top of his flask, and poured some water into his beaker.

'We also know that this particular unsub enjoys taunting us. The tattoo is proof of that.'

'Even so,' said Max, drumming his fingers lightly on the table.

Stone looked at his watch. 'I agree with you, Jo,' he said. 'I don't think we have any option but to check him out.'

'In which case,' she said, 'I hope you'll feel the same about Sam Malacott.'

They all stopped what they were doing and stared at her. Even Dorsey Zephaniah, whose biro was suspended in mid-air. Jo imagined an embarrassing flush starting on her chest and heading north, which was daft because they were only reacting to the fact that she had taken them by surprise.

'It's only just occurred to me,' she said, 'but Malacott visits most of the universities. We actually joked about that making him a suspect. He's now been close to at least one of the victims. And he offered to share his expertise with us if I thought that would be helpful. Plus, he's confident and charming. How does that make him any different from Ginley?'

'At least he has some expertise to share,' said Ram.

'Do you have the same feelings about him as you do about the reporter?' asked the psychologist.

Jo had to think about it.

'I certainly didn't have him down as a chauvinist,' she said. 'Far from it. Most of the charities he's worked with are women's charities. He didn't make me feel at all uncomfortable. And when I told him we had plenty of expertise of our own, he seemed to take that well.'

'You're right though,' said Stone, 'you have to be consistent in applying the criteria that trigger further scrutiny. And it *is* only a background check that you're proposing?'

'Yes, Boss,' she said. 'If that throws up something, or either his or Ginley's name arises in connection with other aspects of the case, such as vehicle sightings or witness descriptions, then obviously I'll take it a stage further.'

She looked down at the agenda.

'Next: Actions.'

Five minutes later, the meeting had broken up and they were back at their desks. All except for Harry Stone. Jo wanted a word with him but couldn't find him anywhere.

'Mr Stone has had to rush back to London,' Dizzy told her. 'Something personal apparently, not work.'

Ram overheard, waved Jo over, and lowered his voice. 'Harry's mum is widowed, in her late eighties,' he confided. 'She's got all her marbles, and is determined to keep her independence. Unfortunately, she's plagued with arthritis. Harry's been trying to persuade her to move into a retirement home or a bungalow. She's not for budging. Doesn't realise the terrace she bought for under a thousand is worth close to a million.'

'That must be hard,' said Jo. 'Especially with him commuting back and forth.'

'That's not the worst of it,' he said. 'He's also got a daughter with a skunk addiction that's led to schizophrenic episodes.'

'God, that's awful.'

'I know. Best not let on that you know. He'll tell you himself when he's ready.'

'Thanks for the heads-up,' she said. 'The last thing I want to do is put my foot in it.'

Andy was the first to leave.

'It's Holly's tenth birthday,' he told them as he wheeled his scooter out from the stock cupboard. 'We're all going to Wagamama for our tea, and then it's the Peanuts movie at the Lowry cinemas.'

'Her choice or yours?' quipped Ram.

Andy slipped his arms through the straps of his backpack.

'Don't mock,' he said. 'The Peanuts comic strip is an intellectual masterpiece that has endured for fifty years. As forlorn as it is ferocious, it plumbs the depths of human misery, and shines a light on the absurdity of man's striving for success and the essential loneliness of social existence.'

'Sounds like a heap of laughs,' said Dizzy.

'As a matter of fact,' Andy replied, as he pushed open the door, 'it is.'

An hour later, Jo was the next to leave. She still had a massive sleep deficit to make up, and the work she planned to do could just as easily be done at home.

Chapter 19

Jo stared one more time at the empty shelves and slammed the refrigerator door in anger and frustration. Under normal circumstances Abbie would have done the weekly shop.

She stormed into the lounge area, and scrabbled through the leaflets under the telephone table until she found their favourite takeouts. Hunters BBQ & Asian Takeaway or Slice Pizza & Bread Bar on Stevenson Square? Pizza won. As she began to punch the restaurant's number into her phone, it dawned on her that a singleton order would fall way below the minimum price for home delivery. There was nothing for it but to put her coat back on and head out into the pouring rain.

The unrelenting deluge made a mockery of the festive lights strung between lamp posts. Reflected globes of coloured light fractured as she kicked her way through the puddles on the pavement. Crossing the square, she passed two council employees exchanging curses as they attempted running repairs to the roof of one of the stalls in readiness for the Sunday Makers Market. She paused between the empty tables and stacks of wicker chairs, timing her dash to dodge the intermittent waterfalls streaming from the colourful awnings.

The bright, warm interior and welcoming smiles of the staff embraced her. Reluctant to return too soon to the empty apartment, Jo took her time choosing. For once she had the bittersweet luxury of being able to choose what she really wanted, without worrying about what Abbie might prefer. Nevertheless, it proved a difficult decision between their unique mozzarella and potato pizza, or the one with aubergine, spinach, goat's cheese and basil. In the end, she made it easy by ordering both. One to eat, the other to freeze for later in the week. *Was this the way that it was going to be from now on*, she wondered?

Jo sat with her pizza on her lap, a bottle of Chianti Classico Reserva on the table and a half-empty glass in her hand, watching the news headlines. Thousands in Brazil join a rally to push for the President's impeachment; there is an outcry against the Tories' decision to drop their plan to crack down on bank chiefs' bonuses; LA officers fire thirty-three bullets into a man holding a gun; *Strictly Come Dancing* dance-off won by a former *Coronation Street* TV soap star. She was about to switch off when a story scrolling across the bottom of the screen caught her attention. A twenty-nine-year-old Oklahoma policeman charged with thirty-six offences of sexual assault, including rape, faced a 263-year sentence. She reached for the remote and pressed the red button. He had collapsed in court, and wept when the guilty verdict was announced. She switched off, and threw down the remote in disgust.

'And he still doesn't have the faintest idea how those women feel,' Jo shouted at the empty screen. 'Or give a damn!'

She took her plate through to the kitchen and placed it in the empty dishwasher. At this rate, it would be another week or so before there was enough in there to justify switching it on. She went back into the lounge and picked up the folder containing the details of the potential suspects she intended to prioritise. It had been a risk bringing it home with her, because were she to mislay it, be mugged or burgled, and it fall into the hands of a member of the public, or worse still a reporter, that would be the end of her career. They all did it, of course, not that that could be used as an excuse. She sat on the sofa, flipped the file open, picked up her glass and began to read.

An hour and a half later, the words were beginning to blur on the page and she had the beginnings of a headache. Perhaps it had something to do with the fact that she had demolished three-quarters of the bottle of wine? She stood up, stretched, and glanced at her watch. Andy would be having a nightcap with his wife about now, the children tucked up, and fast asleep. She half-envied him that. The easy companionship, the unconditional love, even the distraction from his work that quelling sibling rivalries must bring. The irony was not lost on her that this was precisely what she had chosen to reject. It begged the question who she was really angry with, Abbie or herself? She switched off the lights, and went into the bedroom.

Jo opened her eyes. Her headache had gone, but she now had a pain at the base of her neck from sitting propped up against the headboard. The backlit glow from her Kindle bled a ghostly pool of light on to the ceiling. The time was 1.45am. She switched it off, placed it on the bedside cabinet, and picked up her mobile phone. No messages. It irked that Abbie, relying on the fact that Jo had not changed the locks on the door to the apartment, had not even left a forwarding address. She was somewhere in Manchester, but even their mutual friends claimed not to know where she was staying.

Jo was seriously tempted to use the resources available to her as an NCA Investigator to track Abbie down. It would be so easy. A matter of minutes. But to what purpose? To surprise her? To confront her like a pathetic stalker? And then what? With every keystroke recorded on their computers, the inevitable consequence should Abbie complain would be dismissal for gross misconduct. Even if she did not complain, there was now software in place that would throw up anomalies between ongoing investigations, and personal data searches.

Jo switched off her phone, plumped up the pillow, curled up on her side and fell asleep.

Chapter 20

'These three.'

They stood in a semi-circle staring at faces on a display board.

'Where did you get their photos from?' asked Max.

Jo pointed with her index finger. 'These two are screenshots from their Facebook pages, this one is from a staff profile on the university website.'

'None of them with previous then?' guessed Andy.

'Number one has,' she replied. 'But his mugshot was taken years ago. I decided it would be more helpful to see what he looks like now.'

They nodded their heads in approval.

'His name is Nathan Northcote. Caucasian, thirty-eight years of age. Divorced. He was stopped the night before last, at three in the morning,' – she paused for effect – 'on Cromwell Road.'

They looked nonplussed.

'Cromwell Road?' she repeated.

Andy raised his eyebrows. Only then did she remember that none of them had any local knowledge whatsoever.

'Sorry,' she said. 'It passes right by Castle Irwell, the Salford University student village.'

She indicated the locations on the map alongside the photos. 'Ah,' said Max.

'What was he doing there at three in the morning?' asked Ram.

'He told the officers that he had been at a mate's in Moston, up here in North Manchester,' she said, pointing again. 'Playing computer games and then watching *The Bridge* on catch-up.'

'Nothing like a bit of Nordic noir to get the pulses racing,' ventured Ram.

'I assume they breathalysed him?' said her fellow investigator.

Jo nodded. 'He barely registered. Claimed he'd had a couple of pints early on, and a curry. Then he stopped drinking because he was driving home, and he had to run over to Leeds in the morning for work.'

'Very responsible,' observed the psychologist.

'Happy to drive on a couple of hours sleep though,' Ram pointed out. 'Did they search his car?'

'It was clean. No body, and none of the paraphernalia you'd associate with an abduction.'

'What does he do for a living?' asked Max.

'This is where it gets interesting,' she said. 'He works for a security firm, Iskuros Security Ltd. They specialise in the installation and maintenance of intruder alarms, CCTV, fire protection, and access control systems. He does all of that, plus one week in four on rapid response call-outs. DI Sarsfield's team asked for a copy of his work record, and guess what?'

'His work takes him into North West Universities?' Max said.

'Five campuses in all, in the past twelve months, including student accommodation.'

'Any of the campuses linked to our victims?'

'Four of them,' she told him. 'The dates and times don't tally, but that doesn't mean anything. More importantly, he wasn't on call on any of the nights the victims were abducted, so he'd have been free to carry out the attacks.'

'Five victims across fifteen months. He's only on call one week in four. It's not statistically significant,' said Ram.

'It doesn't need to be,' she said. 'On each of those dates he had the opportunity to abduct those women. That's all that matters. Furthermore, he lives in Swinton. That's four miles from the city centre, a mile from the M60 motorway, close to the fifth victim's last known sighting, and the Worsley Woods dumpsite, and well within the circle thrown up by Ram's geographical profile.'

Andy tugged at one of his earlobes. 'You say he has a record. Does it include any precursor behaviours?'

'Not for sexual assault. Unless you're going to tell me that Taking Without Consent and Public Disorder are predictive of rape?'

He shook his head, as she knew he would.

'When he was eighteen,' she continued, 'he was with a bunch of lads the same age. Man City football supporters. They went to watch an away game in Leeds and got involved in a fight with a gang of Leeds supporters. Northcote stole a car so he and his mates could flee the scene, allegedly to escape from the avenging Leeds fans as much as from the police. The car was eventually stopped on the M62. He received a conditional discharge, a £500 fine, and was banned from all football stadiums for five years. Nothing since then.'

'How the hell did he get a job installing security systems?' Max wondered.

'That's one of the things I intend to find out,' she said. 'I'm going to interview him later this morning.'

She pointed to the second photo.

'This one's yours, Max. His name is Zachary Tobias. Twenty-nine years of age. Single. As you can probably tell, he's of mixed heritage. Specifically, second-generation British Asian-African. Born and raised in Blackburn. He works as a motorbike courier for a firm that specialises in scientific supplies and medical emergencies. That includes delivering blood products to hospitals and research laboratories.'

'Including universities?' asked Max.

'Especially university medical and dental schools, labs and science parks. He lives in Bury. Almost the centre of the geoprofile locus. According to his employers, he's visited all of the campuses associated with our victims. He visited two of them on the actual days on which the victim was abducted, but since all of the abductions took place in the early hours that's not particularly relevant. The firm provides the bike. He does have a car of his own. A BMW 3 Series estate.'

'What about his physique?' asked Andy.

'He fits in terms of height and build,' she said. 'They all do.'

'Does he know we want to interview him?' asked Max.

'No. I thought I'd let you break the news and make the arrangements,' she said.

'I think I'll find out where he's going to be today, and just turn up and surprise him,' he said. 'See how he reacts.'

Andy pointed to one of the photos. 'Number three interests me. There's something about his expression. What's his story?'

'Forty-six years of age,' Jo said. 'Married, and American. He's over here on a three-year teaching scholarship funded by the American Creative Writers' International Foundation.'

Professor Harrison Hill stared through piercing blue eyes over his right shoulder, with a smile that verged on a sardonic sneer. His blond hair looked as though it had been blown into a tousled effect intended to convey artlessness. The overall effect was quite the opposite. It looked pretentious.

Jo held up her tablet.

'This is an extract from his bio on the website: "Best known for his short stories including *Around the Moon in Forty Nights*,

Whistling in the Mangroves and *Lion Hunting in Alaska*, he's also the author of three novels: *The Organ Grinder's Monkey*, *Whistler's Father* and *Whatever Happened to Fenella Goodyear?* The latter earned him the Wurlitzer Prize 2013. His work has appeared in *The Edinburgh Review*, *GQ*, *The Cambridge Literary Review*, *Harper's*, *The New York Times*, *Granta*, *Playboy* and *The Atlantic*."'

She stopped reading.

'His current role is as Visiting Fellow in English and Creative Writing for the North West Universities Networked Learning Community.'

'Which gives him access to all of the colleges?' said Max.

'Exactly. He also does a semester teaching at each university in turn. At the moment, he's at Manchester University.'

'How did he come to our attention?' asked Ram.

'His name came up in a number of allegations made following my appeal to the public. Three students from two different universities claim that he not only behaved inappropriately towards them, but that they believed he was also stalking them.'

'In what way inappropriate?' asked Andy.

'Offering extramural one-to-one tutorials. Plying them with alcohol. Implying that he could ensure good grades in exchange for favours.'

'Par for the course then,' said Ram.

'Don't be so cynical,' Max told him.

'Cynical?' Ram retorted. 'I had a psychology tutor who was just like that.'

'Did you report her?' asked Jo.

'*Him*,' said Ram. 'I reported *him*. Didn't do any good though. Apparently it was all a misunderstanding. Cultural differences were cited.'

'What happened?'

'I changed tutors, and majored in criminology.'

'Our gain,' said Andy.

'The most significant allegation,' Jo continued, 'was that he pulled his car up alongside one of these students and offered her a lift. It was gone midnight. She'd been drinking and was obviously unsteady.'

'What happened?' asked Max.

'Her friend pitched up and told him that they were fine. She was with her and they were going to wait for a taxi.'

'Good for her,' said Andy. 'How did he react?'

'Apparently he drove off in a huff. Never mentioned it again. Guess what colour the student's hair is?'

'Blonde?' said Ram. 'And I bet she's tiny?'

'Five three and a half.'

'Bingo!' he said.

Max scratched the side of his face.

'You said he was married?'

'*Is* married,' Jo replied.

'So what's he doing cruising the streets after midnight?'

'We can ask him that together,' she said. 'As soon as we've finished with the other two.'

Chapter 21

The staff lounge was empty except for a woman at the far end working in one of the study carrels. Nathan Northcote looked confused.

'I told you. I was at my mate's. I'm surprised you haven't checked with him.'

He was annoyed on two counts. Firstly, because he thought it had all been sorted the night he had been stopped, and secondly, because it was embarrassing being told that someone from the National Crime Agency wanted a word with him when he was in the middle of fixing an alarm-sensor fault in the Vice Chancellor's office.

'We have,' said Jo. 'I'm not here about that.'

He looked apprehensive.

'So why are you here?'

'Mr Northcote,' she said. 'Sit down, and I'll tell you.'

He slumped on to the chair opposite. Though he bordered on being skinny, his height could easily be intimidating. Was he too tall and too thin to be their unsub, she wondered? He rested his arms insolently over the back of the chair.

'Go on then,' he said. 'I haven't got all day.'

Right, she decided, if that was how he wanted to play it.

'I'm investigating a series of abductions and serious sexual assaults,' she said, a little more loudly than necessary. 'You match the description that we have of the perpetrator, and you also appear to have privileged access to places of interest connected with a number of these crimes. If you'd rather we did this in an interview room back at . . .'

'No! God, no!' he said, looking anxiously over his shoulder. When he turned back, he looked genuinely shaken.

'Good,' she said, lowering her voice. 'I take it you don't mind if I record this? It'll allow me to listen carefully to what you have to say, although I may still need to make a few notes.'

Nathan Northcote looked suspiciously at the tablet, but nodded his agreement.

'Do I get a copy?'

'When we've finished, I will take you through the salient points, and ask you to confirm them as your formal statement. In the event that they may be used at some time in the future in relation to the prosecution of a third party or yourself, then you and your legal adviser will receive copies of both the recording and your statement.'

The blood drained from his face.

'When that other detective interviewed me, he said it was as a witness. He wanted to know if I'd seen anything suspicious when I was driving home. He didn't say anything about me being a suspect.'

'Neither did I,' Jo said. 'If we reach that stage, then I will have to caution you and continue this interview at a police station. In the meantime, this is an opportunity for you to assist my investigation and convince me otherwise.'

The panic returned.

'There's no need for that,' he said.

'So you're ready to answer my questions?'

He glanced over his shoulder again. The woman in the study carrel was now wearing a pair of white earphones. He turned back.

'So long as you keep your voice down.'

Jo pressed record, gave the date, time and place, her name and his, and began.

'You work for Iskuros Security, Mr Northcote?'

'That's right.'

'What does your work involve?'

'I install and maintain alarms, CCTV, access keypad systems.'

'Do you also respond to emergency call-outs?'

'One week in four.'

'It must be sensitive and confidential work requiring the highest levels of honesty and integrity?'

'Yeah, it is.'

His smile was awkward, as though he sensed what was coming. She smiled back.

'I assume then that you told your employer about your convictions for public disorder and theft of a vehicle?'

He squirmed in his seat and struggled to reply.

'Did you tell your employer about your criminal record, Mr Northcote?'

He shook his head, and mumbled. Jo pointed to the tablet on the table between them.

'You'll have to speak up.'

He cleared his throat. 'I didn't have to. It was spent.'

'Your conviction was spent under the Rehabilitation of Offenders Act?'

'Yeah.'

'But security work is one area in which the Act does not apply in relation to spent offences. They must have told you that? Asked you to make a verbal disclosure?'

He shook his head.

'I don't remember that. Anyway, the Criminal Records Bureau check came back all clear, so I didn't think it mattered. What would you have done?'

She didn't give him the satisfaction of a reply.

'How long have you been working for Iskuros Security?'

'Seven and a half years.'

'When did your work begin to take you on to university and college premises?'

Nathan Northcote looked genuinely surprised. *Surely*, she thought, *he's seen the news headlines even if he missed my public appeal on TV. And it must have been something his colleagues talked about at work? Yet he still hasn't put two and two together?*

'Right from the start,' he said. 'My first job was installing key-pads in a new student accommodation block in East Manchester.'

'Do you do a lot of that?'

'Sure. That, and access control and CCTV cameras in sensitive areas like science stock rooms, research facilities, places where radio-active materials are stored. It's important work.'

'I'm sure it is.' Jo paused. 'Can I ask you more about the student accommodation? If you happen to be called to a particular Hall of Residence to sort out a problem, let's say the intruder alarm is going and it won't switch off, is there some kind of override code you use to reset it?'

He sat up and leaned forward. He seemed more relaxed now that he was talking about his work.

'No, it wouldn't keep on ringing. All of our alarms are pro-grammed to reset after twenty minutes.'

'But if there was a problem . . .'

'I'd use our engineer code. Every company has its own engi-neer code that works on all of our common installations. So if we installed the system, we simply use our engineering code to get access to the control panel.'

139

'What if it was an alarm belonging to another company?'

He grinned, and leaned towards her as though sharing a confidence.

'Well, and this is a trade secret, all of us engineers get to know the codes all the other companies use.'

'How do they get to know them?'

'Either because they've moved between companies, or because they've gone self-employed. Whatever, we share them with each other. It makes our lives easier.'

'So if an engineer were to use a code to disable an alarm, how would you know who had done it?'

'You wouldn't. You'd only know that it was someone who knew the engineer code.'

It sounded like all of a burglar's Christmases coming at once, or a rapist's for that matter.

'On the other hand,' Nathan Northcote continued, 'if it were one of the residents using their electronic fob, then you'd know exactly whose fob it was because they're individually programmed and recorded. You could even tell what time it was used.'

Jo paused while she made a written note. Although raising all sorts of questions in her mind, she could not see its relevance to Operation Juniper.

'Are you married?' she asked.

He sat back and crossed his arms.

'Divorced. Why?'

'How long have you been divorced?'

'Three years, but I don't see . . .'

'Was it amicable, the divorce?'

'We're still speaking, if that's what you mean.'

'Any children?'

'Two.'

'Who has custody?'

'She does, but I have visitation rights.' His brow furrowed, and he clenched his fists where they nestled in the crook of his arms. 'Look,' he said, 'what has this got to do with anything?'

'Bear with me, Mr Northcote,' Jo said. 'I'm just trying to get a sense of your personal circumstances, and how that impacts on your movements. For elimination purposes.'

He unfolded his arms and rested his hands on his thighs. There were damp patches under his armpits.

'Elimination?'

'That's right. The sooner we clear this up, the sooner you'll be on your way. When do you get to see your children?'

'It depends. Normally at weekends. I pick them up on a Friday night, and drop them back off at teatime on Saturday. Except when I'm on call.'

'Do you keep a diary, Mr Northcote?' she asked.

He frowned.

'Who keeps a diary these days?'

'Do you have a calendar you write your appointments on? Doctors, dentists, when you've agreed to pick up your kids?'

'My former wife has one in her kitchen,' he said. 'I use this.' He pulled a mobile phone from his pocket, and held it up for her to see.

Jo paused the record button on her tablet, and opened the Word document containing the relevant dates of the abductions.

She pressed play.

'I'm going to read you a series of dates,' she said. 'As I do so could you please find those dates on your phone, and show me any evidence you have that your children were staying with you that weekend.'

Three minutes later, Jo brought the interview to an end, and pressed stop.

'There you are,' she said. 'I told you that if you cooperated we'd be finished in no time.' She handed him one of her contact cards.

'If you could just give me your ex-wife's contact details, you can be on your way. You can write them on here.'

Nathan Northcote looked horrified.

'My ex-wife? What are you going to tell her? I had a hell of a job getting her to agree to my visiting rights. If I can't see my kids, I don't know what . . .'

'Calm down,' she said. 'I'll tell her the truth – that you're a potential witness and you've been helping us with our enquiries. You've been very helpful.'

His relief was palpable. He wrote on the card and handed it back to her. The two of them stood up.

'What about my employers?' he said. 'You won't have to say anything to them?'

'I'm sorry,' she said, 'but I don't have any option. They have to know that you had that conviction.'

'But it was spent! I'll lose my job. What about the maintenance for my kids? I could still lose them!'

He sounded desperate. Jo's conscience pricked her. This man had stayed out of trouble for twenty years. How would it affect his relationship with his kids? And how would he manage to pay their maintenance? Now that he'd admitted lying though, she had no option, she had a duty to report it. Maybe it wouldn't mean him losing his job. Maybe they'd find him something else.

'You don't know how they'll react,' she said. 'Maybe if you tell them that it was an honest mistake. You thought it was spent, and the CRB return confirmed it. You've just had it pointed out to you that they must have applied for the wrong form. I'm sure they'll realise that it was as much their fault?'

'Please,' he said.

'The best I can do,' Jo told him, 'is to give you the chance to tell them first. You've got twenty-four hours.'

Chapter 22

Max lowered the passenger-side window, raised his camera and took a series of covert shots.

Zachary Tobias, twenty-nine years of age, stood at the edge of the pavement outside the main doors. He stretched his arms, and puffed out his chest. Max guessed that it was for the benefit of the two female paramedics standing just yards away beside their ambulance.

At five feet eleven and with a powerful athletic build, Tobias approximated the physical unsub profile that the BSU team had compiled. Predominantly muscular, with an equal but minimal tendency towards fat or leanness, he was a true mesomorph. He worked out, and wanted everyone to know about it. Max could tell because Tobias had his leather biker jacket open to reveal a body-hugging white T-shirt, tight over bulging pecs and the ribbed outline of a serious six-pack.

Tobias began to cross the semicircular roadway in front of the entrance to Accident and Emergency. Black fitted leather trousers showed off firm glutes and toned quads as he strutted towards the car park. If first impressions counted, then he had blown it as far as Max was concerned.

The senior investigator placed the camera in the glove compart-
ment and got out of the BMW. He waited until Tobias had almost
reached his bike, locked up by the entrance to the car park, and
then called out.

'Zachary Tobias?'

The courier stared at Max with a mixture of suspicion and surprise. Max held up his warrant card.

'Police,' he said.

Experience had taught him that it paid not to elaborate. Then
it was up to the person you wanted to interview to draw his or her
own conclusions. More often than not it showed on their faces.
Total surprise, for example, shock or anxiety. The latter was not
uncommon, of course, and easily misinterpreted. It was surprising
how many people associated the police with the imparting of bad
news. You could always mitigate that impression with a smile and
a neutral tone of voice. It was when they were not surprised that it
was most telling.

Tobias's face told a story. In the first few milliseconds, it registered surprise. This morphed into comprehension and concern, and
finally a mask of uncomprehending innocence.

'Officer,' he said, 'what can I do for you?'

Max stood his ground and waited. The courier walked towards
him. He held a bottle of water in his left hand. Up close, Max could
see beads of sweat on his forehead and a patch of damp in the centre
of his chest. He was all of a twitch, as though his whole body had
restless leg syndrome.

'My name is Max Nailor,' he said. 'I'm a senior investigating
officer with the National Crime Agency. I'd like a word with you
about an ongoing investigation.'

The courier's pupils dilated. Max knew that it was not because
he was attracted to him, far more likely then that his brain was
working overtime.

'National Crime Agency? That's Serious Crime, yeah?'

'You've heard of us?' said Max. 'Very few people have.'

Tobias searched for the right response.

'Must've seen it on TV. *Crimewatch*, yeah?'

'You watch it a lot then? Why is that?'

More discomfort.

'Cos it's interestin', yeah? And cos I get around a lot. Might see somefin' worf reportin', yeah?' He unscrewed the top of the bottle, took a swig, and screwed the lid back on.

'An honest and upright citizen,' Max said, 'in which case you won't mind answering a few questions.' He opened the rear passenger door. 'It'll be warmer and more comfortable in the car.'

Tobias took a step back.

'What's this about?'

'In the car!' said Max. 'Please.'

Reluctantly, the courier ducked into the car and positioned himself in the centre of the rear seats, one leg in each footwell. Max closed the door and climbed into his own seat. Then he reached up to the rear-view mirror and pressed a button on the tiny black unit fixed beneath.

The courier leaned forward, one hand on the rear of each of the front seats.

'What's that?' he said.

'Sit back, Mr Tobias!' Max told him. 'Take your hands with you, and keep them where I can see them.'

He waited for the man to comply. Then he pointed to the box.

'This is a dashcam. It records to the front and rear, including everything we say. It means I don't have to take notes.'

Right on cue, the screen lit up. Two images appeared. The larger of the two showed the view through the windscreen. A smaller image, top right, captured the two of them. Max pressed a button and the interior view filled the screen. It showed the courier wiping his face with a handkerchief.

'Do you really have no idea why we need to speak with you, Zachary?' Max said, watching the screen for his response.

The courier shook his head, put the handkerchief on the seat beside him, and picked up his bottle of water.

'No,' he said, 'I don't.'

He unscrewed the top and had another swig, not bothering to screw the lid back on.

'Your employers didn't tell you?'

'My employers?' Zachary Tobias looked genuinely surprised and sounded worried. 'No, they didn't. What's it got to do wiv them?'

'The reason I need a word with you, Mr Tobias,' Max said, 'is that your work has taken you to places from which students – female students that is – have been abducted, and seriously assaulted.'

The courier's eyes widened. His mouth became an O.

'Shit!' he exclaimed. 'Them girls wot got raped, innit? You can't fink I had anythin' to do wiv that? No way, man! No way.'

'So you know about these incidents?'

'Course I do. All over the news, innit. Everyone's talkin' 'bout it, bruv.'

'Everyone?'

'At work. Down the gym. Everyone.'

'So you'll appreciate why we want to talk to anyone who regularly moves around the places where these young women live? People like you?'

'S'pose.' He took another drink. His arm shook as he did so.

'Are you alright, Mr Tobias?' Max asked.

The courier put the bottle down in a footwell, picked up his handkerchief and mopped his brow.

'Yeah. It's hot, innit?' he said.

Max didn't think so, and he wasn't going to invite him to remove his jacket and get sweat all over the back of the seats.

'In which case, let's see if we can get this over with as quickly as possible, shall we?'

He waited for Tobias to nod.

'Good. Let's start with your work. Just remind me, what is it you do?'

'I'm a courier. I deliver specialist supplies to hospitals, labs, medical schools and science parks. That kind of fing.'

'What kind of supplies?'

'Scientific supplies. Medical products.'

'Such as?'

'Tissue samples, blood, radioactive products, chemicals. I just pick up a package and drop it off. I don't have to know what's in it.'

'Is the bike yours?'

'No, the firm provided it, with training in road safety, traffic regulations, spillage management, security, delivery arrangements, use of insulated transportation boxes. It's specialist work, yeah?'

'Do you ever drive another vehicle at work?'

'Yeah. Sometimes I drive one of the vans. All depends on the size of the delivery. Why?'

'Do you own a car, Zachary?'

He relaxed at the use of his given name, and placed a hand on the back of the front passenger seat.

'Hand!' Max warned.

The hand was quickly withdrawn. Zachary Tobias was twitching again and appeared to have forgotten the question.

'Car,' said Max. 'Do you own one?'

'Yeah.'

'And?'

'And what?'

'What make is it?'

'A Beamer.'

He was nervous, and evasive.

'A BMW?'

'Yeah.'

'Hatch, saloon or tourer?'

'Saloon.'

Max was swiftly losing his patience.

'Just tell me the registration,' he said.

Max entered it into the on-board computer. The response was almost instantaneous. It was a four-door 2011 BMW 3-Series Saloon 330d M Sport. Registered owner and keeper Mr ZM Tobias. No outstanding warrants. Max switched back to the camera view.

'Nice car. What did that set you back?'

The interviewee's response was mumbled.

'Say that again,' said Max. 'For me, and the camera.'

'It was two years old. A bargain.'

'How much?'

'Ten grand.'

'I bet it's quick?'

'Yeah. Nought to sixty in under six seconds.'

'Top speed?'

'Hundred and fifty-five mph.'

Max nodded.

'That must cost you well over a grand for insurance?'

'Yeah.' Zachary Tobias put the water bottle to his lips, found there was only a drop left and put it back down on the floor.

'How much do you earn, Mr Tobias?' Max asked.

'What's this got to . . .?'

'Just answer the question, please,' said Max.

For a moment it seemed that Tobias might refuse. Then he mopped his brow with the sodden handkerchief.

'Eighteen grand,' he said.

Max turned to look directly at him.

'Does it have tinted windows?'

'What?'

'Tinted windows. Does your car have tinted windows?'

'No, why? Should it?'

'Are you married?' Max asked, ramping up the courier's confusion.

'No.'

'Girlfriend?

'No.'

'Boyfriend?'

The courier launched himself forward. His hands gripped the seats in front, just below the headrests. On the screen, the tension was evident in his face and the rope-like veins on either side of his neck.

'What you sayin'?' he hissed.

Max calmly turned to face him, and pointed at the dashcam screen.

'Hands.'

He waited until Tobias had slumped back in his seat.

'I'm not implying anything,' he said. 'I'm merely attempting to establish if you're in a relationship with anyone. Are you?'

The courier shrugged.

'No.'

'So you live alone?'

'No. I live in an HMO.'

'A house of multiple occupancy.'

'Yeah. There are six of us. We share the rent.'

'All male?'

'Yeah. So what?'

'What do you do in the evenings, Zachary?'

'Go down the gym.'

'Every night?'

'Yeah. Five mornin's a week too.'

'You never miss?'

'No. I'm trainin', innit?'

'For?

'UKBFF competitions, innit?'

'BFF?'

'United Kingdom Bodybuilding and Fitness Federation. I'm a regional winner. I'm training for the Nationals, yeah?'

'What time do you finish?'

'Gym closes eleven thirty pm. Then we go for something to eat.'

'Every night?'

'Yeah. Protein-loading, yeah?'

'This gym. Do you have to sign in?'

'Yeah. Fire regs, innit? Guy who runs the gym is hot on that, yeah?'

'And is there CCTV in this gym?'

'Outside, not inside.' He laughed nervously. 'Not in the gym. We're not a freak show.'

It was a weak joke. Max wasn't even sure that it was a joke. Wasn't bodybuilding in any case a freak show?

'What's the address of the gym?' he said.

Chapter 23

'How is it at your end, DI Sarsfield?'

'Fine,' Sarsfield replied, 'like you were right here with me.'

Ram turned to Jo. 'We're ready to go, Ma'am.'

They were seated in the BSU satellite incident room on the Quays, using the live video link, secure in the knowledge that all of their voice, video and file transfers were encrypted. Gerry Sarsfield was in the incident room at Central Park.

'I take it that you've read the reports Max and I filed?' Jo said.

Gerry Sarsfield leaned forward and nodded. His face filled the screen. 'You've been busy, the two of you.'

'Do you have any thoughts for us, Gerry?' she said. 'Or questions?'

'Nathan Northcote,' he said. 'Given he could have used any one of the engineer codes to gain entry to student accommodation and even to their rooms, why would he go to the trouble of taking those girls off the street?'

'I wondered that,' Jo replied, 'but then he more or less answered it for me. Every time a code is used it's recorded by the keypad. He'd have been one of the first people we'd have looked at, together with his work colleagues.'

'And when we checked the CCTV on the campus, it would have narrowed it down to him,' Max pointed out.

'Good point,' said Sarsfield, leaving Jo to wonder which of their points he was referring to. 'I've got another one,' he continued. 'How come his DBS report didn't flag up his convictions?'

'It was before the Disclosure and Barring Service took over,' Jo told him. 'The firm applied for a Basic CRB check – his conviction was considered spent by that time so it didn't show up.'

Sarsfield raised his eyebrows.

'I thought security firms were supposed to apply for a Standard or Advanced check? That would have included his spent conviction.'

'They should have. Someone cocked up. It happens.'

'Are you going to tell his firm about the non-disclosure?'

'I don't have a choice,' she said. 'I gave him twenty-four hours to tell them first.'

'He'll almost certainly lose his job.'

'I know,' she said, 'but he shouldn't have lied.'

'Where do you want to go with Northcote?' Sarsfield asked.

'You'll have read that his time sheet checks out for the night he was stopped?' Jo said. 'And according to the calendar on his phone, he had his kids staying over on all but one of the dates when those girls were abducted?'

'Alibis have been known to lie. And one of them's his ex-wife.'

'Precisely,' she said. 'That's why I want you to get one of your team to double-check with the wife, and another one to take a hard look at the mate he was supposedly with most of the night.'

'No problem.'

'And,' she continued, 'I've asked for an ANPR data mine in relation to his car and his work van. That'll tell us if he was any-where near the last known location of any of the other four victims.'

'Good move,' Sarsfield agreed.

'Moving on,' Jo said. 'Zachary Tobias.'

'He sounds an interesting character, Max,' said Sarsfield. 'I get the impression you're thinking the same?'

'I could tell from his reaction when I told him who I was that he had something to hide,' said Max. 'My hunch is that if he's not our unsub, then it's to do with the use of illegal bodybuilding and weight loss supplements.'

'Using or dealing?'

'Probably both. He's mobile. He competes locally and nationally. His work takes him into places where there's a predominant youth culture, and we all know lots of kids obsess about their body image.'

Sarsfield chuckled.

'Kids? Sounds like you've got one foot in the grave. These are eighteen-plus adults you're talking about.'

'Like I said. Kids.'

'Were those the only reasons he raised your suspicions? Because he's mobile and evasive?'

'No. It's also because throughout our conversation he was restless. And thirsty. He drank an entire bottle of water while I was with him. And he was sweating.'

'Must be hot, wearing tight-fitting leathers,' Ram observed.

Max shook his head.

'It was seven degrees Celsius. Even colder with the wind chill. His jacket was undone. I didn't have the heater on in the car. Everything I've described is consistent with drug use. Something that speeds up the metabolism.'

'Such as?' said Andy.

'Steroids, ephedra, high-dose caffeine, DNP.'

'DNP?' said Andy.

'Dinitrophenol, also known as Solfo Black,' Jo told him. 'It's highly toxic and has been known to cause fatalities.'

'How come you know about it?'

'Someone at the health club I go to left some in a locker over-night with his kit. Grant, one of the gym instructors, found it. He waited until the next session the guy attended was full then made everyone stop and gather round.

'"*What did I tell you when you joined?*" he said. "*This is what I expect: a balanced diet, targeted exercise, and total commitment. No drugs, no supplements. It's not negotiable!*"

'Then he pointed to the guy, held up the container of pills, rattled it and threw him out.'

'Sounds like my kind of place,' said Ram.

'One more thing,' said Max. 'In my experience, most body-builders are overcompensating. And if Tobias is on steroids or any of these other supplements, he'll almost certainly be suffering from erectile dysfunction.'

'For all we know, our unsub is impotent,' Jo pointed out. 'In the absence of seminal fluid, anything is possible.'

'All of the victims were raped,' said Sarsfield. 'There was penetration.'

'But we don't know with what,' she reminded him. 'Some of them suffered vaginal tears and there was spermicide present. All that means is that whatever was used was covered with a condom.'

'Very careful, our unsub,' Andy said.

'Either way, we need his alibi checking out again,' said Max.

'That's something else I'd like you to arrange, Gerry,' said Jo. 'If he's in the clear over the girls, but it turns out he's dealing, you can pass it on to the Drugs Squad.'

'I'm on to it,' he said. 'And while we're doing all this, what will you guys be doing?'

'Professor Harrison Hill,' she said. 'Max and I will be paying him a little visit. Three allegations of improper behaviour and stalk-ing, plus a midnight kerb crawl, puts him firmly on our radar.'

'Ours too,' said Sarsfield. 'Whether or not he's your man, Operation Talon will want a word.'

'You'll get your turn, Inspector,' Jo told him.

'Is that it then?' he asked.

'For now. I'll update the shared online Policy File document. I assume you'll do the same?'

His face filled the screen again.

'Absolutely. It's a bugger having to maintain the original one as well though, isn't it?'

He was referring to the A4-bound book, with numbered pages in which all of the SIO's major strategic and tactical decisions relating to the investigation were recorded.

'I don't have a choice,' she said. 'Any defence team is going to look for the tiniest hole in our procedures, even if it means putting a serial killer back on the streets. That's the price we pay for protecting innocent members of the British public from unsafe convictions.'

'Sometimes I wonder if the trade-offs worth it,' said Gerry Sarsfield.

Don't we all? thought Jo. *Until it's one of us in the firing line.*

Chapter 24

'I apologise for the state of this room,' said Harrison Hill. 'As a Visiting Professor with only one semester in each of the universities, this is all they could manage, I'm afraid.'

Jo took in the surroundings. Given her experience of university staff accommodation, Hill had landed lucky. The book-lined study was at least as large as her lounge. Despite the massive desk and the coffee table, there was enough room for a seminar of at least six students. On the bookshelf directly opposite her and Max, a collection of Hill's own books was ostentatiously displayed alongside a framed photograph of the author. The professor misread her expression.

'I know,' he said, 'you should see the one they gave me back home. I could practically hold lectures in that one.'

He laughed, and with perfectly manicured fingernails flicked back from his forehead an artful curl of hair, and ran his hands over the thighs of his earth-toned chinos. Jo's intention to give him the benefit of the doubt was rapidly eroding.

'National Crime Agency,' he said looking from one to the other of them in turn. 'How exciting. What is that, some kind of FBI?'

'Not quite,' she replied, 'but as analogies go, it'll do.'

Both his smile and his tone were condescending.

'That would normally be my cue to begin a deconstruction of your use of the word analogy,' he said. 'As opposed to simile, comparison or even metaphor. But I don't suppose that you're here for a lesson in semiotics?'

'You suppose right, Mr Hill,' said Max, deliberately denying him the use of his title. 'We'd like to talk with you about a series of complaints made about you by three female students.'

The academic looked genuinely surprised. When he spoke, there was no trace of his confident, almost supercilious tone. He looked and sounded seriously flustered.

'I've only just been apprised of those complaints,' he said. 'They're subject to an internal enquiry. The universities involved are still trying to agree on how to proceed. It has nothing to do with the police.'

'Actually, it has everything to do with us,' Jo told him. 'The complaints were first made to the police in response to a public appeal regarding a series of assaults on female students. You may have seen it?'

She saw the moment of recognition in his penetrating blue eyes.

'I knew I'd seen you somewhere before,' he said. 'You were on the television. Talking about those girls, those dreadful rapes.'

The two of them let him fill the silence. He looked at Max and then at Jo, gripped the arms of his chair and shook his head violently.

'No. No! You can't seriously think I had anything to do with those heinous crimes? On the basis of what? A couple of misunderstandings blown up out of all proportion?'

'Three,' said Jo. 'Three allegations from three students in three different universities, none of whom as far as we can tell were even aware of the existence of the other two.'

'As far as you can tell?' he said, attempting to sound scathing. 'Have you checked all of their social media accounts? Have you even heard of six degrees of separation?'

'I saw the film,' said Max. 'I wasn't convinced.'

'Mr Hill,' said Jo. 'We're not here to investigate those three complaints. Colleagues from Greater Manchester Police will contact you shortly to give you an opportunity to respond to the allegations that have been made against you. Investigator Nailor and I are solely interested in seeing if we can eliminate you from an investigation into the abduction and serious assault of a number of other female students.'

He stared back at her.

'Eliminate? Or implicate?'

'That all depends on how you respond to our questions.'

He shook his head again.

'This is ridiculous. I'm a married man. I have two young children.'

'Neither of which facts, Mr Hill, of themselves form the basis of a defence,' said Max.

'Where *are* your wife and children?' Jo asked.

'Back home in the States. Why do you ask?'

She shrugged.

'Just context.'

He moved to the edge of his seat, his posture combative.

'I get it,' he said. 'You assume that because I'm over here on my own, I must be desperate for female companionship?'

'The crimes that we're investigating go way beyond companionship,' said Jo. 'And the only assumptions that I've now made are as follows: the fact that your wife is not here with you means that she's unlikely to be able to confirm your whereabouts on the days and at the times in which we're interested, and it also means that you're more likely to be a free agent in the evenings and at night.'

He thought about what she had said, and eased himself back into his chair. She could tell that he had decided that the best way to get rid of them was to answer their questions.

'Tell me what you want to know,' he said. 'I have nothing to hide and I've done nothing to be ashamed of.'

'Thank you,' said Jo. 'My colleague will now hand you a sheet of paper on which are printed dates and times of interest to us. I'd like you to tell us where you were at those particular times on those dates, and who you think might be able to confirm your whereabouts.'

Hill took the A4 sheet from Max, tipped back in his chair, gave it a cursory read, sat up and tossed it down on the coffee table.

'Twenty-two hundred hours through to two am in the morning?' he said. 'I guess I was tucked up in bed.' He stared straight at Jo as he added, 'Alone.'

'I'm afraid that "guess" won't do it, Mr Hill. We need to know for certain exactly where you were.'

For a moment she thought he was going to refuse to take it, but he relented.

'I'll need to consult my diary and my cell phone,' he said.

'Do you have them with you?' she asked.

'I do.'

He didn't move. The two investigators waited patiently, as though they had read each other's mind. Eventually he lost the battle of wills as they knew he would, got to his feet, and went over to the desk in the bay window. He opened a drawer, took out an A5 diary and placed it on the desk. Then he reached into the inner breast pocket of the tan corduroy jacket over the back of the chair and withdrew a mobile phone and a Mont Blanc pen. Finally, he pulled a notepad mounted on a silver and black slate bed towards him, and sat down at the desk with his back towards them.

Max stood up, went over to the shelf where Hill's collection of titles was displayed and selected two of the books. The one he handed Jo was entitled *Lion Hunting in Alaska*. He sat down and began to leaf through the other one. Jo was surprised to discover from the foreword that there were mountain lions in Alaska, but that sightings were as rare as those of Bigfoot. The novel it transpired was about a disillusioned academic's attempt to discover his true raison d'être by spending a winter alone in the frozen wilderness. One reviewer had described it as a tour de force. Jo turned to the final chapter and began to read. It took less than two minutes for her to arrive at a totally different conclusion. This was the kind of self-conscious, narcissistic navel-gazing that gave literary novels a bad name. Not a patch on *Brooklyn* by Colm Tóibin, the most recent one that she had read. More of a tour de farce, she decided. Max noticed her smile.

'That good?' he whispered.

She shook her head and mouthed, 'That bad! Yours?'

He held it up so that she could see the title.

'Same here, but very interesting.'

Before she could ask Max what he meant, Hill pushed back his chair and stood up. He turned towards them, clutching several sheets torn from the pad. He saw them holding the books and smiled smugly.

'Who'd have thought you guys had a literary bent?'

He handed Jo the sheets. 'Here you go. I can't account for two of those time slots because I was, as predicted, tucked up in bed. But I'm in the clear for the other three.'

He stood there, leaning against one of the bookcases while Jo read his notes and then handed them to Max.

'As you can see,' Hill said, 'on the second of those dates I was at the Cheltenham Literature Festival. I was carousing until the early hours in the bar of the Cheltenham Regency Hotel. I can recommend it,' he smiled knowingly. 'You two would love it.'

He pointed to his notes.

'You've got the contact details of two of the guys with whom I chewed the cud that night. Same for the other two in Lancaster, and right here in good old Manchester. Folks will be only too happy to swear that we went from the restaurant to a pub, and then back to my hotel for a nightcap and a very long comparative critique of modern English and American literature, culture and morals.'

Max handed the notes back to Jo. Their eyes met. His nod was barely perceptible.

'So that's it then?' said Hill, looking from one to the other, trying in vain to interpret their expressions. 'You check 'em out, I'm in the clear?'

'Do you drive a vehicle here in England?' Jo asked.

He looked confused.

'A car,' she said. 'Do you drive a car in the UK, Mr Hill?'

'Oh, right,' he said. 'A car. Actually, no, I don't. I use a pushbike to get around campus. I use public transport if I'm going any distance. And I bum lifts from my colleagues where possible.'

The two investigators looked at each other and then back at him.

'What's the matter?' he asked. 'Something I said?'

'One of those allegations of which you have only recently been apprised by the university,' Jo said, 'includes a statement that you offered a student a lift in a car. A car that you were driving?'

For the first time, he looked visibly shaken.

'Oh, right – that car, Arthur's car.' He sounded flustered.

'Arthur?' said Max.

Hill pushed himself away from the bookcase, thrust his hands in the pockets of his chinos and attempted to appear relaxed.

'Arthur Bartholomew, also from the States. He teaches at the Centre for New Writing right here in Manchester. We know each other from way back. He lets me drive his car from time to time.'

'You've just stated that you don't drive a car in the UK.'

'Jeez, I thought you meant my own car, you know, or a hire car. This thing with Arthur, it's random, occasional, not a regular arrangement. Nothing like that.'

Jo pointed to the pad on his desk.

'We'll need the licence number of Mr Bartholomew's car, Mr Hill. And his telephone number and email address.'

He looked as though he was going to object, thought better of it, scribbled a note, and handed it to Jo.

'Is that it?'

'For the time being,' she told him, 'at least as far as our investigation is concerned. However, you should expect a visit from Greater Manchester Police officers with regard to those allegations.' She smiled thinly. 'Don't leave town.'

She turned to go.

'I have no reason to, Detective,' he said, 'since my conscience is clear.'

Max pointed to the coffee table.

'What *did* happen to Fenella Goodyear? Nothing bad, I hope?'

Hill studied his face for a moment expecting irony, and found only the inscrutable countenance of a seasoned investigator. He picked the book up and handed it to Max.

'You'll have to read it to find out. Let me know what you think.'

Max accepted the book. 'Thank you,' he said. 'I may just do that.'

Hill opened the door for them. Max paused in the doorway. 'Incidentally,' he said, 'would it surprise you to learn, Professor, that we also engage in deconstruction?'

Hill raised his eyebrows. 'Really?'

'Really. To the extent that meaning includes not only the content of a discourse, but what is left out, ignored or suppressed by it.'

Before the stunned academic had a chance to reply, Max turned and followed his colleague out into the corridor, and through the fire doors towards the stairwell.

'I didn't know you'd studied literary deconstruction, Max,' Jo said as they exited the building.

He grinned.

'I didn't. It's something one of the trainers chucked in on a Met advanced investigative interviewing course.'

Jo smiled. Max actually had a sense of humour.

'Well, you certainly shut him up,' she said.

Chapter 25

'So that was Harrison Hill,' said Jo.

The team were assembled in the incident room. They'd all come in, even though it was Saturday, including Dorsey Zephaniah. Jo and Max had finished reporting back on their visit to the university.

'Where does that leave him?' asked Andy.

'A less likely suspect for Operation Juniper,' said Max. 'But right up there as far as the other allegations are concerned.'

'I agree,' said Jo. 'Three separate allegations, together with him lying about having access to a car. Operation Talon are going to have a field day when they go calling.'

'Plus he came across as exactly the kind of sleazeball you'd expect,' said Max. 'Look at the way he stroked you with his thumb when you shook hands, Jo. And you must have noticed how he kept looking at you?'

She nodded. 'Until I put him under pressure, and he had something other than lechery to worry about. I'm going to have those alibis checked out, and an ANPR data mine on the licence number he gave us for the relevant dates and times. But I doubt that he's our unsub.'

'Assuming the other allegations are sustained, what do you think will happen to him?'

'My understanding is that none of them went beyond inappropriate propositioning,' she said. 'Not that I'm minimising the impact of that. He'll probably receive a warning and an injunction to stay away from them. I can't speak for the universities, but my guess is that he won't see out his sabbatical year as a Visiting Fellow. What do you think, Max?'

'The same as you. In my view he'll be getting off lightly, especially if it's true he was dangling better grades in exchange for sex. Were he a permanent employee of one of our universities, they'd have him for gross misconduct, and terminate his contract.'

Max scratched his cheek. 'If it was my daughter, I'd be happy to terminate him.' It didn't sound as though he was joking.

'Moving on,' Jo said hurriedly, 'Ram, where are you up to on that background check you were running on Sam Malacott?'

Ram handed round a two-page report. 'I started with the Police National Computer, the Disclosure and Barring Service, and HOLMES2,' he said. 'I know that's overkill, but in my experience it pays to cross-check. He came back clean. Then I checked his education, training and employment records. They're exactly as described in his various autobiographical accounts. Importantly, there were no unexplained gaps. HMRC confirmed that he pays his taxes. No nasty little tax avoidance or tax evasion schemes associated with his company.'

He paused and looked up.

'Although that's so rare that I'd have thought it was suspicious in its own right.'

They laughed on cue.

'Then I double-checked his birth certificate, NHS number and passport details. He is who he says he is. But I'll tell you one thing that is rare for a man approaching forty: he's never been married and describes himself as single.'

'I agree that's unusual,' said Andy, 'though not suspicious in its own right.'

'What about Malacott's concern for the sexual victimisation of women,' Jo asked, 'and his work as a *Say No And Stay Safe* trainer? Did you get any sense of where that came from?'

'Ah,' said Ram, his eyes lighting up. 'Now that *is* interesting. As far as I can make out, this obsession with serious sexual assaults on females is the result of a family member having been a victim of rape.'

'How did you find that out?' Andy asked.

'He mentioned it in response to a question in an interview with a women's magazine, *Millennium Woman*.'

'What's a Millennium woman?' Jo wondered.

Ram consulted his notes. 'Women who are concerned with values rather than materialism, and esteem ability and authenticity over celebrity and artifice. They're powerful, confident, sexy and self-reliant.'

'Post-post-modern then,' said Andy.

'Sounds like pretentious claptrap to me,' said Max.

Jo was sorry she'd set this particular hare running.

'Did it say which member of his family?' she asked.

'I don't think so, or I'd have written it down. I'll see if they'll send me a copy of the interview if you like?'

'Do that,' she said.

'What if they ask why we want it?'

'Don't tell them. In fact, there's no need for you to mention the NCA at all. The article has already been in the public domain so it's hardly a secret.'

'What if they insist on knowing why I want it?'

'Then you'd better come clean. Say it's in relation to an investigation that does not involve *Millennium Woman*. Just background context. And warn them not to let Malacott know we've asked for it.'

'Human nature being what it is, the more secretive you make it sound, the more chance someone will tell him,' Andy cautioned.

Jo thought about it. He was right. And even if they did alert Malacott, she was hardly going to charge the magazine editor with obstructing the police. A hollow threat was no threat at all.

'I take your point,' she said. 'Forget about warning them, Ram. Just make sure we get the article. While you're at it, get on to the National Archives. Give them Malacott's details and get them to provide you with details of his immediate female relatives. Then you can use that to see if any of them actually reported a rape.'

'Where are you going with this, Jo?' asked Max.

'I'm not sure,' she admitted. 'Just flying a kite, I guess. Malacott is almost certainly the upstanding altruistic person he appears to be. I just don't like loose ends. He was on our list for a reason. The sooner Ram can eliminate him from our enquiries the better.'

She noticed that Ram seemed preoccupied. He was slumped in his chair, staring at his hands. She wondered if he'd heard a word she'd said.

'Is that okay with you, Ram?' she asked.

It made him start, and sit up.

'Ah . . . yes, Boss.'

'Yes what, Ram?'

'Yes, I'll get that article. In the meantime I'll get the sister's details, and then find out if she ever reported having been raped.'

'Good.'

Jo checked her action list.

'DI Sarsfield has logged a dozen stops by the ANPR cars in and around the university towns and cities we're targeting. None of them have raised red flags, but they're all being followed up. I suggest that Max and I have a look at the rest of that list of persons regularly moving between those universities, and decide if any of them are worth interviewing. Unless, that is, any of you can suggest more urgent priorities?'

The three of them looked at each other, and shook their heads. She could tell that they were as disappointed as her that there had still not been a major development in the investigation.

'Let's stay positive,' she told them. 'Sometimes we simply have to grind it out, you know that. A breakthrough will come when we least expect it.'

Max and Andy muttered their agreement. Ram was busy collecting his papers together.

'Are you okay, Ram?' Jo asked. 'Only you seem distracted.'

'Not your usual bubbly self,' added Max.

Ram smiled thinly and shrugged. 'Sorry guys, you got me. It's my maataaji. She's been visiting family in Mauritius. She's flying back for Christmas. Coming straight up here to see me.'

'Your mother?' said Jo. 'I'd have thought you'd be glad to see her?'

He shook his head. It was the first time that Jo had seen him look and sound so miserable.

'She's on a mission. Been on it for the past five years. Only now she's ramped up the pressure. Wants me to get married.'

'Don't all mothers?' said Max. 'And in your case I'd have thought it was about time?' He grimaced. 'Not that I'd wish marriage on anyone.'

'You don't understand,' said Ram. 'I'm not against marriage, eventually. But my mother's a traditionalist. She's pushing for an arranged marriage. To a woman I've never even met.'

'What does your father say?' said Jo.

Ram smiled wryly.

'I get the impression he's on my side, but he's never going to tell my mother that.'

'You could do worse than an arranged marriage,' said Max. 'It's a lottery whatever way you do it. I thought arranged marriages were supposed to shorten the odds?'

'Don't listen to him, Ram,' said Andy. 'Marriage is like any relationship. In my experience, you get out what you put in. Love grows if you cultivate it. If you don't, it withers and dies.'

Ram shook his head.

'I don't disagree. But I'm a modern Asian man. I value freedom, independence and choice over tradition.'

'I think you'll find that's post-modern,' said Andy.

'I doubt your mother will care,' Max told him. 'You'll have to come up with something better than that.'

Jo picked up her tablet and slipped out of the room. She regretted having pressed Ram to reveal the reason for his unhappiness. The team's exchanges had left her with uncomfortable questions. *Did I neglect my relationship with Abbie?* she wondered. *Did I let it wither? More importantly, am I prepared to let it die?*

Chapter 26

Jo found nothing in the list of names to excite her interest sufficiently to pursue them personally. She made the decision to leave it
to DI Sarsfield's foot soldiers. She was about to check how Max was
getting on when Dorsey Zephaniah stood up, and waved, pointing
at the phone pressed against her ear. Jo told her to put it through.
It was DI Sarsfield.

'Gerry,' she said, 'I was just about to call you.'

'There's been a development,' he said. 'Another rape.'

'Is it him? Our unsub?' Her pulse began to race as anger and
excitement competed for attention.

'We don't know yet. I've just been told that she's at St Mary's.
Been there for a couple of hours. Walked in off the street apparently.'

'The Hospital or the Sexual Assault Referral Centre?'

'The latter.'

'She's a student?'

'Living in a rented house off Platt Lane.'

'Was she abducted?'

'No, but she's blonde and there's a tattoo. Of a bird of prey.'

'When does she say she was assaulted?'

'Last night, I think, early hours of this morning.'

'Why has she only just reported it?'

'I've no idea, Jo. She hasn't been interviewed yet. They've only just finished the medical tests.'

'Who's dealing from your end?'

'DS Watts, one of the Talon team trained officers. I've told her to hold off until you get there.'

'Tell her to expect me, Gerry,' she said. 'And thanks.'

It took twenty minutes for Jo to reach St Mary's. She'd had plenty of occasion to visit the facility before. It was the first ever such medical centre in the UK, before the Serious Sexual Offences Unit took over all of the rape cases, including Operation Talon.

By the time she got there, some nagging doubts had started to form. There was the fact that she had not been abducted. That was completely out of character. On the other hand, there was her hair colour and the tattoo. Of course some serial predators were known to vary their modus operandi. Refining their methods as they went along, or simply adapting to circumstances.

A detective was waiting for her in one of the medical offices. She stood as Jo entered the room.

'Ma'am,' she said, 'I'm DS Watts. This is Dr Hollis. She examined the victim.'

They shook hands.

'Please, it's Jo,' she told them. 'I'm not officially part of GMP and I'm not really comfortable with Investigator. Maybe it'll grow on me.'

'I'm Millie,' said DS Watts.

'And I'm Carol,' said the medic, 'although Doc, or Doctor, will do fine.'

'I don't think our paths have ever crossed, Jo,' said DS Watts, 'but your reputation goes before you.'

'Shame we had to meet like this,' said Jo.

'I've only just started explaining where we're up to,' said Dr Hollis. 'Is that okay?'

'That would be really helpful,' said Jo.

The doctor picked up an envelope from her desk. 'This is the standard package: a brief account of what I was told by the patient about the circumstances of the assault, a summary of my findings, and an outline body diagram.'

Unsure which of them to hand it to, she held it out between them.

Jo nodded to DS Watts. The Talon officer accepted the envelope.

'If you could spare us a few minutes, Dr Hollis,' said Jo, 'I'd really appreciate it if you could take us through your notes? You see, this may be part of a much larger investigation involving a number of young women. The smallest detail could prove crucial.'

The doctor frowned. 'This is most irregular.'

'I realise that,' said Jo.

She decided not to push it. That would be unfair, and Dr Hollis was right. She was under no obligation to cooperate further, and Jo did not want to compromise her in any way. The silence stretched out. Finally, the doctor relented.

'On one condition,' she said. 'Anything that I say that is not in my notes you will have to verify through your own enquiries, including the interview with the patient.'

Jo nodded. 'I understand.'

Dr Hollis looked at the other detective.

'Me too,' said DS Watts.

The doctor folded her arms and sat back in her chair.

'At sixteen thirty-two hours, Laura Razero, aged twenty-two, arrived at Reception saying that she believed that she had been raped.'

'I'm sorry to interrupt, Doctor,' said Jo, 'but were those the actual words she used? She *believed* that she had been raped?'

'That's what I was told,' Dr Hollis replied. 'All of the staff here are extremely aware that everything we hear, do and say is potentially part of an evidential process that could end up in court proceedings. So I think you can take it as read that was what she said.'

'Thank you,' said Jo. 'I apologise for interrupting.'

The doctor smiled.

'You already did.'

Medical professionals and scientists shared a lot in common, Jo reflected, such as pedantry. Mind you, she'd also heard that said of police officers.

'Laura spent half an hour with one of our crisis counsellors,' the doctor continued. 'Following which, she decided that she wanted to proceed with a formal allegation and was prepared to undergo the necessary medical examination and forensic evidence gathering, and then to be interviewed by the police.'

'How did she seem to you, Doctor?' asked DS Watts.

The doctor raised her eyebrows.

'That depends on what you mean? Physically, emotionally, psychologically?'

'All three,' said Jo. She looked at DS Watts. 'Preferably starting with the second two since I'm sure you're going to take us through the forensic evidence?'

DS Watts nodded her agreement.

'Very well,' said the doctor. 'Emotionally, she was fragile. She was badly shaken, and it had taken a lot of courage to come here and complain. She told me that herself. Psychologically, she seemed of sound mind. Very much so. But, judging by her manner, body language and hesitations, she was clearly conflicted.'

'About whether she had done the right thing?' asked DS Watts.

'You'll have to decide that for yourselves,' Hollis replied. 'I'm a little uncomfortable about straying into the realm of conjecture. My role is to make a medical assessment, gather forensic evidence and provide a therapeutic service. I'm neither a psychiatrist nor a detective.' It was said in a gentle matter-of-fact manner, but it still felt like a rebuke.

'She is fit to be interviewed though?' asked DS Watts, saving Jo from having to respond.

'Absolutely.'

'No drugs or alcohol?'

'One almighty hangover. She had twenty milligrams per hundred millilitres of blood twenty minutes ago. You'll have to wait for the tox results. I've asked for them to be fast-tracked.'

Well below the drink-drive limit, Jo reflected. But even if she hadn't stopped drinking until the early hours, it still meant that she must have been heavily intoxicated.

'And how did the medical examination go?' she asked Dr Hollis.

'By the book. There is clear evidence of intercourse having taken place. There was slight external bruising to the upper arms consistent with them having been lightly held, or leant on with the palm of the hands. There was no abnormal internal bruising. I took the full range of swabs, and also retrieved loose strands of what appeared to be pubic hair, foreign to the victim.'

'Nothing to indicate forcible penetration then?' asked DS Watts.

Dr Hollis tilted her head, and stared over her glasses at the detective. 'No, but then you'll know as well as I do that does not preclude the possibility of rape. Especially if she was not in a position to consent.'

'Did you recover any semen?' asked DS Watts.

'Yes,' said the doctor. 'She told me that she'd showered after the assault, but there was still seminal fluid in her vagina.'

'There was mention of a tattoo?' said Jo. 'Could you describe it for us?'

'I can do better than that.'

The doctor swivelled to face her computer, brought up a series of pictures and selected one.

'This is the inside of her right thigh. One of the shots routinely taken in such cases.'

She leaned back so that the two detectives could see. According to the scale on the side of the photograph, the tattoo was a little over one and three-quarter inches wide and half that in length, in shades of black, brown and white. They had to crane forward to make it out.

'Can you zoom in please, Doctor?' asked Jo.

It was indeed a bird of prey, but not a falcon. Possibly an eagle. The wings were spread wide as though in flight. It had little in common with the one the unsub had used to mark his victims.

'Is that a permanent or a temporary tattoo?' Jo asked.

'Permanent. It's been there for several years at least. I'll email my report to whoever you tell me is the SIO, as well as providing a hard copy. You'll also find a copy of these photos on an SD card in one of the evidence bags.'

She pointed to a collection of brown paper bags on the shelf behind her.

'Is there anything else we should know at this stage?' Jo asked.

'I offered her emergency contraception, even though she's already on the pill. She's thinking about it. I also explained the potential risks of infection and offered her post-exposure prophylaxis for HIV and Hepatitis B. She agreed to the Hep B, and I've already given her the first of the injections.' Hollis pursed her lips. 'She wants to think about the HIV medication. I told her she'd better not leave it too long.'

Jo knew what she was thinking. If the victim was waiting for HIV test results, she was wasting her time. It would take up to a month at the earliest for any infection to be detected, and if she didn't start taking the preventive medicine within 72 hours of the attack, it would be too late.

'You've counselled her to talk to the Independent Sexual Advice adviser?' she said.

The doctor frowned.

'Of course.'

Jo didn't care that she might have offended her professional dignity; it was always better to be sure. She turned to DS Watts. 'Was there anything you wanted to ask?'

'Did you carry out a self-harm risk assessment, doctor?' said Watts.

'I did. You'll see from the notes that I categorised her as low to moderate risk. Although you probably know as well as I do that it is nigh on impossible to predict how a victim of serious sexual assault may respond in the short and medium term.'

The two police officers nodded. They had both known victims who had managed to pick themselves up and get on with their lives, as well as others whose lives were never the same again. Worse still, a few who had taken their own life.

'If it's okay with you, one of us will collect the evidence bags after the interview with Ms Razero,' said Jo.

'Of course,' Hollis replied. 'That's thoughtful of you. The fewer reminders she has, the better.'

'Thank you, Dr Hollis,' said Jo. 'You've been most helpful.'

Carol Hollis smiled wearily. It was the look of someone who'd seen it all, and knew that she'd see even more before she was done.

'Just doing my job,' she said.

Chapter 27

Laura Razero and Maureen Bellamy, her crisis worker, were in the police interview room.

To any outsider, the room was indistinguishable from a comfortable lounge, with upholstered chairs and a coffee table, the discreet video cameras, microphones and recording facilities blending in like normal hi-fi accessories. Three glasses, a jug of water and a box of tissues lay on the table. The two detectives had agreed that DS Watts would conduct the questioning. Until proven otherwise, this was a case for the Operation Talon team, not for Operation Juniper.

A quick appraisal told Jo that although she was short, Laura had a size 12 frame, larger than any of the other victims, and the true colour of her shoulder-length blonde hair was betrayed by auburn roots along the centre parting. Jo assumed that she must have brought a change of clothes with her because the pullover, jeans and pumps were a perfect fit and the colours suited her.

They introduced themselves and sat down. Jo deliberately took the chair furthest from the victim. She moved it so that she was not in her direct line of sight. This was DS Watts's interview. It also meant that she could observe unobtrusively.

'Laura has requested that I stay with her,' said the crisis worker. 'She understands that I won't be able to say anything or take any part in the proceedings.'

'That's fine,' said DS Watts. She turned to the student. 'So, Laura,' she said, 'I take it that Maureen's explained what happens next, and after the interview, if you choose to go ahead?'

Razero glanced at her crisis worker as though seeking permission to respond, and then nodded.

'Yes, but I'm not sure if I want to involve the police.'

Her voice was querulous, and Jo detected the slightest hint of a Spanish accent. It was the way she emphasised her Rs. She also looked confused. Conflicted was the word Dr Hollis had used, and it seemed about right to Jo. It wasn't a surprise – far from it. Many victims of serious sexual assault, both male and female, wavered at this stage. They would be asking themselves so many questions. *Was I responsible? Did I encourage him? Is he going to claim it was consensual sex? Did I imagine it? It's only his word against mine. I was drunk. Will anyone believe me? Am I going to have the whole of my sex life dragged up in court? What will my parents think?* And on and on, round and round it went. No wonder she was confused.

'Well, I can tell you, Laura,' said DS Watts, 'that it's perfectly normal for you to feel like this. It has to be your decision. Nobody can make it for you. But it generally helps if you tell us why you're in two minds. We'll respond, and then you can ask us anything you want to about the implications of going ahead with the interview, and what will happen if you don't. What do you say?'

Once again Laura looked at her crisis worker, realised that she was unable to help and turned back to reply.

'Maureen has already done all that,' she said. 'What I really want to know is what will happen to him if I do go ahead, and he's found guilty.'

'That will be down to the courts,' said DS Watts.

Laura frowned. 'But you must be able to give me some idea?'

'I'm afraid not, Laura. You see, it all depends on the degree of cul-pability of your assailant, the amount of harm caused, and whether or not there are any aggravating or mitigating circumstances.'

'Such as?'

'I can't tell you that either. It could be construed as my having coached you. I need you to tell me what happened, and then I'll be able to answer part, but not all, of that question.'

A textbook reply. Jo was very impressed, despite the fact that DS Watts was a highly trained specialist officer. Laura took a tissue from the box, blew her nose and dropped the tissue into a small bin by the side of the table.

'You'll be able to change your mind at any stage in this process,' said the Talon detective.

Laura's eyes registered surprise.

'Even after you've interviewed me?'

'Yes. Right up to, and including, any trial.'

The student looked up at the ceiling, down at the floor, at Maureen Bellamy and then decided.

'I'll do it,' she said.

The next ten minutes were spent establishing a little about Laura Razero. It served the dual purpose of giving them some idea about who she was, her background and lifestyle, as well as eas-ing her gently into the interview proper. Her father was Spanish, her mother English. They were both teachers and had first met at Barcelona University where her mother was on an exchange. Laura was bilingual, having lived all of her life in Guildford in Surrey, and three months a year in Spain with her grandparents. She had a first-class Honours degree in Spanish, Portuguese and Latin American Studies, and was one year into an MPhil in Latin American Studies. She worked part-time in a tapas restaurant and bar in Manchester, as she had done throughout her time at the university. She still lived at home, but in term time shared a three-bedroom house with three female postgraduate friends opposite Platt Fields Park, at a weekly rent of £70. She was single, not currently in a relationship. None of this had any direct bearing on the alleged offence, but it was useful context. And it meant that they were listening to a person, not just a victim.

'Thank you, Laura,' said DS Watts. 'Now, could you tell me about last night?'

'Where do you want me to start?'

'At the beginning?'

The student had a drink of water, sat up straight on the edge of her chair and began.

'I'd done a ten-hour shift at the restaurant. I should have done the full twelve hours, but the manager agreed I could finish early because it had quietened down and I'd promised to meet my flatmates in town.'

'What time was this, Laura?' asked DS Watts.

'I finished at ten thirty pm, then I went to join them at All Bar One.'

Jo knew it well. A stylish wine bar with a long list of beers, wines and cocktails. It was a favourite of Abbie's.

'When I arrived, I discovered they had company. Three guys they'd met earlier in the evening. One of them was Meredith's latest boyfriend. The other two were his mates. They claimed it was coincidence they'd bumped into each other.'

She paused and looked directly at DS Watts.

'I did wonder if Meredith had known all along where they were going to be and had set it up. Anyway, we all got on really well. I already knew Meredith's bloke, Tom, and the other two were bright, funny, articulate and good-looking. Mel, that's our other housemate, was clearly taken with one of them. Zac, I think it was.'

She winced, and reached for her beaker.

'Are you alright, Laura?' the crisis worker asked.

She took a sip and nodded.

'It's this bloody headache,' she said. 'Serves me right. I shouldn't have been drinking on an empty stomach.'

'What were you drinking?' asked DS Watts.

The student cradled the beaker in her lap, like a comfort blanket. 'A couple of cocktails. Then we shared two bottles of sparkling wine. It's only fifteen pounds a bottle on Fridays.'

'When you say *we* is that the six of you, or just the girls?'

'Just the girls.'

'And what were the three men drinking?'

'Beers and shorts.'

'Okay, then what?'

'We stayed chatting until last orders. That would be close to one pm. I wanted to go home because I was really tired, but the others insisted on going on to a club. Zac, I think it was, said he was a member at one of those upmarket guest-list clubs in the Northern Quarter. I don't remember what it was called, but the others will know. It was near Stevenson Square. I wanted to get a taxi and go back to the house, but the others persuaded me to go with them. They said I'd be queueing for ages, which was probably true. And Meredith said it'd be safer if I stayed with them.'

She shook her head dolefully.

'So much for her power of prophecy.'

She stared down at the beaker in her lap, and swirled the water round. DS Watts decided to gently prompt her.

'So you went to this club?'

Laura nodded, and looked up. 'It was packed. There was a DJ on, and it was really noisy. They showed us to a booth upstairs. I didn't want a drink, but I was starving. I asked if they'd got any nuts, or crisps, anything like that. The waiter brought bowls of each with the drinks. I only had a few mouthfuls because the three guys scoffed the rest of them. They ordered a cocktail for me too, even though I'd insisted I was fine.'

'Did you drink it?' DS Watts asked.

She nodded.

'To wash the nuts down. And the salt left me feeling thirsty. Then I must have dozed off, because I remember Meredith waking me and saying we were going. Mel and Daz were staying, but Tom had ordered us a taxi. While we were waiting, I asked for a bottle of water. I drank most of that, and perked up a bit.'

Mention of the bottle of water reminded her that she had some left in the beaker. She lifted it to her lips, drained it, and put the empty beaker on the table.

'On the way back in the taxi, Meredith and Tom began snogging. Justin, that was his name, Tom's other mate, had his arm around me. He kissed me on the cheek. Then he kissed me on the lips.'

She faltered, and looked down at the floor.

'Did you respond, Laura?' DS Watts asked.

There was a slight nod of the student's head.

'It doesn't make a massive difference whether you did or not,' the detective told her. 'It has nothing to do with consent to inter-course. But I do need to hear you say it for the tape?'

Laura Razero looked up, as though only now aware that she was being filmed. For the first time she looked close to tears.

'I let him do it,' she said. 'Kiss me. I can't swear that I responded. I'd had quite a lot to drink, so who knows? I may have done. A bit.' Her voice tailed off as she reflected on how pathetic that must sound.

'How many times did he kiss you?'

She shook her head.

'I don't know. Two or three?'

'Were they short kisses, or long ones?'

She shrugged.

'Quite long?'

Jo felt so sorry for Laura Razero. It was a familiar story. A night out with friends and new acquaintances. A good time had by all. Plenty to drink. A grope or fumble in the back of a taxi. A few drunken kisses. Nothing remarkable. Until it all went wrong.

'What happened next, Laura?' said DS Watts.

The student glanced up to the right.

'The taxi pulled up at the house. The two guys were supposed to be carrying on to Hale where they both live, but Meredith must have invited them in. I said I was going to bed, and I did.'

'How did you say goodnight to the two men?' asked the detective.

Laura looked puzzled. 'I just said goodnight, I think. And thanks.' She sounded apologetic. 'After all, they'd bought most of the drinks. And I must have had a good time, until it all got a bit too much for me.'

'No last kiss then?'

'No. I was really woozy, and I felt a bit sick. I just said good-night, and went upstairs.'

'What time was this?'

'I'm not sure. Three o'clock. Maybe half past? Meredith will know. I undressed, got into bed and went straight to sleep.'

'Did you put any pyjamas on, a nightie?'

'No. I just left my thong on.'

'Okay. You just tell me what happened next, Laura,' said DS Watts. 'I promise not to interrupt.'

The student clasped her hands together in her lap, and looked at a spot high up on the wall over the detective's shoulder.

'I woke up,' she said. 'It was dark. I was on my back. There was this heavy weight on my chest. I tried to move, but I couldn't. Then I realised there was someone on top of me. I could hear this heavy breathing in my ear. A cheekbone rubbing against the side of my head.' She paused, took a deep breath, and exhaled. 'Then I realised that he was moving inside me.'

She switched her gaze to DS Watts.

'I tried to push him off. Told him to stop. He put one hand on one shoulder, and an elbow on the other, and a hand over my mouth. All of his weight was on me.'

She looked past DS Watts, and directly at Jo. Her eyes were filling up, and her words were a plea for understanding.

'I couldn't do anything. I tried, I really tried.'

Jo nodded to show that she believed her, and that she understood. It was as much as either she or DS Watts could do without appearing to influence her testimony. The student looked down at the coffee table, saw the box of tissues, took one and dabbed her eyes. It was the first sign of real emotion since the interview had begun. It was almost as though the full horror of what had happened had just begun to dawn on her. She held the crumpled tissue in her hands.

'It was all over within seconds after that,' she said. 'He just pushed himself up, rolled off me and lay there on the bed. I went to get up and found that my thong was around my ankles. I kicked it off and got out of bed. The top sheet and the duvet were on the floor. I climbed over them, went into the bathroom, locked the door and was sick in the toilet.'

She wiped her mouth with the tissue as though reliving the experience.

'I stayed in there until the light began to come through the blinds. Then I had a shower.'

She looked up. 'I know I shouldn't have. But I couldn't help it. I wasn't thinking.'

DS Watts nodded.

'Then I got dressed and went downstairs. Mel was having breakfast. "Where's Meredith?" I asked. "In bed," she said. Then she rolled her eyes. "With Tom." I asked her if Tom's mate Justin was still here. She frowned. "I didn't know he stayed over?" she said. Then she stared at me with these big wide eyes, and said, "Laura! You didn't, did you?" I began to cry. She got up, put her arm around me and that's when I told her.'

Chapter 28

'So it was the friend who persuaded her to come in,' said DS Watts. 'Good for her. I don't think she would have done otherwise.'

'I'm not sure about that,' said Jo. 'That other housemate, Meredith, clearly didn't want her to. Probably felt guilty about introducing them through her boyfriend. And he wasn't much help either. Going on about Justin being a decent bloke really, and how it would finish his career if she told the police.'

'He's a legal executive. He should have known better.'

They were standing in the car park. DS Watts held the brown paper evidence bag containing all of the samples individually sealed in one hand, and in the other a small case holding the original tapes and SD cards on which the interview had been recorded.

'He must have known how it would play out,' she continued. 'Acquaintance rape. A few kisses. No foreplay. Not that that would have changed the fact that she didn't consent. He used minimal force, but it was still force. So, no mitigating circumstances. If the jury believe her, he'll get six years minimum. If the full impact dawns on her before the trial, and the harm he's done becomes more evident, it could be more.'

The Operation Talon detective nodded. 'I hope it doesn't, for her sake. That's one of the crap sides of this job. Knowing that the man getting the punishment he deserves depends on how much the woman suffers.'

'And providing she doesn't back out,' said Jo. 'She's too nice for her own good. Can you believe that she actually felt guilty about reporting it?'

'I know,' said DS Watts. 'I do hope she sees it through. The message needs to be out there. No means no. If we don't get more convictions, then the culture is never going to change.'

She frowned. 'There is one thing I'm wondering about. I know we'll have to wait for the tox results, but did she come across to you as though she may have been drugged?'

'No,' said Jo. 'I was thinking the same. She was far too lucid. There were no gaps in her memory, no haziness. Nothing more than you'd expect of someone who's had a heavy night, and is suffering from a hangover.'

'And that's another thing,' said DS Watts. 'I did a running score. According to her she had two cocktails, shared two bottles of fizz, then had a third cocktail. I know you can never be sure what's in a cocktail, but taking the average, and assuming she had a third of the fizz, I make it around thirteen point five units between ten thirty pm and two thirty am. She'd have had about eleven units in her system when he assaulted her. But that doesn't explain why she still had twenty milligrams per hundred millilitres in her blood thirteen hours after her last drink, and seventeen after she started drinking.'

She disarmed the car, stowed away her bag and case, and opened up her tablet on the car roof.

'This is something I've found really handy,' she said as she punched in the password, 'and not just for work.'

The menu screen filled with apps. DS Watts tapped one with her finger and began entering data straight away.

'It's a blood alcohol calculator,' she said, as she beavered away. 'You just enter the approximate number of ounces consumed, the average percentage of alcohol in the drinks, the body weight in pounds, and the number of hours spent drinking. Or in this case the time elapsed since that first drink.'

DS Watts looked up at her colleague. 'What would you say her weight was?'

'Nine stone max,' said Jo. 'So, a hundred and twenty-six pounds?'

DS Watts nodded her agreement, entered the figure, and pressed a key. 'I upped the units to fifteen, and averaged the percentage of alcohol out to twenty point four per cent. That's on the high side.'

'Here you go,' she said, handing Jo the tablet. 'The BAC percentage result reads "*Negligible amount*". And the box labelled "*Your BAC analysis*" states "*You are below the safe driving limit and not legally intoxicated*".'

Jo nodded, and handed the tablet back.

'I see what you mean,' she said. 'Either she wildly underestimated how much she'd had to drink, which is not unknown, or her drinks were spiked. All it would take would be for someone to tell the barman to put another couple of shots in her glass.'

'Or come prepared with a hip flask,' said DS Watts. 'She would have needed to have downed one and a half bottles of wine, and eleven shots of forty per cent spirits to register twenty milligrams when the doctor checked her blood. That's more than double what she claims she drank. In three and a half hours? My hunch is that he did spike her drinks, assumed that she'd be spark out when he went upstairs, wouldn't be capable of resisting and would only have a hazy recollection of what happened. We see that over and over again.'

'You'll only know for sure when you've spoken to her housemates,' said Jo. 'And hopefully had a look at the CCTV in those bars.'

'When *I've* spoken to them?' said the detective sergeant. 'I take it that means you don't think this has anything to do with your investigation?'

Jo shook her head.

'Never say never,' she replied. 'But there's not one single point of comparison other than the possibility that he spiked her drinks. This isn't the work of a serial rapist. This is your everyday arrogant, selfish, sexist chancer who sees it as no more than an entitlement. He's like an oversexed adolescent, with no sense of consequence.'

DS Watts nodded. 'Well, if I have anything to do with it, he'll have plenty of opportunity to ponder the consequences.'

Chapter 29

It was early evening when Jo arrived back at the Quays. Max was seated at his desk, staring at the computer screen.

'Where is everyone?' she asked.

He looked up and swivelled to face her.

'Ram has gone to pick up his mother. Andy's gone home to his wife and family. Dizzy left at lunchtime. She only came in as a favour – it is Saturday. How did you get on? Any luck?'

Jo dropped her bag on the neighbouring desk, and pulled a chair up close to his.

'Not for the victim. She woke up in bed and found the friend of her housemate's boyfriend was helping himself. They'd spent a little over three hours in town drinking together. Talon are dealing with it.'

'Date rape?'

She shrugged.

'Acquaintance rape, but it comes down to the same thing.'

'I thought there was a tattoo?'

'There was, a small one, on the inside of her right thigh. It was supposedly based on David Beckham's Guardian Angel. The one across the top of his back? But the tattoo artist made a mistake, so he finished it off as an eagle. She had it done on her eighteenth birthday. Regrets it now.' She shook her head. 'Not as much as she regrets being introduced to Justin.'

'A dead end then?'

'You could say that. At least as far as Juniper is concerned. How did the rest of you get on while I was away?'

It was Max's turn to shake his head. 'Not good, I'm afraid. Ram and I haven't got anywhere with that list we've been trawling through. Nothing jumped out at us that would merit being prioritised. We'll just have to wait for Sarsfield's team to work their way through them.'

'What about the ANPR check on Professor Hill, and the follow-up on those dozen vehicles they stopped?'

'Still waiting on those,' he said. 'They told Ram it would be late Monday, or Tuesday morning at the earliest.'

He logged out of his computer and sat back. 'Look, Jo,' he said. 'There's bugger all we can do right now. I'm calling it a day. I suggest you do the same. It's nearly two weeks since you had any time off. And we've both been working long days. Let's go home, enjoy Sunday, and we can come back with clear heads on Monday morning.'

Max was right on both scores. There was nothing more they could do until either the spadework paid off or they had a lucky break, and right now she was too tired and angry to think straight. Jo stood up.

'I think I'll pay the gym a visit, then have a soak and crash out. How about you?'

He stretched his arms, and yawned.

'I intend to have a catnap. They reckon it lowers your blood pressure. Then I might have a jog around the Quays, followed by a big juicy steak with a couple of beers, catch up on some mindless TV programmes and then sleep until midday tomorrow.'

Max levered himself to his feet, and sat on the desk so that their faces were level. He smiled wearily.

'Or whenever it is I happen to wake up.'

The apartment was in darkness. Jo went through to the bedroom, lobbed her bag on the bed, took her gym bag from the wardrobe and realised that her kit was still in the spin dryer. She retrieved it, found a towel, then packed and zipped up the kit bag. Having checked the phone for messages and finding none, she stormed out, slamming the door behind her. In her haste, she failed to spot the note underneath the TV remote on the kitchen table. A hollow echo scolded her down the staircase and out into the atrium.

It was a short walk through the Northern Quarter to the gym. That was one of the reasons she had chosen it. The other was that it operated twenty-four hours a day. That had been a bonus when Abbie was working nights. Now that Abbie had left, it meant that Jo no longer had to keep any evening sacrosanct. It was a bitter kind of compensation.

Despite the fact that the health club was quiet, Jo had to hunt for a locker. There were too many members ignoring the regulation that forbade them storing their kit when they were off the premises. She resolved to complain on her way out. All it needed was for management to empty everything into bin bags and make the recalcitrants root through the damp and sweaty garments when they next came in. That would put a stop to it.

She made her way to the room set up for the various forms of martial arts training that had become so popular among the twenty- to forty-year-old residents of the city centre, as well as those commuters who came for the pre- and post-work sessions. This was not a programmed session so she elected to put herself through an intensive workout using her own bodyweight. It was the best way she knew of increasing one's lactate threshold and developing explosive power. Not to mention releasing some of the tension she knew had built up inside her.

It was a punishing routine. Twelve burpees, twelve mountain climbers, and twelve tuck jumps in quick succession. A one-minute rest, then a second set with double the number of reps. And a final set identical to the first.

She sat cross-legged on the floor, wiping the sweat from her face and shoulders. Her heart thumped in her chest, her limbs protested. *Good pain*, Grant their instructor called it. The muscle burn that told you that your own particular physiology was being adequately stressed. *If only*, she thought, *there was an emotional equivalent. One that leached away the heartache.*

She heard the door open, and turned. It was a guy she knew as Nat, another Krav Maga enthusiast. Late twenties. He worked in one of the banks in the Spinningfields financial district, she seemed to remember.

'Hi, Jo,' he called. 'All on your own?'

'You should be a detective,' she said.

He grinned, and draped his towels over the upright rower. 'What a sad pair of bastards we are,' he said. 'Look at us. Saturday night, and nowhere to go.'

Jo nodded. It didn't feel like a joke to her.

'Do you fancy some floorwork?' he asked.

She stood up.

'Why not.'

Nat was good, very good. Eight minutes in, Jo was becoming increasingly frustrated. His extra reach had given him the advantage in the initial set of moves, but her low centre of gravity had given her the advantage in the throws. When it came to the floorwork, his weight and upper body strength was proving difficult to overcome. He was already up three submissions to her one.

'You're doing fine, Jo,' he said, as they squared up for the penultimate time.

It was to prove a costly mistake. She was in no mood to be patronised. He feinted with a straight-arm strike to her left temple, following with a swift jab to the right side of her body. Anticipating the jab, she stepped aside, grasped his wrist with her left hand and pulled him off balance. Looping her right arm around his neck as she fell backwards, she pulled him down on top of her, wrapped her legs around his waist, and completed the choke by forcing her left forearm against her right tricep. As he tried to buck himself free, she tightened the hold and locked her ankles across his groin. He continued to resist.

'Submit!' she shouted. 'Come on, Nat, submit!'

She was angry with him, with Abbie, with the bastard who was going round abducting and raping young women. With herself . . .

She was vaguely aware of someone shouting. But it wasn't Nat. Why the hell didn't he submit?

'Stop, Stuart! Stop! For God's sake!'

A hand grasped her hair in a vice-like grip and pulled, causing her to release the choke to stop her hair being torn from her scalp. She looked up.

Red-faced and angry, Grant stared back. He released his grip, pushed her aside, and knelt beside a semi-conscious Nat. Only then did Jo appreciate the enormity of what she had or might have done.

'Oh God!' she said. 'I'm so sorry, Nat.' She stood up and looked down on them both. 'Is he alright?'

'He'll live, no thanks to you,' said Grant, sitting back on his heels. 'What the hell's wrong with you? I thought you knew better than this. What am I always saying? You don't train when you're tired. And you never come here to work off your anger. Leastways not on your gym buddies.'

Nat was sitting up, gulping deep breaths and massaging his neck.

'I'm so sorry, Nat,' she said again. 'I don't know what came over me.'

He nodded, and carried on massaging.

'Why didn't you submit?' she asked.

Grant turned on her angrily. 'Don't put it all on him!' he said. 'You know the rule: any chokehold, three seconds maximum. Then you release, submission or no submission.'

She knew Grant was right. There was no such thing as a safe choke-out, especially a blood choke-out. There was a risk of stroke, seizures, short-term memory loss and coma. Even death had been known to occur. She had been fortunate that Grant had come in. Nat had been luckier still.

They helped her gym buddy to his feet.

'No hard feelings,' he said, holding out a hand for her to shake. 'You were right. It was male pride. I should have submitted.'

'Yes, you bloody well should,' said Grant. 'But that doesn't let her off the hook. She was the one in control. It was her call. If it ever happens again, you'll both be barred. Now bugger off, the pair of you.'

Jo had a shower and fled back home. She went straight into the bedroom, dropped her kit bag on the floor and threw herself down on the bed. She was still mad with herself. Grant had been right. She should not have agreed to combat-train in her current state of mind.

Perhaps it was time she went back to see the force counsellor. After all, as a secondee, she was theoretically still on GMP's books. And the counsellor had told Jo when she signed her off that she would put her down as having an open appointment. That meant that she could ring up to see her, should the need ever arise, without having to go through the rigmarole of applying through the Human

Resources team. It was a conundrum that continued to plague her through supper, and into the night.

———⌣———

It was still on her mind the next morning when she woke to discover that she had slept through the alarm. Jo swung her legs off the bed and sat up. If she did ring up, what was she going to say? Her partner had walked out on her? She was beginning to personalise the hunt for the perpetrator she was investigating? She was concerned that she might be developing anger issues? How would that be received? And would the counsellor have to let the NCA know? Would Simon Levi find out? What would Harry think? She shook her head. Was it really that bad?

The phone rang. It was Gerry Sarsfield's deputy.

'I'm sorry, Ma'am,' he said, 'but we have a body.'

Chapter 30

One mile west of Bury on the A58. Twelve and a half miles by major road and motorway. It should have been a breeze, but dawdling Sunday drivers who never looked in their rear-view mirror and were oblivious to her strobing lights above the bumper made it achingly slow. In the end, she had to call for a blues and twos to escort her for the final four miles with their blue lights and irritating siren.

Two police vans, a traffic car and a motorcycle blocked the road eighty yards from the scene. Up ahead, she could see a paramedic bike, an ambulance and a GMP fast response car. Beyond that, more vehicles. Closer still, a black Mercedes was front end on into a crushed steel and glass bus shelter, bonnet crumpled, windscreen shattered.

Jo parked up, showed her ID to the uniformed officer turning traffic around, and walked the rest of the way. This was not what she had been expecting. Had they caught the unsub in the act of moving the body, she wondered?

Facing away from her, a woman wearing walking boots, light-weight khaki hiking trousers, and a light grey waterproof jacket was talking to a uniformed officer. The officer spotted Jo, and spoke to the woman who turned and stared at her.

'SI Stuart, National Crime Agency,' Jo said, holding up her ID as she advanced.

The woman waited for her and then held out her hand.

'DS Hatton, Ma'am.' She looked down at her boots and grimaced. 'I was just about to set off for a Sunday morning walk up to the Peel Tower with the family, then lunch at the Hearth of the Ram.'

'We're not the only ones whose Sunday was spoiled,' Jo replied. She nodded towards the ambulance. 'Is she in there?'

DS Hatton half-turned. 'Oh, no, Ma'am, she died on the way to hospital. You see, we had no idea this might be linked with your investigation, Ma'am. As soon as we did, I had her moved to Oldham, to the regional pathology forensics facility. She should be there by now.'

'Don't worry,' Jo told her. 'That's as it should be. Just tell me what happened here.'

Twenty yards away, two road traffic officers were measuring skid marks.

'It's a classic RTA pedestrian fatality,' said DS Hatton. She nodded over Jo's shoulder. 'Driver of that Merc was doing thirty-eight in a thirty-mile-an-hour zone. According to him and several witnesses, she came out of there.'

She pointed to a wide tarmacked lane on the left that sloped away downhill, accompanied by a footpath sign. 'Stumbled straight into his path. Poor sod didn't have a chance.'

'Neither did she,' Jo reminded her. 'If he'd been doing thirty, she might still be alive.'

The detective sergeant nodded sagely.

'Do you want to talk to him?'

'No,' said Jo. 'I'll read his statement.'

DS Hatton smiled.

'Happens you won't need to, Ma'am. He's got a dashcam fitted. We found it dangling in the passenger footwell – that's how we know what speed he was doing. He thought it might help reduce his insurance, only now it's gone and provided incriminating evidence.'

Jo took a BSU card from her ID wallet and a biro from her pocket. She underlined Ram's email address and handed the card to DS Hatton. 'Can you get them to copy the recording ASAP and send it to my colleague?'

'Of course, Ma'am,' DS Hatton replied.

Jo had decided not to discourage the DS's insistence on calling her Ma'am. Their paths were unlikely to cross again, and given names seemed inappropriate in the circumstances.

'Tell me about the girl,' she said.

'Student who'd been abducted. They know because her student card was in her anorak pocket. Susanne Hadrix. Nineteen years of age. Student at Accrington and Rossendale College.'

She dug in her pocket, produced a transparent evidence bag and handed it to Jo.

'College?' Jo said. 'Not university then?'

'Sixteen- to nineteen-year-olds and adult courses, including degrees,' said DS Hatton.

Jo nodded. If this was him, he was widening his net. Making it even more difficult for them to track him down. She studied the photo. Young. Smiling eyes. The world her oyster. It wasn't a lot to go on.

'Describe her,' she said.

'Four foot eleven, slim, long blonde hair, blue eyes.'

Jo took out her phone, took a photograph of the card, including the girl's image, and handed it back.

'I'll need a copy of this too.'

'No problem.'

'How did you know this was connected with our investigation?'

'As soon as we entered her name into the Police National Computer it showed her as having just been reported as a MisPer.

It also referred us to HOLMES2. When we checked that it told us that she fitted the victim profile for Operation Juniper and directed us to contact the relevant force major incident team.'

'Who reported her as missing?'

'Her mother. Nine thirty this morning. She didn't come home from a night out with her mates. Mother assumed she'd stayed over and hadn't bothered to tell her – it wasn't unknown apparently. When she'd heard nothing by nine o'clock, she rang round all her daughter's contacts. Finally she rang Burnley nick.'

'Burnley, that's where she lived?'

'Yes, Ma'am.'

Jo pointed to the lane from which the victim had stumbled into the road.

'Where does that lead?'

'Mile Lane? Takes you past the back of those two houses, then between fields past a farm, and turning right to reach another. If you follow the footpaths straight ahead where the lane bends, you end up at Elton Reservoir.'

'How far?'

'Just under eight hundred yards to the reservoir. Half that to where the lane turns.'

'Anyone driving down there in the middle of the night unlikely to be spotted then?'

'Providing they don't leave it too late. You know what farmers are like. Early to bed, early to rise. Mind you,' she added, 'there's no saying that's where she was dumped, if that's what you're saying?'

Jo nodded.

'In which case, you need to know that there are seven different ways you could drive a car or a van close to the reservoir. She could have been taken down one and come back up another.'

It paid to have someone with local knowledge at the scene, Jo reflected. Unfortunately, it looked as though the unsub shared that knowledge. Either that or his planning was meticulous.

'How many of the roads that lead to those access points for the reservoir have cameras fitted?' she asked.

'Just this one. There's a speed camera facing the Tesco garage just before you get to St Stephen's church. You must have passed it on your way here.'

'What about fixed ANPR cameras?'

DS Hatton shook her head.

'Nothing this side of the motorway. Division relies on mobile units. We had a blitz last month. Five arrested and thirty-five uninsured vehicles taken off the road. But I doubt you'll get lucky today, with it being a Sunday. I bet we'll only have had one car and maybe the odd bike actively using automatic number plate recognition, and they'll have been checking on unsafe drivers, unsafe vehicles or known criminals. If your guy is clean and driving safely, the odds of him having been stopped won't be far off winning the lottery.'

'No, but the number plate will still have been recorded. If he passed or was in front of a mobile unit, he'll be in there somewhere.'

DS Hatton shrugged. Jo knew what she was thinking. Even if he had, it would be like looking for a needle in a haystack. There were raised voices from behind her. Someone was calling her name. She turned to see who it was.

Anthony Ginley, the investigative reporter, was attempting to wave to her over the shoulder of the burly officer holding him back. Jo swore.

'How the hell did he get here so fast?'

'Someone you know, Ma'am?' said DS Hatton, an amused smile on her face.

'Which hospital was she taken to?' Jo asked.

'She was being taken to Bury General, Ma'am, but as soon as we realised it might be a suspicious death, I diverted them to the Royal Oldham. On account of the regional forensic unit.'

Ginley's voice forestalled Jo's response. 'SI Stuart!' he shouted. 'Can you confirm that this incident is linked to Operation Juniper?'

Jo turned her back on him.

'Don't tell him anything,' she said, 'and make sure everyone else working at the scene understands that if they so much as smile at him, there will be consequences.'

'Right, Ma'am,' said the DS.

'Get that lane sealed off. And all of the other access routes to the reservoir. I want to know where she was left. There may be tyre tracks or other evidence. I'll make sure there's a Tactical Aid team out here as soon as possible. They'll conduct the search and relieve your people. And make sure we get that dashcam footage and the copy of her student ID within the hour.'

'I will, Ma'am.' DS Hatton hesitated. 'Look, I need to know, Ma'am, for the paperwork if nothing else, is this one yours or ours?'

'I won't know for sure until I've seen the body,' Jo told her. 'Maybe not even then. In the meantime, can you deal with it as a fatal RTA, but accommodate the Tactical Aid Unit when they arrive? Once we know for sure, we can talk again. GMP will confirm everything with your divisional commander. Can you get him or her to contact the coroner, and request that he direct that a post-mortem be carried out?'

'Yes, Ma'am.' She didn't look happy. That Sunday lunch was fading into the sunset.

Jo nodded. 'I'll follow that up with a specific request to the coroner for the Home Office pathologist to collect specific samples for analysis. In the meantime, I'm off to the mortuary.'

She began to move away and then stopped.

'Thank you, DS Hatton,' she said. 'I'm sorry I was so abrupt. But if I'm right, and don't repeat any of this, she was his sixth victim and the first one to die. It doesn't make for idle chit-chat.'

DS Hatton smiled. It took years off her. 'I understand,' she said.

'You mentioned family,' said Jo. 'You have children?'

'Two girls.'

Jo nodded.

'Look after them,' she said.

DS Hatton nodded back. 'Don't worry, I will.'

If only it was that simple, Jo reflected as she walked back to her car.

The Manchester Evening News crime reporter had arrived, together with a photographer. She could also see a BBC outside broadcast van slowly approaching the police cordon. It was point-less trying to hide her face. That always backfired. It made you look furtive or embarrassed – either way, it implied you had something to hide.

'Is it him?' demanded Ginley. 'The Falcon?'

Jo clenched and then unclenched her fists. It was the first time anyone had called the unsub that. Now it would be the headline in tomorrow's papers. Even sooner on the media websites and Twitter feeds. It was exactly what the unsub sought, what he fed off: the mystique, the notoriety, the fear that media frenzy generated.

'Who is this Falcon?' asked the MEN reporter. 'Is he referring to the serial rapist, SI Stuart? The one who tattoos his victims?'

She brushed them aside, and then paused as she reached her car.

'As far as I'm aware,' she said, 'this is a tragic road traffic acci-dent involving a motorist and a pedestrian. If you wish to know any more, I suggest you speak with the officer dealing with the incident.'

She climbed in and slammed the door shut. 'Good luck with that,' she muttered, as she started the engine.

Chapter 31

DI Sarsfield was waiting for Jo at the morgue.

'I didn't see any point in going to the scene of the accident,' he said. 'Didn't want both of us hassling the SIO. I've arranged for a Tactical Aid search team to go up there, plus Jack Benson and his scene of crime officers.'

'I'm not holding my breath,' Jo told him. 'If we're lucky, we might get tyre prints. He's never used the principal crime scene as his dumpsite, and I doubt he's going to start now.'

'Me neither.' He raised his eyebrows. 'Is it him?'

'I don't know, Gerry,' she said, 'but we'll soon find out. From what the SIO told me, I'd say this one is number six. If so, he made a massive miscalculation.'

He shook his head. 'You said it was an accident waiting to happen, Jo. He's been playing Russian roulette with their lives. This morning the chamber had a bullet in it.'

The assistant practice manager slid back the glass screen, and waved them over. She pointed to a square grey pad on the wall beside a pair of fire doors.

'If you press the pad, the door will open. Go straight down the corridor in front of you, and you'll find Alex Brough, one of our anatomical pathology technicians, is waiting to take you down to the mortuary.'

Both Jo and Gerry knew Alex Brough of old. While Home Office pathologists came and went, the mortuary technician was one of the few constants in regional forensic pathology units. She stood waiting for them in her white scrubs, blue gloves and matching boots. They matched not only each other, but also her electric-blue hair. It was an eccentric look. Jo thought it suited Alex. It also served to brighten up the otherwise depressingly bland surroundings.

'DI Stuart, DI Sarsfield, good to see you again,' said the technician with a broad grin on her face.

'It's SI Stuart now,' Sarsfield told her. 'With the National Crime Agency, no less.'

The technician responded with a curtsy. 'Congratulations, Ma'am,' she said. 'It's an honour to welcome you to our humble abode.'

'Don't be daft,' said Jo. 'You have the body?'

Alex straightened up.

'Very good,' she said. 'Habeas corpus. I've never heard that one before.'

'We need a quick look,' said Jo, 'that's all. Time is of the essence.'

'We have reason to believe that this is connected with a series of attacks on young women,' Gerry Sarsfield added. 'If so, her death will be categorised as involuntary manslaughter.'

Alex's brow wrinkled.

'Recklessness or criminal negligence?'

'Both.'

'I understood she walked into the path of a car?'

'Stumbled. We suspect that she'd been drugged,' Sarsfield said.

The technician nodded. 'As good as murdered,' she said. 'And initial indications are that someone had sex with her shortly before she died.'

'Initial indications?' said Jo.

'You can't quote me, but bruising on the inside of the thighs and what looks like traces of seminal fluid. I bagged her undies separately. You'll know more after the PM and the forensic tests.'

The two detectives glanced at each other. This was a first. More importantly, it held out the possibility that they might finally have some DNA.

Alex Brough turned and led the way down another corridor to an anteroom where she handed them a set of scrubs, including a mask and booties. This was after all not any old morgue, but a forensic unit. Then she led them into the storage facility.

Gleaming stainless steel cabinets lined one wall. Alex wheeled a hydraulic trolley over to one of the cabinets, and opened the door. Jo shivered as the temperature fell dramatically. There were two vertical stacks of trays, side by side, with only one of the trays occupied.

'We keep those awaiting a post-mortem separate from those pending the decision of the Coroner's Court,' said Alex as she slid the tray containing the body out and on to the hydraulic trolley. She smiled cheerfully. 'Works fine, so long as we don't have a multiple pile-up, or a Sarin gas attack. Not that we've had one of those lately.'

The two detectives stared in silence at the shape beneath the sterile modesty sheet. They were both thinking the same thing. Twelve hours ago, she hadn't a care in the world and a lifetime ahead of her. A career, boyfriends, a husband, children, grandchildren. Now she had been reduced to this: a piece of meat on a slab. A puzzle to be probed, dissected and pored over. And for what?

'The paramedics cut away most of her clothing,' said Alex. 'I removed the rest, and bagged it up for forensics. Don't worry; I took photographs first. Professor Flatman will want to have a look at her clothes before they're sent off.' She paused and took hold of the sheet. 'Ready?'

They nodded. She lifted it back to reveal the head and upper torso.

Jo inhaled and breathed out slowly, her breath damp against the inside of the mask. It was far worse than she had expected. The top of the young woman's skull had been crushed, presumably by direct impact with the road surface. Her hair was completely matted with dried blood so that it was difficult to be sure if her hair was blonde or auburn. Jo put her hand through the false pocket of her scrubs and took out her phone.

'No pictures!' said Alex abruptly.

'It's okay,' Jo told her. 'I have a copy of her student ID card. I just want to check if this is she. It wouldn't be the first time someone was found carrying another person's ID.'

She expanded the image. Gerry Sarsfield peered over her shoulder.

'It's her,' he said.

'I agree,' said Jo. 'But I'm afraid her parents are going to have to get a damn sight closer than the viewing gallery to be certain.'

'That's the beauty of the trolley,' said Alex. 'I can wheel it close to the window.' She reached for the sheet. 'Are you done?'

'One more thing,' said Jo. 'Does she have a tattoo?'

'She has several. Why, what are you looking for?'

'Something that looks like a bird? A bird of prey?'

The mortuary technician's eyes widened in recognition.

'It's him, isn't it?' she said. 'The bastard that's going round kidnapping women and raping them?'

'Abducting,' said Sarsfield.

'We can't confirm or otherwise,' said Jo. 'You know that, Alex.'

The technician was already folding back the sheet. There were livid bruises all over the young woman's body. The right shoulder and right forearm had grazes that had peeled off the skin. The left arm was covered with a tattoo. It looked like an elfin woman holding a spear and a dagger, encircled by the bodies of two wild dogs.

'That's Princess Mononoke, heroine of the epic Japanese film,' the technician informed them. 'Brilliant animation.'

On the left side of her stomach, there was also a delicate swallowtail butterfly that straddled the panty line where her tan ran out.

'I don't see a falcon?' said Sarsfield.

Alex circled the trolley. She placed one hand under the left shoulder, and the other under the right buttock. Ever so gently, she rolled the body towards them.

'Here you go,' she said.

The two detectives joined her on the opposite side of the table. There were bruises across the whole of the left side, and a dark purple discolouration across the lower back where the blood from post-mortem lividity had pooled.

'Where are we looking?' Jo asked.

Alex nodded with her head.

'Bottom right,' she said. 'Across the gluteus medius and the start of the gluteus maximus.'

They leaned closer.

'Hurry up,' Alex urged. 'This is harder than it looks.'

'There it is,' said Sarsfield pointing.

High up on the buttocks, it was barely distinguishable against the bruising.

'It's him,' Jo muttered.

'Can I put her down, please?' said Alex. 'You'd be surprised how heavy she is.'

'Do you know when the post-mortem is scheduled for?' asked Jo, as they scrubbed and dried their hands, and applied the sanitiser.

Alex shook her head.

'Our resident Home Office pathologist is on leave. In the Bahamas, lucky devil. The locum called in sick on Friday and won't be back till Wednesday. We're waiting for one to arrive tomorrow.'

'Who is it, do you know?'

'Sir James Flatman.'

'God,' said Jo. 'I thought he'd retired.'

The technician grinned.

'No such luck. He was up here twice last month. Arson with intent to kill, in which they succeeded, and a nasty case of poisoning. The routine post-mortem said emphysema. The coroner asked for a second post-mortem when suspicious circumstances were raised. Professor Flatman found otherwise. It turned out the wife got tired of caring for her husband, and laced his ibuprofen with potassium cyanide.'

'Nice,' said Sarsfield.

Alex stopped. 'Now you've told me what the urgency is, I'll make sure she's moved to the top of his list. He insists on having a full English breakfast first, so I'm thinking it'll be around eleven am. If you ring first thing, the practice manager will know.'

It was raining stair rods. The two detectives stood under the shelter of the entrance canopy while Jo phoned DS Hatton.

'It's our man,' Jo told her. 'Can you handle the RTA investigation and arrange for the parents to identify the body? If you email me their address and the name of the family liaison officer, we'll have someone go over and break it to them that their daughter was not only run over and killed, but also abducted and raped.'

The detective sergeant sighed. 'Rather you than me, Ma'am.'

'I suggest we both cover the post-mortem, but I'd like to send my own exhibits officer. Apart from the tox results, which we'll share with you, I doubt the other exhibits will add anything to your investigation, but may prove vital to ours. Especially any foreign DNA. As long as we both state the reasons in our policy book, that should be fine with your boss and with mine.'

'I agree, Ma'am,' said DS Hatton, even though Jo sensed that she was far from happy.

'I also need to find out who the victim was with last night and interview them too,' said Jo. 'Given that Mrs Hadrix rang round her friends, she should be able to point us in the right direction.'

Gerry Sarsfield touched her lightly on the elbow. 'If she's up to it,' he said, pointing to the other side of the car park where a short plump woman was being helped from the back of a patrol car. She was clearly distraught, barely able to stand.

'Got to go,' Jo told DS Hatton. 'I think this is her now.'

A tall, gaunt man, presumably the woman's husband, had a hand beneath her armpit and the other arm around her waist. He was struggling to keep her upright. A woman police officer emerged from the driver's side and came round the car to assist him. To add insult to injury, they were getting drenched.

'I may as well stay and see if I can get those names from her,' said Jo. 'Just one will do for starters. Why don't you get back to the incident room, Gerry? I'll have Ram copy everything over to you. Then when I've established who she was with, I'll need all of them interviewed, and all of the bars they went to last night visited. Always assuming the pattern was the same. Staff interviewed, CCTV footage obtained . . .'

He held up his hand.

'I know the routine, Jo,' he said. 'It's becoming all too familiar.'

'Sorry, Gerry,' she said. 'Force of habit.'

They watched as the woman was gently manhandled through the doors to the morgue. Two more victims to add to the scores of people whose lives had already been damaged by the senseless and sickening obsession of this aberration of a human being.

After Sarsfield had left, Jo followed Susanne Hadrix's parents into the viewing room. She stayed well back, not wanting to intrude on their private grief.

It was every bit as harrowing as she had expected. If anything, she felt that the father had been most affected. The mother collapsed on to a chair, wailing and bucketing tears. He stood erect, his hands on the rail, staring with abject incomprehension. Gradually, as reality dawned, he seemed to shrink before her eyes, his shoulders slumping, his entire body appearing to collapse in on itself. Tears began to stream down his cheeks as he gazed in silence at the broken body of his only child.

Jo had to brush away a tear of her own with the back of her hand. It was often this way. Not at the sight of the victim, but of the grief of those left behind. DCI Caton, her mentor, had once compared it to coping with the shock of an earthquake, and then being consumed by the tsunami that followed it.

Forty minutes later, she emerged from the relatives' room with the names she had been waiting for. Fortunately, the mother had her mobile phone with her and it was a simple matter of copying down the contact details from the last four calls she had made before she rang the police.

The downside was that Jo had been the one to tell them how it was that their daughter had ended up miles away from Burnley town centre, where she'd been on a night out with her friends. It had not been necessary to fill in the gaps. Media coverage given to the disappearance of the other five students had made sure of that. In Jo's experience, the imagination was a much more destructive medium than her dry procedural account could ever have been. And so it proved. She was relieved when the family liaison officer arrived, and she was able to make her apologies and leave.

Before she left the morgue, she went to find Alex Brough.

'Those body fluids you mentioned,' she said. 'I'm going to have DI Sarsfield send over the mortuary exhibits officer first thing in the morning. I'm also going to have the forensic submission ready to go. Do you have a DNA identification facility on-site?'

The mortuary technician's eyes lit up.

'We've just taken delivery of the latest-generation portable unit. You're looking at as little as ninety minutes and no more than two hours to process a sample and get a hit, if there's a match in the system.'

The rain had ceased temporarily, but the temperature had dropped close to freezing. Despite this, there was a spring in Jo's steps as she crossed the car park. Was this the break they had been waiting for?

Chapter 32

On the way to the Quays, Jo decided to call Ram and Max on the hands-free. She was not going to tear Andy away from his family, but the other two were both single, although Ram had his mother to contend with. Ram answered on the first ring.

'Jo,' he said, 'what's up?'

She told him.

'I'm on my way,' he said.

'I'm sorry to tear you away from your mother, Ram.'

'No problem,' he replied, although it sounded anything but.

The call to Max went to answerphone; she left a message.

To dispel the mental image of Susanne Hadrix's broken body, she switched on the radio. Mike Sweeney's rasping Salford accent told her that it was his Eighties Classics slot. *Was it that time already?*

'Phil Everly and Cliff Richard singing "She Means Nothing To Me" – what an amazing combination!' the DJ said.

His voice dropped a register and adopted a sombre tone. 'And now we're going to depart from the normal format. I doubt there's anyone out there unaware of the recent spate of attacks on female students across the North West. We've been inundated by calls from listeners who want to know why we haven't given the issue serious coverage. In response, my producer has invited an expert on to the show for a short interview with yours truly to find out how our female listeners can make themselves less vulnerable to attack. So, here with me this afternoon from the *Say No And Stay Safe* charity is Mr Sam Malacott. Welcome, Sam.'

Jo's listened intently and with increasing unease. It was not so much what Malacott was saying, which was more or less the advice he had given at the Chancellors' conference, as the impression she had that he was enjoying the whole experience. It reminded her that she had not yet received the information about his relatives that she had asked for.

It started to rain again. She switched to Smooth Radio, flicked the windscreen wipers to rapid, and put her foot down.

Ram was already there when she arrived. He pointed to his screen.

'I assume you asked them to send this over?'

'What is it?' she asked.

'The footage from the driver's dashcam. The definition's brilliant.'

She pulled a chair up alongside him.

'Ready?' he asked.

She nodded. He pressed play.

'It's quite busy for a Sunday morning,' Ram observed. 'Must've been plenty of witnesses.'

'People returning from church,' she said. 'Picking up their papers and croissants, or off to visit relatives.'

They watched as the Mercedes approached a sign indicating a cycle lane ahead, and then a bold SLOW sign painted in white on the surface of the left-hand lane.

'He's over the limit,' said Ram pointing to the 30mph circle in the top left, and then the analogue read-out of the vehicle's speed. 'Close to forty mph.'

Jo nodded.

'Enough to turn a serious injury into a fatality.'

The car was passing a row of trees in the verge on its nearside.

'She comes out of a side road just up ahead,' she told him.

'Can't see it yet,' Ram responded.

Jo wondered if the trees had obscured his view until the last few seconds. It certainly looked like it.

'There she is,' he said.

Jo craned forward. Susanne Hadrix was just coming into view up the slope of the lane. Four ponderous steps, and she was at the kerb, standing immediately between the bus stop and the oncoming car. A white transit van was turning out of a side road immediately opposite the lane. Suddenly she appeared to sway and stumble into the cycle lane. The driver of the Mercedes steered to the left, heading directly for the girl. Then the car decelerated rapidly, but not before striking the student. They watched in horror as she was swept off her feet, and across the bonnet, struck the windscreen, and was hurled into the air. They lost sight of her as the car careered forward into the bus shelter, and the screen went black, then a fuzzy grey.

'The dashcam was dislodged,' Jo told him. 'We're looking at the carpet in the passenger footwell.'

Ram pressed pause and sat back.

'She never had a chance,' he said.

Jo nodded. 'Can you take it back to just before she steps into the road, and pause it there?' Jo said.

She had him zoom in on Susanne Hadrix's face. There was no doubt about it, she appeared dazed and confused. Her focus was straight ahead, on the van turning out of Mile End Road. She seemed oblivious to the oncoming Mercedes.

'Can you zoom out a bit, and run it on in slow motion?' she said.

'Look,' said Ram. 'Her foot is right on the edge of the kerb.'

He was right. Her left foot was teetering on the kerb in a three-inch strapless mid-court shoe. Her other foot was in mid-air. She seemed to be trying to maintain her balance but failed, toppling directly into the path of the car as it swerved towards her.

'The driver was too busy watching the van,' Ram concluded. 'He overcorrected and didn't see her until it was too late.'

Jo nodded.

'It looks that way.'

She sat back.

'Had he been doing thirty,' she said, 'he'd have had time to start braking, and the impact would have been that less severe. She'd probably still be alive.'

It was the second time that day she had said that. It changed nothing. Ram closed the video down. In its place was a magnified image of Susanne Hadrix's student card. She looked so young and hopeful, full of promise and expectation – neither of which would ever be realised.

'The bastard,' Jo said softly.

Ram looked up and followed her gaze.

'Do you think that's why he's going after students?' he said. 'Because in some sick way it intensifies his sense of achievement, of power? You know, shattering all that confidence and optimism and opportunity?'

'Who knows?' she said. 'You'd be better asking Andy.' She gritted her teeth. 'Better still, you can ask the unsub, when I bring him in.'

She tore her eyes away from the screen.

'Speaking of which, have you got anything for me on Anthony Ginley?' she said. 'The investigative reporter? He turned up at the scene today, suspiciously early.'

'Did he now?'

Ram immediately began routing through his out tray.

'It was the last thing I did before I left yesterday afternoon. I'd gone before you came back in. I had to pick up . . .'

'Your mother,' she said. 'I know. Just tell me what you've got.'

He slid out two A4 stapled pages, and handed them to her.

'See for yourself. He worked for a red top and then for a broadsheet. Highly regarded in the industry as an investigative reporter. He's covered financial malfeasance in the City, political corruption involving the rigging of local election postal ballots, and the illegal trafficking of young women to work as au pairs for Arabs in the West End. He's best known for his covert work investigating cash-for-crash firms. It was made into a Panorama documentary that narrowly missed out on a BAFTA four years ago.'

'All that tells us is that he's a slippery character who's good at his job. What I now need to know is what he was doing last night, and in the early hours of this morning.'

'Right, Boss.'

'And while you're about it, do the same with Malacott. Incidentally, Ram, I'm still waiting on information about his female relatives.'

'In hand, Boss,' he said. 'I have found a sister. Waiting on her details.'

Her phone rang. It was Max.

'Jo, I just picked up your message. I'm in Birmingham, catching up with some former colleagues from the Met. But don't worry, I'll be back bright and early in the morning. What was it you wanted?'

'It'll keep till the morning, Max,' she said.

There was a long pause.

'There's been another one, hasn't there?' he said. 'I can hear it in your voice.'

She shook her head, despite the fact that he couldn't see her.

'Like I said, it'll keep.'

'You may as well tell me, Jo,' he insisted. 'I promise not to drop everything and dash back, but you can't leave me wondering.'

She sighed.

'Very well. It looks as though he followed his usual MO, but this time he was either careless or unlucky. He dumped his victim near a reservoir, but she stumbled out on to a main road and was hit by a motorist. She landed on the top of her skull. Massive brain bleed. Her body's in the regional forensic morgue in Oldham.'

'It was only a matter of time,' he said.

'I know.'

'It's not your fault, Jo.'

'I know that too. But I'm the one who's supposed to stop him.'

'*We*,' he said, 'not just you. There's the team, the Agency, three different police forces.'

'That's not how the press and the public are going to see it,' she murmured.

'Sod *them*!' he said. 'What do they know?'

She laughed hesitantly. He seemed to have an unerring knack for knowing how to cheer her up. It was just a shame he couldn't, or wouldn't, apply it to himself.

'What do you want me to do?' he said. 'Tomorrow morning?'

'If it's okay with you, I'd like you to attend the post-mortem, only it's Professor Flatman and I'm not sure I can take him right now.'

He laughed.

'*Fingers* Flatman? Leave him to me. We have history.'

'Thank God for that,' she said. 'You've no idea how much of a relief it is. And Max, there's something I haven't told you.'

'Go on?'

'The mortuary technician says they have substantial seminal fluid on her clothing.'

'DNA!' he exclaimed. 'That's bloody amazing. It's what you've been hoping for.'

'Not if she'd already had sex with someone else before he took her.'

'Playing devil's advocate doesn't suit you, Jo,' he said. 'You should leave that to me. Mind you, when you said he'd been careless, I didn't realise it extended to spraying his DNA around.'

'I know,' she replied. 'It doesn't make sense. He's been so careful up until now.'

'They all make mistakes sooner or later,' he reminded her.

'Only those we catch,' she said. 'Only the ones we catch.'

Chapter 33

Jo managed to contact the coroner about the trace evidence exhibits. He was surprisingly helpful, considering that he was in the middle of a family roast dinner. She had barely replaced the phone on its charger when she took an incoming call. It was Harry Stone. He listened patiently while she brought him up to date.

'The pressure is going to pile on now that one of them has died,' he said. 'I'll get the NCA Public Relations team to give you a ring. They'll want to be ready with a statement for the media, particularly since you were spotted at the scene.'

'I'm sorry, Boss,' she said.

'Harry,' he reminded her. 'There's nothing to apologise for. I'll get them to run your draft statement by me. There's no reason you should have to handle all the flak.'

'Thanks, Harry.'

'And I'll come up to Manchester in the morning on the milk train.'

'The milk train?'

'Old habits die hard,' he said. 'Just like old cops.'

No sooner had she ended the call than her phone rang again. It was Gerry Sarsfield.

'The news from the search team is not good, I'm afraid. It didn't help that it started raining shortly after you left and before they got started. It's proved impossible to definitively identify the spot where Susanne Hadrix was dumped. There are plenty of indications on the tracks leading down to the reservoir of vehicles from cars and vans to cycles, and off-road bikes, but most of those have been obscured by farm tractors and the vans used by the water company. There are so many, it'll take weeks to work through them all.'

'She didn't drop anything? Leave anything behind?'

'Not that we know of. There's tons of people's detritus though. Fag packets, tissues, food wrappers, crisp packets, discarded fishing line, and dog shit in and out of plastic bags. It's a pity the unsub didn't bring a dog. We could have identified it from its DNA.'

'We don't know that he didn't.'

'Don't say that. Whoever is going to have to sort through that lot will love you.'

'What about the speed camera on the A58?' she asked.

'Being checked as I speak. I wouldn't hold your breath though. He's too clever to have triggered the camera, even if he did go in that way, which I doubt.'

'Do we know where she was last night?' she said.

'Pretty much. She went out with five mates. Three girls from the college and two of her other friends. They all knew each other. Four of them have already been interviewed, and we've corroborated accounts of where they went. They never left the town centre.'

He paused and she could hear him on his computer. When he started again, she could tell that he was reading it out.

'They kicked off with a meal at Planet Pizza, moved on to Smackwater Jacks for a couple of hours. Then they visited a pub, a wine bar and a club, before heading home around two forty-five am. Two of them went to a taxi rank. Two left early to catch the Manchester Witch Way X43 at twenty-one fifty-four. Susanne

Hadrix and her best friend walked home together. They live half a mile from the town centre.'

He corrected himself.

'*Lived* half a mile away. Three streets apart among the terraces near Turf Moor.'

'The football ground?'

'That's right.'

'The friend lives closer to the town centre?'

'Correct.'

'So we know, to within two rows of houses, where he must have abducted her?'

'Correct. Unless she took a detour?'

'Unlikely.'

'I agree.'

'Cameras?' she said, more in hope than expectation.

'Don't know yet. I've got people looking now.'

'Door to door?'

'We're on it. Nothing yet. That time of the morning, there won't have been many people about.'

'Someone might have heard something. Looked out of their window.'

'Hopefully.'

He didn't sound hopeful.

'If it turns out she was drugged,' Jo said, 'how did he know to pick her? How did he know that she and her friend would be the only ones walking home, and that she'd cover the final stretch on her own?'

'I was wondering the same thing,' he replied.

Something about his intonation struck her.

'Was?' she said.

'Until I was told that one of the other girls, one that was in the taxi, was also drugged. With GHB.'

'How do you know?'

'Because she was that bad when she got home that she fell down the stairs and woke up the entire house. She was vomiting and had muscle spasms. Her parents called an ambulance. They checked her bloods. She had close to four thousand milligrams still in her system. That's two hundred times more gamma-hydroxybutyric acid than occurs naturally in a bottle of red wine. Enough to kill her.'

'How is she?

'She's fine but sedated. That's why we haven't been able to question her.'

'So he didn't know which of them he'd be able to isolate,' she said. 'He tried to cut down the odds by drugging more than one.'

'Looks like it.'

'In which case, it became a game of chance. Just like the fact that he leaves them close to roads or water. He's planning everything except which girl it will be, if any, and the final outcome.'

'He wouldn't be the first serial killer or serial rapist to go down that route,' said Sarsfield.

That was true, but it was also the case that most serial killers also had a vision of the perfect victim in mind. Up until now that seemed to have been the case as far as this unsub was concerned.

'CCTV footage from all the places they visited?' she said.

'On to it. And I've arranged for all of the bar staff to be interviewed, along with any punters who turn up tonight who were also there last night.'

'There's not a lot more we can do,' Jo said.

'I agree,' he replied. 'We'll just have to hope that something turns up.'

'It already has,' she reminded him. 'It's called DNA.'

Chapter 34

That evening, Jo had her best night's sleep for over two weeks. She awoke at 6am and was on the Quays by seven. A quick check with DI Sarsfield at eight o'clock confirmed that nothing useful had come up so far on the Susanne Hadrix abduction and RTA. At ten to nine, Harry Stone arrived.

He hung up his jacket and balefully regarded the globules of water dripping on to the floor.

'Bloody global warming,' he moaned. 'It hasn't stopped raining up here since October.'

'Morning, Boss,' she said, 'I wasn't expecting you this early.'

He grimaced. 'The six sixteen am from Euston. I was up at five, but at least I had breakfast on the train.'

She scooted her chair back and stood up.

'You won't want a cup of tea then?'

He grinned. 'Make it a bloody great mug and two sugars. I don't suppose you've got any whisky?'

While she was making them both a drink, Andy arrived. The three of them went through to the small meeting room.

Stone blew across the surface of his tea. 'So, he's gone for a college student this time. Not one from the universities?'

'The universities broke up last week,' Jo said. 'He had a choice of waiting until they came back after Christmas, or targeting random groups of females in the same age range. I think he went for the latter.'

'So you believe the fact that she was a student was incidental?' She shrugged.

'I'm only surmising. But if I'm right, it means that he's losing his patience. He's no longer prepared to wait for the perfect target.' Andy nodded.

'It's a typical escalation pattern,' he said, 'whether we're speaking of serial rapists or serial murderers.'

'How do you think he's likely to react to the fact that his latest victim has died?' Stone asked. 'Albeit that from his point of view it was unintended. Could he panic? Might he become more violent?'

Andy pursed his lips. 'There's no reliable evidence from research on which to base predictions. However, in this case I'd place him somewhere along the power-reassurance power-assertive continuum. The only things these two types share in common are their disdain for women, whom they regard as mere playthings, and their urge to dominate. The former uses minimum force, in this case drugs, and does not intend to harm beyond the effects of the abduction and the rape itself, both of which he's able to minimise in his own mind. However, his ego is likely to be fragile, and if thwarted he could erupt into unpredictable violence. The latter is more confident, macho and consistently violent.'

Jo was uncomfortable with the assumption that abduction and rape didn't really classify as violence. She understood that it was relative in the minds of the researchers, but it certainly wasn't for the victims themselves. Nor had it been for her when she was abducted and almost killed.

'Our unsub seems closer to the power-reassurance rapist,' she said.

'I agree,' said Andy. 'In which case, if the drugs were to wear off and his victims' behaviour spooked him, it's impossible to rule out him killing them. Equally, if he feels that he needs to kill to evade discovery, he may well do so.'

'Is there any good news in all of this?' asked Stone.

The psychologist nodded. 'There is one thing. Statistically, serial rapists average seven victims before they're arrested. Susanne Hadrix was his seventh.'

Stone raised his mug.

'Here's hoping he's Mister Average,' he said.

Jo shook her head.

'He's anything but that.'

There was a knock on the door.

'Come!' said Stone.

The door opened. It was Dorsey Zephaniah.

'There's a call for SI Stuart,' she said. 'It's SI Nailor. He says it's important.'

'Go take it, Jo,' Stone told her.

'We have a match!' said Max.

'That was quick.'

'Flatman was in a good mood. He was too busy charming DS Hatton to argue with me. He agreed to harvest the samples first, and let one of the registrars run a specimen through the state-of-the-art machine they use to help put a name to unidentified and unidentifiable corpses.'

He enthused like a little boy with a brand-new chemistry set. 'You should see it, Jo. It's the size of a small photocopier and . . .'

'Max – just give me the name,' she said.

'Jason Dalmeny,' he told her. 'Forty years of age. One previous, for affray. I've emailed you the details.'

'This hasn't compromised the evidence in any way?' she asked.

'Absolutely not. All done under the supervision of DS Hatton's exhibits officer. Besides, the bulk of that particular sample has been bagged and recorded for separate analysis.'

'Max Nailor, you're a star,' she said.

'Took you a while to recognise it,' he said with a smile in his voice, 'but you got there in the end.'

They huddled around the computer screen as Ram scrolled through the details he had garnered from various sources.

Jason Dalmeny, Jo read. Forty years of age. Address from the electoral register shown as 27 Ashington Road, Morpeth. Self-employed painter and decorator. Married, with two children. His conviction for affray was back in 2010. He was sentenced to one hundred hours of community service.

'It was a fight in Newcastle city centre, following a Sunderland and Newcastle derby match,' Ram told them. 'Reason he got off lightly is that he claimed he and his pals were set upon by a mob of away fans. He had neither provoked the attack, nor willingly engaged with his attackers. CCTV supported his claim. However, it also showed him felling two Sunderland supporters. Hence the reason he got to redecorate a few council properties free, gratis, and for nothing.'

'Morpeth,' said Jo. 'That's what, a hundred and eighty miles?'

'One hundred and sixty-three,' Ram told her. 'Three hours fifteen minutes by road using the A19.'

Jo shook her head.

'That's way outside the locus you constructed for our unsub. He'd have to travel twice that distance to plan his attacks, and the same again to execute them.'

'It also means he must be away from home for a minimum of twelve hours each time,' Andy pointed out. 'A regular pattern like that is going to be hard to explain to his wife.'

'Unless he tells her he has a contract on the other side of the Pennines,' said Stone. 'Maybe he does have one. One that involves the universities.'

'Would you like to see a photo of him?' said Ram.

It was such a no-brainer that he had already pulled one up.

'This is his passport photo,' he said. 'It doesn't do him justice.'

The man stared back at them with a bald head, alert brown eyes, a neatly trimmed ginger moustache and matching beard.

'How do you know it doesn't do him justice?' asked Stone.

Ram replied by bringing up Dalmeny's Facebook page.

'You're right,' said Jo as Ram scrolled through images of him clowning around with two young girls and a border terrier, bouncing on a trampoline in a garden, sharing a pint with friends. As far as she could judge, he was around five foot eight, twelve stone, with the beginnings of a paunch.

'Where's the wife?' asked Andy.

Ram continued to scroll through random videos shared by friends, photos of friends, the odd party or two, and scores of images related to Newcastle United, with accompanying banter in the comments below each image. It was not until he reached a video of Dalmeny taking the Ice Bucket Challenge for charity that a woman variously described as 'Mags', 'Maureen', and 'The Wife' appeared.

'That's over two years ago,' said Jo. 'Either they split up shortly after that or she died, and there's no indication of that on there.'

Stone turned to Andy. 'What do you make of him?' he asked. 'Could he have done it?'

'If it was as simple as studying a suspect's social media pages, it would make my life a lot easier,' he replied. 'The truth is these people are like chameleons. Their ability to change persona and even their appearance explains why they're so difficult to catch. If you were to push me . . .'

'I *am* pushing you,' said Stone.

'Then I'd say that certain of the behaviours he exhibits on there would be consistent with our perpetrator. He appears charming, sociable and gregarious. The videos he chooses to share, his own posts, and the comments he makes on other people's posts, indicate a judgemental frame of mind, and at times quite a cold and cynical bent that doesn't square with some of the photos of himself with his children and friends. However, that could be said of a number of people I know who wouldn't dream of hurting a fly.'

'And how many of those would end up with their seminal fluid being found on the body of a girl who's been drugged, abducted and raped?' Jo asked.

Andy nodded.

'Point taken,' he said.

Chapter 35

It was ten to seven in the evening when they pulled up outside the three-bed semi. The arrest team consisted of Jo and Max. They had brought their own search team. A family liaison officer provided by Northumbria Police and a social worker had joined the convoy at a rendezvous half a mile away.

On the drive stood a silver Fiat Scudo van with twin sliding doors. There was a light on in one of the upstairs windows. A large Christmas tree lit up the downstairs front room.

'How do you want to do this?' asked Max. 'He might be putting the kids to bed.'

'On Facebook they looked a bit too old to be going to bed just yet,' Jo replied. 'Another hour at least I'd have thought.'

'In which case, just you and me to start with?' he suggested.

'I agree,' she said. 'No need to scare them. We can call up the others when I've explained what's going on.'

'Let's do it,' he said.

They exited the car. Jo walked over to the other three vehicles in turn and updated the occupants. Then she and Max approached the front door. A dog began to bark. She rang the bell and a man's voice shouted from inside the house.

'Myra! Get back here.'

They glanced at each other.

'Myra?' muttered Max. 'Who names a dog after a Moors Murderer?'

The door opened. Jason Dalmeny stood there dressed in tracksuit bottoms and a Newcastle United football shirt. His feet were bare. One hand held the collar of a little border terrier that was desperately trying to leap up at the two police officers. They held up their ID cards.

'Joanne Stuart and Max Nailor,' Jo told him. 'We're senior investigators with the National Crime Agency. May we come in, Mr Dalmeny?'

There was a flash of resignation in his eyes.

'Of course,' he said, backing down the hall, dragging the dog with him as he went.

They followed him into a lounge at the back of the house where two young girls were curled up on the sofa watching television. The elder of the two stared over her shoulder at the visitors, was rewarded with a smile from Jo, and turned her attention back to the TV.

'Perhaps we should discuss this somewhere else, Mr Dalmeny,' said Jo. 'The kitchen, or the room we just passed?'

He nodded and led them into the adjoining kitchen, closing the door behind them.

'Now,' he said, 'what the hell is this all about?'

'You'd better sit down, sir,' said Max.

Dalmeny shook his head and balled his fists. 'I'd rather stand if you don't mind. This is my house.'

The change in his tone and manner put Jo on alert. The initial risk assessment had not flagged up anything suspicious, and with the two girls in the house, surely he was not going to kick off? She scanned the room for potential weapons, then moved slowly around the kitchen table, placing herself between Dalmeny and a crowded wooden knife block.

'Be that as it may,' said Max. 'It really would be better if you were to sit down.'

They looked as though they were about to square up to each other, a pair of rutting stags.

'Please, Jason,' said Jo, 'think of your daughters.'

Dalmeny hesitated for a moment, then pulled out a chair and sat down.

'Thank you, Mr Dalmeny,' Jo said. 'To answer your question, we are here in relation to an investigation into the abduction and rape of a young woman.'

His jaw dropped. Shocked and uncomprehending, he stared at her and then at her colleague. If it was an act, it was a pretty convincing one.

'What the hell . . . ?'

He seemed unable to complete the sentence.

'Furthermore,' said Jo, 'I have a warrant to search these premises and I'm now handing you a Notice under Section B of the Police and Criminal Evidence Act setting out my powers and your rights, in relation to that search.'

Dalmeny stared blankly at the words in front of him.

'I'm also arresting you on suspicion of involvement in the abduction and rape of Susanne Hadrix, on or about the nineteenth of December two thousand and fifteen, in the County of Greater Manchester. You do not have to say anything. But it may harm your defence if you do not mention when questioned something which you later rely on in court. Anything you do say may be given in evidence. Do you understand, Mr Dalmeny?'

He stared up at her.

'The girls . . .' he said.

'Do you understand, Jason?' she said.

'No,' he said, 'I don't understand. I don't know what you're talking about?' He began to rise. Max placed a hand on his shoulder and firmly eased him back on to the stool.

'Did you understand the caution?' Jo said. 'About your being under arrest and about your rights?'

'Yes,' he replied. 'And I can't wait to get it sorted, and have you get the hell out of here.'

'When we do leave, you'll be leaving with us,' said Max before Jo could respond. 'You'll be questioned at the station.'

Now Dalmeny looked panicked. 'But what about my girls?'

'Is there someone you could leave them with?'

'My wife,' he said. 'She'll go spare. It's my turn to have them this week. And what's she going to think?'

'I suggest you ring her now,' said Jo, 'and ask her to come immediately. I'd much prefer not to search the house while they're here.'

There was a phone in the kitchen. While Dalmeny rang his wife, Max drifted into the lounge to check on the girls. He sat down in a vacant chair, and pretended to be watching the video. The elder of the two looked across at him.

'Are you police?'

Max smiled. 'No flies on you then,' he said.

'While you were talking, I went into the front room and had a look,' the girl told him in a very serious voice. 'There's a police car out there. That's how I know.'

'Well done,' he said. 'You'd make a good detective.'

She leaned closer and lowered her voice.

'What's our dad gone and done?'

'He's just helping us with a problem we've got,' he told her.

He sensed that she was going to ask a follow-up question and got in first.

'Why's your doggie called Myra?' he said.

233

She ran over to a stack of DVDs beside the television, found the one she was looking for and brought it back. She handed it to him and pointed to one of the characters on the back of the sleeve.

'Mira,' she said. 'From the *Silent Hill* movies.'

He stared at the cute little dog sporting a pair of headphones.

She lowered her voice. 'Our dad says it's not really suitable for us, but we watched it with one of the babysitters. You won't tell him, will you?'

Chapter 36

Dalmeny turned his head, and stared into the camera lens high up in the corner of the interview room in the North East Regional Operations Unit building.

'I don't understand what I'm doing here.'

The two investigators exchanged a glance. Was Dalmeny attempting to claim procedural weakness in their investigation? Was that why he had refused legal representation?

'You do remember my telling you that I was arresting you on suspicion of having been involved in the abduction and rape of Susanne Hadrix?' said Jo. It was too early to talk of manslaughter. Not without the Crown Prosecution Service having taken a view.

'I remember you saying something like that,' he replied, 'but I wasn't really concentrating. I was in shock. I don't even know any-one with that name.'

'And you'll recall that I repeated it again in front of the custody sergeant when we arrived at this station?'

He folded his arms. 'That doesn't mean I know why you arrested me.'

Play it by the book, she reminded herself. *Spell it out for the camera.*

'Because I have reasonable grounds for suspecting that you committed the offence in question, and I arrested you to allow the prompt and effective investigation of the offence, and to prevent the possibility of your harming another person.'

'On what grounds?' he said.

Jo looked at Max. It had not been part of their interview strategy to tell him this early on. On the other hand, it was such an incontrovertible piece of evidence that it would either force him to confess or to construct some implausible alibi. Max must have been thinking the same thing because he nodded.

'Very well, Jason,' she said. 'Perhaps you can explain how your DNA came to be found on the person and the clothing of Susanne Hadrix?'

Dalmeny flinched as though she had slapped him hard. He searched her face and that of her colleague for evidence that this was a joke. Finding none, he slammed his hand down on the table.

'No! You can't do this!' he shouted. 'I told you, I've never even heard of her.'

His face was pale with shock and his hands were shaking. It was a while since Jo had seen a reaction like it.

'Calm down, Mr Dalmeny,' said her partner. 'Now is your opportunity to sort this all out.'

Jo signalled to the constable standing by the door and asked him to bring their suspect a beaker of water. They waited for the water to arrive and for Dalmeny to take a drink.

'That's better,' she said. 'Now, I need you to account for your whereabouts between ten pm on the evening of Saturday 19th December 2015 and nine am on the morning of Sunday 20th December 2015.'

He took a moment to process it, then he smiled with relief.

'Saturday?' he said. 'You're talking about Saturday?'

'That's right. Saturday evening, and all night right up until nine am.'

His smile became a grin. 'There you go then. It can't possibly have had anything to do with me. I never left the house.'

Out of the corner of her eye, Jo saw Max shaking his head in disbelief.

Dalmeny leaned forward, both forearms on the table, urging them to believe him.

'I had the girls with me. The wife dropped them off on Saturday morning. I took them to McDonald's for lunch, and then we went to the cinema in Cramlington to see the *Peanuts* movie. After that we picked up a KFC Double Bucket Deal, went home and never went out again till around lunchtime Sunday so they could play in the park.'

He sat back and crossed his arms defiantly. 'You can ask them. Go on, ask them.'

'You could easily have slipped out while they were asleep in bed,' she said.

He shook his head vehemently.

'I wouldn't. Besides, after they'd gone to bed I had a mate round. We had a few cans and watched the Barclay's Premier League review and then a late-night movie.'

'Which movie, Mr Dalmeny?'

He looked embarrassed and his cheeks reddened.

'It wasn't strictly a movie.'

'What was it then?' said Max, knowing full well what he was going to say.

'One of the adult channels, alright?'

His eyes brightened as he remembered something.

'The wife rang me on the landline about eleven o'clock Saturday night to check the girls were okay. Then again Sunday morning at eight o'clock to remind me that I'd promised to take them both to the park.' He pulled a face. 'Silly cow woke me up.'

'At what time did your friend leave the house?' she asked.

'Three-ish.'

'Can you be more precise?'

'Roundabout three am.'

'Before or after three am?'

He studied her, trying to gauge which answer was the right one. He made up his mind.

'After?'

'Your friend,' said Jo. 'I need his name and contact details.'

Max wrote them down. He handed them to the constable and whispered instructions in his ear.

'PC Bozdoğan is leaving the room,' Jo said.

She waited until the door had closed.

'Now then, Mr Dalmeny,' she said. 'I'd like you to explain how you think it was that your DNA was found on the body and clothing of a woman you claim not to know?'

He was about to reply with another vehement denial when something clicked in his brain.

'Hang on,' he said. 'What do you mean, body?'

Neither of them replied. He sat up straight and placed his hands on the table, gripping the edge as though to support himself.

'What are you saying – that this woman is dead?'

'That's exactly what I am saying,' Jo replied.

Now his face was ashen. He stared from one to the other and then back again.

'No,' he said. 'You're not pinning this on me. I told you I never met this woman.'

'Perhaps you knew her by another name,' said Max. 'Perhaps you never took the trouble to find out her name?'

'This DNA,' he said. 'Maybe I brushed up against her somewhere, in the movies, McDonalds, KFC? That's it. They were all packed with people.' He sat back triumphantly, as though he thought he had cracked it. 'There you go.'

'There are two problems with that,' Jo said. 'Firstly, we know that the victim was nowhere near Morpeth or Cramlington yesterday and secondly, the samples containing your DNA could not possibly have been transferred to her person or her clothing in the way you describe.'

Dalmeny stared at her. It was clear that the penny had still not dropped.

'Let me spell it out for you,' she said. 'How do you account for the presence of your seminal fluid both inside and on the body of Susanne Hadrix, as well as on her clothing?'

His face it seemed had been through the full gamut of emotion. Now it was fixed with an expression of total disbelief. It was a full half a minute before he managed to respond.

'That can't be,' he said, his voice almost a whisper. 'It isn't possible.'

'Let's see if we can help,' said Max. 'When did you last have sex with a woman? With anyone of either gender come to that?'

Jo expected him to take offence, but he did not. The full import of what they were accusing him of had finally hit home. He shook his head slowly and stared straight at her. His voice and his expression were full of anguish and self-pity.

'I haven't,' he said. 'Not since the wife left me.'

'When was that?'

'Twelve weeks on Friday.' He stared down at the table in front of him, and slowly shook his head. 'But the writing was on the wall for months before that. We hadn't had sex in over a year.'

———

'I don't believe it.'

It was two hours since they'd suspended the interview and had him taken back to his cell. The friend who allegedly spent the evening with him had been and gone. Max sat on the edge of the desk kicking his legs to and fro.

'That's it then,' he said. 'His alibi stands up. There's absolutely no way he could have made it to Bury and back. His wife confirmed the phone calls. So far, the search has turned up nothing apart from a stack of porn magazines in his wardrobe. The first indications are that his van's clean. So how come his semen's all over the victim?'

'I have no idea,' Jo admitted. 'We need them to take another look at those samples and double-check the DNA analysis. Hopefully, we'll be able to get them to make it a priority. The same with whatever they manage to retrieve from the van, including soil samples from the tyres and the tread pattern.'

'I assume,' Max said, 'that you're going to keep him in custody until the forensics come back?'

'Absolutely. What if his friend's lying? What if Dalmeny left immediately after we know that the victim left for home at two forty-five pm? Given the condition we're assuming she was in, it could have taken them half an hour to walk the half a mile to Turf Moor. Her friend was hazy about what time she actually got in. If Dalmeny left immediately after his wife's first phone call at eleven pm, he could have driven over to Burnley in time to snatch her off the street, take her to wherever he takes them, drop her off at the reservoir, and belt back home before the wife made that second phone call.'

'Assuming that was the case,' Max said, 'it would have been unplanned. A random opportunist rape. There's no way he could have spiked her drink or followed her from the pub.'

'He could have had an accomplice?' she said, thinking of the man who had arranged her own abduction. Knowing that she was clutching at straws.

There was a knock on the door. It was the custody sergeant.

'Excuse me, Ma'am,' he said. 'There's a solicitor arrived in the custody suite wants to speak with Jason Dalmeny. Apparently his wife asked him to come.'

Jo sighed.

'Tell him I'll be with him shortly, would you? Until then he's to have no access to Dalmeny.'

'Right, Ma'am.'

'What are you going to do, Jo?' asked Max.

'Tell him that despite our having twice reminded him of his right to be represented, Dalmeny has declined the services of a law-yer. Given the gravity of this case, I don't want anyone trying to unpick the way I've handled the investigation so I'm minded to let him see Dalmeny in my presence, and he can ask him himself if he wishes to be represented.'

'Fair enough,' he said. 'The DNA's enough to hold him over-night, even if he does agree to a solicitor.'

He slipped off the desk and stretched.

'While you were emailing the forensic service, I booked us two double rooms with breakfast at the Travelodge. A hundred and eight quid in total.'

Jo smiled wearily.

'You really know how to treat a girl,' she said.

Chapter 37

'My client has asked me to state that he is completely innocent of the offences in relation to which you arrested him, and since he has nothing to hide, he is more than willing to respond to any questions that you wish to put to him. I wish to place on record that this is against my advice as his legal representative.'

Dalmeny's solicitor looked at his client to give him a chance to change his mind. When nothing was forthcoming, he picked up his biro and waited for the interview to begin.

'Thank you,' said Jo. 'I'm sure that with your cooperation, Jason, we should be able to sort out this mystery in no time at all.'

'Good,' Dalmeny said. 'That's exactly what I want. Then I can get home to my girls, and get on with my life.'

'Let's start where we left off last night,' she said. 'You stated that you had not had sexual intercourse in over a year. Do you stand by that statement?'

'Yes,' he said, 'I do.'

Jo smiled sympathetically.

'Given that you and your wife had not been sexually active for over a year, and that you have now separated, no one would blame you for having an affair.'

'I haven't.'

'Or for using the services of, say, a prostitute or an escort?'

He shook his head vigorously.

'I haven't. I wouldn't. I never have.'

The solicitor was scrutinising his client as closely as the two investigators.

Jo nodded her head as though accepting Dalmeny's assurances.

'Very well,' she said. 'Let's move on. I'm going to show you a list of names and addresses of universities and colleges in the North West of England and in West Yorkshire. I'd like you to have a look at this list and tell me if you have ever had cause to visit or work at any of these places, or any student halls of residence or other forms of accommodation associated with them?'

She slid the list across the table. His lawyer raised his hand.

'I'm sorry,' he said. 'I don't see the relevance of your question to the matter on which you detained my client.'

'I can assure you that it is connected,' she replied. 'Your client has agreed to answer any questions that we wish to put to him, and this is one of them. Should it become necessary to explain the connection, I will be happy to do so.'

She switched her attention to the suspect.

'Well, Jason? Do you recognise any of them?'

He looked up, and shook his head.

'No, I don't. To the best of my knowledge, I have never been near any of them.'

There was a knock on the door. Max stood up and went to see who it was. He came back and whispered in Jo's ear.

'It's the lab,' he said. 'They say they've discovered something important, something you need to know.'

Jo turned to face the video camera. 'I'm suspending this interview,' she said, 'for operational reasons at ten fifty-two am and fifty seconds.'

'It's about the nature of the sample we tested, not the DNA match,' said the forensic scientist.

'So it is still definitely a match to his DNA?' said Jo.

'Absolutely.'

'So what are you saying, that it's not semen?'

'No, I'm not saying that. It is his seminal fluid. But it's not just his seminal fluid.'

'You're saying there are traces of someone else's?'

'No, I'm not saying that either. Look,' said the scientist, 'just bear with me. It will all become clear.'

'I'm sorry,' said Jo, 'go ahead.'

'Right. When your colleague had the initial sample tested yesterday at the morgue for a match on the DNA register, that's all he and the pathology technician were interested in. They knew it was seminal fluid. They could see that it contained sperm. What they weren't attempting to do was to analyse the constituent parts.'

'I get that.'

'Good. Well, now we have. And in addition to what we would expect to find, there were other trace elements. Specifically, glycerol, sucrose and soy lecithin.'

'And that's not something you'd normally expect to find?'

'No, not in that combination and not in the proportions or quantities that we found.'

'So what's their significance?'

There was a dramatic pause. 'The most common use for these substances in this combination,' he said, 'is as a cryoprotectant.'

Jo had experienced cryotherapy for a muscle injury following a training session.

'You're saying his sperm was frozen?'

'Semen is either frozen through a slow cooling method,' the scientist continued, 'or is flash-frozen. In either case, it's important to protect the motility and DNA integrity of the sperm both when it is frozen and, even more importantly, when it is thawed – that's the role of a cryoprotectant.'

Jo tapped her head repeatedly with the handset.

'He's a sperm donor,' she said. 'Why didn't I think of that?'

⌣

'Why didn't you tell us, Jason?' she said. 'It would have saved us all a lot of time and trouble.'

Relief had flooded his face as soon as she asked him if he had ever been a donor. Now he was even more eager to help.

'It never occurred to me,' he said. 'It was years ago. And anyway, I thought it had been destroyed. How the hell was I to know it would end up where it did? How the hell did it?'

'That's what we need to find out,' she told him. 'Where and when did you donate your sperm, Jason?'

'I was nineteen, playing for a football team in the Morpeth Sunday League. It was after one of the games. We were celebrating in the Black Bull after thrashing Stobswood Welfare six-nil. Our centre forward was bragging cos he'd scored a hat-trick. Someone called him a wanker. He said the laugh was on us because he got paid for it. Turns out he was going to a sperm donation clinic and getting twenty-five pound a time as expenses. I was skint at the time – I decided I'd like a piece of that. So did two of the other players.' He grinned. 'Only they didn't make it through the tests.'

'Where was the clinic, Jason?' she said.

He told her. While she wrote it down, he babbled on, 'It was more complicated than you'd think. I had to check my family medical history, fill in forms, have an interview, and provide three separate samples for them to test. They told me I'd have to go back after six months so they could check I hadn't developed any medical conditions that might be dormant in the ones I'd donated.'

'When was this, and over what period were you donating?' Jo asked.

'Spring of 1995. But I pulled out after I'd given the four proper samples.'

'Why was that, Jason?'

He shrugged. 'When they told me it could be used either for research, or to father up to ten families, I said research.' He looked embarrassed. 'I just didn't fancy the thought of all those kids wandering round looking just like me. Besides, I was only doing it for the expenses, and by the time I'd paid the bus fares and taken time off work, I only had a tenner left each time.'

'And you were told that after they'd finished with your samples they'd be destroyed.'

'That's right.'

They sat there in silence staring at each other, both asking themselves the same question.

———⌣———

'Have you let him go?' Max strode towards her holding a blue cardboard folder.

'On police bail,' Jo said. 'His solicitor wasn't happy, but as I pointed out there could be other explanations.'

He handed her the folder.

'Well, you may want to stop him before he leaves the station.'

She opened it. There was a printed list and a set of photographs.

'What is this?' she asked.

'While you were interviewing Dalmeny, I had a call from the search team. This is the list of the contents of a large cardboard box found in the loft, containing rather a lot of jewellery. As you can see, there were rings, earrings, necklaces, three women's watches, four men's watches, a couple of iPads, two iPods, three Kindles.'

'Not stuff the wife would leave behind,' Jo said. 'Eclectic taste too.'

He looked at her.

'You thinking what I'm thinking?'

'He's a painter and decorator,' she said. 'In the words of Sam Spade, "What better way to case a joint?"'

'That's what the search team thought. Despite the fact that the warrant did not explicitly give us the right to search for such property, they seized it as potentially the proceeds of crime.'

'It would explain why when you told him who we were, he looked as though he'd been expecting us. No wonder he was surprised when you cautioned him for abduction and rape.'

'What do you propose to do about it?' Max asked.

'I'll get Northumbria CID to see if they can link any of this stuff to their unsolved cases,' she said. 'If they do, then they'll have to carry out a separate search and re-arrest Dalmeny.' She shook her head. 'Those poor kids. First their parents separate and they're shuttled back and forth between them, then their dad's banged up, let out, and now he's likely to be banged up again.'

'We don't get to choose our parents,' he said. 'If we did, then the childless couples would outnumber the rest.'

Jo was tempted to call him cynical, but she knew that he was right.

'I suggest you head back to Manchester,' she said. 'I'll see what the clinic has to say and then head back myself.'

'By the way,' said Max. 'I checked in with Ram and Andy like you asked. Ram told me to tell you that he's managed to locate Malacott's sister. She's alive and well, and living in Christchurch.'

'She's in Dorset?'

He shook his head.

'Christchurch, New Zealand.'

'Well, I need to speak with her,' Jo said. 'I don't care how. Tell Ram to set it up. Preferably for tomorrow. I should be back by then.'

He gave her a mock salute.

'Yes, Ma'am. Certainly, Ma'am. Thank you, Ma'am.'

It was done without the slightest hint of sarcasm or rancour. It set her off laughing for the first time in days.

Chapter 38

It was exactly as she had envisaged it. A former Victorian mansion, presumably commissioned by a wealthy businessman. A mine owner perhaps, intent on enjoying the fruits of his labour and ensuring that all and sundry were left in no doubt of his talent and importance.

Jo parked in the only remaining space on the gravel car park, alongside a 2015-registration gold Bentley. A modern form of conspicuous consumption that she guessed must belong either to the chief executive or the senior consultant. Her money was on the latter.

The receptionist studied her ID, and the consent form Dalmeny had signed enabling her to see the records pertaining to his donation. The receptionist rang for the senior laboratory technician.

'I don't have the authority to respond to this,' she said. 'I shall have to call Mr West, the Chief Executive.'

'Tell him,' Jo said, 'that if I do have to come back, it will be with a search warrant and I can't promise what it may extend to.'

She hadn't lied exactly, but the threat wasn't something she would be able to carry out. The magistrate would see to that. Fortunately, the expression on the technician's face when she returned told her that the bluff had worked.

'Could I see that letter again, please?' she said.

She pushed her glasses higher up the bridge of her nose and peered at the name. Jo wondered how she managed looking down microscopes. Maybe that helped to explain why she closed one eye as she read.

'When exactly are we looking at?' the technician said.

'The spring of 1995. Late March to early May.'

The lab technician sniffed. 'The records from before 2001 are still in paper form. We haven't had the staff to enter them into the computer software. Please, follow me.'

She led the way down an oak-clad corridor and stopped outside a door. Entering a code into a keypad, she opened the door and stepped inside. Jo followed. It was an office that looked as though it had been constructed by portioning off a former library. Banks of chest-high metal filing cabinets lined three of the walls. The technician took a bunch of keys from her overall pocket, unlocked one of the cabinets and pulled out a drawer packed with buff manila folders.

'There were more donors than potential recipients in those days,' she said as she leafed through the files. 'Now it's the reverse. You wouldn't believe it, but last year there were only nine registered British donors to the National Sperm Bank. Almost all of the donations now come from America or Denmark. Their banks are overflowing, if you'll pardon the pun.'

She pulled out a manila folder.

'Ah, here we are: Dalmeny J. No 77986.'

She took the folder over to the desk beside the fourth wall, opened the folder and read it, slowly turning the pages as she went along.

'Application . . . medical clearance . . . trial sample one, two, three . . . donation cycle begins . . . four donations over a three-week period . . . donor withdrawal form. And . . . yes, the samples were definitely destroyed. It says so here.'

She stabbed the page with her forefinger.

'See for yourself.'

Jo walked over and read the note.

'This states that they were destroyed,' Jo said. 'That doesn't prove that they were. Whose signature is this?'

The technician picked the sheet up and studied the signature. She shook her head.

'I don't know. I don't recognise the name or the signature. This was before the clinic changed hands. I wasn't working here then.'

'Can you ask someone who was?'

She sighed, put the sheet back in the folder and closed it up.

'I'll see if the Medical Director, Professor Basillu, is in the building,' she said. 'He's the only one left of the original staff. He may remember.'

The professor was close to a foot shorter than Jo. He wore a shiny grey cashmere suit, immaculate white shirt, red bow tie, and beige, hand-tooled shoes. With his bald crown, curly black hair on the sides, full figure and tinted glasses, he reminded her of Danny DeVito in *Get Shorty*.

'Mary, what can I do for you?' he said, addressing the technician.

'This is Senior Investigator Stuart from the National Crime Agency,' she told him. 'She's asking about a sperm donation that was supposedly destroyed back in 1995.'

The MD raised his eyebrows above the rim of his glasses.

'Supposedly? What does that mean, Miss Stuart?'

'Traces of this particular donor's seminal fluid,' Jo said, 'accompanied by substances commonly used as cryoprotectant, were recovered from a victim of rape.'

Professor Basillu's face clouded over as the import of what she had told him hit home.

'Not possible,' he said. 'Our security has always been second to none. Could it be a coincidence? A mistake?'

'I'm sorry, Professor,' Jo said, 'there is no mistake. The sample contains his DNA. What we need to establish is how it came to be found on a victim twenty years after he donated it at this clinic.'

'Even though it's theoretically possible for samples to retain their viability for up to fifty years, we rarely keep samples longer than ten years,' the MD said. 'We tell the donors that.'

'In this case, the donor withdrew his consent halfway through the donation cycle,' Jo said. 'What I was hoping was that you could tell me whose signature this is?'

Reluctantly, he took the form from her and studied it. 'That's Selma Grainger,' he said. 'She was an administrative lab assistant. Worked with us for about a year. Last I heard she'd gone back to the West Indies.'

'Do you know where in the West Indies?'

Professor Basillu shrugged.

'I'm sorry. I really have no idea.'

'If I show you some faces on my tablet,' Jo said, 'do you think you could tell me if you recognise any of them?'

He shrugged.

'If you must.'

Jo took the tablet from her bag, and scrolled through a succession of images, including those of Nathan Northcote, Zachary Tobias, Professor Harrison Hill, Anthony Ginley, Sam Malacott and Jason Dalmeny.

'Take your time,' she said.

'No, I'm sorry, I don't recognise any of them.'

'Would you need to look at them again?'

Professor Basillu shook his head.

'There'd be no point. I'm certain that I've never seen any of them before. I have a good memory for faces.'

'In which case,' she said, 'I'm going to have to trouble you for a list of all of the employees working at the clinic in 1995.'

'That,' he said, 'will take some time to arrange.'

'I'll wait.'

He shrugged.

'Please yourself.' He turned to his senior laboratory technician. 'Mary, could you ask Rashid to expedite this for Miss Stuart, please?'

As she scurried off, Professor Basillu faced the NCA investigator. 'Whether or not the sample came from these premises, I trust that you will keep this as low profile as possible? It could do a lot of damage to our donor programme. We have precious few home-grown donors as it is.'

'I can't promise that, Professor,' Jo replied. 'If the clinic is implicated and there's a trial, it'll be impossible to prevent the connection from becoming public. Given that it was over twenty years ago and an isolated case, I'm sure your company will be able to manage damage limitation.'

'I hope so,' he said. 'This has been my life's work, Miss Stuart.'

He held out his hand for her to shake.

'Goodbye.'

'Goodbye, Professor,' she replied, 'and thank you for your cooperation.'

'Not at all.'

He turned and walked away.

'Nice car, Professor,' she called after him.

He acknowledged it with a wave of his hand. His life's work had clearly paid off, Jo reflected as he disappeared through the fire doors. She wondered if Abbie and her donor James would be employing the services of a clinic like this, or using a turkey baster as one of their friends had done. The thought caused a wave of gloom to sweep over her. She sighed and headed outside for a breath of fresh air.

She was enjoying the bright winter sun on a bench overlooking the lawns when the receptionist brought her the envelope containing the list of names. There were twenty-two in all. It seemed a lot for a donor facility. Then she realised from some of the job titles that it doubled as a fertility clinic.

There were a chairman, two medical directors, an assistant medical director, a specialist IVF consultant, an obstetrician, one nurse, two scientists, two embryologists, four laboratory technicians, a fertility counsellor, a donor counsellor, a business coordinator, a receptionist, a medical secretary, three admin assistants, a building facilities manager, an electrician, two part-time gardeners and a security officer.

Jo found it difficult to believe that only one of them was still here twenty years later. It was a shame that it wasn't the security officer. He would have some explaining to do. She went through the list of names twice, just to be sure. Not one of them had featured in the investigation thus far.

'Damn,' she said out loud. They would have to check them all for a connection with Operation Juniper. She put the list in her bag and stood up. It would be like looking for a needle in a haystack.

Chapter 39

Black clouds descended as the motorway crossed over the Pennine Way on Windy Hill. Jo switched on BBC2 to catch up on the news and caught the weather forecast.

'*We expect the next few days leading up to Boxing Day to be unsettled with showers or longer spells of rain. The rain will be most persistent in the north and west. Daytime temperatures will generally be above average, although the wind chill on higher ground will make it feel much colder. Odds of a white Christmas in this region stand at four to one, and any snowfall is likely to be limited to high ground.*'

My God, she thought, *the day after tomorrow is Christmas Eve. How did I forget that?* The answer was simple. She had immersed herself in the investigation to the exclusion of all else. Had Abbie still been at home, there would have been no escaping it.

Jo and Abbie had promised to spend Christmas Day with Jo's parents and she had still not told them that they had separated. Worse still, she hadn't even bought their presents. And what to do about Abbie's presents, hidden at the bottom of her tights drawer? A deluxe two-night luxury glamping stay in the Cotswolds, and the exquisite gold Pandora charm studded with turquoise-coloured topaz that Abbie had fallen in love with but rejected as far too expensive. She could try taking the charm back? Or put both presents on eBay and take what she could get?

You're better than this, she told herself. *You know where Abbie's staying. Wrap them up, buy a nice card and drop them off. What do you have to lose?*

It was approaching seven in the evening when Jo reached the outskirts of Manchester. The normal rush hour traffic had come to a grinding halt. The outside temperature had fallen dramatically and was already approaching freezing. Two gritters had just sped past on the hard shoulder, heralding a tricky night ahead. She decided to give up trying to reach the office, left the motorway at the Middleton turn-off and headed for the city centre.

The traffic began to flow again down Cheetham Hill Road. She released the clutch and set off. Her mind wandered back to those two presents. *The worst that can happen is that Abbie will send them back*, she reflected. *If she does, I'll give them to a charity, then at least something good will have come out of it.*

An hour and a half later, following a frenzied shop in Kendals, Jo placed the bags containing her parents' presents on the floor while she found her key and unlocked the door to the apartment. She shouldered the door open and bent to retrieve the bags.

There was a piece of card on the floor in the hallway. She picked it up, went inside and closed the door. Switching on the lights, she went through into the lounge, dumped everything on the floor and sat on the arm of the sofa. She turned the card over. There was a note scribbled in pencil on the back in a barely legible hand.

Delivery next door.

Jo stared at it. She had not been expecting a delivery. Her professional instinct was to be suspicious and concerned. A genuine courier would have left some kind of official card and contact details.

She went to the door, opened it and stepped out on to the mezzanine. Which *next door*? There were two. She started with the one on the left: the woman, a few years older than her, whom she seemed to remember having said that she worked in one of the iconic Co-op Insurance Society Towers. She rang the bell and waited. Rang it twice more and then gave up. She had better luck with the next one.

An older man, whom she had never seen before, stood there with a broad grin on his face. He was holding a large arrangement of white chrysanthemums and black lilies in a silver-and-black box.

'I assume these are for you?' he said.

'Someone pushed this through the letter box,' she told him, holding up the note. 'It just says there's a delivery next door.'

'There you go then,' he said. 'Somebody loves you.'

She thanked him and hurried back into the apartment. The flowers were quite heavy, so she placed them on the coffee table while she searched for the accompanying message. She was unable to find one. Her heart skipped a beat. They must be from Abbie, delivered by the florist. But Abbie had a key – she would have brought them in herself if it had been her. There was only one way to find out. She rang Abbie's mobile, and was surprised to find it answered almost immediately.

'Jo,' said Abbie, her voice an icy monotone, 'I wondered when you'd ring.'

'So it was you,' said Jo, her mood lifting so fast that she almost felt weightless. 'They're beautiful.'

'Beautiful? What are beautiful?'

'The flowers. You did send me some flowers?'

'Flowers?'

Abbie paused, and in that moment Jo already knew what her answer was going to be. Her heart sank in her chest like a stone.

'No, I did not send you any flowers. Maybe you have a new admirer?'

An awkward silence hung between them.

Abbie spoke first. 'I assumed that you were ringing in response to my note?'

'Note? What note?'

'The one I left underneath the remote. Beside the television?'

'Oh God, I'm sorry,' Jo said. 'I haven't been near the television in . . .'

'Days,' said Abbie. 'Three days to be precise.'

'I've been . . .'

'Busy with work? What a surprise.'

Jo was about to say that this wasn't fair. That a young woman had died. That what else was she supposed to do, given that Abbie had walked out on her? But she knew it was pointless.

'By the way,' Abbie continued, 'I rang your parents and gave them my apologies for Christmas Day. Apparently you hadn't bothered to tell them about us. Your mother was gutted. I got the impression that your father was upset too, only he didn't seem at all surprised.'

Jo's heart sank. What was always going to be a difficult conversation with her parents was now going to be ten times worse. How could she have been so stupid?

'What does your note say, Abbie?' she asked. 'If you give me a moment, I'll read it.'

'Don't bother,' came the cold reply. 'I wouldn't want to upset your busy schedule.'

And then the line went dead.

Jo got up, walked over to the television and found the note. It was short and to the point.

Jo, we can't go on ignoring each other. There are things we need to sort out, and in any case I hope we can still be friends when the dust has settled? I'd like that. Perhaps we could meet for a drink and to exchange our Christmas presents? Somewhere neutral. You decide. Abbs X

Jo's hand began to tremble and her eyes welled up with tears. She had assumed that the flowers were a peace offering, a way back from the brink. This carefully crafted note with its bounded reconciliation and closing kiss had a finality all of its own.

She let the note flutter from her fingers. Those damned flowers. If they weren't from Abbie, then who were they from? She dried her eyes with the heels of her hands and went to wake up her Mac.

Chapter 40

The mysterious lilies, Jo discovered, were Queen of the Night and not black but a dark shade of red. She read on. Lilies were universally seen as symbolic of purity with one exception: when left on graves they were a symbol of death. So also were chrysanthemums. On All Souls Day, the *Day of the Dead*, people in Italy left chrysanthemums on the graves of their loved ones.

She logged off, and stood up. The despair she had felt following her exchange with Abbie was turning to anger. Someone was playing a game with her. Sending her a message. There were no spurned admirers nor jilted lovers – this was work-related. Her instinct told her that it was to do with Operation Juniper. If so, it could only mean one thing: she was getting close. Too close for someone's comfort.

It took five minutes to contact the building superintendent, a further five to convince him of the urgency of the matter, and close to an hour for him to arrive at the apartments.

'This couldn't wait till the morning?' he grumbled.

'I'm afraid not,' she told him. 'Besides, I didn't think you'd appreciate being called out then.'

'Very funny,' he replied. 'You thought I'd prefer to come out at eleven pm instead?'

He opened the door to his office, switched on the lights and went over to the desk on which the security monitors stood. He turned to look at her.

'This is police business, right?'

Jo showed him her warrant card.

'*Urgent* police business,' she said.

He shook his head, pulled his chair out and sat down.

'When are we looking at?' he asked.

'My next-door neighbour said they were left with him at around four o'clock this afternoon.'

The superintendent entered a few keystrokes and a blank screen came to life.

'Here we go,' he said, starting the playback at ten to four. He fast-forwarded the recording until a figure with an awkward shuffling gait approached the entrance. He immediately froze the image.

'He's a tramp!' he said.

'Rough sleeper,' Jo said.

'Whatever.'

He zoomed in on the image. A man of indeterminate age, with thick straggly hair and an unkempt beard, stared directly into the camera with rheumy eyes.

'I know him,' said the superintendent. 'He's one of those homeless blokes that hangs around the city centre. Only he normally wears a Man City beanie.'

Jo craned forward.

'You're right,' she said. 'He's a regular.'

He had been outside the Royal Exchange when she and Abbie went to see Maxine Peake playing Hamlet. Abbie had given him a pound and told him to keep the carnation he offered her. That was typical of Abbie. *At least*, Jo reflected, *I know where to find him*.

The superintendent had zoomed out and was running the tape on.

'How the hell did he get the entry code?' he said.

They watched as the man pushed the door open and entered the foyer. It would have been as easy to discover the code, Jo knew, as it was for fraudsters to read pin codes over the shoulder of guileless shoppers.

'What's that he's holding?' the superintendent asked.

'An arrangement of flowers,' Jo told him, 'for me.'

She had seen enough.

'Thanks for coming out,' she said. 'I really appreciate it.'

He stopped the tape and turned around.

'That could have been a bloody bomb!' he said, concern etched all over his face.

'It might be worth changing the code, and reminding all of the residents to shield the pad when they enter it,' she suggested.

The superintendent stood up.

'I will.'

'Have a good Christmas,' Jo said.

'I will,' he replied. 'You too.'

But she had already left the room.

Chapter 41

The narrow beam of light sliced through the ink-black darkness and reflected off a broken bottle on to the ceiling of the brick-lined cavern. Something moved ahead of her. She raised the torch and caught a rat scuttling across the sea of rubbish and into the shadows.

Jo shivered. It had been a mistake to come here alone past midnight. It was not the occupants she feared, but the dozens of discarded needles crunching beneath her boots. There would be many more scattered among the heaps of bottles and cans, the rotting mattresses and cardboard. It had been a wise decision to don her NCA waterproofs and helmet, to clip her baton to her belt, but the thing that she missed above all was a mask. The stench of human faeces and stale urine assaulted her nostrils, threatening to trigger the gag response.

It was hard to believe that human beings lived in these caves, entered through railway arches that turned into tunnels deep beneath the River Irwell. The council claimed that there were properties enough to house them all. Man United legends Gary Neville and Nicky Scholes had even opened up their renovation of the Stock Exchange to homeless persons as a temporary measure. Yet some still chose to make this hell a home. Was it a choice, she wondered, or a desperate last resort?

A large cardboard box moved as she brushed against it with her foot. She swung the torch to reveal a face, and an arm raised to shield the eyes. She stepped back and moved the beam to the right. The arm moved. It was a woman – or was it? It was difficult to tell with the beanie pulled low over the forehead, the face smeared with grime, the body hidden inside the empty boxes.

'Fer fuzz' sake, leave me 'lone,' the woman said, her words slurring each into the next.

'I'm looking for Barry,' Jo told her. 'You may know him as Bazz?'

The woman tried to pull a flap of cardboard over her head. Jo pulled it back.

'Barry,' she insisted. 'Where is he?'

A wavering hand appeared, pointing towards the tunnels.

'Down there?' Jo said. 'Barry's down there?'

'Dunno,' the woman replied. 'Maybe.' The hand retreated. 'Now sod off an' . . . le' . . . me . . . alone.'

Jo backed off and stood up. She was not prepared to go any further into this subterranean underworld. Even sober, it was unlikely the woman would have made much sense. Accepting anything she said in her current state was like believing you could win the lottery. Reluctantly, Jo turned around and began a careful retreat.

She breathed a sigh of relief as a semicircle of half-light appeared ahead. Just a few yards short of freedom from the toxic chamber, she stopped. A narrow shaft of light was advancing across the front of her vision. A shadowy shape filled the entrance. She raised the beam of her torch at the same time as the new arrival, and was forced to place a hand in front of her face and peer through the gaps in her fingers. She was staring into the startled face of Barry 'Bazz' McGinty.

'It's alright, Barry,' she said, lowering her torch. 'I just need a word with you. Can you please take that torch off my face?'

As the beam swung away and down, she walked towards the entrance. She was relieved to find him backing away. Drips of stagnant water landed on her helmet and on the floor beside her. Beyond the arches, she could see a curtain of rain swaying with every passing gust of wind.

'I'm Joanne Stuart,' she told him. 'A senior investigator with the police. But you're not in trouble – I need your help, Barry. Just a minute of your time then you can be on your way.'

Beneath his arm, he carried a rolled-up sleeping bag shrouded in cellophane. In the same hand, he held a plastic shopping bag. He lowered the bag gingerly to the floor. There was no need to enquire as to the contents. The sound of tin on tin and glass on glass was evidence enough. Barry adjusted the sleeping bag with the hand holding his torch and the beam swung wildly across the walls and the gently curved ceiling.

'Go on then,' he said. 'What is it this time? The Great Train Robbery? Oh no, you got them, didn't you.'

His voice surprised her: here was an educated man fallen from grace, Jo guessed. At least he was sober enough to crack a joke. But then presumably he'd spent the bouquet delivery money on the cans and sleeping bag. She raised her torch at an angle so that she could see most of his face in the light reflected from the wall beside him.

'It's about the flowers, Barry,' she said.

He nodded his head, cleared his throat and spat on the floor.

'Excuse me,' he said, wiping his mouth with the back of his hand. 'I used to smoke. Buggered the bronchial tubes. I ought to have sued them – too late now.'

'The flowers, Barry,' Jo persisted. 'Who asked you to deliver them?'

'And buy them,' he said. 'Not just deliver them. Sniffy little madam wasn't going to let me have them. Not till I showed her the money and gave her the name.'

He grinned, favouring her with a mouthful of yellow stumps.

'They were for you, weren't they? Stuart, that's what you said. That was the name. Joanne Stuart.'

'You've a great memory, Barry,' she said. 'So tell me, who gave you the money and the name and the address?'

'It was a lad,' he said. 'Sixteen, maybe seventeen. Never seen him before. He said did I want to earn thirty quid. Fifteen now and fifteen when I'd done the job. I asked him was the Pope a Catholic. He said he didn't know.'

Barry laughed, which set off a coughing fit. She waited patiently for him to recover.

'Where was this?' she asked. 'Where this boy came up to you?'

'I was crossing Great Northern Square,' he said. 'The little toerag had been following me all the way up Watson Street from The Midland Hotel. Didn't know I'd clocked him, but I had.'

There was definitely CCTV on the square, Jo knew. That was something at least.

'Can you describe him?' she asked.

He shook his head.

'Shorter than me, thinner than me, Doc Martens, jeans and a hoodie. I only saw his little pointed nose and his thin tight mouth. Like a weasel.'

'What did he sound like?'

'A kid just out of nappies acting up the Manc' hardman.'

'Manchester, not Salford?'

He chuckled. 'If you can tell the difference you're a better man than I am, Gunga Din!'

'What time was this, Barry?'

He shrugged. 'Do I look as though I keep a track of the time?'

'Within an hour will do,' she said. 'You delivered them to the apartments at four pm. How long before that did he approach you?'

He thought about it.

'It would be about three o'clock then.'

'Did he write down any of the instructions? The kind of flowers, the shop, the address and number of the apartment, the entry code?'

Barry nodded.

'All of that,' he said.

'What did you do with the note?' she asked.

He sensed the urgency in her voice and nodded sadly.

'Sorry. He said to rip it up when I came out, and stuff it a bit at a time down the grids as I went to meet him.'

'And you did?'

'I was worried he was watching me. That I wouldn't get the rest of the money.'

'Which you collected where?'

'Round the back of the Old Smithfield Market.'

Somewhere else to check for CCTV.

'The notes he gave you,' Jo said. 'Have you got any of them left?'

He shook his head again and shone the torch on the two bags.

'I've got a fiver I was given as change, and a pocketful of coins,' he said.

None of which would have on them the DNA of either the boy or the person who had set it all up.

'I'll need a statement, Barry,' she said. 'Is that your real name? McGinty?'

'Didn't I fall into a fortune and buy myself a goat?'

'That was *Patrick* McGinty,' Jo told him.

'Well, there you go,' he said, without a trace of an Irish accent. 'We must both have been labouring under a misapprehension.'

'I can have a word with the GMP Neighbourhood Policing Team,' she said. 'Get you housed?'

'No, thanks,' he said. 'I tried that. They told me I had to stop drinking. Then what would I do?'

'You should get that cough seen to, Barry.'

He shook his head slowly from side to side.

'Too late for that, Miss Stuart. Far too late.'

His voice was charged with resignation, but as it echoed around the arches it sounded mournful, almost ghostlike. He bent and picked up his bag. Jo reached inside her elasticated trousers and pulled out her wallet. She had come prepared to buy his information if necessary. She removed a twenty pound note and held it out.

'I can't force you to spend this on food, Barry,' she said, 'but I hope you do.'

'I'm not a grass,' he said. 'In a former existence I used to be a chartered accountant. I told you what you wanted to know because I'm a concerned citizen.'

She smiled.

'Call this a Christmas present.'

He put the bag back down, took the note, folded it, and placed it in the pocket of his raincoat.

'Thank you, Miss Stuart,' he said with exaggerated politeness. 'I'm only sorry that I cannot reciprocate.' He held up the bag and jiggled it. 'Unless you'd like a can or two?'

'No thank you, Barry,' she said. 'You take care, and have a good Christmas.'

'Fear not.' He raised his torch and twirled it around like a fire stick. 'I have a reservation booked with the Mustard Tree charity. Turkey and all the trimmings.'

As Jo walked off, he called after her, 'Happy Christmas to you, Joanne Stuart!'

The effort set him off coughing again. The echoes followed her out on to Trinity Way where the driving rain merged with her tears, eventually washing them away. She reached her car, climbed in and sank back into her seat, heedless of the water from her clothes seeping into the upholstery. She had, she realised, been crying not just for Barry, but for those seven girls and their families, for herself, for memories of Christmas past, and in dread of the Christmas yet to come.

Chapter 42

Ram saw her enter the room, and came across to meet her.

'I haven't managed to find out a thing about the whereabouts of Ginley or Malacott on Saturday night and Sunday morning,' he said. 'The only way to do that is by asking them. And that's going to alert them to the fact that we still regard them as suspects.'

'Ram,' she said. 'Can I take my coat off first, please?'

His face fell. Jo instantly regretted taking her frustration out on him.

'I'm sorry,' she said.

'No problem,' he replied. 'I'll fix us both a coffee. Give you a chance to catch your breath.'

She hung up her coat, put her tablet on the desk and logged on to her computer. There were twenty new emails since she had cleared her inbox over breakfast back at the apartment. She was halfway through them when Ram returned with the coffee. He placed hers on the Stockport FC beer mat, pulled up a chair and sat down beside her.

'Where is everybody?' she asked.

'Andy's coming in as far as I know.' He pointed to the wall clock. 'But it's early yet. Harry's in Warrington. Dizzy's taken a half-day off to do some last-minute Christmas shopping. Max is over at the Central Park incident room bringing them up to date on your visit to the North East.'

'Oh, God!' she said, reaching for the phone. 'I knew there was something I had to do – thanks for reminding me.'

'You'd better make it fast,' Ram told her. 'That Skype interview you asked me to set up is in twenty minutes.'

The Operation Juniper office manager took the call.

'Ged,' said Jo, 'it's me, Joanne Stuart – can you put DI Sarsfield or SI Nailor on, please? It's urgent.'

'They're both here,' Ged replied. 'Do you have a preference?'

'Whoever has a speakerphone. I'd like them both to hear this.'

'That'll be DI Sarsfield, Ma'am. They're both in his office.'

It took less than two minutes for Jo to update them on the events of the night before.

'Are you alright, Jo?' Max asked.

Her initial response was to wonder if he'd appreciate her asking him the same question had the tables been turned, but it was quickly cancelled out by her surprise that he genuinely cared.

'I'm fine,' she said. 'The reason I rang was that there's still an outside chance that we may be able to track down the sender. I need someone to get round to the florists and see if they still have any of the banknotes that were used to purchase the flowers. And someone else to check the city centre CCTV on Great Northern Square either side of three pm. It should be easy to spot McGinty, and the youth following him. See if they can get a decent image of the youth.'

'I'll take the florist,' Max volunteered, 'then I'll head back to the Quays.'

'And I'll have one of our expert identifiers get to work on the CCTV,' said Sarsfield. He hesitated. 'What do you think about our setting up an observation on your apartment building?'

'Not a lot,' she said. 'I appreciate your concern, but whoever set this up is far too clever to fall for that. I don't see it as a genuine threat. More an attempt to divert us from the investigation.'

'I agree,' said Max. 'Besides, whoever it is would be a fool to take you on.'

She was still smiling as she put the phone down.

'Ram, this Skype interview,' she said. 'How long have I got?'

'Sixteen minutes. Christchurch is twelve hours ahead of Manchester. It'll be eight thirty in the evening there. I'll set it up in our incident room, then you can play it on as many monitors as you want.'

'I don't want her thinking it's a peep show,' Jo told him. 'This has to be just her and me.'

He nodded. 'No problem. I'll feed it into here, then there need be no one else in with you.'

'While I'm in here, I'd like you to keep digging into Malacott's time at university. What did he get up to? What he did in his spare time? Did he have any particular mates?'

'What are you looking for?'

'I don't know,' she said. 'But I will know it when I see it.'

'Fair enough,' he said. 'Now, if you sit here, Ma'am, you'll find it's all ready to go. I've set up the connection. All you have to do is click the blue video icon when you're ready. I set it recording in the office. Mr Swift has arrived, so he can watch it live.'

'Thanks,' she said. 'And I keep telling you, Ram, you can skip the Ma'am.'

He grinned, pistol-pointed at her with both hands, and made like a rapper.

'You're a poet, and you don't know it.'

Jo picked up a pad of Post-it notes and threw them at him. They bounced harmlessly off the back of the door. She turned back to the monitor, took a deep breath, let it out and began to count the seconds down.

Chapter 43

In her mid-thirties, Amanda Malacott shared her brother's oval face and pale blue eyes, but there the likeness ended. She had neither his cleft chin nor his brown hair, and certainly not his brash confidence. What she did possess was a striking physical resemblance to the unsub's prey. Elfin-like, she sat awkwardly on her chair, staring nervously at the screen. Her face, devoid of make-up, looked one-dimensional and pale against the deep-red, pageboy haircut. Jo felt an instinctive sense of compassion for this woman.

'My name is Joanne Stuart,' she said. 'I'm with the UK National Crime Agency. I'm now showing you my warrant card.'

She held it up for the webcam. In the box in the bottom corner of the screen, Jo saw her ID magnified as Amanda Malacott zoomed in on the image. Jo nodded her approval. Sensible or cautious, either way it meant that she was nobody's fool.

'And you are Amanda Frances Malacott?'

A slight nod of the head. 'As was,' the woman replied in a steady voice. 'I'm now Amanda Kelly.' She hesitated. 'I'm married.'

It almost sounded as though she was surprised by her current status.

Jo smiled and softened her tone. 'Well, I'm glad we've got that out of the way, Amanda,' she said. 'And I can't tell you how grateful I am that you agreed to speak with me. Oh, and is it alright if I call you Amanda?'

Another nod, the hint of a smile, but no reply. Jo would have expected her to be asking what this was all about. She had explicitly asked Ram not to tell her in case it frightened her away. Jo's hunch now was that she already knew.

'You can call me Jo. I'd like your permission to record this interview. Then I won't have to take any notes. There is no one else in the room. And I promise not to use the recording outside this building without contacting you first. Is that alright, Amanda?'

Another nod.

'Yes.'

Behind Amanda, Jo could make out a dressing table and closed curtains with a maple-leaf print.

'Are you alone, Amanda?' she asked. 'Or is someone there with you?'

'I'm alone.'

'Are you in your own house, Amanda?'

A shake of the head, a hint of concern.

'No, I'm at a friend's.'

'That's fine,' said Jo, immediately computing the reasons why she had chosen not to do this in the comfort of her own home. There could be a perfectly understandable explanation, such as them not having broadband. On the other hand . . .

'This is about my brother, isn't it?'

Brother, not Sam.

'Yes, Amanda, it is.'

Another nod. This time her voice had a tremor to it. 'What has he done?'

'We don't know that he's done anything, Amanda. He's one of a number of people who have come to our attention in relation to a current investigation. He's what we term a person of interest, that's all. I'm hoping that you may be able to shed some light on his early years so that we can eliminate him from our enquiries.'

'Or otherwise.'

'Yes, or otherwise.'

Amanda flicked the fringe of her hair in an unconscious gesture, and eased herself a little further from the screen.

'This current investigation,' she said, 'is it to do with girls?'

Jo felt her pulse quicken. 'What makes you ask that?'

'It is, isn't it?'

'Well, it involves young women, rather than girls.'

'And are we talking serious incidents?'

'Yes, I'm afraid we are. But I'm not able to give you details at this stage. Not until after we've completed this interview.'

To do so would leave Jo open to accusations of leading the witness, and run the risk of compromising her evidence.

Amanda leaned forward again. Her face filled the screen. Her eyes searched for an answer.

'Murder?'

Jo was rocked by the implications, and by the matter-of-fact tone in which it had been said.

'Not murder,' Jo said, 'not yet.'

Amanda sat back in her chair and folded her arms.

'What do you want to know?' she asked.

'Whatever you feel may be relevant,' said Jo. 'In your own time. There's no rush. Take as long as you need, Amanda.'

Jo watched as she stood up and adjusted something on her chair. *I was right*, she thought. *She's sitting on a cushion. I need to ask her how tall she is. But not yet. Let her tell it her way.* She hoped that

Andy had arrived. She wanted him to be able to see it live. Amanda sat down again. She placed her hands out of sight on her lap, composed herself and looked up.

Chapter 44

'It was just before my tenth birthday,' Amanda began. 'He was fifteen. Our father walked out that summer; he never came back. Our
mother was really unhappy. I realise now that she was suffering from
clinical depression. She cried a lot, except when she took to her bed,
which was most of the time. My brother looked after both of us. He
took me to school and picked me up. He made most of the meals.
He did most of the shopping. He had two part-time jobs: a paper
round and helping a gardener on our estate. He used to give me
weekly pocket money.'

She smiled despondently and looked down.

'We became very close. I needed him; I think he needed me too.'

She raised her head again and stared at the top of the screen, as
though gazing into the distance.

'Around Christmas time our mother seemed to recover, at least
enough to start going out again with some of her friends. She let
him babysit me whenever she went out.'

She paused. Jo was worried that she might not be able to continue. But then she blinked and carried on.

'That was when it began. I remember the first time. "Let's play a
game," he said. "This one is called My Little Pony. It's how everyone

finds out about sex. Lots of brothers and sisters do it if they really love each other, but because it's a secret no one will tell you about it. Trust me, you're really going to enjoy it. But don't tell anyone or we'll both get into big trouble. You do love me, don't you?"

'He started stroking my hair and calling me his beautiful princess. He said my hair was like a pony's mane.'

Amanda raised her hand to her hair and plucked at it self-consciously.

'It wasn't always this colour. I started dyeing it when I met my husband, Jed. Just before I came out here with him.' She paused. 'It used to be blonde and long – right down to my shoulders.'

She lowered her head. There was an even longer pause. Jo held her breath and waited. After what seemed an age, Amanda raised her head and looked directly at the camera. Her voice when she spoke had a harder, bitter, less self-pitying edge.

'Afterwards, he gave me some chocolate buttons.' She shook her head. 'I don't eat chocolate now, it makes me vomit. He said that I was all grown-up now: a proper young woman. That he would never hurt me. It would get easier, he said.'

She spat the words out. ' "You'll come to enjoy it. I promise." '

She shook her head slowly from side to side. 'He had no idea.'

This time the silence stretched on and on. Jo felt she had no option but to intervene.

'How long did it continue?' she asked.

Amanda's pupils dilated and she blinked twice as though emerging from a dream.

'I'm sorry?' she said.

'I was asking how long it went on for?'

'Oh, about three years,' she said. 'He went off to university. While he was away, I started pulling my hair out in my sleep. The school were concerned. They told my mother she should take me to our GP. My mother thought it was alopecia – the GP put her straight. He arranged for me to see a child psychologist.'

She shook her head at some distant memory.

'She didn't have a clue. She just assumed that it must be because I was missing my father.'

'And you didn't tell her the truth?'

'I didn't think she'd believe me. And even if she did, I knew by then that it was wrong what he'd been doing. What he'd made me do. I knew that they'd take him away. And I thought everyone would blame me – that our mother would blame me. That's what he told me when he came home at the end of the first term and found out I was seeing the psychologist. I could tell that he was frightened. Scared stiff. I told him that if he ever touched me again I would tell her.'

That thin smile appeared again.

'He never did. And we never spoke of it again.'

Suddenly her face disappeared as she stood up.

'I'm sorry,' she said, 'I need a drink of water.'

Before Jo had time to respond, Amanda had left the room. Jo waited impatiently, praying that she would return. Even if she didn't, if the interview was over, there was enough to justify a concerted push on Sam Malacott. Jo was more concerned, however, about Amanda. It was important that she finished telling her story. Important for her. She need not have worried. A hand appeared, carrying a glass of water. The rest of Amanda followed as she eased herself into her seat.

'I'm sorry about that,' she said. She seemed different somehow: more at ease, more confident.

'Don't be,' said Jo. 'You're doing fine.'

Amanda put the glass down.

'Where was I?' she said.

'Neither of you ever spoke of it again. You were, what, fourteen or fifteen? He was back from university.'

Amanda nodded.

'I stopped pulling out my hair and started sleeping properly. My grades picked up. I stopped seeing the psychologist. But I was lonely. I hadn't really made any friends all the time I was at high school – I was frightened to let anyone get close. And I couldn't have brought any of them home for a sleepover, could I.'

She looked up, seeking agreement. Jo nodded.

'You didn't want to put them in jeopardy.'

Amanda nodded and repeated the word, savouring it.

'Jeopardy. That's a good word for it.'

She picked up the glass, took a drink and put it back down.

'I got the A-Level grades I needed for university, but I didn't have the confidence to apply. That's something else he robbed me of.'

She spoke directly to the camera again.

'I'd had a holiday job with a florist. She offered me full-time as her assistant. I loved arranging the flowers, and did a lot of weddings and funerals. The funerals made me cry, but then so did the weddings. It was hard seeing people committing to a lifelong relationship. I could never see myself doing that. It was beyond my imagination.'

She stopped, and something in her expression led Jo to prompt her.

'What happened, Amanda?'

'We had two weddings and a funeral on the same day. That evening I was exhausted. I went to bed, but I found I couldn't sleep. I kept going over and over what we'd done together, my brother and I. I couldn't get it out of my head. I tossed and turned all night, consumed with self-loathing and guilt. The next morning, I had this overwhelming sense of sadness.'

'You were seriously depressed,' said Jo.

Amanda nodded. 'Clinically depressed, just like mother. I felt empty. Everything seemed pointless. I started smoking cannabis just to get through the day. Finally, my employer noticed. She sat me down and told me all the problems that she had had in her life – how she had begun to drink and take drugs, but that only made things worse. She persuaded me to see someone who'd helped her – someone the Samaritans had recommended. A counsellor. The counsellor got me to open up. I told her I'd been abused by a family member, but didn't tell her who, and she didn't try to make me. She said the root of my problem was twofold: lack of self-worth and anger.'

Amanda frowned, and shook her head.

'More like self-disgust.'

Then she bowed her head and fell silent.

'Who were you angry with, Amanda?' Jo asked.

Amanda looked up. 'My mother, for not noticing. My father for leaving us. My brother for manipulating me, for stealing my innocence and my youth, for taking away my power to make choices,' she paused, 'and myself, for becoming a victim.'

'I go along with all of that,' said Jo, 'except the last part. You said yourself that your brother took away your power to choose. You did not choose to become a victim.'

Amanda smiled. 'That's what the counsellor said. But knowing and believing is not the same thing. Anyway, she helped me to pull myself together. Saved my life really.'

Sometimes that was all it took. Just one significant other. Someone who enters your life at a critical time and makes all the difference. *I was lucky,* Jo reflected. *I had two: Tom Caton and Abbie.*

'I came off the weed,' Amanda continued, 'applied for teacher-training and went away to university. I had difficulty making close friends of either sex at first, but I got by. It was only when we had a series of sessions about safeguarding children that it all fell into place. The way he had manipulated me, the way he used the situation we were in. The fact that I was too young and innocent and in need of love right then to understand, or to do anything about it. That's when I truly accepted that it was not my fault. That I had been a victim. And that I could choose not to be a victim any longer or ever again.'

She took another drink of water. This time her smile transformed her face. For the first time, she looked relaxed, as though she had shrugged a weight that had been dragging her down from her shoulders. Jo had a glimpse of how beautiful she must have been, and still might be.

'I met Jed during my first teaching post. He was over here on a teaching exchange. When he went back to New Zealand, I went with him. We married the following year. We have two daughters and one son. And I never looked back – until your colleague contacted me.'

She picked up her glass of water and sat back in her chair. Jo realised that she had come to the end of her story. Or at least as much of it as she was prepared to share.

'Do you mind if I ask you a few questions now, Amanda?'

'No.' Amanda lifted her glass. 'Go ahead.'

Jo opened the folder Ram had placed on the desk. 'I'm going to show you a picture,' she said. 'Can you tell me if you've seen anything like it before?'

She held up the enlarged photo of the tattoo left on the first of his victims. Amanda studied it, and then slowly shook her head.

'No, I don't think so.'

'You never saw anything like this when you and your brother were still living at home? A book, a picture, anything at all?'

'No, I'm sorry. Is it important?'

Jo ignored her question. 'Did he ever give you anything as a present – a piece of jewellery, for instance?'

'Sometimes he did. Before I told him it had to stop or I'd tell the psychologist. For my birthday and Christmas. He bought me a silver cross once. Another time, a sparkly bracelet.'

'Anything to do with birds?'

She frowned.

'No, a ladybird, a butterfly. No birds.'

Jo didn't let her disappointment show. It was too much to expect there to be so obvious a connection.

'There was one thing though,' Amanda said. 'Towards the end, before he went away to university, he started calling me his little dove.'

Jo smiled. *That'll do*, she thought.

'Thank you, Amanda,' she said. 'I can only begin to imagine how hard this must have been for you. But you have no idea how helpful you have been.'

'And there's no way he'll find out that I've spoken to you?'

'Absolutely not, unless you decide that you want him to know.' She hesitated. 'However, Amanda, I have to be honest with you, if my investigation should result in your brother facing charges on another matter, the information you have shared with me might be something the prosecution would feel they needed to strengthen their case. If that did happen, then the defence, including your brother, would also have to know about it.'

She nodded.

'Would I have to give evidence?'

'Not necessarily. But if you did, under Section 32(1)(a) of the Criminal Justice Act 1988, you'd be able to give your evidence by live video link, just as you have today.'

Amanda's relief was evident. 'I don't want my husband to know,' she said, 'or my children. I couldn't bear for them to find out. That's why I never reported him.'

Jo took a deep breath. 'I'm truly sorry, Amanda,' she said. 'But even if what you have just told me is not raised in court, if your brother were to be tried and convicted of something, there would be nothing to stop the media from digging into his past, into his family. You need to be prepared for that to happen.'

Amanda Kelly, née Malacott, had remained strong throughout the interview, and it was hard to witness how crestfallen those words had left her.

'It may never come to that,' Jo said. 'But you might want to think about talking to someone. A counsellor. I can give you the contact details for a specialist service right there in Christchurch if you'd like that?'

'Thank you,' Amanda replied, 'but there's no need. I have the details. I looked them up when your colleague contacted me. I've just been trying to find the courage to follow it up.'

'I only hope this conversation has helped,' said Jo.

Amanda smiled. 'Yes, I think it has.'

'One final question, Amanda,' said Jo. 'How tall are you?'

The question took her by surprise.

'Five foot. Why do you ask?'

Her expression slowly changed as comprehension dawned. She nodded her head, her face set hard.

'These women,' she said. 'They're all blonde, aren't they? And petite?'

'Yes, Amanda,' Jo replied, 'I'm afraid that they are.'

The corners of her mouth twitched, and for the first time her eyes began to well up.

'He couldn't let me go,' she whispered, 'could he?'

Chapter 45

'I knew it!' Jo slapped the folder down on the table. 'I knew he was too good to be true. How could he have done that to his little sister, knowing how vulnerable she was?'

'That's precisely why he did it,' Andy told her. 'He was vulnerable himself, remember, but he must also have had sociopathic tendencies. Current research suggests that sex offenders exhibit heightened sociopathy, and an inclination to cognitive distortion.'

'In simple terms,' Jo said, 'he has his own personal moral code, and he lies to himself to justify the evil that he does.'

'That's over-simplistic,' Andy said, 'but broadly accurate.'

'I'd have thought he was more a psychopath than a sociopath,' she continued, 'especially if he's behind these rapes and abductions.'

'*If* he is, Jo, then you may well be right. First you have to prove it. So far all you have is a hunch and his sister's testimony to historical child abuse.'

'How did she strike you?' Jo asked.

'Intelligent, respectable, honest, outwardly tough. She's come a long way from that tragic child and teenager. But under that veneer she still has low self-esteem and exhibits a high degree of passivity. Both of which are characteristic of a compliant victim of grooming and abuse. My hunch is that fear of abandonment following her father leaving her mother led her to develop a dependent personality disorder. Her brother used that to satisfy his own needs and to overcome his own sense of loss. You heard her, they both needed each other. He preyed on that. She's fought like hell to break away from the mould they created together. She's still fighting.'

Jo's eyebrows rose. She was unable to hide her surprise and disappointment.

'I'm sorry,' Andy said, 'but it's true. She needed him. That's why he was able to get away with it for so long, why she didn't report it. She felt guilty – she still feels guilty. What I'm not doing is condoning his behaviour. She was a child; he was on the brink of adulthood. He knew what he was doing was wrong, yet he still groomed and abused her. This is how paedophiles work, Jo. They exploit vulnerability. You know that.'

Of course she did. She had seen it over and over again. Confronted with Amanda Kelly's account, she had lost her objectivity and had been too hasty to judge her colleague.

'I'm sorry, Andy,' she said. 'You're right.'

'The question is,' he said, 'what are you going to do with this?'

'I'm going to enter it into the policy book as substantive evidence of Malacott's precursor behaviour and predilection for sexual abuse. That, taken together with his access to the universities from which six of the victims come, and his obsession with rape crisis charities and training, should be more than sufficient to justify covert observation. I'll also make applications for search warrants as and when I need them.'

'That may be sooner than you think!'

Ram was standing in the doorway, grinning from ear to ear. In his left hand he held a notepad triumphantly above his head.

'Come on, Ram,' she said, 'don't leave us in suspense.'

The three of them sat down around the table.

'I was lucky,' he told them. 'The first person I spoke to at his university put me through to the alumni office. It turned out that Malacott is well known to them because he regularly goes back to give talks.'

'The *Say No And Stay Safe* seminars?' Jo guessed.

'Not just those, but ones on . . .' He consulted his notes. '*Self-Actualisation* and *Marketing Oneself.*'

'That figures,' Jo said. 'Pretending it's all about them, when it's really all about himself.'

'Exactly,' said Andy. 'That cognitive distortion I mentioned? It tends to reinforce negative emotions, to makes us think badly of ourselves. What he's doing is trying to compensate for that – to boost his ego.'

'I haven't the faintest idea what you two are talking about,' said Ram. 'Do you want to hear what I've discovered or carry on a psychology symposium?'

'Sorry,' said Andy.

'Yes, sorry,' said Jo.

Ram grinned. 'You don't need to go overboard. Anyway, the alumni office put me through to one of the profs who's been there ever since Malacott began his undergraduate course. He actually tutored him, and still sees him from time to time when he comes back to give talks. They've even had dinner together.'

'Are they friends?' Jo asked.

'I didn't ask, but I got the impression they get on well together, and Mackay, that's the name of the prof, likes Malacott. Anyway, I told this Mackay that Sam Malacott had offered to assist us with an investigation, and we just needed to check out his background before we took him up on it. A bit like a reference.'

'You devious devil,' said Jo, 'that's sheer genius.'

'Thanks for the genius bit,' Ram replied. 'Obviously, not for the devil. So, it turns out that while Malacott was at university he had a one-term student business placement.' He paused, and grinned. 'Guess where?'

'In a fertility clinic!' they exclaimed as one.

'He said he didn't remember the name, but when I prompted him with the original name of the clinic from which Dalmeny's sample went missing, he confirmed it. Malacott was supposed to be learning about the business side of the work, the systems involved, and because his degree involved psychology, he was learning about the way they counselled patients around IVF, fertility problems and the like. The prof says he remembered it specifically because Malacott also became a sperm donor advocate. He remembered them having a laugh about it.'

'Sperm donor advocate,' said Jo. 'What did that entail?'

'Encouraging others to donate. Explaining what's involved before the start of the formal interview process. Apparently he persuaded some of his fellow students to sign up.'

'Did he donate himself?' Andy wondered. 'It would fit with the unsub's mindset, with his sense of omnipotence.'

Ram placed his notes on the table. 'I didn't ask and I didn't press him any further. I reckoned I'd got enough, and I didn't want him becoming suspicious and reporting back to Malacott.'

'You're probably right,' said Jo. 'Although from the sound of it, I'd be surprised if this Mackay didn't contact him anyway to tell him you'd been in touch. Not that it matters: it's him. Malacott is our unsub – he must be. He'll have known that Dalmeny's samples were supposed to be destroyed. He must have gained access to them. Maybe substituted one of his own. Or falsified the records.'

'How long ago was this?' said Andy. 'Sixteen years. And he's stolen a supply and kept it in his freezer all this time. Waiting for the right moment?'

'It's not impossible, is it?'

'Why not use it sooner?'

'Because he didn't need to. Not until we began to close in on him. Not until he needed a diversion?'

The door opened, and Max walked in.

'Sorry I'm late,' he said. 'What are you three up to? You look like Father Christmas came early.'

'Sit down, Max,' Jo said, 'and we'll tell you.'

'I don't want to spoil the party,' Max said. 'But all of this is still only circumstantial.' He raised his hand to stay Jo's objection. 'I'm not minimising the importance of his sister's testimony, nor the fact that he was at the clinic. I don't believe in two separate and equally bizarre coincidences like these any more than you do. Fifty years ago it might have been enough to secure a conviction. But now? We have no direct evidence linking him to any of the abductions or rapes. We don't have his DNA or his fingerprints, or any other form of trace evidence to prove that he went anywhere near any of those girls.'

'I'm assuming that means your visit to the florist drew a blank?' said Jo.

He nodded. 'I'm afraid so. She remembered the homeless guy. Nearly didn't hand the flowers over till she saw the money. All of which she banked straight after work. I went straight to the bank, but with it being Christmas time, they'd already processed the overnight deposits. It would have been among the cash collected by the security van about an hour before I got there. There's no way we could identify those notes now.'

'But the fact that he was at that clinic at the same time that Dalmeny was a donor,' Ram began.

'Indicates a possible opportunity to steal the sample,' said Jo, 'but Max is right. It doesn't prove that he did, and there's nothing that proves he had the means and opportunity to use it in that way. The defence will ask if we've eliminated everyone else who worked at the clinic at that time.'

'So what are you going to do?' said Andy.

Jo looked at her fellow investigator. 'I think we've got enough to set up covert observation on Malacott himself under my authority, and to apply for authorisation, under section 5 of the Intelligence Services Act 1994 and Part III of the 1997 Act, for directed surveillance on his landline and mobile phones, and potentially intrusive surveillance under the Regulation of Investigatory Powers Act 2000 on his house and car. What do you think, Max?'

'I agree,' he said. 'The sooner the better. It'll bugger up someone's Christmas, but I don't see that you have any choice.'

Jo began to get up, but Andy placed a hand on her arm.

'You haven't asked me about the flowers yet,' he said.

She looked at him. 'What about them?'

'Don't you want to know what I think that was all about? Assuming that they're from the unsub?'

'You're right,' she said. 'I'd just assumed it was an attempt to divert me: to make me take my eye off the ball, to make me start chasing shadows. But you're the expert. I should have asked.'

'Expert isn't the same as infallible,' he replied. 'I agree with your instinctive premise. Distraction is certainly part of it. But it also suggests that the unsub is seriously rattled, either because you're getting close, or because the death of Susanne Hadrix, his seventh victim, has thrown him. That was not part of the plan. He's no longer in control. Sending you those flowers was a way to exercise some control over you – but it may also have been something else.' He paused.

'Go on,' she said.

'It could be a genuine warning, Jo. He may be telling you that he's making this personal. That he's going to target you in some way.

You can't afford to overlook that possibility. You have to be on your guard.'

'I agree,' said Max. 'That's why I'm going to stick to you like glue.'

Jo stood up. The thought of whoever had sent that bouquet, whether or not it was the unsub, had unsettled her more than she was prepared to admit. The thought of him following her, his eyes on her. Her not knowing what his next move might be.

She realised that the three of them were staring at her.

'I don't need babysitting,' she said. 'I'm perfectly capable of looking after myself. Now, I don't know about the rest of you, but I'm exhausted. I suggest that we call it a day, and come in bright early in the morning.'

Chapter 46

He lowered the window a fraction to stop the windscreen fogging up, and checked his watch. It had been over an hour now. Fortune was on his side. Cars were double-parked along the length of this street. He had been able to slot into the one remaining space, twenty-five yards away, beneath a tree and in the shadow between two street lights. He reached across, opened the glove box and felt for the flask of coffee. There was no telling how long he would have to wait.

He paused as a taxi drew up outside the house on the opposite side of the street. The driver switched on the overhead light, and turned to receive his fare. She leaned forward, revealing her face in profile, and the glistening sheen of her hair. She was perfect. This was perfect. His pulse began to race as he watched her hurry up the steps, two shopping bags in each hand. He saw the security light come on. Watched her struggle to find her key. Saw her face light up as the door opened from the inside. Watched as the two of them embraced in the hallway. Saw her kick the door closed behind her. He drew a deep breath, exhaled slowly and began to unscrew the top of the flask. He would give anything to be there and to see the face of that bitch Stuart when she learned what he had done.

There was a distinct change in the traffic now, as city-centre workers hurrying home from their office parties and Christmas drinks were replaced by singletons heading out for a long night in the Manchester clubs and bars. It was raining now, a miserable drizzle that ran in rivulets down his windscreen and pooled in shallow depressions in the road, reflecting the blue-and-white LED icicles strung in the trees and bushes bordering the pavements. He checked his watch again. It was twenty minutes since she had disappeared inside.

There was movement in the hallway. Dark shadows behind the opaque glass panel. He switched on the engine, turned on the windscreen wipers and craned forward.

The door opened. He watched them embrace, their faces framed by the golden glow from the ceiling lights. What began as a hesitant kiss on the lips swelled and deepened. His hands began to sweat. The veins on either side of his neck began to pulse. He tried to wipe away the condensation on the windscreen from his hot breath, and left an ugly smear. He cursed, groping for the wash-leather beneath the flask in the glove box. By the time he had cleared the windscreen, she was getting into a white Toyota Auris parked outside the house.

He closed the glovebox, fastened his seat belt, waited for the door of the house to close, and set off towards the twin brake lights at the end of the road.

He had been surprised to see her drive into this car park. It was a long way to come for a Krispy Kreme doughnut or a visit to ASDA. But now that she was out of the car and waiting to cross the busy Barton Dock Road, it all made sense. Every one of the Trafford Centre car parks had been full as they drove past. Like the thousands of other poor souls who had flocked here, she had some last-minute shopping to do. Something she had forgotten. Unlike him.

His right hand strayed absentmindedly to the deep pocket of his cagoule. He felt the hilt of the knife and smiled. Then he slipped on his black leather gloves and flipped open the brass clasps of the briefcase on the seat beside him. It was time to throw the cat among the pigeons, and for the falcon to take the dove.

Chapter 47

It was a miserable way to start Christmas Eve morning. Jo was angry. With Max, and with herself. With him for thinking that because she had once been the victim of a violent abduction that she needed protection, and with herself for letting it get to her. Or was it simply because she was a woman? It wasn't the sort of thing he was going to say to a male colleague. And she had already demonstrated her ability to look after herself during her very first investigation as part of the Behavioural Sciences Unit. *Get over it,* she told herself – *there are far more important matters to deal with.*

She began by ringing Harry Stone.

'I've just left Warrington,' he told her. 'I'm on my way over to you. I'm on hands-free, so is this urgent or can it wait till I get there?'

'I'll let you decide, Boss,' she said. 'Is your line secure?'

'I've pulled into the inside lane,' he said. 'Unless the caravan behind, or the wagon in front are training an encryption-busting, directional, high-gain antenna on this car, I'd say it's as secure as the PM's direct line to the White House. Although I have no doubt the Chinese and the Russians are already working on hacking into that one.'

'It's someone we've had on our radar,' she said. 'SM.'

She waited for him to let her know that he understood.

'Go ahead,' he said.

'You'll know from the shared drive that I asked Ram to track down the sister. I've just finished a video interview with her. She alleges that he abused her from the age of ten to fifteen. And her physical appearance at the time fits with our victim profiles.'

'Go on,' he said.

'We have also established, Ram that is, that SM had a student placement at the donor facility that was the likely source of the trace evidence found on the body of the dead victim.'

'Shah has been busy,' he said. 'You both have. Well done. What is it you're asking?'

'Approval for covert surveillance on SM.'

'You don't necessarily need my involvement to do that.'

'I do for landline, mobile and Wi-Fi intercepts,' she said, 'and a tracker on his car.'

'Ah,' he said. There was a pause. 'I'm giving you approval for directed surveillance,' he said. 'As for the intrusive surveillance, leave it with me. I'll need to contact the Surveillance Commissioner.'

'Thanks, Boss,' she said.

'Now you'd better get off the line,' he told her. 'Before I get boxed in by this bloody great tanker bearing down on me.'

Jo replaced the phone and punched the air. Before she had time to set everything in motion, her BlackBerry rang. When she saw that the call was from Abbie, she knew that she had to take it. This could be a second chance, or at the very least an opportunity to put right the hash she had made of their most recent conversation.

'Abbie,' she said. 'I'm so glad that . . .'

'You've got to help me, Jo!' Abbie sounded frantic, her words tumbling into each other. 'I don't know who else to turn to.'

'Whatever's the matter, Abbie?'

'It's Sally, she's missing!' There was a sob in her voice.

'Sally? Sally who?'

'Sally! Sally Warburton. James's sister.'

Of course. Abbie had texted her that she was staying with James's sister here in Manchester. But why did Abbie sound so desperate?

'Calm down,' Jo said. 'And tell me what makes you think that Sally's missing.'

'I don't think, I know! Sally is missing. She went to the Trafford Centre yesterday, and she never came back.'

'What time did she set off?'

'At seven pm – I told her it was stupid. That the traffic would be a nightmare, and the shops would be heaving, but she said there was one last thing she needed to pick up. It was something she'd ordered. She didn't want to leave it till today because it would be even more manic, with it being Christmas Eve. You've got to help me, Jo.'

'I assume you rang the Trafford Centre?'

'It was the first thing I did. They said her car wasn't there, and there was no record of it having entered any of their car parks. They're all monitored.'

Jo knew from a multi-agency exercise that she had been on how tight security was at the Trafford Centre. Two hundred and eighty-five cameras, monitored from the state-of-the-art security control room, covered the ten thousand car park spaces. Security officers patrolling the centre were able to speak face-to-face with the control room using videophones. If they said Sally's car had not been there, then it definitely had not.

'You've tried ringing her phone?'

'Over and over again. Last night and this morning. It's switched off. Sally never switches it off when she's out, Jo. Never!'

'Has she been in contact with her brother?'

'No. James is here with me now. We're both frantic with worry, Jo. You've got to help us.'

297

'I assume that you've contacted the local police? Trafford North? That would be Stretford Police Station. You don't have to wait twenty-four hours any more; you can ring as soon as you're worried about someone.'

'I rang them last night when she didn't come home. They asked me for a photo, details of her friends and relatives, places she often visits, whether she has a medical condition.' She paused, and Jo thought she heard her sob and someone comforting her. 'Oh, Jo,' she said, 'they want her toothbrush . . . for her DNA.'

'Don't worry, Abbie,' Jo said, 'that's just routine. It doesn't mean that they believe anything sinister has happened to Sally. They'll be tracing her phone and her car. I'm sure they'll find her in no time. Most people turn up within the first twenty-four hours.'

'This isn't most people, Jo,' Abbie replied, 'this is Sally. She hasn't had a lapse of memory. She's too young for Alzheimer's. She's only twenty-six, for God's sake!'

'You've checked with all of the hospitals?'

'Of course we have. She's not in any of them.'

In which case, Jo thought, *she's right to be worried.*

'Look, Abbie,' she said. 'I'll help in any way I can, but there's nothing I can do that GMP and our Missing Persons Bureau won't already be doing.'

'There must be something else you can do? For a start, you can make sure they're taking it seriously.'

'I will, Abbie, I promise. And send me a copy of the online form the police asked you to fill in. The one with Sally's physical description, ethnicity, mobile number, etc. Oh, and a recent photo. I'll text you the email address to send it to.'

'Of course.'

'I'm sending that text now, Abbie. If I hear anything, I'll let you know straight away. You take care, and try not to worry.'

'I'll try, and Jo . . . thanks, from both of us.'

'Like I said,' Jo replied, 'I'm sure she'll turn up soon. Got to go, Abbie. The text is on its way now. Bye.'

'Bye, Jo . . .'

It was an uneasy ending, with neither of them knowing how best to finish the call. Jo entered her dedicated email address and pressed send.

'Problem?'

She looked up. A concerned Max was standing beside her.

'It's Abbie,' she said. 'The girl she's staying with has gone missing. I think she's right to be worried.'

Max pulled up a chair, and sat down.

'What are you thinking?' he asked.

'That it may have something to do with Operation Juniper,' she said.

He frowned.

'Is there any way,' he said, 'that our unsub might have connected this girl with you? How long is it since Abbie left your apartment?'

'Just over four weeks. But Abbie has a key, and she's been back several times to collect her post and some of her stuff, always when I'm out. But he must have been watching the apartments to know where to send those flowers. He could have seen her and followed her.' Jo's voice caught in her throat. It followed that he must have been watching her too. Studying her. Trying to get inside her head.

'Assuming it was him,' said Max.

'Who else could it be?'

'But she'd left before you took over Operation Juniper.'

'You know how serial perpetrators work, Max. He'll have been doing his research on me from the moment that I gave that first press conference. He'll know I'm in a civil partnership with Abbie. If I was able to track her down, I'm sure he could.'

Jo's computer pinged to let her know that she had mail. She turned to face her monitor. There were two mail attachments.

'It's the Missing Person description,' she told Max.
She printed them off and swivelled in her chair.
'Oh my God!'
'What is it?' said Max.
She handed him the printouts.

Gender	*Female*
Age	*26*
Ethnicity/appearance	*White Caucasian*
Height	*1.57 metres/5'2"*
Build	*Slim*
Ethnic appearance	*White*
Eye colour	*Blue*
Hair colour and style	*Blonde, shoulder length*
Glasses	*None*

But the photograph was the clincher. Sally Warburton could easily have passed as a slightly older sister of Sareen Lomax, the first victim attributed to the unsub.

'I agree,' said Max.

'With what?'

Andy had been attracted by Jo's outburst, Ram was close behind. Max handed them the printouts.

'See for yourself.'

'Her name is Sally Warburton,' Jo told them. 'Abbie's staying with her at the moment, here in Manchester. She went shopping at the Trafford Centre last night and didn't come back. She's been missing for fifteen and a half hours. No phone or text messages. Her phone is off. No sign of her car. It has to be Malacott. This is too much of a coincidence. First the flowers, now this.'

She stood up.

'I'm going to arrest him. Search his house, his office, his car.'

'Hang on,' said Andy. 'Let's think this through. Firstly, it could just be a coincidence. Secondly, since she hasn't turned up, then the odds are that she's probably still alive and he's holding her somewhere. Thirdly, he's either trying to distract you again or he's challenging you. You can't just rush in and arrest him. Let's say you do and he bluffs it out – you may never find her. Besides, right now all you have is a hunch that it *is* Malacott that has her.'

'He's right, Jo,' said Max. 'You have to approach this as you would any missing vulnerable person, not charge in there like the cavalry just because he's made it personal. That may be what he wants, what he's prepared for.'

Jo bit her lip. They were both right. This had to be finessed and done by the book.

'Okay,' she said. 'Ram, you get on to Missing Persons and find out where they're up to with tracing the car and the mobile phone. Impress on them the urgency of the matter. Tell them if they need additional help, we'll offer Operation Juniper resources. Max and I will plan the covert surveillance strategy on Malacott. When the Boss gets here, I'll brief him and see if he can get us some tactical support.'

'Tactical support for what?'

They turned their heads towards the door as Harry Stone strode in.

Chapter 48

'Sally Warburton's phone has been traced to a waste disposal bin on the outskirts of a retail park opposite the Trafford Centre,' Gerry Sarsfield told her. 'That's where her car was parked. As soon as we found it, I sent a DC to have a look at the CCTV on their cameras. It looks like they captured her and her abductor getting into the car, and the car driving off. I've just sent a link to your inbox. I suggest you brace yourselves, because you're not going to believe what you see.'

Jo and Max were seated in the satellite major investigation room at the Quays, conversing with Sarsfield by videoconference. Harry Stone had been called away to take a personal call. Ram had slipped out for a moment.

'I've got it, Gerry,' said Jo. 'Give me a second.'

Jo angled the screen of the second monitor so that the GMP detective would be able to see exactly what they were watching. She waited with mounting excitement as the video began to stream. The first thing that struck her was the quality of the resolution, especially given that it was late in the evening.

'The detail is amazing,' she said.

'That,' Sarsfield told her, 'is because they're using a network visual recording system with IP cameras so they can control the cameras in real time from their monitoring room, and also get good-quality licence plate capture. That way they can send out automatic car park fines and resolve any disputes over accidents in the car park, including false claims for compensation.'

The car park was only half full. There was movement on the extreme right of the screen. A woman opened the driver's door of a Shogun, and got into the car.

'That's not her,' said Sarsfield.

They watched as the lights came on and the car backed out. As if by magic, the camera followed the Shogun until it disappeared from the screen. The camera swung back to its starting position.

'Here they come now,' said Sarsfield.

A couple appeared in the centre right of the screen. A tall figure with a man's gait, and a woman over a foot shorter than him. His left arm enveloped her back and appeared to be clamping her left arm to her side. His right arm was across her front with his hand hidden inside the fold of her open coat.

'That's either a knife or a gun,' Max observed.

'Shhh!' said Jo.

The man was wearing a dark cagoule with the hood up, over dark jeans. Ten strides brought them to a small, white family-size saloon. They stopped beside the driver's door. The man bent so that his head was close to the woman's.

'He's giving her instructions,' said Max, unable to contain himself. 'Telling her what he'll do if she doesn't comply.'

'That's what I thought,' said Sarsfield.

'Shut up, you two!' said Jo. 'I'm trying to concentrate here.'

The car's lights flashed as it was disarmed. The woman opened the driver's door and began to get in. The man shifted his right hand to her right shoulder and pressed down. He was wearing dark gloves. Something glinted briefly in the glow from the car's interior light.

'Did you see that?' Jo asked.

'Yes,' said Max. 'He was too fast for me to be sure, but he was definitely holding something. I'd hazard a guess that it was a knife. Maybe he's concealed it up his sleeve.'

The man opened the rear passenger door on the driver's side with his left hand, and then used the same hand to push back his hood.

'I don't believe it,' said Ram. 'He's black!'

'And he's wearing dark glasses at night!' said Max.

The man slammed the driver's door, ducked his head and slid quickly into the seat behind the female driver. His left hand curled around the driver's headrest, out of sight his right hand pulled his own door closed and then deftly secured his seatbelt.

'The bastard's thought of everything,' muttered Max.

The man leaned forward with his head close to the woman's. She secured her seat belt. The car lights came on and then the white reversing lights. The car began to back slowly out of the parking space. A sequence of three cameras followed the car until it finally turned right on to Barton Dock Road, heading north towards the Ship Canal. The three of them breathed out as one. The two investigators sat back in their seats.

'I see what you mean, Gerry,' said Max. 'A bald, moustachioed man of African-Caribbean heritage?'

'Does anyone else thinks it's odd that he pulled that hood back and looked towards the cameras?' said Jo. 'Especially given how careful he's been in every other respect?'

'I was wondering that,' said Ram. 'It was almost as though he wanted us to see his face.'

'Can you run it again, Gerry,' she said. 'Freeze it at that point and then zoom in on his face?'

'I can't,' he said. 'But I have a techie here who can.'

Thirty seconds later they were staring at an archetypal, almost stereotypical image of an African-Caribbean male face most representative of boxers, rappers and bodyguards. A large, perfectly oval egg of a head, completely bald. Wrap-around sunglasses, a prominent nose and lips. A narrow strip of beard surrounded the lips and filled the crease at the centre of the chin to form a sophisticated yet sinister goatee beard.

'I'm sure I've seen him somewhere before,' said Ram.

'Can you move it on frame by frame, please,' Jo said.

They watched as the man turned in slow motion, and began to duck his head.

'Freeze it!' she said. 'Now zoom in on that?'

She pointed to the lighter grey inverted V-shape running down the back of the skull to the nape of the neck.

'What the hell is that?' asked Max.

'That's a seam,' she said. 'He's wearing some kind of mask, only it's a fraction too small for him.'

'That's why I thought I'd seen him before,' said Ram. 'That's a silicon mask. I nearly bought one last year for a Halloween party.'

The two investigators turned to stare at him.

'No,' he said. 'I really did. Look, I'll show you.'

He leaned across Max, entered something into the search bar of the computer, pressed return, made a selection and pressed return again.

'There you go,' he said as the image flashed up, 'thirty quid on eBay.'

'It's identical,' said Max.

'Right,' Jo said. 'I want that seller contacted. We need a list of everyone who has ever purchased one of those masks.'

'Assuming we can get that information,' said Gerry Sarsfield. 'There could be hundreds, thousands of names, email addresses, credit card or PayPal details to sift through.'

'I don't care,' she said. 'We can prioritise those with UK delivery addresses, and those in the North West of England. I also want to know where that car went.'

'We're already on to it,' said Sarsfield. 'I was about to tell you that we know it headed north and was picked up by ANPR at twenty eighteen last night, two minutes after it left the car park, approaching the junction of the A57 with the M60. No sightings since then. I'll give you real-time updates on that. I can also tell you that none of the other car registrations on that car park belong to Malacott's BMW. So however he got to that car park, it wasn't in his own car.'

'In which case,' Jo said. 'Let's find out if there are any cars registered to that company of his. If there are, we need to find out who they're registered to, the name of the keeper and the keeper's address. We also need to know if he's been using a hire car.'

Dorsey Zephaniah arrived and, seeing them deep in conversation, waited for an opportunity to interrupt.

'He could have parked his car somewhere else,' said Max. 'Travelled in on the metro or by bus, forced her into her own car, made her drive to where his car was parked, somewhere without CCTV, transferred her to it and driven off. That's what I'd do.' He paused, and then shook his head. 'Mind you, he'd have to have known that she was heading there in the first place.'

Dizzy raised her eyebrows.

'Remind me to keep an eye on you, Mr Nailor,' she said. She turned to Jo. 'This arrived for you in the post, Ma'am. It looked unusual. I thought it might be important.'

Chapter 49

Dizzy held an envelope in her left hand. She was wearing a pair of the white nitrile gloves provided for just such eventualities. In her right hand, she held another pair. Jo put the gloves on to receive the envelope.

She saw at once what Dizzy had meant. It was a standard buff envelope, but the name and address had been cut and pasted from a glossy magazine. Her name and correct title, Senior Investigator Joanne Stuart, had been used. Conscious of her colleagues moving back a pace, she felt gingerly around the edges of the envelope for telltale wires, then turned it over. Across the sealed flap in glossy yellow capitals were the words FOR YOUR EYES ONLY A.

'That's the James Bond film,' said Ram. 'Someone's printed out an image of the poster and cut out the title. You can tell because that diminutive letter A at the end was the British Board of Film Censors' rating.'

'You might want to let Forensics open that,' said Max. 'It may not be a letter bomb, but it could easily contain or have been impregnated with God knows what. Anthrax or ricin – it wouldn't be the first time.'

'Puts a whole new spin on poison pen letter,' Ram observed.

'Under the circumstances,' said Jo, 'I think we should find out what's in here sooner rather than later. Don't worry, I'll be careful.'

She took from her desk tidy the wafer-thin plastic ruler that she used as a paperknife, together with a pair of plastic tweezers.

'I really think you should wait!' said Max.

Ignoring him, Jo carried the envelope over to an empty desk beside the windows that looked out on to the Huron Basin. It was a calculated risk, one she was prepared to take. She slid the ruler beneath the top edge of the flap and held her breath as she drew it gingerly down, to the side and across, until the whole of the flap was released. She then teased the flap open with the tweezers and used them to widen the gap so that she could see inside. There appeared to be a single piece of paper, just over three inches square. She exhaled, and used the tweezers to ease it out. It was a portrait photograph on standard printer paper. Jo recognised the face immediately.

'Come and see this,' she said, holding it up in the air.

Max was the first to recognise it.

'That's Ginley,' he said. 'The reporter?'

Jo nodded. 'Anthony Ginley, the IPC investigative reporter.'

'That's the photograph on the IPC website,' said Ram.

'The question is, why has someone sent it to me?' asked Jo.

'More distraction,' Andy suggested.

'Unless someone else is the unsub,' said Ram. 'Ginley, for example. Or someone close to him has decided he's gone too far and is giving him up?'

'Hang on,' said Jo. 'You did the background check on Ginley and started to check on his whereabouts at the time the girls were abducted. I thought you said he was clean?'

Ram was suddenly the centre of attention. He shook his head sheepishly.

'I said I couldn't find anything suspicious about him,' he said. 'Or anything that linked him or his vehicles to the scene of any of the abductions. But I never said that he was definitely eliminated. And the mere fact that he's been investigating all of the cases means that he must have been visiting the campuses. But he hasn't yet been asked for alibis in relation to specific incidents because there didn't seem to be any grounds for that.'

'Shit!' said Jo. 'Have I become fixated on Malacott? Have I got this all wrong?'

'Hang on,' said Andy. 'Why has Malacott become our prime suspect, Jo?'

Jo put the picture of Ginley down on top of the envelope, and began to count off on the fingers of her left hand. 'Because he has previous, because he's linked with the universities, because he has an almost unhealthy obsession with victims of rape, because his sister, whom he abused, is the spitting image of at least one of the victims, because . . .'

'And we haven't yet asked him for any alibis for the evenings the girls went missing,' Max said.

'That's because we didn't have reasonable cause until now,' she replied defensively.

'Well you do now,' said Max. 'So why don't we proceed as planned, and at the same time get Detective Inspector Sarsfield to have a couple of his team question Ginley, based on you having received that photograph? That way nobody could accuse you of having tunnel vision, or of failing to follow up every lead.'

Jo picked up the photograph using the tweezers, put it back in the envelope, and handed it to Dorsey Zephaniah.

'Put this in an evidence envelope,' she said, 'and have someone from Forensics come and collect it. I want anything they can find: DNA, fingerprints, typeface, make of printer, anything. Tell them that it's a priority, an abduction.'

'And that if necessary – we'll pay for it to be brought forward,' said Harry Stone as he walked towards them. 'Whatever it is.'

'It's from the unsub, Boss,' Jo told him. 'A wind-up.'

'You can tell me all about it in my office,' he replied. 'I need a word with you, in private.'

He turned, and began walking towards the door.

'I'll be with you in a second, Boss,' she said.

She turned back to the conference screen, where DI Sarsfield waited patiently for them to tell him what was going on.

'I'm sorry about that, Gerry,' she said. 'I've got to go and have a word with Mr Stone. Max will explain. I'll see you at the Gold Command meeting at Central Park in . . .' She looked at her watch. 'Bloody hell! – thirty-three minutes' time.'

She turned, and dashed from the room.

***

'I'm sorry, Jo,' Stone said, 'but you'll have to attend the Gold Command Meeting without me.' He looked even more tired and drawn than usual. 'I don't know how much you've been told about my personal circumstances?'

'I only know that your mother is far from well, Boss,' she said, 'and your daughter has some issues.'

He massaged his temples with his thumbs, and then passed his hand over his forehead as though wiping something away.

'I've just had a call about my daughter. Half an hour ago, several passengers on the Victoria Line stopped her jumping under a tube train at Warren Street. She's been sectioned.'

Jo instinctively placed a hand on his arm. 'Oh Harry, I'm so sorry.'

'So am I,' he said. 'You've got your own problems, and here am I leaving you in the lurch. But don't worry, whatever you need from our side, you've got it. For a start I've contacted the AKEU, that's our Anti-Kidnap and Extortion Unit, and told them to get in touch with you and give you every possible support.'

'I'm sorry, Boss,' she said, 'I've never heard of them.'

'That's my fault,' he told her. 'You should have had a fortnight's induction while you were introduced to every aspect of the Agency. The AKEU is part of Investigations Command. Small but perfectly formed, like us.'

He smiled weakly.

'Unfortunately, your reputation had proceeded you and I had no hesitation in handing you the first investigation that came along. Now I'm playing catch-up. The AKEU have been handpicked for their experience in hostage and kidnap investigation, negotiation and release. Not just in the UK, but worldwide.'

'That's brilliant,' said Jo. 'I assumed I'd have to go cap in hand to GMP for that kind of support.'

'Anything else you need,' Stone said, 'just give whoever it is my mobile number, and I'll approve it. Any paperwork I'll sign retrospectively.'

'That's too big an ask, Boss,' she said. 'You can't put your career on the line for me.'

He shook his head.

'Look, Jo, my career hasn't got that long to run, and the way I'm feeling right now it wouldn't be that much of a disaster if I was forced to retire – far from it. So don't worry about me, just get this bastard and make my Christmas.'

Chapter 50

'So, SI Stuart,' said the Chief Constable, 'if I've understood you correctly, you want us to throw everything at this Malacott?'

The absence of Harry Stone had left her and a colleague from the AKEU who had dashed over from Ralli Quays in Salford as the only representatives of the lead agency, the NCA. Simon Levi was supposed to be on his way, but had been held up in the traffic made worse by torrential rain as frantic shoppers flooded into the city centre. The Chief Constable and Assistant Chief Constable, together with various operational commanders, including the Head of the Firearms Unit, were already assembled when she arrived. One of the deputy chief Crown Prosecution officers for the North West was also present.

At first Jo had been daunted by the presence of so many heavyweights, but as the meeting progressed she had become more confident. They had now reached the critical point, where the overall strategy had to be agreed and resources allocated.

'That's correct, Sir,' she replied. 'I accept that we have no direct evidence to link him to any of these crimes, but I'm sure that you'd agree that there is sufficient circumstantial evidence to warrant a concerted surveillance operation on him as a prime suspect, especially since we're talking about the abduction of a female whom we all agree is likely to be at serious risk of harm.'

'But you don't know that for a fact?' said the man from the CPS.

Naeem Khan, sitting beside Jo, raised his hand. 'I think we do,' he said. 'The evidence is pretty conclusive.'

The Head of Crime leaned forward. 'Remind us of your name,' he said, 'and what it is you do?'

'My name is Naeem Khan. I'm the on call officer in the Anti-Kidnap and Extortion Unit of the National Crime Agency. As I explained earlier, our job is to support agencies in the UK and worldwide in kidnap and hostage situations with strategic and tactical advice, and access to NCA resources as appropriate.'

'And what makes you think this woman is at risk of serious harm?' the ACC pressed, deftly ignoring the rebuke.

Jo was tempted to tell him that it was blindingly obvious.

Khan was far more tolerant. 'Firstly,' he said, 'because the abductor has gone to a lot of trouble to avoid detection. We have, for example, no idea how or where he first approached and took control of her. He wore a mask that was designed not only to disguise his face but to intimidate her, and taunt the police. And he clearly used force to prevent her from fighting back, calling for help or resisting when he made her get in the car and drive off in a controlled manner. Secondly, it is also a reasonable assumption that the abductor was behind the arrangement of flowers sent to SI Stuart, as a warning and or threat. And finally, there has been no ransom demand, or demand of any kind whatsoever. In our experience, the absence of such demands suggests that the abductor has a purpose other than extortion, blackmail or terrorism.'

'Such as?' said the Commander of the Tactical Firearms Unit.

'Other than extortion, the only other agreed categories are tiger kidnaps and vendetta kidnaps. The former have the intention of forcing a relative of the hostage to assist in a crime such as robbery.

Vendetta kidnaps, as the name implies, are used by criminals to retaliate or resolve a dispute. Since neither of these appears to apply in the case of Sally Warburton that leaves psychopathic ends such as sexual gratification or displays of omnipotence. Or, possibly, to strike fear into others who might pose a threat to the person or organisation behind the abduction. In either of these cases, there is seldom a positive outcome.'

'Meaning?'

'Meaning that the abductee will either be found dead or will never be seen again.'

There was a prolonged silence, finally broken by the Chief Constable. He turned to the Head of the Press Office. 'Where are we up to in engaging the assistance of members of the public?'

'Missing Persons have issued detailed descriptions and photos to all of the North West police forces,' she said. 'They have also been released via our Twitter and Facebook accounts. Radio appeals have already been broadcast. A joint GMP/NCA televised appeal and press conference has been arranged for three pm this afternoon.'

'SI Stuart,' he said, 'are there any firearms or public order implications surrounding this operation?'

Naeem Khan leaned close to Jo and whispered in her ear, before sitting back.

'No, Sir,' Jo said. 'We have no reason to believe that the abductor has a firearm, and neither Mr Khan nor our own behavioural psychologist believe that he would use one if cornered. On the contrary, the presence of a significant number of armed officers might present a greater danger to the victim. However, both I and my colleague Investigator Nailor are registered firearms officers, and have already received approval to carry sidearms during this operation.'

The Head of the Tactical Firearms Unit began to object, and was forestalled by his Chief Constable.

'So long as you have carried out a risk assessment, signed off by your superiors, SI Stuart,' he said, 'I'm content for my firearms officers not to be involved.'

The Chief Constable might just as well have added 'on your head be it,' thought Jo.

'Yes, Sir,' she replied, 'that is the case.'

He nodded grimly. 'Then I'm content for ACC Gates and Deputy Director Levi, when he finally arrives, to assume joint Gold Command, and for you, SI Stuart, to assume Silver Command, with DI Sarsfield to assume Bronze Command. Although, as I understand it, you also intend to operate in the field, SI Stuart?'

'That's correct, Sir,' Jo replied. 'DI Sarsfield and I will both be using command vehicles with integrated communications equipment.'

'Marked or unmarked vehicles?'

'Unmarked. I have secured two further unmarked Interceptor pursuit cars, and five marked vehicles, plus a paramedic, a forensics nurse and a Crime Scene Investigation Unit. ACC Gates has already agreed to provide a Tactical Aid unit in the event that we need to make enforced entry, search premises or pursue on foot.' She hesitated for a moment. 'However, I do have a specific request involving the potential use of air support.'

'Go ahead,' he said.

'As we speak, a tracker device is being placed on the suspect's car. However, we believe that he must have been using alternative vehicles to abduct his other victims. In the event that he did use an alternative vehicle and employed evasion tactics such that we lost visual contact, it would be essential to have air support on standby. More so, because we believe that he holds his victims in a well-hidden or remote location.'

The Chief Constable frowned.

'I can try to prioritise that, however, there are only four helicopters across the whole of the North West Air Operations Group, and that covers a vast area, not only Greater Manchester, but also Cheshire, Lancashire, Merseyside and North Wales.'

'I'm aware of that, Sir,' she began, but stopped when her colleague Khan raised his hand.

'In such cases, a helicopter can turn out to be over-intrusive,' he said. 'If the abductor becomes aware of the helicopter before he reaches the place where he's holding his victim, he could well abort and we may never find her. But I do have an alternative suggestion.'

'Which is?'

'We, the National Crime Agency, possess a number of UAVs – Unmanned Aerial Vehicles – which are used for a variety of purposes, including major drug investigations and kidnap and hostage rescue. I'm sure we can get one up here fairly quickly, but I understand that Merseyside Police and Greater Manchester Fire and Rescue already employ them. Would it be possible to ask for the loan of a UAV and a flight control operator?'

'That's a great idea, Naeem,' Jo muttered under her breath.

'That will not be necessary,' said the Chief Constable. 'We're currently trialling a SkyRanger drone. This would be an excellent opportunity for a live trial in the field.'

'Thank you,' Jo said. She looked at her notes. 'I have just one final request. I believe that we ought to have Dog Unit support in the form of one dog and handler.'

'Would that be a general-purpose dog or a specialist search dog, like a body dog?' asked the Head of Crime.

'General purpose,' Jo replied, hoping fervently that she was right. She dreaded having to face Abbie and tell her that Sally had been murdered, let alone informing Sally's brother and parents.

Chapter 51

'I'm sorry, Gerry,' said Jo, holding up her BlackBerry. 'I'll meet you in the foyer. I have to take this call – it's Abbie.'

He grimaced.

'Good luck with that,' he said as he headed for the stairs.

Jo took a deep breath and answered the call.

'Abbie,' she began.

'When were you going to tell me?' she yelled. 'We had to hear it on the radio, for God's sake!'

'Abbie,' said Jo. 'Please, calm down and let me explain.'

'Calm down? How the hell am I supposed to do that? The bastard that's been kidnapping and raping those students has got her, hasn't he? Hasn't he!'

Jo swore silently. That was not supposed to have been part of any of the briefings. Someone was going to pay.

'Abbie, either you calm down,' she said, 'and let me explain what we're doing to get Sally back safe and sound, or I'll end this call right now.'

She could hear Abbie arguing with someone, then a male voice replaced Abbie's.

'Miss Stuart, this is James Warburton,' he said. 'Sally's brother. Can you please tell me exactly what's going on?'

His voice was rich and authoritative as befitted a privately educated City trader. Jo wrestled with her emotions. She knew she had to set aside her feelings about his role as putative father for Abbie's baby. He was a victim. A dangerous man had abducted his sister. Right now that was all that mattered.

'I have just come from a meeting, James,' Jo said, 'with the Chief Constable and some of his commanders, the Crown Prosecution Service, and a colleague from the National Crime Agency. We're united in our determination to bring your sister back safe and sound as soon as possible.'

'What does that mean?' he asked. 'I'm sorry, but it sounds like a load of platitudes.'

'It means that we're following up specific leads and mobilising all of the relevant resources. We *will* find Sally.'

'You're saying you know who has got her?'

'I'm not going to repeat myself, James, because you'll only accuse me of giving you the brush-off. The truth is that I can't tell you anything more at this point because it might compromise the investigation. You wouldn't want that, would you?'

'No, but . . .'

'Look, James,' she said, 'I'm leading this investigation, so unless you want to hold it up, you really have to let me go right now. Where are you and Abbie at the moment – at Sally's house?'

'Yes.'

'Good. Well, please stay there. Two Family Liaison officers are on their way to you as we speak. They will be my sole point of contact with you. And I promise that I will keep you and Abbie informed, through them, of any major developments.'

'Well . . .'

'I'm sorry, James, but I have to go. Please try not to worry, and do your best to reassure Abbie. I promise we'll get your sister back.'

She pressed *end call* before he could respond, put her phone away and hurried to the lifts. Now all she had to do was deliver on her promises.

Chapter 52

Malacott's house was on a quiet leafy road just off the A56 in Prestwich, an upmarket town three miles and a lifetime away from Manchester city centre. It stood behind a low brick wall, and a row of beech trees that screened it from the road. The residents were sufficiently influential to have ensured that automatic barriers at each end of the street further protected their privacy, and there were traffic-calming measures designed to deter any boy racers who might slip through the net. It was 18.00hrs, six in the evening. The light from the street lamps and gaudy Christmas displays on the houses themselves was barely visible through the skeletal trees and the slanting rain.

There were four of them in the modified Audi Q7. The driver, the communications officer, Jo, Max, and a loggist whose role it was to record every single decision against which Jo, as Silver Command, could be held accountable up to seven years hence. The rear two seats had been folded to provide storage for their clothing and equipment.

'Remind me,' said Jo, 'how long is it he's been in there?'

'Since sixteen thirty,' said Max, 'according to the guys we replaced.'

They could hear the sound of Christmas music being piped around the house.

'What is that?' Jo asked.

The driver turned his head. 'That's *Slay Belles* by RuPaul,' he said. 'Interesting choice.'

The two investigators looked at each other.

'It's one of the top-selling Christmas albums this year,' the driver continued. 'I'm surprised you haven't heard it.'

'Well, at least we know the bugs are working,' said Jo.

They were sixty yards from the house, behind two parked cars. Another hundred yards ahead of them, beyond the house, was the second unmarked car, call sign X-Ray Zebra Sierra, containing DI Sarsfield, his Comms officer, loggist and Naeem Khan from the AKEU. An unmarked Interceptor pursuit car, call sign Tango One Seven One, was parked out of sight around the corner on the main road. Reconnaissance had established that the only exit from the rear of the property was via a garden gate on a path through the woods that led to Church Lane to the east, and Clough Lane to the west, both of which were also under observation. Four unmarked cars were discreetly hidden away awaiting instructions. Malacott was boxed in.

'He's done well,' said Max. 'Who'd have thought that line of work would buy a place like this?'

'It didn't,' said Jo. 'His mother died two years ago. Liver failure. She left the house to him because the daughter had buggered off to New Zealand. In any case, according to his sister, he was his mother's blue-eyed boy.'

The radio bleeped.

'Quebec Base, Quebec Base . . . Quebec One.' It was Ram, using the Quebec prefix they had agreed for all NCA officers engaged in the operation.

'Quebec One,' said Jo. 'Go ahead, Quebec Base.'

'We've established that there are two further vehicles registered to the target's company,' Ram said. 'Both are leased. The registered keeper is the company secretary. I've sent you the details.'

'Thank you, Base.'

Jo punched the back of the seat in front of her.

'I knew it!' she said.

The Comms officer peered around the side of his seat.

'I felt that, Ma'am.'

'Sorry,' she said. 'Can you open that message, please?'

He nodded, turned back and hunched over his keyboard.

'There you go, Ma'am,' he said.

The details appeared on the screen attached to the back of his seat. Jo pointed to the screen.

'One of them's a Vauxhall. There were fibres from a Vauxhall on Sareen Lomax's clothes,' she told Max. She read the keeper's address. 'Radcliffe. That's a stone's throw away from here. Can you map this address, please?'

The Comms officer tapped away at his keyboard. A street map appeared with an arrow over the address. Jo used her thumb and forefinger to zoom out until the map included their current position.

'Two and a half miles,' Jo said. 'That has to be the explanation. He's using one of those cars.'

'We should get a car over there,' said Max.

'Too late,' said their driver pointing to the screen. 'The target is on the move.'

A green blip pulsated on the map that he had now brought up. The tension in the car was palpable. They watched as the BMW nosed out of the drive and turned right towards Gerry Sarsfield's own 4x4. There was no need to let him know that Malacott was heading his way, their radios were on open channel.

'I have visual on the target,' Sarsfield said.

They waited for Malacott to reach the main road, where his left-hand indicator began to flash. As soon as he disappeared around the corner, Jo leaned forward.

'Go,' she said.

The driver started the engine, switched on the lights and set off.

'Tango, Tango One Seven One, the target is yours,' she said.

'Quebec One . . . understood,' Tango One Seven One replied. 'We have visual now. One male up. Can confirm it is the target. Repeat I have visual on the target.'

As the Audi approached the junction, Jo glanced in the rear-view camera display and watched as Gerry Sarsfield's car performed a U-turn and fell in behind them. At the same time, the final unmarked car entered the road in which Malacott's house stood and took up station in the spot he had just vacated.

'Do you really think he may have an accomplice?' asked Max. 'That he's acting as a decoy?'

'Like you, I have no idea,' she told him. 'I think it's unlikely, and Andy agrees. It doesn't fit the profile. But then the person who abducted me was an accomplice none of us knew existed.'

'Malacott's was the only vehicle at the house,' Max reminded her, 'and no voices were heard all the time he was under observation.'

'I know,' she said, 'but I'm not taking any risks. Not when a woman's life is in peril.'

She leaned into the microphone, and pressed the button. 'This is Quebec One. Juliet Two, please execute a clandestine search of the target's property to establish if our MisPer is present. Units Five through Juliet Nine, follow now. Maintain two-mile interval at all times between Juliet Five and Quebec One until instructed otherwise. Please confirm.'

'Quebec One, this is Juliet Two. Understood.'

'Quebec One, this is Juliet Five. Two-mile interval at all times. I confirm, you have a convoy.'

Jo released the button and shook her head.

'We also have a comedian,' she said.

'Two miles?' said Max.

'If the target decides to do a U-turn to throw any pursuers, I don't want him passing a line of marked cars. At least this way they'll have time to scatter into side roads if he does.'

'Good decision, Ma'am,' said their driver.

Before Jo could decide if she was being patronised, he pointed to the display console.

'I'd say the target was deploying evasion tactics.'

The blip that represented Malacott's car was on the roundabout at Junction 17 of the M60 ring road. However, instead of taking either of the slip roads to the west or the east, or going straight ahead across the roundabout towards Bury, he was heading back on himself, towards them. Jo pressed the send button.

'This is Quebec One,' she said. 'All units: prepare to take evasive action.'

Malacott seemed to have stopped at the lights. They waited to see what he would do next. The blip began to move.

'He's going back round,' muttered Max. 'The devious bastard. At least we know he has something to hide.'

'Quebec One, this is Tango One Seven One. I have a visual. I'm holding back until we have a clear sense of the target's route.'

The Comms officer pressed a key and pointed to the second of the larger screens.

'This is Tango One Seven One's dashcam,' he said.

The lead unmarked car had pulled into the Shell garage sixty yards from the roundabout.

'Do you think the target may have spotted him?' Jo asked.

'I doubt it,' the driver replied. 'Not with this rain and his wipers going.'

The traffic had slowed approaching the roundabout so they did not have to pull over themselves, but Jo realised that both they and the second unmarked car were getting perilously close to having to do so. To their relief, on the third pass, Malacott took the eastbound slip road on to the motorway. Tango One Seven One pulled out of the garage and resumed the pursuit.

'What are you going to do about the marked vehicles?' Max asked. 'If he pulls a similar trick at the Middleton turn off and doubles back on the opposite carriageway, he's going to pass them going the other way. He only has to put two and two together, and we're blown.'

Jo leaned forward and spoke to the Comms officer. 'Tell Juliet Five through Nine to pull over before the Shell garage at Junction 17 and await instructions,' she said.

As he did so, she pointed to the split-screen map displaying the tracker blip from Malacott's car.

'What's he doing now?' she demanded.

The blip had slowed dramatically. He seemed to be travelling in the inside lane. They watched as he suddenly pulled out, and sped up for half a mile, before moving back into the inside lane and slowing down again.

'At a guess,' said their driver, 'I'd say he's playing hide-and-seek in between articulated lorries. That way anyone following him would have to do the same and risk losing visual contact.'

They watched as Malacott's car approached Junction 18.

'He's got three choices,' said Max. 'To carry on towards Leeds, to head south towards East Manchester, Cheshire, and the Derbyshire Peaks, or go north on the M66.'

'Four choices,' Jo reminded him. 'He could double back on the M62, in which case you and I will need to duck out of sight.'

'He'll never clock us,' said Max, 'it's too dark, and what with all this rain . . .'

'No need,' said the driver. 'He's nipped on to the M66 north-bound slip road.'

'This is Quebec One,' said Jo. 'Juliet Five through Nine, proceed eastbound on the M62, and then northbound on the M66. Close up to within two miles of Quebec One, and continue to follow.'

For the next six miles, the only sounds in the car were background chatter as units confirmed their positions, the clack of the wipers and the hiss of tyres dispersing surface water. The driver had to continually adjust his speed as cars desperate to get home for Christmas cut in, spraying the windscreen with a grimy film of salt, muck and water.

'Junction One. Target leaving left, left, left,' said the Comms officer.

They stared at their screens.

'Where are you going, Sam?' muttered Max.

'He's got plenty of options,' said Jo. 'Bury, Ramsbottom, Nangreaves, Edenfield.'

'Not Bury,' the driver observed as they watched the blip turn right on to the A56.

'He's not going to his company secretary's place in Radcliffe either,' said Jo. 'Or if he is, he's going a roundabout route. How far are we from Junction 1?' she wondered, staring at the map on the screen.

'Less than a mile,' said the driver. 'Tango One Seven One should be just leaving the motorway.'

'You devious bugger!' she said.

'What?' said Max.

She pointed at the display. 'Look where he's going: Summerseat.'

'So what?'

'Firstly, there are dozens of ways out of there. Secondly, Bass Lane, where he's just turned into, is a single car width, with passing places all the way down. If he doubles back at the bottom, he's going to have all the time in the world to eyeball anyone following him.'

She leaned into the mike.

'Quebec One to Tango One Seven One. Go left,' she said, 'go left, then first right.'

'Tango One Seven One, left then first right,' came the calm reply. 'Rowlands Road.'

Jo sat back.

'There's no way we can cover all of the exits out of there,' she said. 'Not with unmarked cars. Thank God for that tracker.'

'How come you know so much about this place?' Max asked.

'Because it's a popular beauty spot. Abbie and I have been to a restaurant down here loads of times.'

'Target has stopped,' observed the Comms officer.

Sure enough, the green blip was stationary.

'Where is he exactly?' Jo asked.

The Comms officer zoomed in on the map.

'Summerseat garden centre. Looks like he's in their car park.'

Jo knew that she had to make a quick decision. They were approaching Junction One themselves. Tango One Seven One was just entering Railway Road, seconds from the garden centre. She leaned forward.

'Quebec One to Tango One Seven One, lay up south of the target location, with visual on the exit. Please confirm arrival.'

They waited with bated breath. Thirty seconds later, the radio came to life.

'Tango One Seven One,' came the reply. 'Stopping now. Have visual on exit.'

'What's he playing at?' Max wondered. 'It's a long way to come for a Christmas tree.'

'Which way do you want me to go, Ma'am?' asked the driver.

They were at the lights at the end of the slip road.

'Left, then right,' she said. 'The same way One Seven One went.' She studied the map. 'Then take the fourth on the right, at the bottom, Miller Street.'

She leaned into the mike again.

'X-Ray Zebra Sierra, please proceed to the junction of the B6214 with Newcombe Road, Summerseat. Juliet Five through Nine, lay up on the exit slip road at Junction 1 and await instructions.'

Gerry Sarsfield acknowledged the instruction, waited for Juliet Five to do the same, and then addressed Jo directly. He sounded put out.

'Quebec One,' he said. 'What's going on?'

Jo knew why Sarsfield was upset. After all, he was Bronze Command. By insisting on being right here, in the thick of the operation as Silver Command, she had muddied the waters, effectively giving him very little say in anything at all. It was time to redress that before it soured their relationship. She dared not let that happen, not in the middle of an operation as sensitive as this. And not with Gold Command listening in to every word that was spoken.

'Apologies, Bronze Command,' she said. 'It's been full on up here. I didn't want us parking behind One Seven One. If the target were to emerge from that garden centre, he'd make for us straight away. What I'm suggesting is that I wait on the opposite side of the River Irwell, and cover the exits on that side, and you cover the possibility that he might exit towards Greenmount, or Holcombe Brook. What do you think?'

When Sarsfield finally replied, he sounded mollified. 'I agree,' he said.

She sensed his hesitation. 'Go ahead,' she said.

'I was just thinking,' Sarsfield said. 'What if he's picking up a Christmas tree, some baubles, whatever? What if it isn't him?'

She tried hard not to let her irritation show. He had just articulated the unthinkable that she had managed not to dwell on until now. 'Then we'll have to deal with it, and go back to square one,' she said.

Beside her, Max pulled a face and whispered in her ear. 'If it isn't him, I'll eat my hat.'

'You haven't got one,' she whispered back.

'Then I'll buy one specially.'

The driver ventured cautiously on to the ancient stone bridge over the Irwell. The river was seriously swollen and in spate. On their right, the Waterside pub and restaurant spanned the river, forming the left wall of the bridge. On the opposite side, a muddy, swirling, white-crested torrent slapped up and over the bank on either side. On the far side of the bridge, both the road and courtyard of the Spinney's Mill apartments were already a foot deep in water.

'It'll be a bloody miracle if that bridge holds out much longer,' said the Comms officer.

After three hundred yards, Jo instructed the driver to turn off alongside a park and children's playground, and then stop. She leaned forward and tapped the Comms officer on the shoulder.

'Can we have Tango One Seven One's dashcam up again, please?'

The five of them watched rivulets of rain running down the windscreen of the Interceptor car, interspersed by brief moments of clarity as the wipers kicked in. It was one of those watching-paint-dry occasions with which all police officers were only too familiar. Jo stared at the screen, willing something to happen.

Chapter 53

'How long has it been?' Jo asked.

'Five minutes,' Max told her.

It had felt like an eternity. They had seen two cars and two vans leave the garden centre. Both vans, one of which had driven right past the Interceptor, had the tips of Christmas trees protruding from open rear doors. The cars, both of which had driven past their Audi Q7, had two women in one of them, and a male and female with two young children in the other. Malacott's car had still not moved.

'Something's wrong,' said Jo. 'I can feel it.'

Her hands were clammy. She wiped them on her trousers.

'I agree,' Sarsfield chipped in. 'What do you propose we do about it?'

'I think we should send Tango One Seven One into the car park,' she said, 'and have Quebec Three go inside and see if she can spot him.'

A female voice broke in.

'Silver Command, this is Gold Command. Might that not be premature?'

Jo cursed silently. Tactical decisions were down to her and Gerry Sarsfield, not Helen Gates. They were the ones on the spot, stuck out here in the pouring rain.

'That may well be, Gold Command,' she replied, with a calm that belied her inner turmoil. 'But One Seven One is an unmarked car. The officer I have in mind to enter the garden centre is female and not known to the target. I think it highly unlikely he would suspect either her or One Seven One. On the other hand, if he has slipped us, every minute that passes, he could be further and further away.'

There was a long pause.

'Your decision, Silver Command,' came the response.

The loggist bent to his pad and began to write. Jo leaned in to the mike. She was not going to be accused of going it alone.

'Bronze Command,' she said. 'Where do you stand on this?'

She imagined Gerry Sarsfield pulling a face and cursing her. Helen Gates was his Boss. Jo knew that she had placed him in an unenviable position. He wanted to share the decision-making: this was his big chance. It was time he manned up. Squeaky balls time. She could hear him squirming.

'I accept the rationale for your decision,' he said at last.

She had to admit it was a smart response. He had managed to slide out of siding with either of them. Beside her, Max shook his head but held his tongue, mindful of the loggist beside him.

'Tango One Seven One,' Jo said. 'This is Quebec One. Please proceed to the car park. Let me know when you're parked with visual on the target vehicle, without compromising your anonymity.'

One minute passed.

'Quebec One, this is Tango One Seven One. I'm in position. I have visual on the target vehicle. The target is not present.'

'Quebec Three,' Jo said. 'Get in there, and see if you can spot him. Wear your earpiece and lapel camera. Make as though you're buying something, and for God's sake don't wear your NCA cagoule!'

'As if.'

'I heard that,' said Jo.

'Sorry, Ma'am,' said the hapless NCA officer. 'I meant to say, message received and understood.'

'That was a bit harsh,' whispered Max as they waited for the pictures to come through.

'It's easily done when it's pouring down like this,' Jo retorted. 'You reach back on autopilot, grab your cagoule, shrug it on and skip through the raindrops with POLICE emblazoned across your back. We've all done it.'

'Here we go,' said the Comms officer, pointing to one of the split screens.

They watched as Quebec Three dashed to the conservatory-style entrance, stepped beyond the automatic doors and paused before an impressive display of blue and silver Christmas trees. Which way to go? Left into the apparently empty plant hall, or right into the indoor shop? She went right, squeezing past two women standing before a display of poinsettias, and into the right-hand aisle, full of seasonal cushions, cards and baubles. It was empty. The camera wobbled as she bent, picked up a blue shopping basket and placed a cushion in it.

'Clever girl,' said Max.

Jo elbowed him. 'Officer,' she said. 'Clever officer.'

Three aisles and two dead ends later, Quebec Three reached the central display area. It was surprising how few people she had passed, given the number of cars in the car park. A picket fence surrounded the entrance to Santa's Grotto. A mini Big Wheel took centre stage. A gnome stood in the mock ticket office. The door to the grotto was closed.

'Keep going,' said Jo, as much to herself as to the NCA officer.

They watched as she sped through a winter wonderland replete with life-sized polar bears and penguins, a bandstand with Father Christmas musicians, and a food and deli area, before arriving at the cafe, which was closed. She turned and hurried to the Pay Here Zone. There were five people queueing at the two tills. Malacott was not one of them.

'This is Quebec Three,' said the NCA officer. 'He's not here.'

'The toilets,' said Jo. 'You haven't checked the toilets.'

They heard Quebec Three curse under her breath, before turning on her heels and dashing back towards the cafe. They could hear her heavy breathing and the sound of the doors banging as they watched her slamming them back. One, in the men's, was locked. She entered the neighbouring cubicle, climbed on the seat and levered herself up. Her lapel camera was pressed up against the cubicle partition. The screen was a blurry mass of beige.

'Whoops! Sorry, sir,' they heard her say. 'Police.' She began to climb down. 'Nothing to worry about. You carry on.'

She jogged back to the entrance, turned right, and scanned the plant hall.

'This is Quebec Three,' she said. 'He's definitely not here. I repeat, the target is absent.'

'We could check their CCTV,' said Max. 'If he's been in there, they'll definitely have picked him up.'

'I'll get Juliet Seven to come and do that,' Jo told him. 'They can carry out a thorough search at the same time. But you know as well as I do, this means he's done a switch. We've lost him.'

She issued instructions to the Tactical Aid team waiting in Juliet Seven.

'It can only have been one of those two vans with the Christmas trees,' Max said. 'Both Tango One Seven One and us had a good look at the occupants of those cars.'

Another voice broke in. It was Gerry Sarsfield.

'This is Bronze Command,' he said. 'Negative to that, Quebec One. Both of the vans you described exited from Summerseat on to the B6214 from Newcombe Road, turning right towards Holcombe Brook. We had close visual on both. We double-checked the dashcam footage on both. In neither was the target present, unless he was lying down beneath one or other of the Christmas trees.'

Jo stared at the map, trying to suppress the panic that was threatening to engulf her.

'It's about three hundred and fifty yards from the car park across fields to Higher Summerseat, or ninety or so yards to Hall Street,' she said. 'Perhaps he had another vehicle parked on one of those?'

'It's possible,' Max agreed. 'But those fields are going to be a quagmire after all this rain.'

'There is another possibility, Ma'am,' said the driver twisting in his seat.

'Go on,' she said.

'Between us spotting that the target had stopped moving, and Tango One Seven One confirming visual on the car park exit, thirty-five seconds elapsed. Even allowing for ten seconds of visual contact by Tango One Seven One on a car travelling away from that exit, it would give the target twenty-five seconds to transfer to another vehicle and drive away. I could do that comfortably in fifteen.'

It wasn't what Jo wanted to hear, but she knew that he was right. It also meant that Malacott would have had time to get out of the valley in which Summerseat lay before Gerry Sarsfield's vehicle had taken up station. Besides, he would have had four other exit points that did not involve passing vehicles associated with the operation. The silence in the car and over the network was oppressive. Everyone was listening. Waiting for her decision. She tapped the Comms officer's shoulder to ensure his attention, and then leaned into the mike.

'This is Silver Command,' she said. 'I'm about to send details of two vehicles associated with the target to every officer associated with this operation. If either of them is identified, I need to know immediately. Gold Command, could you please ensure that every car fitted with Automatic Number Plate Recognition within a twenty-mile radius of my current location is alerted to look out for the licence plates, together with priority analysis of static ANPR camera footage for the past fifteen minutes.'

While she had been talking, the Comms officer had picked up on her instruction, located Ram's email and prepared to send it as instructed. Jo nodded to him.

'Sending now,' she said.

'Understood,' said Helen Gates, the Gold Commander. 'What will you do if he's using false plates?'

What I'm doing now, Jo was tempted to reply. *Pray.*

'In addition to notifying any sighting of the two licence plates,' Jo replied, 'I request notification of any vehicles meeting the description of those vehicles that are believed to be bearing false number plates.'

'Understood,' Gates responded. 'However, if the plates are cloned, there's no way they're going to be picked up without a stop and search.'

Jo already knew that. It didn't help to have it spelled out.

'Then we'll have to hope they haven't been cloned,' she said. 'Given the trouble he's gone to in order to avoid being followed, I doubt that he would want to draw attention to himself by using either false or cloned plates.'

'You had better hope you're right, Quebec One,' said Gates.

There was an uncomfortable silence, during which they watched as Juliet Seven overtook them at speed, spraying water all over the windscreen and side of the Audi before swinging into the garden centre car park. At least if he was hiding in there they would soon find out, Jo reflected. They would also know if there was CCTV covering the car park that might have caught him switching cars.

'Gold Command,' she said. 'What is the possibility of deploying air support?'

'Checking now,' came the brusque reply.

Thirty nervous seconds went by.

'No helicopter support available at present,' Gates said. 'Home-based India Nine Nine is dealing with a ten-car pile-up on the M6. Merseyside is tied up with a missing child search. Cheshire is experiencing technical problems. North Wales is unable to fly due to severe weather conditions, and none of the fixed wings available to the region are able to fly for the same reason. Even if they could, it's unlikely they would be able to see much with the low cloud cover and torrential rain.'

'Presumably paramedic and motorway police are also dealing with the pile-up?' Jo said. 'How soon might India Nine Nine be free to support this operation?'

'Wait, please,' said Gates.

Another thirty seconds passed.

'An estimated ten minutes on station, plus twelve minutes flying time to your current position, Quebec One,' Gates told her.

Twenty-two minutes. Given the current traffic conditions, that was time enough for Malacott to travel another seven miles or so in any direction. Not that they knew where he was right now, or what they were looking for.

There was a faint squeal of leather as Max eased back in his seat. Beside him, the loggist sat, biro poised. The radio crackled. Rain drummed on the panoramic roof. A new form of water torture.

Jo felt a cold sweat coming on. They were waiting. Gold Command in Central Park, her colleagues on the Quays, dozens of officers in the cars and vans. Waiting for her to make up her mind. Wondering how she was going to dig herself out of this hole. She was beginning to think the unthinkable. That she would have to abort the operation.

Then the radio burst into life.

Chapter 54

'Juliet Seven to Silver Command. We have CCTV of the target arriving in the car park at nineteen oh seven, transferring to another vehicle and then leaving. Second vehicle was out of camera shot within twenty seconds.'

'Details of the vehicle?' Jo demanded.

He read out the licence number. 'That's a white BMW 1 Series, sports hatch.'

Jo gave a silent prayer of thanks. That was one of the two cars registered to Malacott's company.

Another voice broke in. It was Helen Gates.

'Silver Command, we have ANPR capture by a Lancashire Force static camera of said vehicle three minutes ago leaving the A56 west of Haslingden, on to the B232 towards Blackburn.'

Gates followed this with the exact coordinates.

Jo tapped the driver on the shoulder. 'Go!' she said.

As he set off, she leaned into the mike. 'Tango One, Bronze Command, please go immediately to those coordinates and pursue until visual contact with the target vehicle has been established. We will be right behind you. Juliet Seven please secure that CCTV footage as evidence, leave one officer with the abandoned target vehicle, and then follow. All other operational vehicles proceed to the coordinates on your screens. Immediate Priority. I repeat, Immediate Priority. This is a blue light run.'

She sat back and glanced at Max. He smiled grimly and nodded. No words required. She had held her nerve, and now they were back on track.

At speeds touching seventy miles an hour, despite the driving rain, they hurtled up the A56. Way ahead of them they could just make out the flashing blue lights of X-Ray Zebra Sierra, and a mile or so back the convoy of support vehicles. Within three minutes they joined the M66 for a short stretch, where they now touched eighty.

'I daren't go any faster, or we may aquaplane,' the driver told them.

'Given where the BMW was when it was pinged by that camera, he must be sticking to the limits to avoid attention,' Max observed. 'At this rate, we should catch up with him in another ten minutes or so.'

'Oh, God!' said Jo.

'What's the matter?' he asked.

She shook her head and began to speak into the mike. 'Gold Command, this is Silver Command. Please ask the Lancashire Force to instruct all vehicles to report any sightings of the target vehicle, but on no account to stop it. I repeat, on no account are they to stop or follow the target vehicle.'

'That has already been done, Silver Command,' came the cool reply. It felt like a rebuke.

'I should have thought about that straight away,' Jo muttered as she sat back. 'It's textbook.'

'Don't beat yourself up, Jo,' Max replied. 'It looks like your bet on Malacott being the unsub has paid off. That's all that matters.'

'Finding Sally Warburton safe and sound,' she said, '*that's* what really matters. That, and putting him away for good.'

Jo wiped the condensation from the nearside window and peered out. They were now speeding down the slip road towards the B6232. There was a sudden squeal of brakes, and they were all thrown violently forward. The seat belt bit into Jo's ribs as she braced herself against the back of the seat in front. The driver cursed as he wrestled with the wheel, pumping the brakes as the car aquaplaned in towards a tanker straddling both carriageways. At the last moment, the driver brought it under control, steered it on to the hard shoulder and passed the tanker. They could see the white face of the driver staring down at them as they sped by at close to fifty miles an hour.

'Sorry about that, Ma'am,' said the driver. 'Stupid bastard must have seen our lights at the last moment and decided to change lanes. Realised he'd made a mistake and jammed his brakes on.'

Jo knew from experience that this was one of the inevitable hazards of a pursuit. Civilian drivers thinking they were doing you a favour, and making a stupid manoeuvre. She rubbed her bruised ribs, thankful for the slimline body armour beneath her cagoule.

'Don't worry,' she said, 'no harm done. You did a great job.'

They were now on a single carriageway high up on the moors, with 50mph signs and reminders that this was a stretch with record injuries and deaths from dangerous driving. They had now caught up with Bronze Command, and were travelling six car lengths behind. Less from any danger that they might collide than from the spray thrown up by the other 4x4. Gerry Sarsfield must have spotted them in his mirror.

'Good to have you with us, Silver Command,' he said. 'The target must be on the outskirts of Blackburn by now. If we don't catch up with him soon, we could easily lose him once he gets into the city.'

'I agree, X-Ray Zebra Sierra,' said Jo. 'But there will be more cameras and more patrol cars, therefore more chance of him being sighted.'

'I think we should cancel our blues and twos now,' he said. 'Just in case he's closer than we think.'

'Agreed, Bronze Control,' she replied.

It was eerie up here without the flashing blue lights. Clouds the colour of slate obliterated the tops of the moors. A north-westerly wind drove the rain hard against the windscreen, forcing the wipers to battle incessant swathes of water. It was pitch black outside, apart from glimpses of the rear red lights of X-Ray Zebra Sierra, and sudden blinding flashes of halogen headlights as cars sped by on the other side.

The excitement that had come with the reported sighting of the BMW had slowly evaporated, and Jo sensed an air of despondency settling over the operation. It was Christmas Eve, and there were forty-two officers and civilian staff out here wondering if this woman from the NCA had brought them on a wild goose chase. She knew that she ought to say something to energise them. Someone beat her to it.

'Silver Command, this is Gold Command. Target vehicle sighted at the Blackburn Beehive Roundabout, entering the Walker Industrial Estate in Guide. Coordinates fifty-three degrees forty-three minutes forty seconds north, two degrees twenty-six minutes fifty-five seconds west.'

Jo stared at the map on the screen in front of her.

'Two miles straight ahead of us,' said the driver.

Max pointed with his finger. 'Just beyond where we cross the M65 roundabout. Where's he headed?'

'The industrial estate? The Shadworth estate?' Jo said. 'It must be one of the two, or he'd have used the motorway.'

'Gold Command,' she said. 'How was the target vehicle sighted?'

'Silver Command, by a North West Motorway Patrol car parked in The Willows pub restaurant car park, watching cars enter and leave the roundabout.'

'One minute to go,' said the driver.

'This is Silver Command,' said Jo. 'Bronze Command, please pull in and wait for us in The Willows car park. All marked cars maintain a discreet distance from Quebec One until further notice.'

She turned to Max. 'I don't want him seeing a convoy on his tail.'

'I get that,' he replied. 'But if he's holed up in there somewhere, we may need them to flush him out.'

'It's not about flushing him out,' she told him. 'It's about locating Sally Warburton.'

Max grunted and stared straight ahead. The tension had ramped up again. Everybody, she realised, would be getting edgy. It was her job to keep them focused.

'Gold Command,' she said, 'what is the current status of India Nine Nine?'

She had her reply in less than fifteen seconds.

'India Nine Nine is still on station. Expected time of departure ten minutes.'

Including a flying time of twelve minutes, that meant it would be at least twenty-two minutes before it arrived.

They were approaching the roundabout over the motorway. The rain had eased a little, and she guessed that the wind must have dropped. The traffic was slower now and bunching up. It was tempting to use the lights and siren, but far too risky.

'There's the traffic car,' said the Comms officer, pointing.

The Willows stood on a bend between the two roundabouts. A BMW estate car was parked close to the exit, its distinctive blue and yellow paintwork bright in their headlights. Gerry Sarsfield's unmarked 4x4 was parked beside it.

'Pull in,' Jo commanded.

The Motorway Patrol officer was standing by the rear passenger window of the Bronze Command vehicle talking to Gerry Sarsfield. Jo pulled up her hood, opened her door and went to join them.

'Well spotted,' she said. 'Do you think he saw you?'

The officer shrugged.

'I didn't notice him look at me – he was concentrating on the roundabout ahead. And it was raining harder than this. But I'd be surprised if he didn't see me. After all, this car is hardly inconspicuous, is it? One of the reasons we park here is to remind them to slow when they come off the motorway.'

'Are you local?'

'Yes, Ma'am.'

Jo pointed towards the industrial estate.

'What's it like in there?'

'Modern industrial units, warehouses, some manufacture – plastics, drugs, food. There are a couple of empty properties. At the far end, there's a sports centre, the local primary school, school fields, some empty land and then the council estate. Two thousand people. Part tenants, part right to buy. A pub, a small shopping precinct, some lock-ups. It's got a reputation for being one of the most deprived in the country. There are some good people on there, community-minded. But they've got more than their fair share of drug-dealing, alcohol abuse and antisocial behaviour to contend with.'

The radio in Sarsfield's car crackled. It was Helen Gates.

'Bronze Command, Silver Command, where have you both gone? I'd appreciate a sitrep please.'

'This is Bronze Command,' said Sarsfield. 'We're both parked up by the Beehive Roundabout. Will have a response for you imminently.'

He looked up at Jo and raised his eyebrows.

'Your call,' he said.

'*Our* call,' she told him, conscious of the loggist in the back of Sarsfield's car. 'I want your agreement on this.'

He frowned.

'On what?'

She took a deep breath.

'I propose that we box off all of the exits from the industrial estate and the housing estate. If he's in there, we'll find him. If she's in there, we'll find her.'

'I agree,' said Naeem Khan. 'The empty buildings and the lock-ups should be the first priority.'

'That will require a minimum of eight vehicles, Ma'am,' said the traffic officer.

'We'll have none left over to search for his car,' Sarsfield pointed out. 'They'll have to do it on foot. That could take forever.'

'I'll watch this roundabout,' said the traffic officer. 'And I'm sure Division will be willing to spare a couple of cars and a motor-cyclist if your Boss asks them nicely.'

Jo leaned into the open window and spoke across Sarsfield to the man sat between him and the loggist.

'That drone,' she said, 'can you fly it in this?'

'The rain is not the problem, Ma'am,' he replied. 'The wind may be. I can't operate it over forty mph, or if it's gusting over fifty-five mph, but I can soon tell you.'

'Do that,' she said.

She watched as the flight operator exited the vehicle and went round to open the trunk. She joined him and sheltered beneath the trunk lid as he slid a black metal case towards him. Inside was a narrow brown rucksack. From this he eased out what looked like a white metal spider with folded legs. Beside it was a small device, which he switched on, holding it above his head into the wind.

'This is a portable anemometer,' he told her. 'It won't tell me what's going on at a thousand feet, but it's better than nothing.'

Jo found herself crossing her fingers as he lowered the device and held it close to his face. He turned, and looked at her.

'It's close, Ma'am,' he said, 'but I'm prepared to give it a try. However, I have to warn you that if I do fly this, you won't be able to call up a helicopter until we've effected a safe recovery.'

'I understand,' she said.

Jo turned to look across at the industrial estate. Flashes of light from passing cars speeding past the huge silver dome on the round-about lit the underside of menacing clouds. In her mind's eye, she could see Sally Warburton's pretty face, Susanne Hadrix's twisted body and the mask that Sally's abductor had worn. Jo wiped the rain from her face and turned to face the flight operator.

'We don't have time to wait,' she said. 'Let's do it.'

Chapter 55

Jo watched as the flight operator huddled over the tablet. It had two split screens, one of which he used to guide the SkyRanger by touch across the map, while the other provided a constant stream of flight data. He wore headphones connecting him with the command station in Manchester to which telemetry information was being beamed. Outside the vehicle stood an observer making sure that there were no obstructions or potential dangers to human life or property. Jo didn't understand any of it. All she cared about was the incredibly crisp video footage from the eyeball camera slung beneath the UAV.

The operator had been searching zonally for nine minutes now, from a height of one thousand feet. It was five hundred feet below the approved minimum height, he told her, but the cloud cover was so low it would have been pointless otherwise. She had seen the logist recording the exchange. If anything went wrong, her decision would come back to haunt her.

The search had begun at the centre of the area covered by the industrial park and council estate, and was working outwards. Her eyes hurt from straining to identify white vehicles that might be the target car. Each time one was spotted, the camera zoomed in. So far they had had five hits, all of them negative. The radio crackled into life.

'Quebec One, this is Gold Command. India Nine Nine has left station and is proceeding to your coordinates. ETA seven minutes. Please advise.'

Jo tapped the flight operator on the shoulder, and mimed for him to lift his headphones.

'Did you get that?' she asked.

He nodded, his eyes still glued to the tablet.

'So, what do you think?'

'There's not a lot to choose between this and the helicopter,' he replied. 'They have a loudspeaker system and a thermal imager, but on the other hand, this has the advantage of stealth. As soon as the helicopter turns up, you'll have lost the element of surprise. He'll be able to hear it even from inside those buildings, whereas this . . .' He didn't need to elaborate.

She looked across at Gerry Sarsfield who, having exchanged his seat in his 4x4 with Max, was outside, leaning into the open passenger window and listening in.

'What do you think, Bronze Command?' she asked.

He shrugged.

'It's a close call, Ma'am.'

It was the Ma'am that did it. The insinuation of seniority when he knew full well they were of equal rank, and that it was as much his call as hers. She looked at Naeem Khan. He was shaking his head. She gritted her teeth.

'Gold Command, this is Silver Command. Please ask India Nine Nine to hold off, circle out of visible and audible range from our coordinates and await instructions.'

There was a pause.

'Are you sure about this, Silver Command?' said Gates. 'India Nine Nine reports only twenty-seven minutes available flight time before it'll have to return to base to refuel.'

'Understood,' said Jo. 'I *am* sure, Gold Command, and I will be sure to advise of any change in the situation in good time.'

She heard Gerry Sarsfield suck air in between his teeth, in a far too obvious expression of dissent. Presumably for the sake of both the loggist and Helen Gates.

'Do you have a problem with that, Bronze Command?' she said, staring straight at him.

Sarsfield shook his head sheepishly.

'For the record,' Jo said, 'Bronze Command is shaking his head.'

She switched her attention back to the screen. A tense three minutes passed, during which the air could have been cut with a knife.

'What's that?' she said, pointing to a white dot in the top left of the screen.

The flight operator touched the screen with his index finger, and then used two fingers to zoom in. The rear half of a white hatchback protruded from beneath the canopy of a small industrial building.

'Can you get the licence number?' Jo asked, her heart beginning to pump hard.

She watched with bated breath as the drone swooped low, and the operator continued to zoom. Even before the number plate filled the screen, she knew that it was the car from the garden centre car park.

'This is Silver Command,' she said, struggling not to shout. 'Target vehicle located, I repeat, target vehicle located. Stand by!' She turned to the flight operator. 'Can you back up a bit so that we can see the whole of the complex? What is it, anyway?'

'It looks like a series of large industrial locks-ups,' he replied. 'Big enough to take a small container.'

A plan of action took shape in Jo's head. She would need the Tactical Aid Search and Entry team, the paramedic and the forensics nurse, the CSI team, and at least two cars, one at each end of the row of lock-ups. The rest would have to watch the exits from the industrial park in case he tried to escape. Assuming he was still there.

There was a shout and someone banged on the roof. She ducked her head to look beyond the loggist and out of the offside window. It was the UAV observer. He was pointing into the sky, away to the east, talking into his throat mike. She could not see anything, but she could hear it. The growl of an engine. The sound of blades beating the air into submission. India 99. Coming closer. Threatening to ruin everything.

Chapter 56

'Gold Command,' Jo shouted. 'This is Silver Command. Please instruct India 99 to abort, I repeat, India 99 to abort, immediately.'

'Too late,' said the flight operator, pointing to the screen. '*I'm going to have to abort. I can't risk fouling that helicopter.*'

'Don't you dare,' she said. 'Can't you hover nearer the ground?'

He shook his head. 'I'm sorry, even if I did, the down draught from those rotors is going to slam my UAV into the ground. I've no option.'

She cursed as the drone swung back towards them, and they lost sight of the lock-ups. The observer hammered on the roof again. The video stilled as the drone went into hover mode and then swung back towards the lock-ups. Helen Gate's imperious voice burst from the radio.

'Silver Command, this is Gold Command. India 99 has aborted as per your instruction and is returning to base. I hope you know what you're doing, SI Stuart.'

Jo cursed again. Not just at the deliberate use of her name, but because she had never intended the helicopter to leave, only to back off. Before she could reply, Gerry Sarsfield was shouting in her ear and pointing at the screen.

'They've spooked him!'

The roller door of the lock-up had retracted and was now closing again. A man stood in front of it, staring into the sky. The camera zoomed. It was Malacott. Wild-eyed, desperate, confused. He ran towards his car. Stopped. Started again. They watched as he ran around the side of the carport towards the rear of the lock-ups.

'Stay with him,' Jo ordered. She grabbed the mike. 'This is Silver Command. Target located. Juliet Six, Seven, Eight and Nine proceed immediately to . . .' She stared at the screen and read off the coordinates for the lock-up. 'And wait for me. All other units, hold your position and await instructions.'

She turned to DI Sarsfield.

'I'm going to that lock-up with Nailor. Can you stay here and direct the operation to secure Malacott? I'll use your car.'

'Fair enough,' he said, as she opened the door and got out. He watched her sprint to his car and called after her.

'Good luck, Jo!'

There was a knot in the pit of her stomach. She knew exactly what he meant.

———⌣———

'They got here fast,' said Max, but Jo was already out of the car.

There were four vehicles waiting in a V-formation outside the lock-up. A van containing the Tactical Aid Search and Entry team, the police dog van, the paramedic and forensics nurse, and the CSI team. Jo spoke to the Tactical Aid inspector.

'I need that opening now.'

'Leave it with me,' he replied.

'I'd like to go after Malacott,' Max told her, 'with the dog team.'

'Good idea,' she said. 'Clear it with Sarsfield.'

He grinned, checked that his earpiece was secure and began talking into his throat mike as he moved away.

One of the enforcer team was trying to lever open the roller door so that a colleague could crawl under it and find the release switch. He sat back on his heels.

'They've got security locks,' he said. 'We'll need the MVT.'

'Metal vapour torch,' the inspector explained to Jo, 'developed for the US military.'

'How long will it take?' she asked.

'Seconds,' he assured her. 'Like a knife through butter.'

Max was already walking fast past the white hatchback with the dog leading the way, his handler close behind him. The enforcer returned, holding what looked like the handle of a black regulation torch into which he was clipping a shiny silver cylinder some six inches long. He lowered the visor attached to his helmet and approached the doors.

'We need to step well back,' said the inspector.

His colleague held the MVT against the doors at head height, close to the right-hand corner. He pressed a button. A two-second burst of red and orange flame lit up the entire area. Sparks flew and the enforcer disappeared in a thick, white cloud of smoke. He ejected the cartridge and clipped another into place, repeating the operation three times, then stood back, studying the perfect ring of holes.

Jo's throat and nasal passages stung, while her mouth tasted of burnt metal.

'Bloody hell!' she said.

'Copper, aluminium, magnesium and liquid oxygen,' said the inspector. 'Brilliant, isn't it?'

The enforcer took a small hammer from his belt and struck the door at the centre of the ring. The steel plate fell away, leaving a six-inch hole. He reached his arm inside, felt for the cord attached to the manual release and pulled it. Seconds later, the door was open.

'This is Silver Command,' Jo said. 'We've found her.'

Chapter 57

A ceiling strip light lit the room. There were rugs on the floor, photos on the wall, a clothes rack with wire hangers, and a king-size bed.

Sally Warburton lay naked in the centre of the bed, hands secured with cable ties to a Gothic-style iron bedhead, feet tied with rope to the bedposts. There was a set of headphones on her head, a mask over her eyes and a gag in her mouth. She was thrashing from side to side, struggling to free herself. There was a pungent smell unconnected with the burning metal.

'What is that?' Jo asked, resisting the temptation to rush in. 'Do we need a biohazard kit?'

'It smells like bleach,' said the crime scene investigator. 'He's probably tried to destroy trace evidence, though with all this in here, I'd say he was wasting his time.'

'Is it safe to go in?'

'It's your call,' he said, 'but I reckon so. Gloves on, masks on, keep to the left of the bed and keep the numbers to an absolute minimum.'

'Right,' said Jo. 'Just you, me, and . . .' She turned and beckoned to the forensics nurse. 'With me,' she said. 'The rest of you, wait here.'

'One photograph,' she told the CSI, 'then I want you to hang back till we've got a sheet on her and the blindfold off. I don't want her seeing a man staring at her when that mask comes off.'

They stood beside the bed.

'Poor love, she must be terrified,' said the nurse.

As Jo began to remove the headphones, the young woman froze.

'It's alright, Sally,' Jo said. 'I'm Jo Stuart. I'm a police officer. You're safe now. A nurse is going to cover you with a thin sheet and then remove your blindfold and your gag.'

The gag was of a bondage type Jo had last seen on the body of a murder victim. It had small holes to allow the wearer to breathe, but not talk. Sally Warburton made a pitiful whimpering noise as the blindfold was removed. She stared back at them with wild frightened eyes that flicked from side to side. Gradually they settled.

Jo gestured the CSI forward.

'Can you cut those ties and untie her legs, and do what you have to do to secure trace evidence. I'd like her out of here, in that ambulance, and back to St Mary's as quickly as possible.'

She slipped off her own mask.

'My colleague, Helen, is going to untie you now, Sally,' Jo said. 'Then she's going to give you some paper briefs, a paper gown and some booties to slip on. She will also cover your hands. Then she will take you outside to an ambulance, and you'll be driven straight to hospital so that we can have you checked over. Do you understand?'

The young woman nodded and began to reply. Her throat was parched, her words emerging as a series of croaks.

'I don't think he touched me,' she said. 'Not like you think.'

'Good,' said Jo. 'Nevertheless, we need to be sure, for your sake.' She leaned closer. 'Did you see his face at all?'

Sally shook her head.

'No, he was wearing a mask.'

'We know,' said Jo. 'Did he say anything to you?'

'Only when he came up behind me in the car park.'

'What did he say?'

'He grabbed my arm and put something sharp against my neck. "I have a knife," he said. "Do as I say and you won't get hurt."'

'That's it? Nothing else?'

'He told me to get in my car, to drive, and where to go.' She paused. 'There was something else though.'

'Go on.'

'It wasn't anything he said. It's just that while I was driving, he was singing to himself.'

'Do you remember what he was singing?'

'I only remember a bit – I was terrified. I remember it was really creepy: him having a dove, and the sweet dove dying?'

'At some point he changed cars?'

'He made me get out, and then climb in the trunk of the other car. He brought me here and left me like this.'

'He didn't touch you again?'

A shake of the head.

'Did he come back and give you any food or water?'

Another shake of the head.

Jo could see that she was wasting her time.

'Okay, Sally. We'll take you to hospital now. You'll be looked after. I'll come back and see you as soon as I can.'

She turned away, and left the forensics nurse to her tasks. She could hear all the time in her earpiece the chatter involved in the search for Malacott. He had last been sighted scaling a chain-link fence around one of the industrial units. Max and the dog handler had arrived there just as he dropped down on the far side. It was too high for the dog to clear, and the two of them had decided it was better to go round and pick up the trail on the other side. After all, they reasoned, he was boxed in and going nowhere. Jo hoped they were right.

She stared at the walls. They were covered with photos of his victims. In some they were naked, in others clothed. There were head-and-shoulders portraits and close-ups of each of the tattoos. In none of the photos were the victims' eyes open. She counted the portraits: there were three faces she did not recognise. Then she realised that one of the faces, not among the victims they had already seen, was known to her. It was a head-and-shoulders of his sister, Amanda.

'Bastard,' she muttered.

'Sorry?' said the CSI.

'Not you,' she told him. 'Malacott.'

'Oh,' he said. 'Anyway, I've got all I need, she's fine to be whisked off to St Mary's, and I'll start on this lot.' He gestured to the walls, and a table on the far side of the bed.

Jo moved away from the bottom of the bed to allow Sally Warburton and the forensics nurse to pass. As they drew level, Sally stopped. Her body shook with shivers as she spoke.

'You're Joanne, aren't you?' she said. 'Joanne Stuart – Abbie's ex?'

Jo's reaction was visceral. Her fists curled into balls, her heart pounded, she realised that she had clenched her jaw. *Ex?* What gave her the right to call her Abbie's *ex?* Anger was rising up to choke off any pity she felt for this girl. Sod that! This *woman.*

Jo suddenly realised that they were both staring at her, waiting for her to respond. She slowly uncurled her hands, breathed in and forced a smile.

'Yes, I am,' she said.

A reciprocal smile broke out on Sally's face. She suddenly looked innocent and very pretty, despite her lack of make-up and her tangled hair.

'Will you let her know I'm alright?' Sally said. 'And James too?'

'Of course,' said Jo.

She watched as Sally and the forensic nurse walked slowly out of the lock-up towards the paramedic's estate car.

Jo inclined her head.

'Gold Command, this is Silver Command,' she said. 'Our missing person is on her way to the St Mary's Centre. She appears to be fine. Please advise her parents and her brother. Bronze Command, what is the sitrep on the target, please?'

'This is Bronze Command,' Sarsfield replied. 'The target appears to have gone to ground within the search perimeter. We expect to have contact shortly.'

Jo shook her head. What was that dog doing? And what about the UAV? She was beginning to wish she had not been so hasty in sending the helicopter away. This was where its thermal imaging would have come in handy.

The CSI had walked around the bed, and was staring at the contents of the table. On top lay the discarded facemask Malacott had worn. Beside it was a cabin-size aluminium case.

'Be careful,' she said. 'It could be booby-trapped.'

'I don't think so.'

Nevertheless, he was cautious, as he gently opened the lid. Inside, in special compartments, nestled a cordless electric razor, a multiple socket plug, sterilized needles in cellophane wrappers, plastic needle tips, three needle valve seats, three tubes of specialist permanent coloured ink, and various objects she did not recognise.

'This is a portable DIY tattoo kit,' said the CSI. 'It looks like he was upping his game.'

He closed the lid and picked up a small plastic jar with a handwritten label. Unscrewing the lid, he looked inside, screwed it back on and rattled the jar.

'Flunitrazepam – otherwise known as Rohypnol,' he said. 'No wonder she was hazy about the details.'

Jo pointed to a row of industrial-size bottles of liquid beneath the table.

'What are these?'

He squatted down and read the label.

'It says sterilised water. We'll find out soon enough.'

'And this?'

Jo nodded to an opaque spray bottle like the one she used to mist the orchids in the apartment kitchen. Beside it stood another plastic container. The CSI stood up and examined the container first.

'It's sodium percarbonate,' he declared. 'Otherwise known as oxygen bleach. He's been mixing it with water and spraying it everywhere, trying to obliterate any traces of his DNA.'

'Is it safe?'

'To breathe, yes. Undiluted it's corrosive, so make sure you keep your gloves on.'

'Silver Command, Bronze Command, this is Gold Command. You need to hear this. Go ahead, Juliet Two.'

'This is Juliet Two, Silver Command. We have just discovered items in our search of the target's house that suggest that he may be armed.'

Jo's heart began to race.

'What items, Juliet Two?'

'Five antique knives and a modern hunting knife. We also found a selfie of the target holding a revolver. It looks like an old-spec British Enfield, Number two, Mark one, thirty-eight calibre. We come across a lot of these. Usually they're de-activated.' He paused, letting the tension build. 'But we also found a half-empty box of cartridges. There's no sign of the weapon.'

'It'll take us fifteen minutes to get an armed response unit to your location,' said Gold Command. Her voice was steely with reproof. 'I think we should do that, don't you?'

Jo swore silently.

'Yes please, Gold Command,' she replied.

'Contact, contact!' someone bellowed in her ear.

'This is Silver Command,' she said. 'Who is this? And where the hell are you?'

'Sorry, Ma'am, flight control here. The target has broken cover eighty yards south of the BP garage. He's crossing Haslingden Road. Quebec Two and the dog handler are in pursuit. Target has just vaulted a drystone wall into a field.'

Jo took a deep breath. Until the armed response arrived, she and Max were the only two with firearms.

'Quebec Two,' she said. 'Please be aware that the target may be armed with a revolver. Proceed with caution. I'm on my way to cut him off. All other units hold your position. I repeat: *do not approach the target.*'

Before Max had time to acknowledge her command, Jo was already out of the lock-up and running towards her car.

'Flight control, where is he now?' she asked.

'He's heading straight for Guide Reservoir.'

She flung open the door of the Audi and dived into her seat.

'Don't lose him,' she said.

'No fear of that, Ma'am. Now that he's out in the open.'

'Go!' she yelled at the driver. 'Just go!'

Jo hung on to the grab strap as the car hurtled the five hundred-odd yards around two bends and the Beehive Roundabout. It wasn't just that she had to get to him first, it was the thought of losing a second perpetrator to a watery grave, as she had her own abductor. Once had been careless, twice would be professional suicide.

As they sped down by the side of The Willows, she spotted Max and the dog handler, halfway across the field. Both dog and suspect were out of sight. The car squealed to a dramatic halt in front of twin steel five-barred gates that marked the boundary between the tarmac and a sandy path above the reservoir. Jo leapt out of the car into a sudden rainy squall, clambered over the gates and set off running, the comforting presence of the Glock 26 hard against the small of her back.

Guided by the sound of the dog's furious barking, and instructions from the flight controller, she turned left along the path beside a drystone wall, beyond which was a five-foot-high steel palisade fence with wicked sharpened tips. Behind her she could hear pounding feet. Max's shouted words were lost on the wind. The dog had stopped barking now. At the end of the path, she scaled another drystone wall on to the road, ran five yards, climbed over one more wall, and landed on a grassy bank that led down to the water.

Malacott stood facing a second steel fence, looking out across the reservoir. He heard her coming, and turned around, head bent. His arms were down by his side. In his right hand he held a revolver.

Jo stopped, reached behind her, and drew the Glock. She assumed the stance, square to the target, arms slightly bent, support hand locked, strong hand relaxed. The front sight blade centred on his chest.

'Armed police!' she yelled, as much for those listening as for him. 'Drop your weapon, and get down on the ground!'

Malacott turned towards her. His hair was a sodden mass of coiled snakes. Rivulets of rain streamed down his cheeks like tears. Behind him, the wind whipped up white horses on the reservoir.

'Drop it, *now!*'

He slowly raised his head and stared at her. His eyes were wild and full of confusion, as though he had no idea what they were doing here.

'Malacott, drop your gun *now!*' she yelled. 'Do it *now!*'

She strained to hear his response above the wind.

'You won't shoot me,' he said. 'You don't have it in you.'

'Drop your weapon,' she repeated. 'Then get down on the ground!'

He smiled sadly and began to raise the gun towards her.

'Drop that gun!'

Her finger squeezed past the point of resistance that acted as the safety catch.

Fast is slow, slow is fast.

His gun was at hip height, still rising.

'Drop it now, or I will fire!'

She re-sighted, exhaled and squeezed the trigger.

Malacott fell against the fence, the gun spinning from his hand.

Something smashed into Jo's back, throwing her to the ground. A searing pain erupted in her arm.

Across the water, and around the hills, the final echo of her gunshot faded on the wind.

Chapter 58

Jo closed the door of the Post Incident Suite behind her and sighed with relief. The fire doors swung open and Max strode towards her. Concern was etched on his face. Jo anticipated sympathy and got in first.

'How is Malacott?'

'He'll live. A flesh wound. Straight through his shoulder. In and out.' Max grinned. 'You're either a bloody good marksman or a lucky one.'

'I'm never lucky,' she said.

'What about you, Jo?' he asked. 'How are you?'

'Shaken not stirred. I've got a few bruises, and a perfect set of canines on my arm instead of a tattoo.'

He grimaced.

'I bet that's painful.'

'Not to mention the injections in my bum they insisted on.' She grinned. 'I bet Malacott's feeling a bloody sight worse.'

'You can't blame the dog,' he said. 'It's what they're trained to do. They see someone holding a gun who isn't dressed like Armed Response, they're going to clamp down on that arm and not let go till they're told to.'

She tried straightening her arm and winced. 'They should teach them to read.'

He laughed, breaking the tension.

'I doubt he's ever seen an NCA logo before.'

She started to walk along the corridor and lowered her voice.

'You do know we're not supposed to confer or compare notes?'

'We're not doing. Besides, I didn't see what happened.'

'So where were you when I needed you?'

'The handler fell vaulting that wall and cannoned into me. By the time I'd got up, Malacott was slumped against the fence holding his shoulder, and you were lying there with the dog wrestling your arm. I tell you what though – it's a good job you managed to get one off before the dog crashed into you.'

There was an uncomfortable silence while they reflected on what might have been.

'Have they finished with you then?' he asked.

'For the time being.' She shook her head. 'It was like a rugby scrum in there.'

He knew what she meant. Helen Gates, Simon Levi, the investigator from the Independent Advisory body, a solicitor to represent her, the NCA welfare officer, her Federation rep, someone from the Crown Prosecution Service. It must have felt like the Grand Inquisition.

'Have they interviewed you yet?' she asked.

He nodded. 'They took my statement while you were at the hospital. Have they told you what happens next?'

'They said it's got to be referred to the Independent Police Complaints Commission. Discharge of a firearm, resulting in wounding. They don't have a choice.' She smiled weakly. 'On the bright side, that drone captured everything. As far as they're concerned, I'm in the clear. It's just a formality.'

He pushed the fire doors open.

'Are they going to let you interview him?'

'Under GMP procedures I'd have been removed from duty, but since we had the operational lead, Simon Levi argued I was the one that knew Malacott best and I was the SIO, so it was only right that I should conduct the initial interview.'

'And they agreed?'

'On condition that Welfare and the police surgeon ruled I was fit to do so – which they did.'

Max grinned. 'That's brilliant!' he said. 'Andy's waiting upstairs to help us with the interview strategy.'

Jo stopped.

'I assumed that Malacott would be drugged up to the eyeballs on painkillers? That his brief would argue that he wasn't fit to be interviewed.'

'What brief? He's adamant that he doesn't want one. And he's been passed fit to answer questions, provided we wait till the morning. He insisted that he wants to talk to you.'

'The feeling's mutual,' she said. 'But first there's something I need to do.'

Jo opened the door to the St Mary's Centre counselling room. She had been hoping to find Sally Warburton on her own. To check that she was coping and to reassure her that Malacott would go down, with or without her testimony. She should have expected that Abbie would be there too.

They sat side by side on the sofa, a suitcase on the table in front of them: Sally's change of clothes. Abbie had her arm around Sally, her head on her shoulder. Jo's heart lurched. There was more than sympathy in that pose, much, much more. Abbie looked up. Her expression changed in an instant from love to hate. She sat erect and pointed an accusing finger.

'This is down to you!' she shouted, her eyes blazing with anger. 'You're responsible for what he's done to Sally. Nobody else. You!'

'He hasn't actually . . .' Jo began.

'Abbie,' said Sally, placing a cautionary hand on Abbie's arm, 'that's hardly fair.'

Abbie cut her off. Her finger stabbed the air.

'He was trying to get at you, wasn't he? To punish you! He'd made it personal, hadn't he?'

There was no point in trying to explain. In any case, what could she say? Abbie was right. It was down to her. Now Abbie was shaking with anger and conflicted emotion. There were tears in her eyes. Jo wanted to reach out and hug her, but she was transfixed to the spot by this tide of rage.

'You promised me you wouldn't go there again,' Abbie said, struggling to make her voice quieter. 'Look at you. This is you. What you love doing. You need the danger. You thrive on it. Well, it was slowly crucifying me. The worry, the fear, and your total bloody obsession with whatever case you were on. There were times when I thought you cared more about the person you were after than you did about me. It's like you were trapped inside some bloody great paracosm. Well, you'll never put me through it again, and certainly not any child of mine.'

Jo fled the room.

She stopped outside the door. Her hands were shaking. Her heart was racing. She suddenly felt cold. She thrust her hands beneath her armpits and leaned against the wall. Only now did she realise what she had lost and how, deep down, she had been hoping that they could sort it out. There seemed little chance of that now.

Chapter 59

It was 9am on Christmas Day. Everyone wanted to get this over so they could put him back in the cells and get home in time for lunch. All of the preliminaries had been concluded. The tapes and the video were running.

'Mr Malacott, can you confirm that you are happy to proceed with this interview without legal representation?' said Jo.

'I've already made that clear several times.'

'For the tape please, Mr Malacott.'

His face was pale and drawn, despite the painkillers. His right shoulder was thick with bandages, his arm cradled in a blue sling. He leaned forward, winced and sat back again.

'I confirm, for the tape and the CCTV, and especially for Senior Investigator Stuart, that I do not, at present, wish to have legal representation.'

'And could you confirm that you are happy to proceed with this interview, under the caution I have given you, despite your injury and the medication you have been given?'

'Let just get on with it, shall we?' He cradled his right hand beneath his left elbow to add to the support provided by the sling. 'I confirm that I'm willing to have this little chat with you, notwithstanding your having been responsible for the injury to which you refer.'

There was no way she was going to let him wind her up, not today.

'You are being interviewed with regard to the matters that have already been put to you,' she replied. 'Namely, the abduction, unlawful imprisonment and rape of seven named persons, the abduction, false imprisonment and assault of Sally Warburton, and possession of a weapon with intent to kill. We're not here to discuss the manner of your arrest.'

He intended his smile to come across as charming, but it made him look arrogant.

'Ah, but you see,' he said, 'the manner of my arrest is pertinent to your accusation that I intended to kill someone.'

'Then why didn't you drop the gun when you were ordered to?' said Max, hoping to prevent this turning into a game of ping-pong. 'And why did you then point it at SI Stuart?'

Malacott ignored him, keeping his gaze fixed on her.

'I was aiming at the dog,' he said. 'I was trying to protect you.'

Andy's voice was in her earpiece. '*He's trying to rattle you. This is a distractor, like his use of your given name. Ignore it.*'

She knew all that. But he might just be telling the truth. Or had he been trying to protect himself from the dog? Or goading her to shoot him dead? She had been aiming at his chest. That was it. He had gambled on suicide by cop. He was hoping to escape justice, humiliation, the years and years of mindless incarceration. He had known that if she killed him, she would be the one to face the music. She smiled back at him.

'*Don't rise to the bait,*' said Andy.

Malacott raised his eyebrows, feigning surprise and disappointment.

'You don't believe me, Jo?'

They had got it wrong. She was smiling because she knew that there was nothing he could do to touch her now, or any more defenceless young women. Malacott was going down for life, and there was nothing he could do about it. And he knew that. If he was hoping that she would give him the opportunity to argue mitigation, to paint himself as a victim of circumstance, to blame his father, his mother, a genetic aberration, he was going to be disappointed. He was a nasty, evil, egotistical abuser. And she was going to do her best to ensure that was how the world would always remember him.

'It doesn't matter what I think,' she told him. 'The jury will decide.' She paused. 'What do you think they will make of the fact that we have CCTV of you abducting a young woman? That we also have film of you leaving a lock-up in which the same young woman was spreadeagled naked on a bed? That the walls of that lock-up were covered in images of other young women. Images that could only have been taken by the person who abducted them, drugged them and subjected them to the most serious form of sexual assault?'

'*One question at a time, Jo,*' the psychologist cautioned.

She didn't care – for once it didn't matter. There was no way that he could wriggle out of this. It sickened her to look at him. Remembering how he had painted himself as a women's champion. How he had leaned close to an unsuspecting Orla Lonergan at the *Say No & Stay Safe* seminar, touched her arm, whispered in her ear. Listened as she recounted the horrific experience he had put her through. Fed off her account. Had been spurred on to attack, again and again. She could see him preparing to tell the story he had concocted overnight. Some fantasy about being drawn to investigate the abductions himself. Taking the gun to protect himself. Stumbling across the lock-up. All the evidence being circumstantial. Either that, or some psychobabble to deny culpability on grounds of insanity, diminished capacity or irresistible impulse. Either way, she didn't want to hear it.

'*Ask him about the tattoo.*'

'Tell me about the tattoo,' she said. 'The one across your back. The falcon with a dove in its talons? Is that how you see yourself? Preying on the defenceless?'

'It signifies nothing.' His tone was scornful.

Despite her best efforts, Jo found her anger surfacing.

'Is that why you left those tattoos on your victims? As a pathetic parting shot, a final insult? A reminder that for brief moments in time you had possessed each of them? As if they needed reminding. Or was it just the sad signature of an egomaniac?'

'*Jo, we agreed that wouldn't work. You need to invite him to explain. You need to employ empathy, not derision.*'

To hell with that. She didn't want to have to listen to his explanation. She needed his admission of guilt. She leaned across, her hand on the switch that controlled the recording.

'Interview suspended at nine twenty-seven am. SI Stuart is leaving the room.'

She flicked the switch up, and turned to her colleague.

'I'm sorry, Max. I thought I could do this, but I can't. I'm tired. And it sickens me being in the same room with him.'

She pushed back her chair and stood.

Malacott seemed concerned that she was leaving.

'Why did you have to contact my sister?' he said.

He saw the flicker of surprise in her eyes, and smiled. 'When *Millennium Woman* told me that you'd asked about that article, I knew it was only a matter of time.'

She stared down at him, making no attempt to hide her anger and loathing. 'Because I sensed that was where it began for you. The abuse, the rape, the sense of power. Don't pretend that you feel pity for her now, your "little dove".' She shook her head. 'You were never powerful, not like that falcon. You were weak. So weak that the only way that you could feel strong was to prey on those weaker than you. You sicken me.'

She turned her back on him, and went to the door.

'Don't you want to know what drove me to it?' he persisted.

The sneer had gone. Now he was pleading. She turned in the doorway.

'No. Because it makes no difference to me, or to any of those women you brutalised. And it will make no difference to the jury. You're not a victim, no matter how hard you try to convince yourself of that. You'll have the rest of your life to persuade the psychiatrists and the psychologists who'll view you as a specimen in a laboratory. When you're dead, they may even slice up your brain and look for abnormalities. But you and I know that they won't find any. The simple truth is that you had a choice. Nobody forced you. You chose to abuse your own sister. You enjoyed the feeling of power and control. It wasn't that you couldn't stop, it's that you didn't want to. That makes you an evil monster. End of.'

She turned her back on him, and left the room. She didn't need to see what Max and those in the observation room were seeing. The sneer wiped away. The utter desolation that replaced it. The pain etched on his face. His body seeming to collapse in on itself.

Malacott was safely locked up in the cells. He had closed down after she left. Neither Gates nor Levi were best pleased, but they already had more than enough to charge him, thanks to the trophy hoard plastered all over the lock-up, and the fact that in his panic he had failed to sanitise the inside of the mask he had worn. And besides, he'd said enough under caution on the way to the station to incriminate himself.

Andy had ventured the opinion that once Malacott realised that Jo would track down his sister, then he must have known that time was running out. Sally Warburton's abduction had been the last desperate ploy of a man who had lost control, was hitting out, but had no endgame in sight. The plan now was to haul him before a magistrate on the Monday and get him remanded in custody.

'I spoke to Ram earlier,' Max told her. 'I wished him a Happy Christmas from the two of us. He was in the middle of a family shindig by the sound of it, his mother holding forth in the background. He sends you his congratulations by the way. Ditto Andy. He was busy trying to wrap a bike they've bought for his eldest. I told him there wasn't much point. It would still look like a bike, whatever he did.'

Jo smiled wanly. She seemed distracted. She had her phone out and was fiddling with it.

'What are you doing?' he asked.

'Googling something that's been niggling me,' she said.

She studied the response.

Paracosm: a highly detailed world created by one's imagination. A fantasy world involving people, places and things that may or may not exist.

Fair comment, she reflected. *Except that there is nothing imaginary about the cruel world that I move in.* She closed her phone down and put it in her pocket.

'Are you still going to your parents'?' Max asked.

She shook her head.

'I've told them I'll come tomorrow, Boxing Day. I couldn't face it today. The inquisition or the sympathy.'

They started walking down the corridor towards Reception.

'How are you going to spend today then?' he asked. 'You shouldn't be on your own, not on Christmas Day. Besides, how are you going to cook a turkey with your arm like that?'

She opened one of the fire doors for him.

'Get a takeout. Curl up on the sofa and watch the telly. What are you doing?'

He shrugged.

'I was going to stay with a former colleague in Surrey, another sad singleton. But I feel like you. And there's no way I'm racing all the way down there in the pouring rain and then having to come straight back on Monday.'

'Why don't you join me?' she said. 'There's no point in us moping alone, when we can do it together.'

He grinned.

'I'll bring the wine,' he said. 'But anyone caught sulking gets to make a substantial donation to the Police Dependants' Trust.'

Jo managed a smile for the first time that day.

'You're on,' she said.

Chapter 60

Max arrived at midday, clutching two bottles of Cotes Du Rhône and a bottle of champagne.

'This is getting to be a post-investigation habit,' he said cheerfully. He held up the bottle of champagne. 'I wondered about Prosecco, but then I thought sod it! Let's make it a celebration. You deserve it.'

'*We* deserve it,' she said, taking them from him. 'Come on through. Put your coat on the bed in there. Sorry there isn't a Christmas tree, I never got round to it.'

'Don't worry,' he replied. 'That bloody great tree in the foyer more than makes up for it. Put the champers in the fridge for a bit, lob me a corkscrew and I'll open one of the reds.'

Leaving him to uncork the wine, Jo brought the antipasto misto through and put it on the table.

'This looks good,' he said. 'You do know that you're supposed to have fish and vegetables for the traditional meal of La Vigilia? To purify your body before you get stuck into the festivities?'

'Firstly, it isn't Christmas Eve,' she retorted. 'Secondly, I can't speak for you, but my body's pure enough.'

That set them both off laughing. Max handed Jo a glass of wine. As she sipped, she felt the stress and tension of the last few days finally beginning to leach away.

An hour later, they were relaxing on the sofa with a brandy apiece. Max had demolished the minced fillet steak, tomato, cream and chilli that was reputedly Ryan Giggs's favourite, and she the eponymous Linguine Puccini with a crabmeat, crayfish, cream and tomato sauce. The remains of the tiramisu lay in a bowl on the table.

They had watched the Queen's Speech, pulled crackers and managed not to mention the investigation, Max's estranged wife and children, nor Jo's bitter estrangement. Her mobile phone informed her that she had a text.

'Sorry,' she said as she reached for it, 'I thought I'd switched it off.'

'It's probably your mum,' he said.

It wasn't.

It was Abbie.

Jo's finger hovered over the screen. Damn it, she told herself, you mustn't let it get to you like this. You can't be afraid to open any of her messages. She flicked it open and began to read.

I'm sorry, Jo. I never meant it to come out like that. You once told me that there was a limit to how much evil you can experience without it burning you out. That you absorb it. That it changes you. Well, I'm sorry, Jo, but I think that's already beginning to happen to you, and I don't want to be around to see what it does to you or to us. I can't risk exposing a child of mine to it either. But that doesn't mean that I'll ever forget the time we had together, or you. I hope that we will be able to stay friends, and that you will find peace and happiness in whatever it is you're looking for.

Abbs X

She handed the phone to Max. He read the message twice and handed the phone back.

'All that anger,' he said, 'and the tears. And now this. You know it's because she still loves you, don't you?'

Jo nodded.

'I know. The problem is that Abbie's right. I need this: it's what I do. What she needs is a child, more than one. Without that, she's never going to feel complete.'

She reached for the bottle of Italian dressing and held it up to the light. The balsamic a thick chocolate layer above the translucent golden oil. She gave it a shake. They watched the contents swirl into a seductive cloud, and then begin to settle.

'This was Abbie and me,' she said. 'An unstable emulsion, slowly separating. We just couldn't see it.'

'You and me both, Jo,' he said. 'It was the same with me and the wife.'

He took the bottle from her hand, placed it on the table, handed her her glass and raised his own.

'It's taken me a while,' he said, 'but I've finally realised that there's no point in trying to hang on to something that used to make you happy, but now simply makes you sad all the time. Life's too short, Jo. It's time to move on. Let's drink to that.'

She raised her glass.

'Moving on,' she said.

The brandy filled her mouth, scorched her throat, and coursed through her veins. A metaphor for the pain of her loss, and the challenge of a new beginning.

Author's Note

The statistics within this work of fiction relating to rape and sexual crime have been taken from reputable and reliable sources. Those statistics mean that there will inevitably be readers whose lives, or the lives of those close to them, have been touched by these crimes. I have listed below just a few carefully chosen sources of help from the thousands instantly available on the Internet.

Rape Crisis Support
Services set up to support victims of rape, child sexual abuse, or any kind of sexual violence.

RAINN, the USA's largest anti-sexual assault organization, with direct links to sexual assault and counselling services across the USA.
www.rainn.org

Rape Crisis England & Wales is the national umbrella body for a network of autonomous member Rape Crisis organisations across England and Wales.
www.rapecrisis.org.uk

Also, in Scotland and Ireland:
www.rapecrisisscotland.org.uk
www.rapecrisishelp.ie

Staying Safe on Campus, produced by RAINN, is full of practical advice for any student at high school or college, going away to university or leaving home for the first time. The advice is applicable to any setting, anywhere in the world.
www.rainn.org/get-information/sexual-assault-prevention/
campus-safety-sexual-assault

Reporting Rape and Sexual Crime is the Greater Manchester Police online best practice guide on what to do, and what to expect when reporting such crimes, whether current or historical. The information given and the advice provided is what one would hope to find in any modern police force.
www.gmp.police.uk/live/nhoodv3.nsf/section.html?readform&s=A
B606F6E10CE47448025796100403635

St Mary's Sexual Assault Referral Centre, Manchester, offers YouTube videos such as this one, in which clients explain how important the Centre has been in helping them recover from their experiences of rape and sexual assault.
www.youtube.com/watch?v=LxnYa70pDBI

Men are victims too. While the overall percentage of men and boys affected by rape is much smaller than for women and girls, the impact is just as life changing. Organisations designed to support male victims are few, but the number is growing. This is one such organisation.
www.survivorsmanchester.org.uk

Acknowledgements

I wish to acknowledge the following whose specialist knowledge and technical advice has been invaluable: former GMP Officers – Chief Superintendent Brian Wroe and Gordon Ritchie; Anthony Wood, former Scotland Yard Senior Forensic Science SOCO, and Visiting Lecturer at Thames Valley University; Simon Nelson, Her Majesty's Senior Coroner, Manchester North District, specifically for his advice in relation to the role of the availability of HM coroners and their role in directing that post-mortems be carried out; Kevin Murtagh, for advice in relation to legal terms and procedures; and finally, those Rape Crisis organisations whose details and links can be found in my Author's Note.

My special thanks go to everyone at Amazon Publishing UK, and their Thomas & Mercer imprint team. In particular, Emilie Marneur for coaxing me over to the dark side after six years of total freedom; my editor, Jane Snelgrove for leading me through the process with great wisdom and sensitivity; editor Russel McLean, and copy editor Monica Byles for their ability to get inside my head, their meticulous attention to detail and their brilliant advice.

Bill Rogers
November 2016

About the Author

Photo © 2015 Paul Whur

Bill Rogers has written ten earlier crime fiction novels featuring DCI Tom Caton and his team, set in and around Manchester. The first of these, *The Cleansing*, was shortlisted for the Long Barn Books Debut Novel Award, and was awarded the e-Publishing Consortium Writers Award 2011. *The Pick, The Spade and The Crow* is the first in a spin-off series featuring SI Joanne Stuart, on secondment to the Behavioural Sciences Unit at the National Crime Agency, located in Salford Quay, Manchester. Formerly a teacher and schools inspector, Bill has four generations of Metropolitan Police behind him. He is married with two adult children and lives near Manchester.